HORN OK PLEASE
HOPPING TO CONCLUSIONS

Kartik Iyengar

RUPA

Contents

Foreword

I had to do something with my life. This has been an issue for a while now. I also wanted to be rich and famous. Not that I had any real skills in the first place, but I had managed to keep myself busy with God-knows-what-I-was-doing anyways, a career path which, far from being well-planned, was more like one taken by those bouncing balls which have no clue about direction and where to hit.. That was stupid, just plain stupid. So I decided to do something decisively stupid instead. I decided to become an author...not just any author – but an author of this particular book. And I knew I was amazing. My editor had told me so for having made my way into the Guinness book of records for the maximum typographical errors in any manuscript since writing was invented. They were at their wit's end while editing the original manuscript of this book and now they look a lot older since we met the first time.

The first 'blook' in a frivology (five frivolous loo-books), 'HOPping to Conclusions' is a humorous spoof on a journey called 'Life'. In this book, I attempt to describe life in a progressive way that underlines the spirit of freedom, living on the edge like a rock-star and the need for us to stop taking everything so seriously. It is a racy, full-of-punch-lines novel that is part fiction, part reality. Based on my real life experiences in India and abroad, these experiences range from adventure sports to hospital visits to living life on the highway.

It is meant to bring out the outdoor aspect of a nation that is considered to be humorless, self-effacing and living in its past glory. Throughout the book, I portray myself as a moron with low IQ while addressing the reader in the same light... but I'm sure you, dear reader, will at least will be smart enough to know that this is a mere façade.

The names of the testosterone-loaded and thoroughly spoilt characters in the book have been changed to protect the guilty. Of the various facts quoted in this book as part of my research, more than seventy percent has been made up in my sleep. I tend to dream a lot. If they sound like facts to you, then you are as delusional as I am and suffer from severe behavioral problems at work and at play as well. If you bought this book, then I am cool. If you are merely skimming through the contents of this book at a bookstore or have pinched this copy from a friend, then may the curse of a thousand locusts infest your underpants.

'Horn OK Please' (HOP) is meant to look at the sunny side of life and experiencing India through the eyes of an educated and a successful individual in the Corporate Sector. It explores the growing up of individuals in urban India, childhood adventures, adult experiences and the breaking of barriers with emotional maturity and lightened by humor. As the book is targeted toward the educated urban class, young working professionals, NRIs, it delivers hope in terms of aspiration and freedom from mundane, mere existence. It is to be a symbol of pure commercialism, a dream of long drives lived through the book and a positive view of India as a nation that is meant to be an eye-opener for Western media.

It is not a travelogue. It is meant to be a humorous journey across the country. Every chapter starts with a poetic snippet, describes an experience and has a warped moralistic end with pointers from a fictitious community. Through the eyes of a compulsive roadie, I demonstrate translation of the dreams of a bold new India I call India 2.0, a dream translated into a thought to seed the tree of progressive behavior. Add to it a feigned ignorance and usage of acceptable slang that is understood by the 18-40 web-savvy community around the world that is heavily into Social Media. Needless to say, it is aimed at questioning the rudimentary and plain simple existence in every kilometer of the book, and to look at the goodness and prosperity that is evident across a booming India.

Keep that thinking cap aside, dear reader, get inside a talking SUV called Motormouth and let me show you the beauty of my country called India through the eyes of a moron from Urban India. Buckle up, for we are going to drive through canopies on the road, lemonade in hand and a smile in our hearts.

About Chief Red bull, the Author: He says, "Being an author is so cool! I can kill people with a punctuation mark or praise them to the skies. 'Drop dead beautiful' or 'Drop dead ... Beautiful'. And if this doesn't make you laugh, I'll poke you in the eye. I am an avid blogger, a self-proclaimed moron, scuba-diver, bungee-jumper, a pathetic Las Vegas loser, Red Bull addict and a compulsive road-hog and also a writer. In the midst of it all, I found time to listen to my inner calling and decided to write what I hope will become the holy book of the morons. As a cockroach-loving, heavy metal maniac, I now command an army of thousands of morons on Facebook, who are living my experiences of writing my first book, living a 40-day road-trip of the country and living a social cause for underprivileged children. The book is aptly titled 'Horn OK Please'. My sole objective in life is to sell a million copies of the book within a year of release, and I am confident of achieving much more till I become the best President of India after Dr APJ Kalam. Also, I cannot count beyond five and my lucky number is 69. So, since I cannot read, I decided to write my own stuff. I am a puzzle to the world, a jigsaw puzzle with the important pieces missing. The link is missing, if you know what I mean. Perhaps, my reputation now casts a cloak of intelligence around me and creates an aura and hence people call me 'Chief'. Little do they know that behavior is so Un-Chiefly. I love my friends. *Smack!!*"

About Goose Goldsmith, Photographer and professional lecher: He says, "I am a photographer, a diehard roadie and a freak of nature. I am full of fun and shit. I am a dude who loves House Music and Classic Rock. I also listen to Tiesto when I'm down with fever. Armed with my new Nikon D5000, I am also putting together a coffee table book. I usually walk around with stubble. I am fun. And hell, we're going to have loads of fun in this ongoing virtual reality show on Facebook, while I scout around for my perfect life-partner. I like taking pictures that make me happy. It's about India 2.0 and the spirit of our great nation. I love cockroaches too. My dream is to become the best photographer in India, who can depict the real India as we see it, and that's not about poverty, filth, politicians or pathetic leaders. I love my friends. I aim to please. You aim too, please."

About Derek Demonia, the 'Thing': He says, "I am a brawny, aggressive, fun-loving, bashful road-hog. I care a hang about anything. I live my/our life to the fullest and I have absolutely no purpose in life. I join the trip so we can have fun and help the Chief and Goose live out their fantasies as they need my help. I am schizophrenic. And hell, we care a hang as we are the true depiction of Generation of X, Y and Z. Both of us in me watch over Goose and the Chief as they do the Full-Monty of India. We are there, for we define the wild side of India 2.0. I love my friends."

About Motormouth: The talking SUV – A Jeep with superpowers, she has a mind of her own and drives the roadies crazy with her antics. They love her. Everybody does, for she is the beast for the ride.

1 Introduction

Roses are red, violets are blue,
There would never be a day when I shall not curse you;
Remember the time when you didn't listen to me?
You took your noisy ever-vibrating chassis and rammed
into a tree?
As I write this Ode, I feel my blunted nose & a
permanent scar on my face,
You stupid car, you always begged the cops for a chase?
You dumb mangled piece of iron & steel, I have
nightmares when I think of you,
Those ugly silver and black pieces of metal and plastic
pieces that really made you
I long for the day when you shall be melted,
Turned back into a lump of metal & with stones, be pelted
If smiles and imagination make you say 'Cheese'
Drive on, for that's the spirit of 'Horn OK Please'...

India. The last I read up about geography was in high-school. That was eons ago, when we had dinosaurs peeing in our backyard. We had about 22 states then. They are a medley of mountains, deserts and forests. They also threw in a few rivers here and there to make things look pretty. These lakes and rivers attracted a lot of people from everywhere and they settled down here. These folks soon got busy and started building many villages and congested towns. The scenic beauty and good climate of the nation made people breed and swell the population. India now has a population of about 1,179,829,000 (per Wikipedia). I never knew we lived in such a beautiful country where the climate is so conducive for us to breed like rats in a lab. I'm not so sure about the number of states anymore. Surely, it has doubled or something equally close even as this book was being published. Maybe it means that the growth of the Indian population demands new states although the size of the nation remains constant?

As a nation which has been constantly nibbled here and there at the borders, it still remains a large, motorable nation. We drive on the left-hand side of the road, at least we are supposed to, and that is probably why many of us we are leftists. The first known human settlement came up somewhere near the Indus River, about 9000 years ago, and there's been no stopping us since then. Well, at least in terms of population. As a nation, our optimism drives us. On the roads, the honking drives us crazy. Horn OK Please.

Many Indians drive wherever they can find space to squeeze into – be it a footpath/sidewalk or anyplace or any patch that vaguely resembles a motorable path. Since an empty right street may be considered left out if one only drives on the left, we tend to use any space to drive through as we are very impatient people. Many of the folks who live in cities tend to believe that those blinking, colorful lights at intersections are meant for beautification, just like the road authorities paint some white stripes in the middle of the road (No, not the ones that are only meant for zebras to walk across). They tend to make the roads look a whole lot nicer. The white marks on the

HORN OK PLEASE

HOPPING TO CONCLUSIONS

road also reflect some of the glare that helps that greenhouse thing that makes our leaders look smart in front of the United Nations. That's why we are still an "environmental friendly" nation in spite of dwindling forest cover and rising levels of garbage. Of course, the red skid- marks on the road means nothing but road-kill. It could have been you this morning.

We also have a few caves here and there, when the Maharajahs who ruled us had this fetish of mutilating big rocks and carving out nude statues and obscene sculptures meant to spur the population growth within their respective kingdoms. There again, they overachieved, for as the Indian Males of yore swelled, not exactly with pride, the population started to swell too. The Stone Age rock shelters with faded paintings at Bhimbetka somewhere in Madhya Pradesh are the earliest known traces of human life in the country. This tells us that the ancient kings had really pathetic painters and carvers at that time, who used really cheap distempers and emulsions (probably bought from the friendly, neighborhood local Chinese convenience store) to paint with, in the first place. Not to mention some garish interior designers which will hit you smack in the eye, should you choose to visit some of our palaces.

India has battled many invaders and we continue to do so. We succumbed to many invaders in the past and last I remember was when we kicked the British colonists out of our country. Not that I've lived that long, but this is what they taught me at school. Now that we are a secular, democratic, sovereign nation, we also debate if we were better off with invaders than with our own home-grown set of thugs and goons masquerading as political leaders, who are busy looting our coffers as you read this book. Add to that a good sprinkling of mediocre folks running the Indian Corporate sector. Well, that's about what I know, having grown up in urban India. Yet, I am proud of the fact that India is the breeding ground for some of the brightest minds and our nation. Spare us the few who bought this book, India is a nation that holds promise. A dream of a progressive nation we call India 2.0. If you were expecting any more information about India, you have probably picked up the wrong book.

In India 2.0, we use cars and other means of transport, not elephants. Foreign TV channels have thrived on fuelling the ignorance of their audience and increasing the TRP ratings of their channels by showing images of famished children standing in front of the Taj Mahal, weird rituals being performed by a local version of Hannibal Lectar, calamities, floods and everything negative. They continue to underline their ignorance by referring to India as a nation of monkey-brain eating people, considering a majority of folks here are die-hard vegetarians (At least many of us pretend to be). Many foreigners coming to India, having been raised in farms, chewing beef jerky and tanking up on horrible sodas that taste worse than cough syrup, brain-washed by some local moronic TV channels, still try to converse with Indians in sign-language. I agree, there are many such dumb folks in India who do not even see the writing on the wall, forget understanding sign-language, who today run large corporate houses or are highly successful politicians, models or actors or in the board of the Indian Cricketing Association. But then again – which nation does not have its regular set of morons?

Growing up and driving in urban India is like growing up in a microwave oven, without the on-off switch. The pressures of education and success are similar to what a potato would feel like inside the oven. One has to skillfully navigate through patches of road found in the midst of a vast expanse of unending wasteland, resembling a bomb-shelled Iraq in the 9/11 aftermath, a wasteland called a 'City'. Teeming with all kinds of life forms, the sheer statistics of a well-defined city in the world's largest (read densely-populated) democracy as compiled by the National Statistical Institute of India can be mind-numbing. No wonder the National Statistical Institute hides these numbers. As classified State-secrets, these facts are being recorded annually by many such covertly operating Government agencies who provide employment to many politicians, their drivers, servants, watchmen and their mothers-in-law.

Such unpublished and classified information in the hands of Corporate India cried for the formation of a non-Profit Organization called the HOPfans. The facts that this Organization has chosen to reveal through this book will make the hair on the nape of your neck stand on its end. If it does not, then you should probably consider running in the upcoming elections to become a Mayor.

These scary statistics are used by multiple government agencies, as well as many private bodies, but more on that later. Of course, one assumes readers have a minimum IQ of 40, not exceeding 70, to be able to grasp and make sense of the statistics.

Introducing HOPfans (Horn OK Please Facebook Anonymous Network)

HOPfans is the Organization of compulsive road hogs in India, and is squarely responsible for the theme 'India Rising'.

Every reader needs to understand the motive behind this secret, purely nonprofit, Organization. With absolutely no legitimacy and completely devoid of any sense, sensitivity or sensibility, the members of HOPfans are driven by the singular itch to drive without any real reason.

Throughout this book, dear reader, the HOPfans will be publishing startling facts and recommendations as you, dear reader, shall experience with me the torture of living and driving in modern India. You can later use these highly intelligent points for betterment of mankind or just to look smart in front of the people you are trying to impress. It is strongly recommended that you, dear reader, spend some time on understanding the very purpose of this Organization.

You could also consider using these statistics to your advantage (which further justifies your action on buying this book in the first place, rooted in your abysmally low IQ) and use these figures in front of a corporate luminary or a witch-like socialite over a dinner table and make yourself look very smart. The Virtual Headquarters of this Organization is commonly known as the 'HOPfans Sack' Vision: This Organization came into being to address the pains of a roadie in India, which includes mediocrity, lack of humor, Farmville, painful leadership and other such symptoms that cause the Indian urban population to become mediocre.

HOPfans Size: See for yourself, the online community can be found at http://www.facebook.com/hopfans

Startling facts from the Secret HOPfans Diaries

- *38% of Indian population practically lives on the somewhat motorable roads (The Spitters)*

- *2% of the Indian population squat on or very near to motorable roads (The Gawkers)*
- *30% of the population leans on objects placed incongruously near the roads. 10% of this segment has the perpetual stare, 65% are over-eager to out help others, 20% only salivate and drool at every female passing and the remaining 5% comprises of beggars, eunuchs and aspiring politicians (The Lechers)*
- *Only 20% live two kilometers away from the roads (Citizens)*
- *The balance percentage figure, unfortunately, has been withheld by the National Government (We, the Morons)*

There has been an on-going debate for years in our parliament to reveal the balance percentage figure. The HOPfans has been working with the RTI (Right To Information) group and has presented a 'Thought Paper' to the Parliament to disclose the figure. Unfortunately, the ruling majority is winning by a majority of votes and is supporting the secret agencies not to disclose the percentage figure to the general public, citing misuse of this Information as a National Security concern. As can be noted from above, India, as a nation, is very good in Math and Science. Unfortunately – 'Thinking' is not an area where we have truly evolved.

Let us try to grasp the psyche and the idiosyncrasies of each segment of the population from a roadie's point of view.

The Spitters (38%)

This breed is typically spotted roaming near small cubes called 'Paan' shops – that sell anything from betel leaf, tobacco, and medicines to dope and porn. 18% of this segment has been recorded as belonging to the 'floating' variety which can be somewhat classified into the sub-categories of illegal immigrants, credit-card sellers, goons, budding politicians, beggars and aspiring terrorists. The Statistical Institute however failed to segregate the politicians from other sub-categories and therefore, the data-point might be somewhat skewed.

Predominantly male, it is this slice of the Indian population that is being targeted by the multinationals & Indian corporate houses that promote mass consumerism and crass commercialism through all media channels funded by Bollywood, Tollywood, Kollywood, Sandalwood and Morning wood. They are called the 'Spitters', as they are prone to chewing the leaf and tobacco and spitting on roads, walls, banisters and cinema halls. A gentle note, dear reader, is to understand that the figures may vary from state to state, depending upon local progress. The Human Rights Commission along with the HOPfans, is questioning the Indian Government, which would be craftily used by various Marketing agencies to specifically sell copies of this book.

The typical profile of this cross-section of the Indian population includes wearing dull or no clothes, highlighted by either extreme lankiness or extreme obesity, and underlined by the extreme usage of bathroom slippers or cheap sneakers that are worn along with socks that are brown, black or grey. The stench of the sweaty socks mixed with the smell of cheap tobacco-based betel nuts announces their presence. The shirts are typically off-white or dirty or both.

There is also a heavy proliferation of cheap Chinese mobile phones in this section, which can be identified by the most obnoxious ring-tones known to mankind since Graham Bell. They typically use movie-song ringtones that sound worse than the dinky cars that infest the roads of India today. This is a huge market for the tobacco sellers of all varieties to sponsor the local mafia or the goon-brigade of the any political party that dictates the policy-makers in New Delhi. And the goons in the political parties are the mentors for this breed, which sits in the plush offices of Government-owned buildings, chewing 'paan'. A segment which is not to be ignored, this breed is coming in the way of the 'Green Revolution' by painting India red with spit. To win over this community, one must know how to chew the damn thing called 'paan' and learn to spit sharp and straight with force from a car moving at 169 Kmph.

HOPfans Note: The day you have mastered the art of sharp-spitting, you can easily win over 38% of the electorate, once you get used to walking around the city in your pajamas and bathroom slippers.

The Gawkers (2%)

This segment of the population takes a little IQ to understand. Anyone in the range of 40-50 IQ quotients should be able to grasp the figures with ease. This breed comprises of the revelers who live near the roads. Those flashy round things when you zip by in your car at 130 Kmph you see squatted near the roadside with a cut-open tin can of Castrol engine oil? You might have also spotted the round-robins when you look out of a train or a bus window early in the morning. Now this is where the true test of your intelligence comes in – The round-robins are not exactly birds or animals with the tin cans tied to their legs, you see. The rest of the description is not meant to be published in a classy book like this.

HOPfans Note: To win over this segment, you just need to learn the fine art of picking your nose intently while driving past them.

The Lechers (30%)

Typically found in groups or flocks of pea-brained jocks, the profile of this cross section of the Indian populace which dots the road-side of every city, every village, is punctuated by a curable personality disorder brought about by living in repressive small towns, fed on pornography and the proliferation of the internet. This segment views every single passerby (across genders – males, non-males, females and neutral) with equal desire as an object of sexual gratification walking straight out of a porn site. Some are happy and they ogle; some are happy and gay and they lech. Their physical structures would be predominantly portly or very lanky (once again) and they generally come packaged with fake Raybans and borrowed motorbikes. Suffice it to say, the level of sophistication extends to the degree of affordability of more fake Raybans and borrowed cars, slightly bigger than the dinky cars with four wheels one was so used to playing with as kids. All they are good for is wearing jazzy t-shirts with anything written in English, even if it conveys absolutely no meaning.

10% of this 30% of the Indian population are in a state of perpetual stupor and are ardent T-Shirt readers. This is where the textile barons make money. So do the big brands. The demographic split includes mechanics, petty shopkeepers, insurance agents, credit-card sellers, IT professionals and stock-market losers. Everybody's business is their business. I have always had a sneaky suspicion that they also form part of some secret agencies that measure the per capita consumption of clothing of any respectable Indian citizen.

Maybe that's why they stare. They also engage in unwanted social work. This lot is always eager to help anyone and anybody and ask all kinds of pesky intimate questions the moment you have a conversation with them.

I learnt about this repressive behavior when I was a kid. My uncle, who is a psychiatrist, owns a hospital and he has the picture of a brain on his visiting cards. Thank God, he was not a gynaecologist. The Lechers would be sitting in front of his clinic ogling at all the crazy women go by. Later on, the same bunch of Lechers would be spotted right in front an advertising agency. Maybe, they had grand images of the advertising fraternity being full of good looking models that one gets to see on the hoardings.

Another key characteristic of this segment is their changed gait and mannerisms as soon as an attractive person is spotted. Very similar to a peacock, the gait changes into a totally starched-out walk, the arms spread out as though their armpits have been freshly shaved. It is this segment which the multinationals are targeting, based on false-statistics with just one (most likely empty) can of Coke being circulated amongst five friends, and the skewed numbers reflected in an animated power-point presentation on the screen of a plush office in Nariman Point.

The Junta (20%)

It is this segment of the Indian population you get to see on any News Channel. Those extremely irritating ugly-popping heads you've always noted trying to fit into your TV screen, that form the colorless background of any newsreader broadcasting from a public place as you flip through those channels with your remote? It is this segment that makes India seem more populous on TV than it really is. It is this very faction that any sensible newsreader would go after to talk to, be it a natural calamity or a terrorist attack and pop that extremely intelligent and most-used probing question to unearth the sentiment of the common man – 'How do you feel about it'? It is this intelligent segment that always feeds into the extreme creativity of the media. Imagine a poor pesky credit-card collection agent, who has just lost his entire family to a major fire in a building asked this brilliant question exactly twenty minutes after the disaster? Well, what do you expect him to say, you moron? That he is on Cloud #69, in the pink of health and looks forward to a charmed life after the incident?

That aside, statistics are also available on the number of popping heads that surround such poor souls. It has been measured to a level of detail that defies comprehension. Sample this – On an average, there are exactly twenty heads that pop into your TV screen (the newsperson and the victim are not counted) and the average angular tilt of each popping head on your screen will never exceed 45 degrees. Of these twenty heads, there are three heads with glasses. More details exist, but I shall spare you further torture, except the fact that the remaining 10% have some very unique characteristics, underlined by cheap Raybans, have a nasty habit of chewing gum by repeatedly opening their mouth extra-wide and are prone to smoking. And if you are expecting the math to add up here, you should just get off that high chair, flush this book well and get back to your life. That's a job for the Mathematical Institute of India, not for a roadie.

The Morons (Undisclosed %)

As we now have 38%+2%+30%+20% = 87% of the statistics revealed as stated above. As I have pointed out earlier, the balance percentage is not being revealed and is under debate. And you, dear reader, belong to that segment of the Indian populace targeted by the HOPfans. Not sure if you were born lucky. After all, India is a free country and as they say – every good thing in life comes for free. But I've always wondered as to why the second best things in life are very expensive, immoral, and injurious to health or come under the taxable bracket.

With this sound grasp on the demographics of the Indian population, let's explore the segmentation of this population, which is very important in understanding how the very fabric of society takes shape. It is this fabric that defines the rapidly changing culture of the country, which has an indirect bearing on the fabled infrastructure of Indian roads – cities or highways, ports and airports, moths and behemoths..... not sure why I wrote that, but it makes the book sound cool to the reader. It's a different topic altogether as to how this misshapen monstrosity of a moth-eaten fabric of our proud nation is dotted by the many incompetent nincompoops and mediocre monkeys, who have all been chewing at this beautiful fabric.

As a nation, India has progressed despite the poor quality of leadership across sectors. I know it, as it takes one moron to deal with another, and I do it every single day of my work life since the time I started pretending to work, and since the time they pretended to pay me as I am fun to work with. Others work while I have fun. If one were to classify this body count that one euphemistically terms as 'population', they can be easily understood by the very simple following classification by the classic application of the KISS (Keep It Simple, Stupid) Principle from NASA. Why NASA? I don't know, just read on and keep your thinking cap aside. As mentioned in this chapter before, your IQ needs to be not more than that of Neanderthals, and if it is, reading the subsequent chapters of this book will lower your Intelligence quotient by at least 20 points. And, if you think that your intelligence has not been under question till now, I promise to try harder in the subsequent chapters.

The below mentioned data-points would be extremely useful for anyone trying to understand India if it involves driving, mergers or acquisitions, driving competitive advantage in the market or for those who are looking for an extreme book to be used in a public restroom.

With this understanding of India, having grown up in the urban pockets of this vast country, I started experimenting with the fine art of vehicular autopsy before I could reach a double-digit sequential age that can only be measured chronologically. Like any spoilt brat in any part of the world, having tinkered around with small and tiny dinky cars inside the house, graduating to small and dinky cars in the backyard, I finally qualified to driving small and dinky cars on the Indian roads. The Indian automobile sector has always been plagued by the worst set of brains that never could think beyond their lowly-funded innovation labs. No wonder the Indian roads are dotted by these horrible-looking vehicles till date. First, the country was invaded by the marauders and the colonists. Come Independence and democracy, the roads were invaded by eye-sores and olfactory disasters that made more noise than offered speed and fuel efficiency, not to mention the fact that every vehicle being manufactured in India has the extreme potential of singularly burning a hole straight through the ozone layer. Now when the time comes to stop pollution and sign treaties on a piece of paper, we cry wolf!

Smaller towns have their share of problems. Over and above these ugly looking, HOPfans-tearing, gut-wrenching, smoke-spewing & foul-smelling rides such vehicles subject the Indian population to, they have vehicles that look like pigs. Just so they can carry many people at the same time. Never have I seen a bus or a public carrier that did not have a minimum of three persons dangle dangerously holding on to the handlebars, not to mention a minimum of two people sitting alongside the driver. Till date, these horrible auto-rickshaws run on Indian roads, where the driver will always use the 'half-butt' position on the seat as the engine is right under his gluteus maximus. Suffice it to say, if you were ever to be asked to identify an auto-rickshaw driver to save your life, take it from me, dear reader, you can identify him by the way he sits. Give him a luxurious Lazyboy or a sexy swivel chair, he will still sit in his 'half-butt' posture out of sheer force of habit. It is the conditioning that defines the way we shape up as a nation. Do not forget to observe the way your boss sits in the office, and you know who is in the driver's seat.

Thanks to these scrolls that made me a very aware Indian citizen and armed with these statistics that have been hidden since Independence, I decided to dig into their research a bit more to get on with my road-trip. Without a doubt, we roadies have been deprived of such knowledge that exists within the HOPfans.

A Road-trip is a philosophy. With the net-savvy Indian 2.0 emerging community, I would like to make sure we bush-whack some cheap, two-bit, 1/2 a penny politicians someday & help build India 2.0 ... in my sweet, special way. This was a random mind-burp straight from the crotch, thank you very much. It didn't matter to us if we were sun-kissed or sunburnt anymore. Who cares as long as you get close to nature and explore the vastness of India? Hell, we don't even look like human beings anymore. As the stereo played the rock classic 'Born to be Wild – By Steppen Wolf'. It gives one the courage to face the world, pump up the volume to "madness" levels on your stereo, flip the birdie and plough ahead without a look-back as our mind-bubbles vaporized. Thank God, my SUV has a strong windshield; the loud decibel couldn't shatter it. This is life for this is a passion that cannot be defined. It is a love so blind that it cannot be fathomed, an intensity that cannot be measured as the surge of the power behind the wheel coupled with loud speed metal blaring through the speakers makes skins crawl.

Take it from me, it is only sound advice that you shall receive in this book, dear reader – 50% sound and 50% advise. You choose what will keep you alive while driving. Consider these details exposed by the HOPfans last week about Indian roads and highways along with my advice:

1. Every fifth male who crosses a street in India, rubs his crotch. – Avoid every fifth Indian male if you want to avoid watching

2. Every 14th person in India accepts that GPS in India works brilliant. When in need of directions, 24/7, seek

GPS (General Public Service) Roll down your windows and just ask the nearest life – form that approaches your vehicle

3. There is a place of religious worship after every 500 meters. – Slow down and bow every 500 meters to avoid getting beaten up by zealots

4. Every sixth accident on Indian roads is caused because of the inability of the driver to understand the behavioral pattern of the drivers who drive call-center vehicles – Learn psychology

5. Every 7th person who gets lost on Indian roads is because of his/her inability to understand directions. When asked to turn 'Left' or 'Right', they fail to verify if the person providing directions has got his/her 'left' or 'right' right – Learn sign-language; try scuba diving

6. Every 7th person who gets lost on Indian roads does so because of his/her inability to understand directions. When asked to go 'Straight', they fail to understand that there is a curve ahead. If the person swings his hand to the right (the right right), it means you must take a right turn in 600 meters. Corollary is true sometimes (Glitches do happen when 'left' is explained) – Learn to meditate

7. Every 12th person on the road wasted 15 minutes of his/her time while seeking directions when the list of turns exceeds five line items resulting in a time-out and the deciphering costs a good 12 extra minutes (without negotiation) – Keep your watch aside when seeking directions

8. Every 13th accident at night is caused by drivers who do not know how to speak with their headlights & frantic hand – signals. Low-beamers are usually the rookies who

drive at speeds less than 169 Kmph – Drive like a jerk, use high-beam always

9. Every 12th bump with a pedestrian could have been avoided had the driver rolled down his/her windows and played Metallica at deafening volume thereby clearing the road within 55 seconds. (Over 50% of Indian rural population lives on/near the highway) – Buy new CDs

10. Every accident could have been avoided if people gave up driving and surfed the internet looking at exotic pictures of locales taken by others who chose to take the train or fly – Get a high-speed internet connection at home and stay put

To summarize, based upon the above data-points and sound advice, the HOPfans, along with the Author of this book (yours truly) have presented our key recommendations to the NHAI (National Highway Authority of India), for educating drivers and roadies on Indian roads, insisting on strict compliance for safety.

HOPping to Conclusions

▶ When lost and entering an eatery on the highway to ask for directions, be sure to spit very frequently & vigorously as if your very lungs are going to come hurtling out of your mouth

▶ Wash your face in front of everyone as if you've driven for a long time (even if you didn't)

▶ Bang car doors loudly to announce arrival & be a total nuisance to all

▶ Tip heavy at all places; you'd be surprised what a wad of 20-buck notes (INR) can do

▸ Try a word or two of the local lingo – you'd be surprised by the warmth after that
▸ Look pissed, stay pissed or you will be pissed upon
▸ Feign complete ignorance about everything, even the size of your innerwear (if asked)
▸ Ensure you and your vehicle sport the unwashed look. You are respected if you are a 1000 Kms + Easy-rider

Note: All 'Horn OK Please' recommendations in this and subsequent chapters strictly adhere to the HOPfans Scrolls and Standards as prescribed somewhere, someplace, sometime during the course of writing this book

2 Sunny Side Up

When we made paper boats and set them to sail,
A time when we never had to work and life was a fairy
tale,
Playing in the sun, a dip in the pool;
When counting stars in the night sky was just way too
cool
A time when comic book heroes came out at night,
I could hear the silent screams
When the world of Tintin, Asterix, Calvin and others
shaped our dreams
Nostalgia and Imagination makes you say 'Cheese'
Drive on, that's the philosophy behind 'Horn OK Please'...

Growing up in urban India is really not very different from the way kids grow up the world over. (Note: We are only talking about chronological age). What started off as regular camping drives has manifested itself into a passion to get behind the wheel, kiss the roads, make love to the open skies and get caressed by the cool gentle breeze, bathed by sunshine and nurtured by the rains. We all went to good schools, must have had some kind of education, must have failed in Moral Science as a subject, and those formative years of growing up in urban India, especially in a small town, does provide one with limitless courage to face the future and go with gusto for the unknown. It is very similar to going into the forest at midnight tanked up on beer and looking for wild animals. Today, every time I want to show the victory sign, the middle-finger comes up involuntarily. I guess that's how one can identify the compulsive roadie I eventually turned out to be.

The Bird has landed … Goose arrives

It was midnight and we were at the airport, waiting for Goose. Listening to Derek clear his throat now, I got it all figured – Bryan Adams doesn't gargle in the morning, instead he cleans his throat with sand paper. I must try it sometime too and then I can try yelling my way through rush-hour traffic in Bangalore and not honk the horn. There are no rules against yelling anyways and any conversation with Derek and Goose was similar to wild animal grunts. It's just that we were a lot louder than those dumb animals in the forest. It's always painful to wait for anyone at an airport; the pain intensifies when Derek is around. The eagle had landed; we were waiting for our goodie-bag, full of travel-accessories from a potato-growing country called Finland. Galileo, our guide, navigator, who would not be physically with us on the trip, but was helping us with the latest gizmos to be fitted inside Motormouth, had very clearly instructed Goose's to get all that he needed if he was to be allowed to set foot on Indian soil again. Things like the infamous 'Russian-camera' kind of heavy-duty stuff that was impossible to break. Remember the violent flash? Those things would leave any woman looking like 'Helga'? Maybe that's how the name 'Helga' was born, and right now it was one of these 'Helgas' getting us dinner at an airport food joint. The pizza tasted like a grilled raincoat and the coke tasted like formalin. Maybe she had drooled all over our pizza and spat in my drink. As she gleefully hovered around us waiting for a tip, Derek took a spare tissue paper, neatly scribbled 'Tip of the day' on it and said, "You should go far … the farther away from us, the better."

Chewing on my raincoat-crusted pizza still, I couldn't help but notice this guy at the next table. We shall call him 'Dork'. We reveled in eavesdropping, an art we had mastered way back in high school as peeping-toms and voyeurs. Dork kept on repeating to his date, "You know what I mean?" at the end of every sentence, filling up his boring sentences with the use of the sexy verb "like" ever so often. I had hoped that Dork would cut out on those histrionics and waving arms as he was now giving me a nasty headache. We couldn't even eavesdrop in peace. Topped with a funny, fake accent acquired after just a few visits to some remote part of the world, he had come back to ask for a 'Bawdle of Vaader' when I went to pick Goose up from the airport. With a fake accent like that, the Dork was sure to die of thirst. Nobody would understand what he wanted. As we wait for his Avian Highness at the arrival section, I realize that I've been talking to my Facebook wall all the time. I was slowly turning into Derek's clone and becoming a budding author and a blooming moron. You can call me 'Quasimodo' now, thank you very much. After all, man is a social animal. Send him on a road-trip for a few days; you can drop the 'social' word – Nancy Thursday. Fate determines who walks into our lives. The heart determines who stays … Socrates. But when I drive, I decide everything, and to a road-hog like me, that's life. Maybe, that's what was happening to me. Too many road-trips and we just couldn't get enough. A mere irritant like a tire-puncture opened up the dungeon door in my mind where I could see a 'nut', a few loose screws and bolts and out popped a sentence that would come together as 'Nut screws and bolts…'. It tasted like burnt toast that was tougher to swallow than truth and tasted worse too. And the truth was Derek and Goose had definitely become a part of my life – The Chief's life… How un-Chiefly! *Duh!!*

Growing up with these guys, I'd like to highlight some experiences from my childhood to you, dear reader, so they can have the same effect, that of cheap beer, on your system. So read on, dear reader, for this is going to be more painful than watching a chick-flick like 'Sunshine Calling'. Keep the barf-bag ready by the side and buckle up.

Tarzan was just an ape, Man!

It was raining that night. I can barely remember Aerosmith playing in the background as we were so smashed. I don't even recall how many bottles of beer we had demolished near that ghastly tree that was right in front of the graves we were sitting on. We were somewhere in a graveyard at a hill station in Madhya Pradesh. It had been a crazy night. We had gone hunting in two Gypsies along with a friend, whose father was some hotshot in the Forest Department. We had pinched some guns (12-bore), manned two Maruti Gypsies (4WDs) and were smashed beyond repair. It was tough trying to 'borrow' the keys to the two cars. The flash-lights that are used by the Forest Department folks connected to the battery of the lovely beasts. We were pumped up with adrenaline having demolished a crateful of beer and were hungry. And we wanted to be 'real men', hunt, shoot, cook and eat. We all knew that hunting is illegal in India, but for a bunch of youngsters pumped up on adrenaline and loaded with testosterone and messed up with alcohol, the term 'illegal' meant nothing more than a sick bird i.e. Goose.

It was around 10 pm and we had managed to escape the forest quarters and were somewhere deep in the jungle with two forest drivers. Down twenty minutes into the forest, we chanced upon this very pretty sight – that of a deer and a fawn. Guns pointed at them, having blinded them with the flood lights, we felt 'man', or so we thought. The entire image was so captivating and touching, all of us remained quiet for a good seven to eight minutes before we lowered our guns and turned the jeeps back to the quarters. Barely out of high-school, had we to prove to each other that we were men? Growing up in one of the good Jesuit schools in the country, our hearts took control and we couldn't do it. Back in the camp quarters, we tanked up yet again, tied a chicken to a post and shot the shit out of it, made the cook roast it and serve it to us. It tasted awful as a 12-bore gun just sprays pellets and it had messed up the chicken so bad, we wished we hadn't killed it. I didn't know if I chewed chicken or pellets or a few of my teeth then. Maybe we all grew up that night...

Wanting to let the softies within us take over, we decided to do what we always loved to do. After all, this was one of our 'Night outs' and no amount of begging, pleading, cajoling or scolding from our parents could ever stop us from getting together at our rendezvous, which, unfortunately, was a graveyard. Sitting on graves was our demented idea of a 'graveyard shift', having failed many times earlier with the Ouija boards and calling the spirits from the nether world. That was reason enough for us to shift our focus to the friendly earthly spirits, which seemed to be more under our control, like whiskey, beer, rum and blowing up tuition fees on the same and coming back home more drunk than enlightened. My father caught me a few times like the night we pinched the whiskey bottle from the cupboard, polished it off and demolished the evidence in the nearest pesky neighbor's courtyard. Unfortunately, my friend had left the bottle cap in the cupboard, a tell-tale sign and we got caught.

Or the time when I had taken an advance out of my tuition fees from my father under the pretext of paying for an evening class before a term exam. Having got smashed in the bar, I had taken the menu card from the bar home and left my syllabus on the table. The owner called up home and I was grounded for a week. Still, it was much better than the times when we experimented with cough syrup and used to be stoned for hours on end. The trip was good, the kick was cheap and it was all that we could afford by the end of the month, having so totally run out of pocket money. With no part-time jobs (the concept never really existed in urban India during that time), I had no choice but to be a big parasite on my parents.

Growing up also meant a mandatory visit to the local haunted house with creaking stairs and swishing windows, but drunkenness made us very brave. With the scariest being in the room being one of my friends, who had this perpetual frown on his face, the lightning had scared the hell out of us before we thought he was possessed. We finally reached our favorite spot near a dam, which was close to a water body and till today, I swear, we heard the growl of a tiger that left us really scared. Not that the forest over there was known to have tigers; it was that or it was someone who was burping real loud after a few sodas in the dead of night in a thick forest at two a.m.

HOPping to Conclusions

▶ *Never enter a forest at night unless you are totally smashed*

▶ *Never have chicken for dinner if it's been tied to a pole and shot*

▶ *Never carry your syllabus to a bar. Once drunk, at least, do not carry the menu card back*

▶ *Before throwing out an empty bottle, ensure the lid is in place*

▶ *Never enter a haunted house with ugly friends*

▶ *If you hear strange sounds in the dead of night in a forest, burp loudly*

▶ *Sitting on a grave and throwing empty beer bottles makes a lot of noise. Use cans instead*

▶ *A smoker can be easily identified by the way he/she taps a cookie*

The fun is in the journey, never the destination. That's why roadies love to drive. It is a philosophy and we experienced it that night. Just pick up the car and just drive. Funny things happen down the road when you don't plan, and let life take over.

Been a long time since I Rock 'n' Rolled!

Growing up as an '80s child, you know what Heavy Metal is all about. Classical music and all that nasal stuff made me barf. Not that it doesn't anymore; it's just that I don't talk about it. I turned smarter, so I write about it now. Me and my metal-head friends used to follow the Heavy Metal brigade all over India and I had the most enviable collection of tapes and I still pride myself on that. For us, the best way to let our dreams float and allow imagination take over was to pump up the volume and play imaginary guitars, drums, bass, leading vocals and do all the antics that would even put Ozzy Osbourne to shame. It was really cool; we guys would actually take positions and let the world become our stage. Needless to say, we were the coolest and the best Rock band known to all humanity at that point in time. Our dress code always used to be 5-pocket blue-jeans, sneakers, denim jackets and a t-shirt. (Darn! It still stays the same!) Anybody in high-school who doesn't have grand delusions of having his own rock band and a set of groupies is either lying, demented or is fit to work for an Indian IT organization. I've learnt that growing up and growing right are two different things. The difference is similar to the definitions of a man and a biological male. It is the same difference between going on a vacation and going on a road-trip.

The standard perceived image of a young boy or girl growing up in India typically includes growing up chronologically to either become an engineer, a doctor or a scientist, get a job, no affairs, get married, have kids, buy a house and squander away your life till you grow old and die of diabetes and high blood pressure before you put your kids through the same sausage-maker. If this image were to be typecast and turned into a corollary, we must have grown up to become someone every mother warned her daughter not to associate with. And horrors, we did just that.

It was our Annual Day and we had this stupid line of geeky basketball playing high-schoolers and we decided to use them as our launch pad into super-stardom of Rock and compete with the likes of Iron Maiden and Metallica. We were horrible singers and air-guitar players in a country where 'Rock' had nothing to do with music but with pornographic sculptures and sexy statues of big-breasted women, places of worship, gardens and mining instead. But a dream is meant to be chased and we were neither good singers nor guitar players. What made matters worse was that we couldn't even pass off as sculptors, artists, gardeners, religious folks or miners. But we did our practice sessions at school, encouraged by our Dean who liked us for some strange reason and he was not even a pedophile. We managed to do a number and moved the audience with our sheer talent. They moved out in droves before we could even complete a song. Somehow we managed to lick the wounds to our badly bruised ego, which took a lot longer to heal than the physical wounds caused by the throwing of empty beer bottles by the audience. And that was the start and end of our music career. We were better off as Air-bands, the most successful ones, and we still jam occasionally at the privacy of our homes to avoid any further injuries to mind, body and soul.

Of course, being the lead singer of the most successful rock-band on Planet Earth does have its side-effects which tend to rear their ugly heads once in a while. Symptoms include head-banging while the mind-radio plays on in a boring meeting, which often makes me seem demented and I invite strange stares from many geeks in monkey-suits in formal gatherings.

Did it turn us into lesser Indians with no sense of patriotism in us? Hell, no. It's just that I didn't turn out to be a jingo. Were we influenced by other cultures? Mercifully yes, and it made us all successful in our regular lines of work by turning us into global citizens, rather than being jingoistic about India. After this page in our lives, we evolved as smarter beings. Like right now, when I want to sell a million copies of this classy book, I pretend to be an author.

HOPping to Conclusions

▶ *If you want to be a rock-star in India, become a sculptor*
▶ *If you want to play in an Air-band, make sure that the floor is not slippery*
▶ *If you want to move an audience to your guitar, it is better to imagine you have an audience*
▶ *It is a lot safer to play in the privacy of your car or the shower, than to get on stage*
▶ *If you must get on stage, ensure that the organizers sell beer only in flimsy plastic cups*
▶ *You cannot lick the wounds on your soul, even if you are Gene Simmons from KISS*
▶ *If you are a roadie, it pays to be an Air-band star as pedestrians tend to move away from drivers who look deranged and make constipated faces while driving*

Spread your wings and fly, sweetie…you got the concept all wrong!

Growing up in a small town of Urban India includes a lot of clandestine dates, porn-filled pads of friends taken on rent for a few hours, extremely boring and uninteresting love-lives of overly emotional friends and batch mates when I had no choice but to turn entrepreneurial just to ward off the evil spirits that used to take control of some of my friends. It is hard to listen to someone's sob story; it's harder to look sympathetic and understanding and nod your head every few minutes, but it's hardest not to laugh straight at their woes and self-inflicted pains and miseries and walk away and make the other person pick up the tab. I mean, how long can you listen to someone infected with 'Whine-flu' till your plastic smile starts to hurt and your angel halo starts to look like a noose around your neck? They should charge such folks for abusing so many words and resorting to obscene honking into disposable tissues in public. It is enough to make your stomach turn. Having run out of pocket money on the second day of the month itself (which was never anything new for most of us), we decided to make a quick buck out of these suckers and relieve them of their pocket change so we could go out and buy a few cans of beer and go out of town for the weekend.

Having identified a specimen who was loaded with cash, my friend picked up enough courage to go and listen to her sob story. I decided to accompany him – for sure I must have been really broke and desperate then as I was destined to find out shortly that I was about to pay a heavy price for having been broke and desperate. The two hours of whining about her two-timing boyfriend, coupled with my hunky buddy staring intently at her chest was straight out of a movie. The conversation went from inane to ridiculous to sublime. I was having these vivid images of my putting my fingers through her nose, every time she honked into her lacy pink hanky, and scratching the back of her head with a fervent hope that some bulb would light up in her pea-sized brain. For us, she was a walking, talking and honking ATM machine, that's all. My hunky friend was my ATM card and all I cared was to get the cash so we could buy bare essentials like beer and petrol for our weekend trip.

The pink-laced hanky was beginning to irritate me no end. What can be counted in minutes, seemed like hours. But before I realized, I was asked to arrange for a room for a couple of hours so they could have some privacy. Privacy? What about me? Did I look like a pimp to them? Maybe, yes, judging by what happened next. I made my demand and got the cash from her to get a place from one of my equally stupid and enterprising friends for the usage of his pad. And I increased my demand and added the pink-laced handkerchief to the list. The deal was struck. I was to pay my other friend, make a hefty margin; these two would get to use the room and as a bonus, my friend promised to pinch the pink-laced handkerchief from her and pass it on to me. As an added bonus, I was rewarded with an option to watch through the window, which I declined. So while they made out, I was to keep a watch before the other friend's mother came home and I could have a whale of a time burning the pink-laced handkerchief. To add to my woes, there was this stupid little puppy in the garage which my other friend's mother had recently acquired.

Unfortunately, while they were making out in the name of consolation after a very complicated discussion on the fine art of multi-tasking (read multi-timing here), I was the pimp looking for a can of kerosene to burn the pink laced-handkerchief, now neatly wrapped in a doggie-bag, pinched from the coffee shop. As I left my watch tower in search of kerosene, my other friend's mother must have finished off her work before time and slam! – she lands up. It was too late to let out a scream and a bit difficult as well, as I had the garage lock in one hand, the doggie bag between my teeth and a can of kerosene in the other as I saw two naked figures, clothes in hand, making a mad dash out through the gate and into the car. I don't recall how much thrashing I got from my other friends mother. She just wouldn't believe my story, given that I was there in her garage with her precious little pup, jerry can in hand, doggie bag between teeth and the lock in the other hand. She considered me nothing less than Hannibal.

When I reached the coffee shop, all I had were scratches on my face, a black eye, a small doggie bite and the blasted pink-laced handkerchief. Still, we had made a killing that night; so what if it was at the risk of getting killed ourselves? The weekend turned out much better than we thought it would. We had the forest, the lake, a campfire, a barbeque and a pink-laced handkerchief which was finally burnt along with the doggie-bag. We watched the darn thing go up in flames and we all had a hearty laugh.

HOPping to Conclusions

▸ *If you are two timing, please increase the count and multi-time*

▸ *Never ever trust a woman with a pink-laced handkerchief*

▸ *Every break-up is an opportunity to make extra cash when you are invited to listen to them whine*

▸ *The Doggie-bag is one of the best inventions ever*

▸ *Avoid people who whine or cry; simply ask them for their credit/ debit cards*

▸ *Never be friends with people who don't know when their parents come home*

▸ *Always keep a spare set of clothes in your car*
▸ *The size of a dog does not correspond with the intensity of its bite*
▸ *Never tell your friend's mother the truth, especially if she's just got back from work*
▸ *Life is all about choices – smarter people choose to bury pink-laced handkerchiefs*

I don't know how to behave myself … even in a jungle!

It was a lazy Saturday afternoon and we had spent so much time in the water we were worried about growing fins. We were bored and were having inane conversations about something academic, so totally uninteresting I was contemplating rolling over and playing dead. Since it was our summer vacations and most of the interesting people had skipped town, we were saddled with some residual stupid and dumb animals. Given that we were anyways stuck for a plan, we decided to head out to a forest and check out some stupid and dumb animals over there instead. As we debated about the destinations to drive to, we somehow managed to zero in on three.

Well, there were three people, so aren't there supposed to be three opinions? All that we needed was a three-sided coin to flip, and our decision would be made. Unfortunately, all three of us were somewhat equally built, so muscle-power was out. And all of us loved to drive, so psychological warfare was not an option. That left me with only one choice and that was to beg and grovel at their feet to go to where I wanted and they caved in to emotional blackmail.

We had absolutely no idea what a safari was. After all, we had always gotten to see those big dumb animals on posters of travel offices or on big hoardings that were used to sell tea-leaves. So, we had absolutely no clue about how one needs to behave in a forest. But we had several hobbies, owing to our very fine upbringing in urban India, and we named them after real and fictitious albums of one of our favorite rock-bands, Def Leppard. HOPfans classifies the moronic behavior of roadies in India as below:

Pyromania: One of the several hobbies that I'd learnt to skillfully master with my friends was pyromania. Every time we saw something that could be set ablaze without harming anyone, we would set fire to it and watch the flames leap. We became skilled in this art by setting fire to many haystacks, garbage dumps, thorny shrubs, bushes and heaps of newspapers. For us, it was nothing short of a soul-cleansing exercise that used to purge us of all the forthcoming sinful acts we were about to undertake in the very next hour. It was a fine and a very classy hobby.

Hysteria: Another one of our pastimes involved a bike. Two of us friends and the rider would swerve very close to a stray mongrel, while the pillion rider would stand up on one bike rest and use the other leg to whoop the stupid mongrel's butt. Of course, administering this technique to a goat never needed much practice or skill and we wouldn't have tried the trick with a cow or a bull or an elephant. We were pretty sensible that way. The inspiration for this hobby is attributed to many Hollywood flicks where they used to hunt people using cars and bikes.

Dementia: One of my personal favorites was to take midnight walks inside our gates community post midnight, just when it had stopped raining. The place used to reverberate with the croaks of those big horny toads all over the place, looking for a mate. We would arm ourselves with sticks and stones in heavy jackets, walk close to the sound and pound the place with stones till the sounds died. This particular hobby was a result of watching too much war on TV during the Iraq bombing days. That's how we were inspired.

Kleptomania: Another gem that we were forced to master owing to the high-priced junk and trinkets that were meant to be gifted to girlfriends. It was always unfathomable to me and my friends as to why some idiot would buy flowers, cards, bunny rabbits, and other such unspeakable junk to be gifted to chicks who need to be appeased and kept in good humor for various reasons. This gruesome ritual of offering precious gifts to such deities is known only to the civilized world. Our forefathers, the primitives, had this simple theory of using a thick wooden club which kept life simple. And soon man progressed and the wheel was invented. To save cash for more useful purposes like buying petrol and beer that would keep the spirit alive, we had no choice but to master the art of pinching these cheap cards, smelly flowers and ugly dolls from gift-shops. This kept the chicks in good humor as the hunger of the beast was appeased with the offerings, and we could go camping and road-trips.

While there were many such hobbies that are pursued across various towns and cities of India, this does not perchance include any normal behavioral pattern as recorded by all the moronic TV channels across the globe, as stated earlier. These go beyond the standard activities such as games and sports, billiards and snooker, cricket and football, girl-ogling and bird-watching, drinking and doping or hunting and fishing. So, armed with grit and attitude, some extra cash and a moronic friend's father's car, we checked into this place which offered these safaris, where they would drive us deep into the forests, spot animals and come back. Our first day was tame and lame. We saw some trees and leaves, some more trees and leaves, and much more trees and leaves. Exasperated, we returned only to crib about the similarity between all the trees and the leaves we had seen. We wanted to see animals, real mean and wild animals, of the four-legged variety. So the next day, money exchanged hands, we crossed a few palms with silver and managed to get into thickest of the restricted forest areas where the two-legged beasts are usually not entertained; instead, they are considered nourishment.

We did everything we were not supposed to do, as we later discovered. With absolutely no intention of gaining any knowledge, we learnt the hard way. Imagine lying on your stomach near an anthill in just your t-shirt and shorts. Well, a man's got to scratch when a man's got to scratch. Not allowed. Waiting for a dumb tiger near a water hole from atop a 'machaan' (a treehouse), without smoking – not allowed. Opening a can of beer in the sweltering sun while watching an elephant horde having a bath and going 'Whee-whee' while they playfully throw water all around, well, not allowed. Leaping from the jeep upon spotting pugmarks of a tiger and making a dash into the bushes, two pegs down, and calling out 'Kitty! Kitty! Good pussy, come to papa! Daddy's here to kick your butt!' You guessed it right! See? Your Intelligence Quotient is dropping at an alarming pace already. Opening a bag of chips to feed the chimps is a strict no-no. So is making faces at deer and fawns. Tempted to call elephant names of people whom they resemble from behind? Nix it.

This trip changed many things for me as I saw animals in different light. I had only seen them in cages with dim-bulbs, or within concrete enclosures where they would be treated better than us, or in travel brochures and posters. This was the virgin trip and over a period of time, this was only to become an obsession as I started my brush with the corporate sector, where I have met some really fierce and ugly beasts. Today, I feel more at home in the forest, with the beasts in the open, as we have switched places. It is I who sit in a closed, concrete enclosure, under dim bulbs and am taken good care of. God sure moves in mysterious ways

What I learnt during our first real trip into the forest taught me some invaluable lessons for a lifetime that I would, dear reader, like to share with you. I am pretty confident that you will find the tips below useful.

HOPping to Conclusions

▶ *Never look at elephants when they are having a bath. They get pissed.*
  How would you feel if an elephant walked into your bathroom while you were taking a shower?
▶ *You always know if there is a tiger in the vicinity simply by its growl – try downing 3 Red Bulls in a row and let out a loud burp....that's how it sounds*
▶ *A deer is a dandy animal. When you try to take a picture, they stand dumb*
▶ *A bison is a very big animal. You'd know when you can take a picture without zooming*
▶ *A leopard is a very tricky animal. You know you've spotted one when you see many spots together at the same time*

▶ *You know you are sitting on a crocodile when the log on which you just stubbed your cigarette, moves*

▶ *You know you've spotted a wild boar when your jeep moves downhill despite your brakes being locked*

▶ *In a jungle, prefix everything with the word 'Wild'. Wild-boar, wild-pig, wild-people, wild-animals, wild-anything … it makes you feel good; your money is being well-spent*

▶ *Never try to use a cell phone in deep forest. Chances are, you won't get the signal*

▶ *Never try to spit on monkeys, they jump around so much, usually it all falls on your t-shirt*

3 Alternative Theories

Stunted growth in the hallowed halls of learning,
A wild heart that's always yearning;
A pit stop needed when I must unwind,
Break away those chains, get away from the grind;
From dreadful schools to corporate cages,
As I keep on writing more trashy pages;
A sense of freedom makes my heart go 'Cheese'
Drive on, that's the spirit of 'Horn OK Please'...

Theoretically speaking, one could turn any argument into a conspiracy theory. We all learn so much from the dumb idiot box and even more idiotic leaders. It is important to understand here that we all run the risk of turning totally sane by the 31st of Feb, 2012. They even made a movie out of it. To save the world, from this impending calamity, I've decided to do my bit and so the purpose behind the book stays. After all, you are yet another moron who has been set back by a few hundred bucks with this book. Not only does that reflect on your diminishing level of intelligence, it also reflects upon your bank balance as I grow richer with every sucker who buys this book. And as I do not read, I decided to write. And so, I just wrote this crap and never read it. And you probably have been thinking about the various (mis)adventures of the author as I go through the trivialities of life, expanding my horizons by taking off like a moron to do a full-Monty of the nation over and over again. But the spirit of the nation can best be understood and fathomed by the people whom one meets on the way. And given the startling statistics published by the HOPfans at the beginning of the book, the majority of the Indian population (48% to be precise) is found on or near the roadside in India.

The point I'm trying to make over here, my friend, is this – I have no point to make, no morals or messages to be delivered. And so that leaves me a lot relieved and devoid of any sense or some moral-laden message to be delivered. I can afford to be all over the place with many scatter-brained thoughts running in parallel at the same time. I guarantee you 100% pure absurdity, devoid of any intelligence, and unadulterated crap that will change the way you think, feel or behave, by reversing your intelligence by at least 3 years. Isn't it moronic to listen to people or read books about them, who always have a point to make? Well, I've done worse (I am sure you've done too) – like trying to read trash written by some stunted bonsai manager about leadership and crap like that – especially when they try to sound intelligent and successful, usually when they've reached the very pits, the nadir, of their mediocre existence. My ass, to think we slave for such mediocre idiots in every field without giving it a thought and trashing our entrepreneurial instincts....

From Scuba diving to Vampires to Meditation to Farmville, all of which appear to have no threads in common to the untrained mind. I guarantee you this – you will see how it all comes together; how easily you understand the spirit of the philosophy 'Horn OK Please', as I patch up the pieces with feeble theories by the end of this chapter. Reading this chapter is like sitting under a tree and meditating – you simply let your thoughts wander all over the countryside. If a bird poops on your head when you reach the end of the chapter, take it from me.....you are enlightened.

Scuba diving is like driving an 800 cc car. Slow!

It was a boring Friday morning and the mechanic had come home to pick up my car for the regular mooching off, euphemistically known as servicing. Servicing? I just couldn't wait for the evening when I was to drive down for some eight hours with some of my friends to a secluded beach. We were to take a boat from there and get to an island where we could go scuba diving and snorkel like tadpoles. The sun was up, the climate was brilliant and my blackberry was not working since last night after I fished it out of the swimming pool. What else could one ask for? A heavy amount of Facebooking had got a few of us together and we had decided to skip town and get around for some serious fun after a week of dull and inane work.

As I was getting the car hauled up for the drive in the evening, the engineer seemed to be creating a very long list of items to be changed. It didn't look like a 'To-do list' anymore; rather, it looked more like my will or a desperate plea for a new car. It was obvious that I would not be able to take my car for the road-trip and my friend had an equally rickety SUV for the weekend. We decided to take the bus and along with the others, go on this trip with complete strangers, which was a much better idea as my friend-list had slowly started shrinking. I was beginning to find that my friends act very strange after marriage. Suddenly they were exposed to the world of free-sex. I guess, to many of them, it meant that they didn't have to reach for their wallets after sex as it came free. It was like one of those offers where you buy a new car and you get a year's insurance for free. And as I was soon to find out, it was going to be a brilliant trip as I was well prepared by watching 'Finding Nemo' over five times as homework.

Armed with loads of energy bars, some cash and beer cans, we boarded the bus after a rickety auto-rickshaw drive which, I am sure, has the potential to be turned into an adventure sport in itself. Making new friends and meeting new people is like trying out a wide variety of beer. The bus ride was peaceful and I just had to punch my friend twice in his face to make him stop snoring. After reaching the beach, we headed straight for the resort's pool, gear on; we were like the bunch of ugly tadpoles in the water as stated before, kicking up a storm. Practice sessions over, we headed for the island, loaded with anti-barf pills so as not to dirty up the boat in the two-hour boat-ride as I enjoyed Mother Nature in full splendor. Actually, this is the part which, although it sounds very romantic, is also the most irritating aspect of the boat. One has a 'starboard' and a 'portside'. Why does it become so difficult to call it 'right' or 'left' when it means the same thing? Why tax the brain by learning unwanted new-fangled (for this particular brain, that is,) jargon? It's actually worse trying to pick up sea-language than to learn a local language in India or abroad – at least you can put the latter to some use when you get lost some place. At sea, it makes no sense to learn another new set of terms as it will be of no use to you if you got lost. Take it from me, dear reader; no one is going to understand directions as one would on Indian roads. Imagine asking someone to take a sharp starboard turn right after an island, before taking a port turn and explaining things in latitudes, longitudes or depth. The damn sea, unlike the roads, looks the same everywhere and is perpetually wet. (Also applies to those with severe hydrophobia). It is better to just give up like Tom Hanks in 'Castaway' and start talking to your pet basketball.

The island is home to the great diversity of fish life common to Goa and the Arabian Sea. It is also well known for regular sightings of Turtles, Barracuda, Wrasse, Empty Beer Cans, Cobia, Small Sharks, Stingrays, Floating Underwear and Starfish. Mercifully, these names sound more dangerous than the fish themselves.

As the island neared, the clothes came off faster. As the anchor was dropped into the sea, me and my friends dived into the sea and swam to the shore, a feeling so invigorating that it cannot be explained. The reef was beautiful and the island was alive and breathing as we donned the snorkel masks and spent over five hours exploring the rich fauna that lay underneath. I think the fish get scared when you hover around looking scarier than a barracuda. To avoid growing gills and fins, we decided to take a break and go for scuba diving. Donning the scuba gear is fun as it can make you look like a superhero, barring the underpants that superheroes tend to don over their spandex.

I covered my eyes with those big nerdy glasses to prevent them from getting salted before donning my Donald Duck shoes. My friend had a small mishap as his cylinders were leaking and while testing out the depth, he had his ears ringing like Mariah Carey in full spate while attempting a mere 21 meters. This particular phenomenon makes driving better than scuba diving. One gets to change the songs and the artists while driving whereas while diving, one has no choice but to listen to Luciano Pavarotti in full spate. Another important difference that you, dear reader, may want to know of is whether drinking and diving is far more dangerous than drinking and driving. Underwater, I realized that bubbles make a racket. With two more divers, it is sheer cacophony. Staying calm in the face of mishaps is probably the most important thing. As my oxygen tube had the nasty habit of dissociating itself from my mouth repeatedly, the experience gained in training was put to its ultimate test. Drawing a parallel to the world above sea-level, this particular irritant is comparable to driving on city roads when one tends to roll-down the windows constantly and describe to the other person his entire family tree and the nasty things you want to subject them to. (It wouldn't be out of context here to state that power windows were actually the brainchild of a roadie who used to drive in Bangalore, where you need to constantly repeat this exercise of rolling down and cussing).

Of course, the most painful thing for a roadie, who is so used to flipping the middle finger at the drop of a hat, is that sign-language used underwater can be a very painful experience for you just can't flip the birdie to expect others to save your life after that. Bored after an hour and thoroughly pissed with the slow body movements underwater, I was mighty relieved to get out of the Donald-Duck gear and hit terra firma before taking off for an evening of kayaking, waterscooters (to get back my sanity after zero driving for over 24 hours), campfire and a few rounds of dumb-charades, before heading back to civilization. Looking back, the only way in which scuba diving helped me, was in my becoming better at dumb charades thanks to all the new-fangled sign language I learnt under water.

HOPping to Conclusions

▸ *Only try scuba diving if you want to find out how Donald Duck feels*

▸ *There is no term as 'drunken diving'; underwater you move like a drunk*

▸ *Sign-language is a pain in the ass, the middle-finger has no use underwater*

▸ *When under water, do not slap the other person if he/she stares at you and makes faces at you*

▸ *There is no pit-stop needed if you need to pee, which is the only good thing*

▸ *Full cylinders make more noise underwater, empty ones make you zoom like superman*

▸ *Do not fiddle around with cylinders if you want to avoid going off like a torpedo*

▸ *Never try to spit underwater, it increases your chances of living longer*

▸ *Never ever show the middle finger to your trainer under water if you are an amateur*

▸ *Earplugs don't work underwater, the pressure will have Mariah Carey sing in your ears*

Sky-diving is like the fabled 2-minute Indian noodle. It is over before you know it!

According to Osho, there are 112 techniques of meditation in his little black book of secrets. Music is one of them. I would apply it as a good, pulsating rock in my life. I must be close to attaining nirvana then. Driving could be another form of meditation, so I must be getting there at an accelerated pace? By that count, every person on Indian roads must be applying at least twelve techniques on a daily basis, and I just counted twenty-four that I use. With this stupendous math, I must be twice as much closer to attaining Nirvana. No wonder, driving at 150 Kmph comes easy to me on the highways, where one should typically be doing 70-100 Kmph. I surely do have to wear the seatbelt to prevent the halo from falling off......one could sense that such moronic thoughts had started to darken my mind as my face became more twisted and contorted with the savage guitar of Metallica in the background. It was time to pull over and let sanity take control before the moron took over completely. Every individual has many such random thoughts. Ever think about them deep enough to hear the call of the wild? When one honk on the city road wakes you up from the stupor? I had reached stratosphere, and I was about to jump off the building. I needed the twenty-fifth form of meditation after a 120 mph ride on I-5 North.

Other forms of stupidity known to the roadie are bungee jumping or its mutants such as sky jumping, free fall, base jumping or what have you, all of which can prove very painful experiences for a roadie. For a novice, they are akin to bondage, except, there is no pretty chick with a whip. Instead there are trained instructors (who are far more dangerous), who harness you up, take you to the top of the crane and let you free fall. Although I have done this more than five times, I still do not get the idea behind being strapped into nothing more than a seat belt, and being helplessly flung over a cliff or from the terrace of a government-building. It is worse than being fed Chinese takeaway everyday for a month at a stretch and being made to watch the chick-flick 'Sunshine Cleaning', over and over again. I must have been really bored out of my skull for having agreed to subject myself to this extreme stupidity over and over again. I loathed the very idea of being trussed up like a chicken, surrounded by braggarts and motor-mouths, whose very idea of fun was tying up dumb people and throwing them off a cliff, and getting paid to do so.

This gut-wrenching, bowel-loosening sport is actually not far removed from the feeling of helplessness experienced during an auto-rickshaw ride on Indian roads. Just that bungee jumping is a far safer thing to experiment. They strapped me up into a harness and a jumpsuit while I tried to go 'boing-boing' on the trampoline we stood on. Once they were done tying and gagging me up, I felt more helpless than as a pillion rider with one of my crazy friends from high school. I was hauled up 850-odd feet and the feeling I was very close to was that which one experiences in a 'Slingshot' (yet another stupid sport which I'd done thrice in Orlando – but that's very tame). The 'descender machine' has guide-wires that prevent you from spinning like a loose nut in the sky. I guess the folks were convinced of my lunacy as they hauled me up about 400 feet and I started singing very loudly as the excitement grew. It was after that that I realized that I was being hauled up real quick for the balance 450 feet. Even at that altitude and in my condition, as I continued to sing and go 'whoo-hoo', I could sense the people down below didn't quite fancy my singing. Maybe, they just wanted me to shut up or stay out of ear-shot or both. And so, as a punishment, they just dropped me from there and I was on a free fall.

The only challenge I faced while coming down was that I wasn't allowed to wear my spectacles and I wasn't carrying my contact lenses. Any blind-bat like me in the world would know how it feels to be growing up with one of the major faculties being challenged (and I'm not talking about the brain here) and still insisting on trying out all things that any other person would. It's like being a cross between a bat and Tarzan (An ape-man, who's got great eyesight here as a real swinger in loin cloth gets a real hot chick) and am reminded of the days when I used to jump from 14 feet high up at night and dive into the deepest part of the swimming pool. From the top, the water always looks solid at night without spectacles or contact lenses. But the fun was in doing it over and over again till you outgrow the fear. Of course, the free swings after the free fall remain etched in my memory consuming 2% of my brain (a fact that substantially reduces my IQ).

Maybe, it was the fear factor which drove me to try this dumb sport over and over again till I was set free and back behind the wheel on I-5 back toward San Diego. Of course, not to mention the cute little badge which I earned proudly proclaiming 'Extreme Sky jumper'. When I left the ring, I could hear sighs of relief and cries of joy. Turning back once, I could see the instructor wiping his brow, and passing on a tissue to a colleague who had tears of relief in her eyes. A sight so beautiful that it made me want to first kiss the road with utter glee as I drove toward the sunset.

HOPping to Conclusions

▶ *Empty bladders before they haul you up. 850 ft high, dangling in mid-air, the urge alone can kill*

▶ *Never laugh at a trussed turkey before you attempt the sport.*
You won't laugh at it ever again

▶ *Kill the braggart in you, or the instructor will kill that*
braggart, up in the air

▶ *Once again, drinking and diving don't mix*

▶ *Do not attempt Facebooking on your iPhone mid-air. Carry a*
blackberry instead

▶ *If you want to feel like Pierce Brosnan jumping off Hoover*
Dam, do a 500+ ft jump at least

▶ *Base jumping is for people who do not find anything better to*
live for

▶ *It is similar to Scuba diving in the sky*

▶ *There are no airbags in case of a mishap when you land,*
another reason why driving is safer

▶ *There are easier ways to die faster. Cheaper too.*

The Vampire Strikes back!

My first trip to a hospital happened when, I think, a vampire
bit me on my butt as it was much more than a pain in the
neck. I hadn't performed any heroic feat to save the world
like the heroes in Hollywood flicks nor was I in Iraq or any
of those places where people drop bombs for a lark and kill
millions (Is that an extreme sport known to the civilized
world?). I had just fallen off a dumb dune buggy on a bumpy
track which was far more motorable than the roads I take
every day to get to work in Bangalore. For a regular city-
driving professional in India, this would rank the lowest. It
was a very lame reason to go to a hospital. And the reason
for falling off my buggy was actually a conspiracy. Being a
compulsive roadie, to show the victory sign, my middle-finger

would come up involuntarily. As I was way over my 7th lap, I had to get off the track and when I was being flagged to get off the last lap, I gleefully chose to acknowledge the flag-bearer, in the best-known manner known to me, half-way through my last lap. The next few seconds are a haze as I chose to show him the victory sign and made the classic roadie mistake of flipping the birdie. I would know as to why I was flagged into the puddle area when I was not experienced enough to do water thing before. I could feel the sound of my helmet kissing the used tyres around me, which are meant to ease the crash. I got up and drove my car back to the resort loaded on energy drinks and testosterone. Next morning, I was walking around like the living dead with a tilt that asks for a tight slap.

It was during one of my year-end stretches which I pulled across the beaches of South India that I decided to subject myself to one of the most inane sports known to the motor-savvy world. A nutcase vehicle like a dune buggy is like a cross between a Maruti 800 and a moped gone mad. You either give me a power-packed car with roads to explore or nothing at all. After a nasty bump over predefined dirt-tracks somewhere in the south of India during one of my beach-trips, I thought I would give this sport a shot. Two things – it isn't what a roadie in India would quite call a sport. Second, the only shot that I got was from this wicked vampire masquerading as nurse. Actually, nurses and lab technicians of the world are vampires who walk on this earth. They just grew sophisticated over time, and they drink our blood after sucking it out in those thick-needled syringes and storing it in bottles. They do not inject anything in us; they just suck out our blood, neatly pack them in pouches or bottles and brand them as various beverages and sell it in the black market. This is to increase the population of vampires on earth, which had started dwindling over a period of time owing to coagulation amongst vampires sucking the wrong blood groups from their victims. An analogy can be drawn to our world as we read and hear much about spurious alcohol and people going blind or dead or both. Anyways, coming back to the point, here I was, feeling as if a vampire had bitten a bit of my butt.

The Lame-brains tried their level best to tie me down to the hospital for two nights, but I managed to flee from there, somehow. The MRI test was performed on the high field (1.5 tesla) magnet while multiple sagittal slices were taken through the neck utilizing T1 weighted spin echo and a T2 weighted inversion recovery sequence. 8mm axial slices were then taken through a T2 weighted inversion recovery sequence er… yeah, Great! Huh! Dude! I didn't know it was that simple and cool? Of course I understand, wouldn't anybody?

Going through a stupid range of tests simply because I carried a fat insurance card, having a nurse who looked like Grace Jones puncture my gluteus-maximus with painkillers that were called "Wolverine" or something, dealing with the post-traumatic-stress of having gone through a range of x-rays and realizing that I looked better in x-rays than in real life – that hurt. The Bone-collector with kinky hammers and tongs on me, save stuffing me into an iron maiden – that hurt. The vampires gleefully sucking me dry and breaking out into maniacal laughter for all they were worth – that hurt. The only fun part was the massive commotion I caused ever so frequently at the hospital ward with my whims, fancies and tantrums. Heh! Loved that part! The ENT guy made me sit on a monstrous throne with lights shining bright from all over – reminded me of the House of Wax. Thank God, I was spared the hand-cuffs, the electric shocks or Chinese food (read torture). The fun part was the MRI – like a silver coffin, they put me into this round tomb-like structure, and after that they made me go through the agony of listening to Trance music inside. I can now bet my life on it – every single DJ on the planet who plays Trance has been through an MRI scan. Lame-brains tried their level best to tie me down to the hospital for two nights, but I managed to flee from there, somehow. I hope I can escape tonight again before any white-coats come knockin' on heaven's door.

Of course, the best part was the truck-load of Hollywood/Bollywood movies and having this stupendous wave of sympathy sweep across my family and friends, all for nothing! Leaving the hospital a free man, post my check-up from the neck-up, I was taken home by my freak-buddies – Derek, Goose and Galileo. I suspect I heard the sound of celebrations as I left the asylum. Looking back, it was only my whims, fancies and tantrums that helped me escape the dark castle with a promise to self that I would never do a dune buggy again.

HOPping to Conclusions

▶ *The size of the tablet is inversely proportional to its potency*
▶ *Sleep deprivation can lead to very interesting things*
▶ *All Vampires don't have sharp teeth & look menacing; some wear spectacles too*
▶ *Nurses in movies are always prettier*
▶ *While grim faces and heavy talk can scare the crap out of anyone, just heavy talk is much worse*

▶ *Never make any wise-ass remarks to a doctor*
▶ *One always looks a lot more handsome/prettier in an x-ray*
▶ *MRI Units are run by Trance-lovers and they hate heavy metal*
▶ *Do not believe a nurse when he/she tells you it won't pain, especially when he/she smiles*
▶ *10. Never tinker around the doctor's room when waiting. Things often tend to go beep*

You like Farmville on Facebook? Well, then use this book to hide your face!

HOPfans revealed another startling fact in the rise of Social Networking in India, Facebook, one of the fastest growing social networking sites in India and the world, recently beat Google as well, clearly indicating that like Twitter and LinkedIn, games on Facebook are potentially more dangerous than swine flu or AIDS. The highly qualified researchers at HOPfans, who recently concluded a study on the increasing breast-size of women in Britain, also shared some ugly truths about the rising menace of the online Facebook game 'Farmville' and other such vile acts indulged in by the Indian population. Honestly, 'Farmville' scares me much more than jaywalkers, call-center vehicles and auto-rickshaws on Indian roads. They are as evil, if not more, than the drunken truck drivers on the Indian highways. HOPfans figures indicate crime figures exceeding 32 million players (and rising steadily) of this stupid game on Facebook all across the world. Agreed, India is an agrarian economy, but this is taking things a bit too far.

Though Social Media was bringing together a lot of like-minded people, I sometimes do worry about posterity. Surely, a few years down the line, if someone were to ask a person where they grew up, I'm sure the answer would be 'Facebook', 'Orkut', 'Farmville', 'Twitter' or something stupid like that, instead of the place of birth. In fact, I have this strange and recurring dream every night which includes me running like a maniac, over a small fuzzy animal called 'Twitter', to avoid getting bit on my butt by a sharp-toothed fur ball called 'Digsby', stepping on a small 'Orkut' before crashing into my 'Facebook' wall and passing out ….I needed this break and I needed it bad. The scarier part is the presence of yet another nerdy Indian behind the game, who created this deadly virus in five weeks from Conception to Launch. HOPfans is pursuing Interpol for an extradition treaty with the Government of United States to have the dude deported. There are way too many Indian women seduced by this virtual farmer, who has the potential to replicate the Chinese population on Facebook.

HOPfans further revealed the top three concerns on which they are currently working on:

1. There is a baby born to a Chinese woman every 36th hour, who is a Farmville addict
2. There is a baby born to an Indian woman every 48th hour, who is a Farmville addict
3. Farm animals in Farmville are doubling in population to wipe out humans in 17 months

Based on the above statistics, HOP concluded that these two women must be found and stopped immediately before they clutter the world with more babies.

HOPping to Conclusions

▸ *Driving keeps you off Farmville, if not off social networking sites altogether*

▸ *Always keep extra cash to pay off traffic cops in India, also known as the Social Networking tax*

▸ *Battling cows on roads is far more exciting than Farmville*

▸ *A real farmer or a driver need not have to worry about picking crops, seeds or cow dung*

▸ *Unlike Farmville, where you must design a farm with efficiency, you can buy an efficient car*

▸ *It is cheaper to be a roadie with just one car, than a dumb farmer buying buildings all the time*

▸ *Do not try Farmville if you are pregnant. Especially, if you are an Indian or a Chinese*

▸ *You can drive a small car, you cannot drive a small farm*

▸ *A roadie will never have to worry about ugly virtual smells of a farm in the future*

▸ *A roadies never has to worry about mystery eggs, only speeding tickets and road-signs*

I have a sneaking suspicion that you may have understood by now that this chapter was a red herring, just as the book is a Trojan horse. But the Trojan virus I implant in you (if you read the book till the end), shall make you a proud moron. Well, no one ever said you are picking up a classic here.

A roadie just needs a reason to drive. To grab that extra bit of sun, wind, sand and exploring various cities – it is a philosophy. Even if it means conjuring up a totally warped image of talking to a pregnant Facebook addict in China, there cannot be a cause nobler than the pregnant woman's.

The true vagabond heart of a roadie is underlined about being a rebel without a cause. All you need is a good car and some cash. It is not my problem if a bird didn't poop on your head.

4 Day in the Life of a Moron

When you live in a box, you want to break free
Feel the wind in your hair, the world is there for you
to see,
Just stay safe, drive with care,
ATMs, Medics and mechanics, just beware
The rise of the moron is an impending curse,
Thank your stars for it could have been much worse;
India Inc. is a gruesome scene,
Bright young professionals in an evil machine;
If you are a moron, say, that's cool,
So, what are you – a bad manager or a pathetic fool?
India 2.0 holds promise,
I just don't know what rhymes with this.
An exit from the grind makes you say 'Cheese'
Drive on, that's the philosophy behind 'Horn OK Please'...

I'd like to play indoor cricket, hit the cuckoo clock and watch the dumb bird drop dead

It is two a.m. now, I am staring at the cuckoo clock, waiting for the dratted bird to come out, so I can wring its stupid neck. It's been a hard day, just like any other day.

The cuckoo clock has been a bane of my life. May the wrath of a thousand locusts infest the underpants of the inventor of the stupid cuckoo clock. I hate cuckoo clocks. Thinking it was five am and that I was late, I got up, all woozy. Within ten minutes, I realize, two hours have passed and it is now seven am. God almighty! I got the pointers wrong! And so I woke up at one-thirty am!!..... I never wind it to make a racket every hour.

I have a five am flight to catch and there has not been a single instance when I have not been the last person to board the aircraft, no matter how early I've got up. After all, consistency is the name of the game and I have always been consistently messed up. Getting ready to get to the airport and watch those constipated faces print out my boarding pass, with equally constipated security guards at the security gate, who never tire from making me feel so special. Step aside, please, Sir? Somehow, I always seem to be the random guy. That random statistic. The computer always chooses to pick me out with that uncanny ability, that thirty-odd single male, traveling alone, terrorist-looking and having that stupid smirk on my face that seems to distinguish me from all those regular travelers who seem to revel in standing in a queue for hours, while I make a dash to the hallowed portal to the sanctum sanatorium called the waiting area post security-check. Trust me on this, dear reader, the people at the security gates do not have a sense of humor, which I have often discovered in the most unpleasant way. The lady making the announcements seems to have an acute case of verbal diarrhea compounded by severe mental constipation. Why else would she continue to rant the same thing over and over again? Yes, woman, I shall board at my will and wish. And if you run out of seats, I do not mind standing and traveling. Or for that matter, lean from the door as they do in those over-crowded public transport buses on Indian roads.

As I am packing, I realize that suitcases have a nasty tendency to bloat up every time I put stuff in them. It only gets worse when one tries to repack. iPod – Check! iPad – Check! Apple Mac – Check! Darn! I just bit into my laptop and tapping on my apple that was supposed to be my prebreakfast snack. Apple is confusing the hell out of me today, while I realize that my wallet is empty and I have no money as usual. I decide to make a mad dash to the nearest ATM near my house and I suddenly get inspired by all those marvel comic super-heroes. You know those jocks who wear their underpants on top of their trousers? Yeah, like that. As I make a mad dash to the ATM, I get these vivid and horrific images of Spiderman trying to use his confounded webbing and taking a short-cut to the bank. Hell, if Spiderman were to try out his stunts in India, he would be scraping his butt, his webbing stuck behind an old truck with a sign-board proudly proclaiming the classic Indian philosophy "Horn OK Please". God only knows what it means. There are no tall buildings around and Bangalore looks like a post-war Afghanistan, bombed out and desolate in the wee hours of morning, with absolutely no semblance of civilization, except for all those under-construction flyovers and roads. The perils of trying to fight crime in a developing country, I am sure Spiderman would be mauled across the street, caught in his own webbing with a thousand cars honking at his scraped-red butt. And so the super-heroes wear their underpants like that, I conclude. Imagine Batman, stuck in his stupid bat mobile in any of the Indian towns. He would be caught in a jam for hours on end, stopping at each signal and melting in his black underwear.

Superman, from way above, would never be able to spot any city from the skies, and would fly right over them, as they are so dark and it's a miracle how flights land and take off in the dead of night.

Somehow, I reach the ATM. I insert my card and punch in the amount. At the precise moment when I try to take out the cash, the stubborn dispenser bites my middle-finger and scrapes the skin off, straight to the bone. Born greedy and impatient, I could never repeat the procedure of withdrawing cash in installments and save my fingers from the flesh-eating, bone-chewing cash-dispenser of a big, dumb robot called the ATM. (Appendage Tearing Monstrosity). I collect the cash, wipe the floor clean of blood-stains, mouth my choicest obscenities to the dratted machine that seems content after chewing my fingers to the bone as I get a sinking feeling in my stomach (very similar to Monday morning blues) that I might end up being late and miss my flight. As usual.

I dash back to my house, in the dead of night like the Flash, running at break-neck speed before I bleed to death. Somehow, I get into my car and try to breathe life into the old one. Like a necrophile, I insert the keys and she groans like Medusa shown the mirror, although I don't feel like a gladiator fighting demons. As if I am having a whale of a time bleeding to death, trying to arouse this beaten down-old bucket of bolts of mine at three am. She does me a favor and whines back to life and I start driving like crazy. Only, this time, it's for survival and not for fun. Right now, the mechanical voice of the lady in the car is irritating the hell out of me as she asks me to buckle up. Constantly. Imagine making love to the woman in the GPS. When it's all done, she would say "You have arrived"… How romantic!! I wonder when these smart engineers in the design department of these automobile manufacturers are going to start paying attention to folks like us who are in desperate need of a keyboard instead of the horn to help us Facebook while driving. Or let's change the voice of that witchy woman inside the GPS, who sounds like a completely disgusted mother-in-law.

It is so exasperating to explain to a traffic cop that I am not using the cell phone, Mister, I was Facebooking. Is that a crime? Is there a tweet on that? Show me the rules that are published somewhere on Wikipedia. What prevents those idiots who manufacture cars in India to rip-off the horn and put in a keyboard? I could simply tweet if I want the jerk in front of me to drive faster or get out of my way. If they are so smart, why couldn't they have put the steering wheel in the middle of the car, world over, instead of getting dumb people like me all confused every time I travel to the US or Europe? I think the first thing we need to do is to make those people in the United Nations forget about global warming and wars and make them focus on core issues like these which impact the life of an Indian 2.0. All this liberal use of the noisy horn can be eliminated if they just surgically removed it like the appendix, which is a vestigial organ like the human brain. Horn OK please.

The Botox Scare

Having been successful in waking up the dead-beat post a successful vehicular autopsy, I am now faced with the grumpy face of a nurse with thick lips as if some patient in pain had beaten her black and blue after a few rounds of painful butt-puncturing games. Now, I start to writhe in pain – not by my hurt, but just looking at the nurse is very painful. The Vampire, I shall christen her 'Botox'. Why 'Botox'? I don't know, but it sure sounds scary and cool. Her teeth look like a crude coconut scraper used in rural India, I'm worried she's going to chew off what remains of what was once my middle finger. Anyways, I show her my middle-finger and feel a sense of triumph. Cheap thrills. Come on, lady, nurses in those kind of movies look a lot prettier and you ain't really any fantasy come to life. And this ain't that kind of a book, anyways. All chirpy now, I show her all three fingers as I have half-a-mind to tell her to read between lines. But I want my middle-finger to be restored or it's going to be really tough to drive on Indian roads, roll down the windows and flick the birdie. The middle-finger is a very important part of the hand if you happen to be a roadie.

The charlatan arrives; they call him the doctor. More like a witch doctor with a mask. Hold on, that's no mask, that's his face. If I were the President of India, the first thing I would do is to cordon off this hospital, just like Area 51, and dip all the hospital staff in big bottles of formalin and put them up on display. These are blood-sucking vampires, as I have stated earlier, dear reader. But considering your low IQ (a fact as you obviously have more money than brains for having bought this book), I dare to repeat my words. I suspect he has an Iron Maiden in the torture chamber and I'm going to be subject to some real torture. As he makes me go through an X-Ray, I realize how awesome my middle-finger is to now have grown in prominence, owing to constant usage over the years of driving. Grumpy psycho charlatan seems to scribble something that looks like a hieroglyphic that needs to be inscribed on a tomb. I break into a cold sweat imagining what my pyramid is going to look like once Frankenstein here is done with me. Botox arrives with what vaguely resembles a poisonous arrow from Xena's quiver and a bottle of what seems like spray-paint. I now know what's going to happen to my behind. Botox is going to ram that needle into my gluteus-maximus, suck out a gallon of B+ (for her weekend orgy with the other vampires who shall feast upon my blood) and once the deed is done, she will spray paint my backside with 'Horn OK Please' and make me look like a banged-up ambassador car on NH17. For all the agony I made her go through, she would then mummify my finger and crucify it on a splint. The bandage on my hand now looks obscene with a perpetual 'Up Yours' sign. Horn OK Please.

It is five a m now and no way can I make it to the airport; the driver of the bird is now left high-and-dry. As I walk back to my car post this horrendous experience, my sixth sense (which is the only one I have and I can talk about as no one understands it – at least you won't) warns me that my ol' bucket-of-bolts is about to die on me. And she does. She refuses to show any signs of life in her – just like Botox. With the borrowed help of a few Good Samaritans who perpetually live on the roads or by its side (The Lechers), we push the car and reach the garage which is to open at ten a m and I have good couple of hours to kill, waiting for the mechanic to come and yell at the engine and make it come to life. A monkey-suit in India is no fun and that's what I'm wearing. I run a high-risk of being accused of being wealthy at the garage. Mechanics world-over, as a breed, have the uncanny skill of bloating up effort, replacing things that are working fine and leaving cigarette butts in the car as a trademark. Unlike doctors, mechanics are mechanically inclined and tend to screw-up anything that's working. My bucket-of-bolts is no exception. It now looks like a fossilized dinosaur from the Mesozoic or Paleozoic era, which Fred Flintstone would have abused in a drag-race on primitive roads. Though my car and the roads in India are still from the same era, I'm not. And, hence, the mismatch and the inconsistency in my thought processes, which is a true reflection of the spirit of urban India. An urban Indian or an Indian 2.0 has no clue if a chicken has two or four legs. If you, dear reader, disagree, then your IQ is way too high for this book.

Two hours of down-time. They say an idle mind is a devil's workshop, a surgical ward or a closed garage in this case. I decided to light up my life with a cigarette, which obviously was a very stupid thing to do. I was fooling myself with the thought that I had been smoking for many years and had still not gotten addicted to it. When I decided to quit smoking, I realized how easy it was so I started doing it repeatedly. I flicked the lit-up cigarette, which had a mind of its own. Like a homing device, it found its way to the nearest stack of old newspapers which the pyromaniac in me enjoyed for a good fifteen minutes. Not that I had any intention of starting a fire, but the small little puff of smoke gave me a sign that it was to be another one of those days, so might as well enjoy it.

And on came a barrage of garbage thoughts. I had woken up at two am, yet missed my flight. I had packed my bags, but was at a garage. I had managed to get money out from the ATM, but at the cost of a finger-bust. Why did life have to come to me at a discount? Those little, fine prints which one tends to overlook become suddenly very prominent when one faces one of those days. God, give me patience, but give it to me now! These random thoughts that plague one to madness (read as incubation of desire to write a damn book) are making me take on a full-Monty trip of India.

Here I was, wondering if work is a four- letter word and life is not, why does the corporate world talk about a work-life balance? A botched-up meeting today, I need to be back at work to ensure that while they pretend to pay me, I pretend to work. After all, diplomacy is not something that I had mastered and Corporate India is replete with snakes, cockroaches, leeches and every other disgusting life-form known to humanity. Which idiot invented the concept of a workplace? And I was surrounded by people who would ask me to go to hell in such a smooth way that I would actually look forward to it. They were the diplomats, and I had to learn how to handle them.

Then there are the butt-kissers, who would surgically glue their lips to their bosses. Beating them is tough, as this coterie is like a swarm of bees. One prod by Winnie the Pooh would have the bees stinging you in all the wrong (or right) places.

Then you have the leeches: they will suck you dry with off-loaded work that you would have to do for them, yet ensure that the credit is blissfully passed on to the leeches.

And of course, you have the chauvinists at workplace, who refuse to take orders from the superior sex. Just because a male has an extended outgrowth of a body-part doesn't automatically render him worthy of being a man. There is a huge difference. In order to sound neutral, let me take on the women at workplace as well. There are some at the workplace who will perpetually whine about how difficult it is to work in a male-dominated workforce, make doe-eyes and perpetually use this as a lame-brain sympathetic wave to climb the social and corporate ladder. Keep gender aside, woman, It is difficult to work – period – especially when you are not used to working. All in all, there are three kinds of people who, in the Indian corporate sector – the males, the non-males and the females. These are mostly mediocre monkeys, born to defy Darwin at every point in time, going against evolution in every way and hallucinating that this is what life is all about while performing their day-to-day Mickey-Mouse rituals at the workplace while continuing to destroy creativity with regular carpet-bombing of mundane work while successfully decimating progressive young and impressionable minds, thereby turning them into slaves to the grind. You want loyalty? Get a lap dog.

Give me a break, you fool! It's just a phone call; they are not playing the national anthem nor is it a 21-gun salute. So, why are you standing up and talking? I need some change, not the kind that goes into a piggy bank. And the only change I have right now, today, is loose change in my pocket. And it makes a racket when I walk; so I don't like it. And anyways, I'm sick of the corporate lingo which is a language spoken by people with forked-tongues. Sample this:

HOPping crazy corporate talk

▸ *Can we 'Touch-base' now? (And create a scandal?)*
▸ *Shall we take this 'Off-line' (Means I don't like your face and you better shut-up)*
▸ *Why don't you 'take a dump' from her? (Do I look like a septic tank to you?)*
▸ *I am running on low bandwidth (Means can you do my job for me while I goof off?)*

▶ *'Let us not externalize the issue' (Means you better do it as best you can and I'm the boss)*

▶ *Can we 'park it'? (And run the risk of a traffic jam of issues?)*

▶ *I need 'data-points' (Means I cannot nail you so help me screw you)*

▶ *'Will you debrief' me? (What kind of a pervert are you?)*

▶ *You 'might want to consider it' (Means if you don't, I'll screw you)*

▶ *'Spare me the details' (Means you better put a lid on it before it blows up in your face)*

That's the sausage machine a grown-up has no choice (or so one thinks) but to conform to and I was no exception. Right from high-school, when I wished my grades would smoke weed to go higher, drooling at our math teacher who would be talking about figures of the wrong kind, to the moral science moron who flunked me up saying I had no morals. The more I studied, the harder it became for me to tell them what they were looking for in an answer and I felt less sure of getting good grades. Well, my question is – is there a page on Facebook that has a list of all the dos and don'ts of life? Or a book?

So, dear reader, this piece of garbage, accumulated from the fountain head of trash, is written when the septic tank inside my head was full of crap and I decided to vomit it all out as words. Well, if you thought you bought a literary master-piece, you are sadly mistaken. However, since you bought it, you might as well choose to make it your loo-book, if nothing else works and you cannot go through all the chapters. I have consistently maintained that this is a book for the left-brained people, who have left their brains behind while making the decision to buy this at the bookstore. Right-brained? Well, you rightly left your brains behind. And the behind decides everything. Like a rear-view mirror or the back of a truck –with a brightly painted 'Horn OK Please'.

Well, the brain is an organ with which we think we think and I don't think that is correct as thinking is pretty much forbidden while reading this book. Did I make any sense here? No? I thought as much. Anyways, that was my feeble attempt at sounding deep and intelligent and I failed miserably, I guess. This is what happens when the septic-tank in your head (medically termed as the 'brain') is kept in a cage called the skull for such a long time that it stunts one's growth. And that's why one tends to think in a box. I guess when folks ask you to think 'outside-of-the-box', you are expected to stop thinking, pout some gibberish, look very serious and people will think you are deep. After all, such is life and this is the lifecycle of an Indian, who grows up with a tricycle, graduates to a bicycle, then moves on to a motorcycle before getting trapped in the vicious cycle of mediocre existence. Now I realize how badly I need to go on a road-trip.

Behold the Mechanical Moron

Here comes the magician. What? No cape like Mandrake? How are you going to fix my car, dude? No, I don't have a monkey wrench; do I look like a monkey to you? And why should I worry about the engine oil? Do I need a technical manual to talk to you now? Or do I use sign-language to converse with you? It's a curse! Why do I get saddled with morons? Horn OK Please? Were you 'Born OK Please'? No, I don't remember my cell phone number, I never talk to myself.

I'm staying here till you fix my car. Do you understand? And your face belongs in an obituary column if you don't fix it in the next half-hour. It's close to noon and I need to get back to work, which is a four-letter word on a day like today and I want my life back and no, I do not mean Bacardi...well, that too, but let's get to the heart of the matter and get down to some serious post-mortem of my car? Like please? Pretty please? With lots of cream and cheese? Anyways you look like someone straight out of Mandrake's 'Rogues Gallery'.

It worked. The miserable monkey of a mechanic climbed all over the car, showed a lot of attitude, while I stood there pretending to be awed while he pretended to work his magic. But this miserable flea-bag in moth-eaten work-clothes seemed to have cast some strange spell on my car and he brought it back to life, back from the other side. Every mechanic the world over looks at a customer as a sucker with two heads, eight arms, four legs and a thick fat wallet. Since customers with the above anatomy are fictitious exaggerations and figments of my imagination, ignore that, dear reader and just consider the 'big fat wallet' part to be true.

A Wok with Chung? Why should I wok with Chung? Psst! Who *is* Chung?

I was hungry, tired and irritated now. My stomach was making obscene sounds and demanded to be fed. I had the choice of a Subway snack or Chinese takeaway. Tough choices of life, back at the cross-roads of critical decision-making with my wisdom being clouded by hunger and my stomach having a life of its own. On one hand, Subway sandwiches are clumsy and I've learnt that there are two ways to unwrap the cover – the right way and the wrong way. I've always opened the wrapper and realized halfway through the sandwich that wrappers with ketchup don't really go easy on the stomach. And one makes very angry faces while eating a Subway sandwich. The same applies to pizzas, burgers and all the oil-dripping junk-food which needs to be gobbled in a hurry. After finishing my sandwich, I've always had to clean the carpet, the table, my hands and feet, They're that clumsy and demand a near-bath experience after eating. On the other hand, I had to to appease my hunger. And the fire in my belly turned into a major case of acidity after a round of poisonous Chinese food.

I wonder why it is called Chinese takeaway. I mean, they've taken away half the jobs in United States, half of India in the surrounding areas of Ladakh, and half of the cyberspace population with Baidu. Maybe their next planned move is to take over my stomach. And that is just not done. They can keep what they have taken away but also take away some of our leaders as well. But not my stomach. I'd rather eat my pride and have a Subway sandwich. It was way past noon, my finger was aching as I cursed Botox under my breath before I got behind the wheel to head to work and keep things unbroken so they don't need to be fixed later on. My wallet had suffered a huge burn and my pocket had a hole the size of a crater as big as one of the craters on the moon and I was waiting for the next dole or what they call euphemistically – payday. Since I do not think much, I also went to the Chinese joint and had something which I cannot pronounce. The only embarrassing part was when I mistook the Chinese tea served after lunch to be a finger-bowl and promptly dipped my fingers in and felt very happy with myself. Hell, who cares? This is India, after all, not China. I can not only ask for a finger-bowl after my meal, I can also ask for a bed-pan if I feel like it. This is my country.

The human mind is a septic tank of crappy thoughts

I was thirsty and I needed a Red Bull. I stopped at the nearest supermarket where the counter was manned by a very thin lady. Had she gotten any thinner, I would have taken photocopies of her and you could have used it as a book mark for this book. On the other side was a customer woman, who seemed to have taken in all the meat from the thin one and she alone would have needed five bookmarks for her multiple double-chins. Since I cannot count beyond five, I would say it was two times five double-chins. This is India, it has nothing to do with me doing anything with a chick called Dia. On one side you have poverty; on the other side you have the rich. It's better to become rich and stay rich, I suppose. And so, dear reader, I wrote the book. While I glanced at the TV, there was news of some volcano which had erupted somewhere in Europe. Europe is full of English spelling mistakes. This volcano was called "Eyfafjallajokull" and saying it was more horrific than the volcano eruption itself. If I took my laptop and banged my head on the keyboard repeatedly and wrote down what came on screen, this would be it. Or if I gargled real hard and spat it all out noisily, this is exactly what it would sound like.

Hell, now that I knew that I had the power to name a volcano, I knew I was good for something. Something else. Well, everything else than what I am doing right now, living in a box. There it was, working and spewing out smoke as

I imagined what it would be like if I were to lay down in a park doing nothing, smoke a cigarette. Then, people would say I'm working. That's the subtle difference between man and a volcano, I guess. Well, at least, this day was lighting up those tiny dim-bulbs inside my head and now I was more sure that I would do a road trip and that it would span the nation end-to-end. And there would never ever be any correlation between what I thought, what I said, what I imagined and what I wrote in this book. So if you are hunting around for a reason or a meaning or some deep crap, you might as well perish the thought now.

Random names the world over

Back in the car, I was worried about my scheduled meeting with a French gentleman whose name sounded like 'Guacamole' and a Portuguese lady whose name sounded like 'Anaconda' being skipped. I had no choice but to call up my Indian colleague named 'Gopal'. He prided himself in calling himself 'Gopendra'. Imagine the plight of any American or a Brit when they shook hands with him, asked him his name, and he'd ask them to take a leak! I thanked my stars that I wasn't Chinese or I would have called myself 'You' or I might have called you 'Mee'. Well, anyways there is my fellow Indian colleague called 'Balasubramanian' who didn't like to be called 'Balls' just like my Amercian colleague who didn't like to be called 'Dick'. And I thank my stars we didn't do any business with Arabian Sheikhs called 'Mehboob'. Every nationality has its share of funny names, but we Indians take the cake, the bakery, the baker and the baker's wife. And if we don't remember names, we just rudely snap our fingers or make funny smooching noises to call people. You, dear reader, could be next, if you also fall in the category of world's greatest nobodies, like so many other morons who have bought a copy of this book. As you might have noted, morons are neither racists nor feminists nor chauvinists. We are just confused, we are liberal. We take any shit. And today, that is why in our nation, anything goes. We call it 'Chalta hai' (It's alright), which is reflected in the deep-rooted philosophy etched behind vehicles on Indian roads as 'Horn OK Please'.

As I cut across one end of the city to another, all kinds of domesticated animals, weird people, stupid and irresponsible drivers, angry people and monstrous trucks carrying turbines – are all on the same road. It's a circus out here and I must get to the other end of the city in another hour. When I look at a cow crossing the road, I realize that though considered sacred, it has to be a very scared animal on Indian roads. Maybe it was a typo-error in the olden days and we started worshipping it. Cool, we worship anything and anyone, not just our Gods. Beyond our gods, we also worship fat movie-stars, ageing celebrities and politicians. We have Gods for everything, except the roads. I'm not an atheist, I'm a believer and subscribe to the noble thoughts that are written as part of the Indian legal framework, but it beats me when I cross places of worship smack in the middle of a traffic snarl. We are a very holy nation and these places of worship all over prove it. The goon-brigade, which heavily influences the political vote-banks of the nation, seems to misinterpret the Indian Constitution in as many ways as possible. If anyone takes any offence to anything written in this book, I'm sorry, just let me write in peace for I want to be rich and famous.

Too late for anything and totally pooped out, a few of us decide to get together at the local pub. The waiter, who knows us as regulars, eagerly asks us if we will have our regular 'Baccadi with Cock'. Apply mind over a small matter? Never mind. Better to have 'Baccadi with Cock' so we can all live happily ever after. The classic post-colonial English remnants have mauled the language. The Brits must be ruing the day when they decided to colonize India. Now we are getting even with them with our English. Imagine a world when the right diction in English would be dictated not by the ol' bat, but by Indians and Chinese – and that would be the appropriate usage of the language. Yes, we gloat over such matters. And that's when we started debating what the trip and this book must be called. We arrived at 'Horn OK Please'

These three words packed the entire knowledge available in the whole universe -whether it was on the need for anger management, thanks to the constant honking of the vehicles on the road; the increased palpitations of the heart as a result of some loud musical horn; the sheer exasperation caused by a cyclist or an auto rickshaw driving in the opposite direction, on the high-speed lane of a highway – straight onto your car; the sheer disgust caused by the perverse fetish of the local residents of some village for using the road-side as their toilets for core-dumps in the morning as they would otherwise be constipated without the sights and sounds of all those trucks from across different states passing by, or whether it was the test of your reflexes caused by a lazy villager crossing the road in clothes barely covering his crotch and staring at you as though you have committed a crime of the highest order by disturbing the gent by honking while His Highness takes a stroll on a National highway. It also symbolized the sheer apathy of all those truckers, who defied all senses and sensibilities by blatantly painting the back of their trucks with these three words clearly stating that thou shall have the right of way only if I hear thee honk.

Horn OK Please

These words had been etched in everyone's mind since childhood, something I could never make any sense of before, but tonight, we had been granted the entire wisdom that the universe had to offer. For a person who derived the least pleasure in reading books on philosophy or anything remotely spiritual, for someone who had grown up on technical manuals, the world runs on a geeky open-source platform on a super-computer, and night happened when God took a bio-break and the screen-saver came up. Seasons, to us, were caused by changing of the shifts in the IT department working over there somewhere in the Cloud, and natural calamities were the result of power-surges that caused tripping where people were the bits and bytes of the world. And land was a mesh of wires. These networks were called 'Roads'. Some were clogged & rough and some were high-speed and cruise-worthy. All we needed to do now was take a piece of paper, draw out a crude map of the cities we would cover, get going with the right set of friends who were equally messed up as us, if not more, and start planning. We were now enlightened, with those pearls of wisdom which our Indian saints and Yogis have spent years pondering. And we discovered spirituality while driving on city roads. This is further evidence that they didn't have cars or roads then and it's for us to drive and make all the lost souls rest in peace.

And you, my rickety old car – may you rust in pieces! We made no sense that evening. But those inane talks make up our daily lives. India 2.0.

Crash! Boom! Bang! That's an awful sound when you try to reverse your car while leaving the pub. Darn! I need to visit Mandrake yet again and I don't feel so good anymore. Thinking and driving just don't mix! Now, I'm surer than ever before that the road-trip must be done. India 2.0 holds promise. We can bring about a positive change, and we shall try with the 'Horn OK Please' trip and be do-gooders, trying to make it count. So says Count Duckulla.

It is two a m again now. I am staring at the cuckoo clock, waiting for the dratted bird to come out, so I can wring its blasted neck. It's been a hard day, just like any other day.

HOPping to Conclusions

▶ *People management is about winning hearts. It does not mean killing people and collecting their hearts as trophies*

▶ *The human mind harbors curiosity and creativity. Curiosity did not kill the cat, it merely bruised it to rise and shine, eating yeast and shoe polish for breakfast everyday*

▶ *Preparing for a life is like preparing for a urine test. You cannot do much about it*

▶ *Thinking and driving do not mix. Thinking does not make sense, and is worse than drinking*

▶ *5. Use three fingers on the road to avoid conflict. Smart people will read between lines*

▶ *Rear-view mirrors are useless if you are into butt-watching, It's a misnomer*

▶ *A moron is a person with polish lacking even on his/her shoes*

▶ *Loads of bird poop is not called bird peep*
▶ *When faced with a difficult situation in life, forget your lessons, do a U-turn, run like the wind*
▶ *Georgio Armani is not a Sindhi businessman*

5 All Roads Lead to Nowhere

*Your mind is my fuel tank; and I shall fill it up with
trash,
And so I wrote this book for fame and some extra cash;
There are no morals, there is no learning,
There's just fun on the road, there is a yearning;
A quest for freedom, a desire to explore,
Step into my car, dear reader, as I open the door,
You spent money to buy this trash and now your smile
starts to fade,
I have taken your all money and you've just been Leh'd;
A sense of freedom makes my heart go 'Cheese'
Drive on, that's the spirit of 'Horn OK Please'...*

There is a huge difference between listening and hearing.
Sometimes I wonder if my ears are only meant to support my
glasses. Why wasn't I paying any attention to her when she
was explaining the route to me and I for one, like a moron,
was fiddling with my BlackBerry and Facebooking? Maybe
I didn't understand Spanish and was way too worried with
the sign now put on my door which read 'No Moleste'. Did
that mean 'Do not molest this person'? What kind of a dump
was I staying in anyways? My GPS had died on me and I
couldn't get a single peep out of the lady inside the dratted

instrument. No amount of charging would help and I was rendered directionless somewhere south of San Diego that had nothing to do with English. To add to my woes, all the roads looked the same and I had done the complete circle of life in the arterial roads with no sign of the freeway. It was hot. So hot that my ice cream melted before the cone could touch my mouth, the slip between the cup and the lip was widening and I'm not talking about her clothes. We all have a very Freudian way of looking at things when it comes to instinct and survival. For example, I remember this pillar in front of a mall which I circled twice, simply because it had a phallic appearance.

I had come to mediate peace between a few of my friends in Southern California and we had smoked the peace pipe to weed out any evil remnants of malicious misunderstandings and got ourselves back on the high ground of pure friendship. And I had to get back to Los Angeles quickly, now that I had prevented World War III from happening. Just like the Americans, I had saved the world. I had somehow managed to scrape up some dinner at a sushi joint where they served me something that tasted like a chewed up, smelly shoe fished out of the nearest fish-tank, served with some sea weed. I cunningly spotted the barf on my plate in the name of the sauce which the cook must have slyly sneaked in, as we had pained the hell out of them while placing the order. The waiter had looked like a scarecrow, so scary that had you placed him in a rice field in Punjab, the crows would have brought back the rice they had stolen last year. On hindsight, I think they served me a dead crow and not a shoe. Crows are those obnoxious bird-like freaks that come hitched to witches in fairy tales. God made crows with the left-over meat after carving out Adam, Eve, Satan and Moron.

We were all recovering IT professionals; we were tall and dark (so what if not handsome? A score of two out of three wasn't bad at all), we were dirty, rotten, filthy and stinking (again, not rich, so what? A score of four out of five wasn't bad at all) with a finger-in-the-electrical-socket approach to life. Definitely not the 'Duh!!' types as we had managed somehow to stay afloat doing something that gave us money. It's a different debate that we all were doing everything else than what we were really good at. Like my specialty was mooching off people and living on their money. You, dear reader, are a sad specimen, a victim of my experiments with writing, having bought this book. Work, to me, like most of us, was like an unwanted pregnancy. We had decided to do something else, and we had decided to bury the hatchet and do it together.

The mediation was just a pretext but at the end of it all, we did decide to bury the hatchet – into each other's necks. We had come a long way, since childhood, since we had had our own Rock Band once upon a time. We sucked and we were more like a rubber-band with zero elasticity to tolerate each other's cacophony. We were totally disillusioned with our Rock idols as some of those idols had died of a drug-overdose, some had turned gay and the remaining had turned gay and died of an overdose. We wanted a new lease of life and it sure wasn't a rock band. And today, two of those guys were at a stage in life, having been thrown out of a job, without a career, they would be grateful to be anywhere. But the last thing I wanted on a road-trip was to hang out with a bunch of losers who refused to come back to India. And so we had decided not to proceed any further with the plan and just stay cool. But we did have a good time as we pondered over the follies of the past and the present, also the ones we were destined to commit in the future. And here's my rendition of how we can approach the road to nowhere.

Sticks and stones do break my bones, and such names do pain me

A friend of mine had a girlfriend who was called 'Lucky'. Going by what a loser he was, the name had nothing to do with her fortune, looks or any other department of her anatomy that is worth being discussed in this book. I was lucky enough not to get Lucky that night, but I did watch someone get Lucky one night. It was like watching a bout of pathetic Indian porn. I remember vaguely being exposed to a movie called 'Bombay Fantasy' and I had lost my mojo for a week after a bout of severe barfing, again for a week, trying to get those horrific images out of my mind. Sometimes, I still wake up in the middle of the night, dripping in cold sweat when those horrendous images from that movie flash in my dreams. I have written off those two weeks of my life to that movie and the third week was written off after this peep show. Guys have this 'Librarian chick' fantasy and like any other guy, I had one. So, we'd go hopping from one library to another and come back totally disillusioned after having our fantasies run over like road-kill by those banged-up old cars. The last feeble attempt was to check out the 'Library Bar' at the Leela Palace in Bangalore, and again, there was nothing of importance over there, only monumental prices of the drinks being served. Also, there were no books, same logic as the name 'Lucky'. When God was distributing brains in heaven, I must have baled out, too busy smoking pot. Now, let's extend this logic to India. I have had a haircut in 'New Delhi

Hairdressers' in Calcutta, dined at the 'Lakeview Restaurant' which didn't overlook anything beyond a fish-bowl, eaten fish called 'Bombay duck', 'Peshawari Chicken' in a place called 'Khyber pass' in Pune, which incidentally tasted like Chinese cuisine and have driven down to meet a friend who lives at 'California' in Bangalore. Truth be told, we threw out the British not because of any power-struggles, but because we simply hated their cooking. We are ready to let them come back and colonize a few pockets of our nation, but only if they promised not to cook.

As I mull over creating the route plan for the road trip, I'm aghast at the obscenities that are written all over. I just spotted a place called 'Asansole' in the North East, a place called 'Burnpur' in the east, a city called 'Wankener' and not to mention 'Shag Falls' in the Indian Ocean. Think of any silly goodie and we have the name of a place. By the way, Siliguri is the name of a place in West Bengal.

Still better are some names outside India where one can simply gargle and spit and you have the name for a volcano. But as Indians, we are a very proud nation, We Indians are proud of our culture – be it agriculture, horticulture, sericulture, floriculture, apiculture – but since this book is about pop culture, we're proud of that too. In tune with the philosophy of meaningless rants in this book, allow me to highlight how the post-colonial leftovers in India decided to mangle some English names as well:

1. *Deks (An object to place books on, write a book like this)*
2. *Ecscra (Those see-through black and white pictures taken at a hospital)*
3. *Shervolett (Supposed to be a car manufacturer)*

4. *Shopner (Instrument one uses to sharpen pencils with)*
5. *T-rain (Runs on a railway track)*
6. *Dicky (Bonnet of a car)*
7. *Travera (Another car maker)*
8. *Ankal (Father of your friend)*
9. *Government (The morons who rule)*
10. *Riks (Whi*ch one takes while crossing the road on foot)

I have often been accused of thinking; the allegation is false and the alligators know it!

I had hopped off one of those long-haul hopping flights which take you all over the world except to the place you want to quickly get to and I was jetlagged. It was then that the ultimate truth dawned on me that the best way to beat jetlag is to get drunk and beat it down with a hangover. A couple of drinks down in my belly and I was seeing those hallucinations and garages or whatever. Anyways, the point I'm trying to make here is, dear reader, there are so many alternative theories out there as we realize that all roads lead nowhere. Forget the farce that all roads lead to Rome, damn, that would be a very long drive. Also, they are liars. Which moron said that Rome was built in a day? Untrue. It took exactly three months, six hours, four minutes and twenty three seconds. The project was delayed due to bad Roman roads, red-tape and scotch-tape, project overruns and excessive thinking and a host of meetings that destroyed the creativity of those very minds who named the place 'Rome'. That's dumb. It's a four-letter word. They should have named it Acropolis or Necropolis or something really cool. The clash was not between Titans (if that happened in Rome), but was between the Diplomats and the Consultants who executed the job. While the Diplomats were trying to make everything sound simpler than it actually was, the consultants would make everything sound more complicated.

And so they built Rome with cobblestones, as it was right after Stone-Age and they had a lot of jobless cobblers and a helluva lot of stones and they were plunging into a recession just like Greece today. And so one gets to see such roads in Rome. It was a job more pathetic than the Bangalore International Airport. The HOPfans are fighting tooth and nail with the United Nations today to make people consume more olive oil and eat kebabs as that would strengthen up the Euro and bring Europe back on track. I have personally written to all the Global leaders to take in all the currency, get a few jobless writers like me to scratch out all the currency notes and change their denominations to a higher value so we can make people richer in Europe, while creating new employment opportunities for one and all. Have they ever asked us? The Vox Populi is there on the Facebook wall of HOPfans. I mean, the people are right out there. And the people out there are always right. Just like in India, where we have people all over, including many on currency notes and big, ugly statues. And if you believe what I just said, dear reader, you will believe anything. But if it makes you put your fingers up your nose and want to scratch the back of your head, then we're right on track. All the concocted gobbledygook that's been talked about in this chapter will start making absolutely no sense once you decide to open up your skull and keep that appendage medically known as the 'brain' aside and read. So read on, dear HOPper, or the curse of the morons will plague you for life.

The more you think, the worse-off you are. Why thinking causes headaches.

As the sheer apathy of these World Leaders plagued my thoughts, I was getting bored. If I got bored any further, I would be selling sheep and buying cows in Farmville. My travel companion walked up to me and chirpily asked me 'Wassup?'. Dumb. Isn't the answer to a question like that always 'Nothing'? Maybe the extra bit of sunshine which was due to me today was wrongly delivered by the Indian postal service to him this morning. It was a very bright, sunny morning. One of those mornings which clearly tell weathermen that it will rain in the evening and the night would be dark. If one extends the logic of a light bulb (Thomas Edison be spared), those dratted things have a tendency to give that extra bit of light just before a fuse-out. Today was exactly like that. I had passed out in the name of sleep, but it had lasted for only a couple of hours. The day had included two hours of sleep, an hour of workout, five hours of work and three hours of intensive eating. And again, if you expect the math to add up, you picked up the wrong book. You should have invested in a calculator instead as anyways, I cannot count beyond five, I start all over again the moment I reach five.

Those two hours of sleep was a sheer waste of my time when my mind conjured up vivid images of everything I didn't want to see, hear, think of or dream about. Someone ought to make a 'pay-per-dream' machine and start charging. There's a huge market out there for such inventions which have absolutely no use. Like a door stopper nailed to the ground, they should be banned. Ever try walking around in any bathroom without busting your toe on one of those things? Or ever ponder over why they made those toothpaste tubes with a narrow neck instead of being able to scrape the stuff out with a scoop and start brushing? We need to think out of the box, if we need to think at all. So give me a bigger box so my mind can wander in peace without being contradicted by another thought. Thoughts are like atoms, those funny particles that collide and create a mess called an idea. Same applies to those smaller elements that created the universe, similar to molecules which keep banging into each other like those folks in a local train in 'what's-the-name-of-the-place-again-after-they-changed-it?'

So, a bigger box or fewer thoughts – both work to keep the world in a healthy balance. Too much thought is bad for us, as you might have experienced in the previous paragraph. A state of thoughtlessness is also called 'Nirvana' per Indian philosophy? (and if that's not what it means then we just made it mean that, as I'm doing all the dirty writing). A state of 'nirvana' is also what the ancient sages call 'continuous orgasm'. So, I gather, that a moron who doesn't think is a happy person. I guess that's what made me write this book; that's what made you buy the book. So I conclude that thinking leads nowhere, just like those Roman roads. It is full of contradictions and leads to nasty outcomes like ideas and collision of particles which is what gives headaches, before you try to cure yourself by hitting yourself on the foot with a hammer and turn all chirpy again.

A cloudburst happens when God sneezes

It was a cold, clammy Sunday morning when I woke up and let out a sneeze that measured 5.2 on the Richter scale, followed by a jaw-breaking yawn. I swear I heard something crack inside my mouth. Thanks to my Neanderthal-influenced bone-structure, I survived. I must have been pooped out last night. I had a cough and was spreading the germs of joy in the world. Crawling out of my bed, I scratched my wound after a fall from the stairs the night before. The scratch reminded me of my first ex-girlfriend. It was painful. Not the break-up, but the girlfriend. I wondered what had bitten me in my crotch for having gone totally ga-ga over her. A typical loser thought, post being dumped. It had turned cold as it had rained last night. There had been a cloudburst, as I vaguely remember. That's when I wondered if God was a typical Indian male. Two minutes and it was over. Noodles were invented much later.

When you have a splitting headache, hit yourself in the foot with a hammer

Loaded up on oodles of testosterone, college days are real fun-days for most of us. A few of us had got together, and we had pinched this cheap bucket from a supermarket and we had to do something with it. We had collected anything and everything that could sedate, numb and could be administered through the mouth. A hose pipe was acceptable. We had also pinched a few bouquets as we weren't the kind of people who would be given bouquets, just spare us the brickbats. My friend and roomie was a dude from Punjab. He had taken his turban off, donned a Rayban, turned into a chick and we posed for wedding snaps. We wanted some bouquets as they looked cool in a group picture. I don't remember a thing after my first dunk-in-the-bucket with a stolen mug from the nearest Archie's Gallery. And now, I had this headache and a cold. I think the best cure for a headache right now would have been to hit myself on the foot with a hammer and distract my brain from the headache so we could all get on with the day. It actually works for a person like me as

I also suffer from foot-in-mouth-disease. I tend to take one foot out of my mouth and put the other one in with uncanny precision, enough to make me qualify to become a leader of a nation, or a CEO of one of these successful Indian companies. Of course, putting your foot in the mouth does help you clip your toe-nails without paying through your nose for a pedicure, but we can ignore that fallout.

After all, getting struck by a thought gives any moron a headache and I had mixed thinking and drinking with my driving that night. So much of stuff written about the perils of drinking and driving, it's enough to make one give up reading and get on with life.

The more populated a nation, the smaller are its people.

Scientists have overlooked one fact that hits you smack on the face. It has to do with population and the average size of the populace. This thought has always haunted me in my dreams. As scientists trace back the history of mankind, well, what about the future, morons? Here's my hypothesis. As the per-square feet (some idiot out there wants us to believe that people have square feet) lessens as the population thickens, it is a direct result of what we do or how we are. If we have more people in a nation, the per capita space lessens and it directly results in shrinkage of the population. By shrinkage, I mean the forces of nature come into play and we all start to shrink. Look at China, one of the most populated nation in the world – the shoe sizes say it all. Or India, where there is a drastic drop in the average height of a person by a horrific one millimeter every decade. If we went on like this, our wars will be with cockroaches and the insect world. Look at Finland, for example, a land of potatoes, worse than Idaho in the United States.

The people are bigger as they have more space to grow and expand. Now, enhance this theory with obese people. The fatter the people become, the more square inch of space they would consume and there would be lesser space to grow. Compounded by the fact that India gets nibbled on the borders by all our extra-friendly neighbors, whose love for us is so overwhelming that they just want to take over us, the total cubic feet (here I go again to confuse you more, dear reader) lessens and we will only get smaller. And that's the reason why the HOPfans Community is filing a writ petition to the Government of India to start talking about the perils of overpopulation in a different light. I strongly urge you to be a part of this community on Facebook for the greater good for all humanity. If that doesn't excite you, well, you better sign-up to lose weight and gain height, for today, you might be over-height (euphemism for skinny like a bookmark) or under-height (euphemism for overweight).

Being tall is good; you get cleaner air to breathe

It is good to be tall. Anywhere in the world. Especially if you live in a polluted place which is equivalent to smoking two packs of cigarettes a day and may die soon. Of course, you have the choice of moving to a less polluted place if you are short and smoke two packs of cigarettes per day and die at the same time as the tall guy in a polluted place. Of course, tall people run the risk of turning into lightning conductors on a dark, rainy night and it is advisable for them to stay at home when it rains. I remember taking a walk somewhere on the crowded streets of Calcutta. There are so many people out there and everybody seems to be in your face and on the street. The population bomb seems to have been tested out there and it must have been another crazy experiment gone out of control. It's like they exploded the population bomb in Calcutta and all the people came out as shrapnel and landed up on the street. I wonder what we are planning to do with our nuclear bomb now.

As I walked around, I thanked my parents like never before, for they gave me that extra foot (not another one to walk with, you moron) of height so I could breathe easy. Since carbon dioxide is what we exhale, and is heavier than oxygen, I can get more oxygen than many others thanks to that extra advantage of one foot above the average five-foot tall population. Probably, my frequent trips abroad all my life prevented me from shrinking. And anyways, most of the Indian cities look better on the internet, but that's a separate discussion altogether. Of course, if you are one of those who are too tall, you run the risk of trying to breathe in rarefied air that kind of addles up the mind. Would that make people who live in mountains addle-headed? So, dear reader, if you happen to be a scientist, you may want to stop and think and do a thesis on this theory; and since you are a scientist, that anyways makes you good for nothing except for writing dumb research papers, having been declared unfit for the real world. And if you happen to be a scientist living in the UK, dear reader, I say you stop measuring the expanding breast sizes of women and focus on the real in-hand issues that demand immediate attention, such as this one.

The easiest way to avoid beggars on Indian roads is to look like one

I remember once in college when I was completely broke on the tenth day of the month, like every other month, and I realized there was a pattern here. It is a very important finding, very useful for all the trash that comes to visit India without any money in their wallets. Every month, my dad used to wire some money into my account which I used to blow up in the first week of the month on bare essentials like cigarettes, liquor, petrol, condoms and music CDs. The rest of the month I would live like Tarzan on bananas for breakfast, more bananas for lunch and many more bananas for dinner. My friends' circle used to turn into a straight line made up of just my equally starved roomie, who had no choice but to talk to me when he was not talking to himself. I was living in a banana republic alright. Unfortunately, after the first week of every month, hygiene used to go out of the window, as there was no money left for luxuries like razor blades, deo-sprays, mouthwash and shampoo. Needless to say, I used to end up looking like a beggar, a cross between Jimi Hendrix and Akon, and to make myself look good at no cost, I used to hang out with uglier people. The theory of relativity, you see. Like all these actresses from Bollywood who surround themselves with out-of-shape chunks of meat so they can look better in comparison in those groupie-songs.

Come end of the month, I used to be so broke that even beggars would start avoiding me. It was that survival instinct in me that used to make me break my piggy-bank and scrounge for all the loose change so I could date a chick with money. It helped me develop a very liberal outlook towards life as I grew up not getting unduly worried about how she looks, the fun I could have in her company or her niceness. All that mattered was the size of her purse and not the sensuousness of her anatomy, at that point in time. Else, dear reader, why on earth would I attempt to write the world's greatest loo-book and relieve you of your money? So, the Casanova in me rose from my stomach to date any chick with money close to month-end. It's a different matter that such girls would have no choice but to spend to get a date. Like this date of mine who claimed to be from a prestigious college known as Miranda House in Delhi University.

I cared two hoots about the fact that she looked more like a pork sausage from a slaughter house. Mirinda House or slaughter house or a whore house, it didn't matter as long as I could be fed and burped and left to wander the streets like a puppy who overate. Ever notice those puppies with eyes bigger than stomachs who try to walk? They go teetering to one side before trying to totter back to their original planned trajectory. Looking back, I realize that I scraped through my (non)education not on scholarships, but by schmoozing and glib talk. Those in-between twenty days, between the first ten days of wanton delight and orgy and the last ten days of the month playing gigolo was the period of hunger, starvation and begging. For all you know, dear reader, if you happen to see a beggar cross the street, there's a good chance that he might just be your future boss or your CEO. So spare that change or at least be nice to him.

Alibaba's muse was a sadistic freak and Lewis Carroll was a junkie

Morgiana, the sadistic slave girl, who used to hang out with Ali Baba, took pleasure in disposing off her enemies in the most barbaric manner, with Alibaba abetting her in the crime. Didn't she deep-fry a few thieves in hot oil? Later in the story, didn't she also plunge a knife into the robber-chief's heart and stab him repeatedly? This gruesome story is what people call a fairy tale today, how perverted have we become? Consider Lewis Carroll, yet another pervert. His real name was Charles Lutwidge Dodgson. Maybe, he was perverted because his parents gave him such a name. But what made him strange was that the guy was a poofy weed-head. There have been theories in the past about his sexuality. Scholars over the years have certainly questioned his apparent fondness for very young girls, so one accusation (although never proved) was that he was a paedophile. There have always been theories that Carroll was a drug-addict, Again, there's no real evidence, but substances like laudanum (typical of that era) and cannabis have been suspected, especially with all those references to teas and mushrooms in his book. No proof, though. But does one really need any proof after reading his stuff? You decide.

It is quite stupid to look back and say, "Hey, was that the stuff that you taught me, teacher, calling them Arabian Nights and fairy tales and classics?" Give me a break. I mean, no sane person would now read about a gruesome act of boiling forty people inside jars filled with stolen stuff and that's where they were all killed. A gory tale about robbing the robbers, killing them in the most horrible manner and still accept this person's claim to be a good person. Someone try that out now in a world where we can keep terrorists alive at the cost of the tax-payers pension fund and still be worried sick about human rights! What kind of stuff makes a good story that is told to young and impressionable minds? Here's another example. Imagine a pervert weed-head writing trash about big mushrooms (the kind of stuff Amsterdam is made up of) and talking frogs, walking cards and a little girl with a persecution complex? It is a clear depiction of a hallucinating mind that we read out to kids thinking this is an imaginative, childish dream. Are you dumb enough to believe that? I don't know about you, dear reader, as kids we never thought about such things, but as grownups, we do.

Today, if I told you there is a controversy erupting somewhere in the planet because some freak author was writing (sex)toy stories and the nation had brought down all Social Media sites because of that, you would believe me. 'Fairy-tales' today would be looked upon as the sexual escapades of a story teller whose sexual preferences are in doubt. Let's not worry about private lives of individuals, rather, let's focus on ensuring that the children learn the right stuff. I propagate the moronic mind, where thought takes a backseat as I sit back, drive without a cause, publish a book and become all rich and famous. I would rather have the wind caress me, the sunshine kiss me, the rains make love to me and have the music take away any random thought blurb that could poison my mind. In short, thinking and driving do not mix, and so the trip must be undertaken.

Come together. Right now

As I looked at my coffee mug being filled to the brim by the waitress who looked as though she was in a perpetual state of burping, the sage saying of a moron filled my pretty much empty skull: "The pleasure is in the journey, not in the destination". I had pretty much run out of battery as I decided to call my friends and my friends' friends and line up the morons who would join me on the full-Monty trip spanning forty days and forty nights. I was desperate to call Goose and Derek who had now confirmed they'd join me on this trip. The beast for the ride would be a brand new SUV, a rugged Scorpio with the engine of a jeep and she talked and irritated the hell out of me every time I would forget a trivial act like fastening my seat belt. She shall henceforth be called 'Motormouth', the talking car. The four of us all we needed now was a plan. But first, I needed to charge my cell phone. I had heard they are planning to make cell phones which can get charged by the human body. As I sipped on my coffee, I wondered where the hell are they going to ask me to insert the charger if I have to charge it on myself? Gulp!!

I must now get talking to my guide, whose name sounded something like 'Nitwit', the Chief Dork of a school in Leh, which we plan to do something good for, and of course myself, nicely called the 'Chief', as that's what they call a person who leads a pack of morons on a cross-country drive.

6 The Maiden Run

Birds of a feather flock together, works better with tar,
The best plans are always made when one sits in a bar;
Roses are red, and violets are blue,
You are hell bent on making it all rhyme, dear reader,
aren't you?
Crazy antics and loads of follies make you say 'Cheese'
Drive on, that's the philosophy behind 'Horn OK Please'…

Here comes the fake photographer and crappy roadie – Goose

A moron once said "When you get to sleep all you want, you will wake up at 4 am." Bang at 4 am, Goose was lost in this thought as he was checking his credit card bills, having paid through the nose and every aperture in his body for his new Nikon D5000 camera. He wondered why they didn't make bigger credit cards and smaller bills so he could spend more and pay less. The radio was playing in the background. His favorite station – he liked it as he enjoyed the sense of humor of the radio jockeys on this station, as it was a perfect match for his IQ. "I passed a kidney stone this morning….a pimple at the wrong place, eh?" As the radio jockey started playing one of his favorite Trance songs, he wondered why some people thought that Indians don't have a sense of humor, especially since his life was one constant joke. Haven't we been humoring our neighbors all this while in spite of their unexplainable urge to keep nibbling at our nation's boundaries like hungry piranhas? Or being dumped thrice in a row and still being haunted by his ex-girlfriends? Or having one's brand new car getting banged up the day it was bought – that too, when it was innocently parked? It was unexplainable, not at all funny, and God seemed repeatedly kicking him below the belt.

He quickly stuffed his super-spent credit card into his dry wallet when he saw the traffic light turn green. He was happy at least something turned green with envy when he fished out his wallet. As his car started to move, he saw a bunch of drunken college kids coming out of a pub, lurching toward his car like those Neanderthals crawling from their burrows, who always came straight to his car. His instinct told him to accelerate and he did, scattering the kids like a bunch of wild rabbits for cheap thrills. It was a bit like bowling, a game he always lost. After all, Goose was a man with keen senses, sight, smell, taste, touch and hearing, minus horse and common, which made him the perfect candidate to play a leading role in the road trip.

Anger management in progress, he wondered why he couldn't take his dog to the studio, especially since his pet looked a lot better than his boss. They always seemed to hate the idea of him being watched upon by a huge German shepherd whom he called 'Imhotep', I mean, one has to be seriously demented to name a dog 'Imhotep'. It sounds like a good English word spelt backward and cut halfway through by a sneeze. Imagination certainly wasn't at a premium for Goose for that's why he was an upcoming photographer, but an over-paid and under-worked geek. However, his bank account was a stark contrast; he had loads of imagination and practically no savings. His ego had taken a wallop as he had tried to climb the ladder of success in the field of photography. It was a dog-eat-dog world out there and there were only dogs of different varieties – poodles, stray, thoroughbred and hot.

He would have Imhotep take on the dogs and show loyalty so he could focus on his career and hone his skills. That's why he had a dog. It was a sycophant-dominated industry where mechanically-inclined dodos with zero-talent would screw anything to straddle the ladder of success. Imhotep had to be careful too, for he too would need to watch his back. The powers-that-be were dominated by a crowd of incompetent and mediocre nincompoops who would beat the young ones with experience, drag them down to their level of stupidity and beat them again with experience.

A gizmo freak, his world comprised of the latest models of mobile phones, the latest in takeaway music paraphernalia, and used to come to a grinding halt when the batteries ran dry across gizmos. The last time he was left high and dry – literally, was when he ran out of batteries on a mountaineering trip close to Himalayas and his batteries had died on him. Goose had lost his mojo for a week after that. Maybe for him, erections were caused by batteries.

Goose smiled as he thought about the idea of 'Horn OK Please', remembering how the Chief had called him up the night before, excited over his attainment of Nirvana while reading the back of a truck. He was no different. Not very successful at dealing with people, Goose's patience and anger seemed to be rising high whenever he had to deal with levels of stupidity perceived than his own. He was becoming a regular athlete at his work by flying off the handle, throwing tantrums and jumping to conclusions. He didn't care as long as he did whatever made him happy. He knew he needed a break to get away from it all. He was on; the dumb bird was going to be my co-pilot.

Introducing Derek

Derek was feeling too lazy to hit the gym. He was a miracle worker. It was a miracle when he worked out. In his late twenties, his New Year resolution was to fight flab and work on his six-pack abdomen. Instead, he was into guzzling six-packs of beer this evening. Derek figured that watching a Rambo movie was a far easier way to work out than burning calories on a treadmill and playing Forrest Gump. Of course, the same logic didn't apply to porn. Getting him to visit the gymnasium was like taking a horse to water. But getting him on a treadmill was like getting the damn horse to float on its back.

But today, he was dazed as though a thought recently struck him. Thinking was not his forte, and unfortunately, he was the only one who could think amongst us. It was something that he used to do from below the belt. Derek had never been to a classroom, a meeting room, an RTO Office or the PWD (Public Works Department) or any room of significance, so higher education was out of the question. His hyper renegade nerves and pathetic upbringing only made his attitude worse. He was the kind of guy over whom your mom would probably have a seizure or two by just looking at him. He was the fountainhead of trash and his knowledge about the world could give stiff competition to a paper-weight kept in the office of a semi-retired bureaucrat. Somehow, Derek had a lot of money in the stock market and he had invested it wisely. Well, at least some of it seemed sensible. And since he was rich and crazy, he made it into the A-Team. He was tall, dark and all the girls wished he were hands-off.

The self-styled Casanova knew how to handle girls who liked to have a good time. He had recently broken off a couple of engagements as the girls wanted to go too far, like wanting to get married. With his fundamentals in life as clear as mud, not only was he a great leader of men, he was also an ardent follower of women. A carefree person; he didn't care as long as it was free. Hanging around with Derek, I had to be very careful not to end up writing this book from prison. Mercifully, we always got away with bribing the cops and not going to jail. Maybe, we awed people with our corporate backing and our superpowers or maybe we were considered too pathetic to be in jail.

Goose and I (The Chief) were particularly drawn to one of Derek's posts on Facebook, when he had put forth the need for people to chew food well before swallowing it. His logic was so simple, even we could understand. He said, "If you don't chew, it gets stuck in your jaw and you get a double chin. Ever wonder why cows don't have double-chins? Or why one should always eat more carrots? I haven't seen a single rabbit wearing glasses". We had started eating carrots and chewing our food since then.

After a few drinks, Derek used to turn all filthy and obnoxious; not that he wasn't otherwise, but just that little bit more. Like those pesky kids at the airports with their equally dumb mothers, who would start talking loudly to their children trying to attract attention? That kind. Such parents should be chained to the seats of their airplane seats as punishment. You could make out his level of drunkenness by the number of public walls he used to start irrigating. I'm talking about real walls, not those see-through, perforated Facebook walls. He came from a place which was devoid of any signs of intelligence for he showed no such quality. Derek was of the firm belief that it is not rash driving, but driving with a wallet, which is a magnet for traffic police. An ardent animal lover, Derek always prefers to have them served on a platter, piping hot, well done and served with dollops of strawberry icecream.

Ask Derek to pee in the corner of a circular room, he would take ten seconds to respond with a highly intelligent answer…. "Duh!!" He plans the route for us. God bless us.

Meet Motormouth, the talking SUV

She's a crazy, powerful, mountain climbing, yakkety-yakking, fuel-guzzling SUV. She has superpowers. She converts oil into carbon monoxide. Nobody fights wars over polluted air. And so, 'Motormouth' brings peace on earth. She likes to be cleaned only with spit. By the time Derek, Goose and I reach Leh, we will be ready to challenge camels and llamas and their spitting abilities. She hates those tiny cars from the Flintstone-era, which infest Indian roads today, probably because she is as big as Helga. Helga, dear reader, is any big, well-endowed woman and since I don't know any other Russian names, hence the analogy. She particularly hates those battery-operated, funny-looking cars. The automobile advisor told me not to mix any additives to the diesel that Motormouth would guzzle. I wonder if he's a mind-reader or something.....how did he know that I was planning to mix Red Bull in the fuel in the absence of any octane boosters? And now, Motormouth was to be our beast for the Full-Monty road-trip of India. With a very powerful engine, she whines like crazy.

Introducing Chief Red Bull

I went to McDonalds, they don't accept cards. I went to Subway, my card didn't work. I was hungry, so I ate my card. Now I don't feel so good anymore. So I'll quit the blabbering or I'll be coughing up a lot of money. The good thing is that now I can empathize with an ATM machine. I guess this is what they mean by rich food. I shall swipe my nose or something the next time I need to pay. That's me, they call me Chief Red Bull...probably because of my addiction to that dratted syrupy poison. There was a time when I didn't know which one was the steering wheel among all the five wheels for a car and I cannot count beyond five. There was the sixth wheel that lay in the back of my car which confused me no end. I always wondered why a step-knee was considered to be a wheel and not a battered up knee. The less you know about me, the happier you shall be.

Planning the Maiden Run. But *why* should the maiden run? Duh!!

Derek, Goose and I were sitting at the local Barista, guzzling coffee, leching, drooling as we asked for more coffee. The waitress was nice and talented. With a pout like a vacuum cleaner, she was bound to have a talent the world may not know of today. She was what one could call a Venus fly-trap and she wasn't a plant. We were from Mars, alright. We got back to the map spread out in front of us. The trouble with maps is that they have way too many lines in them and you can never figure out where they start and where they end. Of course, the roads in India are no bigger, so there is no scale mismatch.

The maiden run is from Bangalore to Kanyakumari, which is barely 669 kilometers from the place where we were having coffee now. To get there, all we needed to do was to get into Motormouth and go via-Chandapura-Hosur-Krishnagiri-Karimangalam-Dharmapuri-Omalur-Salem-Rasipuram-Namkkal-Karur-Vedsandur-Dindigul-Vadippatti-Madurai-Tirumangalam-Virudnagar-Sattur-Kovilpatti-Kayattar-Tirunelveli-Munradiaippuo-my-ugly-soiled-paper-plate-Nanguneri-Kanyakumari and if you can read the names of the places listed out, you must be smart. All we could understand was get on to NH7 and drive, stop when you see a big statue, or you fall into the sea. Come back the same way if you don't fall into the sea. See? We are smart too. Or so we thought before we did everything that we shouldn't have. Like Derek getting behind the wheel and shutting down the GPS. Or Goose trying our various shortcuts. I am usually calm and composed, but these two morons left me to decompose. We had started off the evening after coffee, without a hint of a proper plan or any such complicated phrase, which I have carefully avoided in this book. Needless to say, the maiden run was a big fiasco and we knew it. We did everything wrong. Like starting up Motormouth and getting on the road, for instance, was the biggest mistake. His Awesomeness, Derek, got off the highway in exactly two kilometers.

Stranded

The national bird of India – the much-feathered and tasteless peacock. The very basis of its existence is questionable. Maybe God had some meat left over, having made crows. He decided to give man the ultimate form of colorful decorations as a feather-duster, frequently used to supposedly scare away lizards in rural India. The scene resembled a scene straight out of a Bollywood horror (read horrible) flick made by the Ramsay Brothers of yore. The fabled Ramsay Brothers made such primitive monsters, probably because they themselves hadn't evolved into human beings. If ignorance is bliss, Derek was divine. Goose had bought one of these feather-dusters and we stood by Motormouth as we tried to figure out our way back to the highway. And clearly, peacock feathers can seem really scary at midnight, with those fake eyes on them, no wonder they used to scare away lizards with them. But I wasn't a lizard and yet I was scared. Scared like a cow on Indian roads.

The sacred (scared) Indian cow stands on those frail and fragile legs on the road, eating a bunch of newspapers from last week, topped with polythene bags, served in broken down garbage made of concrete, with the poster of some vague South-Indian hero stuck on it. He must be a famous dude and a star, alright. Those shaking legs are more like appendages holding up a mass of visibly outlined bag-of-bones, which can barely hold up the physical structure at eye-level while one sits in a sunken Maruti 800. And this sight is a familiar sight every morning for many of us. Of course, staring at anyone having a meal is not good manners, and that includes cows. But I've been out for many dinners with so many cows, it doesn't bother me anymore. Anyways, back to the feather-duster. The epitome of stupidity, Derek's eyes were glowing in the dark like very dim zero-watt bulbs about to fuse, as he narrowed his eyebrows, came very close to my face as he concluded ever so wisely. "We are lost", he said.

Here we were, stranded, about two hundred kilometers from somewhere and another hundred kilometers from elsewhere. We had no choice, but to take in the scenery on a full moon night. I can never understand what people see in these sceneries anyways. Unlike pine trees, which know how to grow and look all pretty, the moon-kissed trees looked more like cobwebs. And Goose was busily clicking pictures of them in the forest. I couldn't figure out what there was about them to take pictures of, because after ten minutes of looking at those trees, they would be crying out to you to be cut and razed to the ground. They were like those cobwebs that one gets to see in police stations all over India. Since we had to get 'yes-where' and by dawn somehow, we decided to muster up our collective non-existent courage to stop a passerby villager who looked like he used to drink a few gallons of arrack to get his heart started every morning. Unfortunately, he wasn't dumb enough to understand our moronic frantic gestures or our incoherent speech.

We had driven for about four hundred kilometers in a no-lane highway, had done only two pit stops at breakneck speed (I think my neck was broken after the bumpy ride), broken many speed limits, jumped over traffic lights and were proud of the distance covered in such a short span of time. We were tired and weary as we had run out of Red Bull and were forced to stop over. Motormouth needed to rest. She was whining as her shock absorbers had by now been turned into shock observers by a frenzied lunatic called Derek. Anyways, driving late night is no fun in India and one needs to have a death wish to do so. Tonight, it seemed that we did.

We were near a place which we couldn't pronounce at all and it sounded worse than having someone say the name of that volcano somewhere in Europe, twice. We chose to refer to it as 'My-ugly-soiled-paper-plate' as it sounded like that. From what I could see in the dark, it also looked like one. You know those kind of names that you see deep down south, which you can barely read the first few alphabets of while driving a mere sixty Kmph, so that by the time you get to see the signboard and start reading, you've passed it and you couldn't read the whole thing? Well, we were lost in exactly that kind of a place. You would need to drive at a speed lower than ten Kmph just to figure out where you were lost and still not be able to pronounce the name of the place to anyone on your cell phone as to where you were. Maybe, they deliberately invented such names to get you lost and keep you lost.

Still, there was absolutely no sign of human life beyond the three of us and the signs of life in us seemed to be getting bleaker as we were really tired and hungry and completely out of Red Bull, ready to drink each other's blood. Maybe, this is how vampires are born. We need to get there soon.

I tried to close my eyes and open them again, just so I could pretend it was all a bad dream. Or maybe I had passed out and would get a glimpse of heaven if I opened my eyes now. I saw Derek talking to himself while Goose was doing some strange things with his belt. Surely, these sights do not make up heaven. Heaven was ruled out; this was reality and it was right there – smack on my face, the kind of reality one gets to see when a dumb goat gets in front of your car, hits the windshield and rolls over your roof and you hear that dull thud behind you? Well, it was always that kind of reality I got with Goose and Derek.

This was the forbidden, deepest part of South India and we had to get to Kanyakumari by dawn and we wanted to watch the sunrise. I wonder why. We could have easily watched it on the internet or in a documentary or bought a few post cards from somewhere. But no, we had to experience the follies and there could be no better bunch of fools than us.

How we got back on the highway will always remain a mystery to us as Goose drove Motormouth towards the North Star. The guy was luckier with a car than with love. Maybe, he should marry Motormouth and settle down in the backseat, make babies there and let them loose on the Indian roads as tiny little morons. We just wanted to get out of here and go there, and get to 'My-ugly-soiled-paper-plate' soon.

Closing in on a town somewhere close to Madurai, we drove through what one would call the human network of people connected by electrical wires and glowing heads. In the South, people get married in the morning, real early morning. Morning in the South also means a little past midnight. In India, we call it a tradition when the victim is placed on a high-horse, decorated with flowers and garish clothes, with Neanderthals performing some kind of a voodoo ritual, seemingly dancing in front of a very tired-looking and a confused animal with blinkers on. In South Indian movies, they play tribal music at very high screeching decibels and Sandalwood stars with their troupe of background dancers perform a dance that reminds one of a bunch of crabs on the seashore, trying to avoid the wave. Though this ritual is strictly followed in Northern India, movies have confused the hell out of us and the town 'My-ugly-soiled-paperplate' was no exception. If you will believe this, dear, you are capable of believing anything and you must be living somewhere near Ohio in the US, where some folks still believe that Indians take their pet elephants to work, pass the fakirs on magic ropes as traffic signals, before retiring to bed early, a bed made out of nails, burped out on a platter of monkey-brains.

What made South India different from the rest of India was very evident now. This was the rest of India which was different from any other part of India. The frenzied noise was certainly not what one would term as 'music' and it's probably one of the reasons why people in the South tend to suffer from high blood-pressure at an early age. Not only do people in this town have a nasty habit of making a beeline towards your car, their favorite pastime seems to be drinking and throwing wild-berries at you and cursing you if you look like an outsider, anything to pick up a fight with you, especially if you don't understand the local language. Derek did educate one drunk and told the drunk something about his mother, after which he sobered down a bit and Derek had a huge smile on his face, a smile that made him look like a cross between Bart Simpson and Julia Roberts.

We found a place to halt and unfortunately, it was one of those places where one shouldn't be halting. It was not a good idea; after all it was Derek's idea. The place was a dump. Garbage collection to the civic authorities of this town meant to display their garbage in front of their houses and shops. Certainly, the ladies were highly social over there and each one carried a vase-full of flowers on their head. Getting to the front-desk was not an easy task. If only they had Segways in India. We were felt all over, groped, semi-raped and abused, called homosexuals till they finally gave up on us. We were tired and we needed sleep. Not even Viagra could get a rise out of any sane person with these ladies, not even a shoe-horn would work on any of us with them. The room was like a cage where they would probably be conducting strange and secret experiments on humans. There were more cockroaches than mosquitoes in the room. Since I cannot stand mosquitoes, this was a big consolation. At least I could step on the cockroaches, enjoy the crackling and squishing sound, hop about with glee till the room was filled with gooey stuff that looked like peanut butter all over. That's why I prefer cockroaches to mosquitoes. They filled me with glee. More so, it's practically impossible to step on mosquitoes, or get any crackling sounds or make them go 'squish' or get the butter out of them and have so much fun. And the place in which we decided to spend the night probably served this stuff for breakfast. Every object in the room seemed to serve a purpose – any purpose as long as it was not worthy. But just to be fair, the room wasn't really what I had expected it to be; it did have a latch and I could bolt it from inside to keep the ladies of the night outside the door. Having lived in a dormitory in my student life, I was used to bed-sheets with stains, creaking beds, banging on the walls leaving nothing to imagination, and just a few pet rats around.

Another thing about cockroaches is that they only walk slower after pest control. Those tiny intoxicated pests seem to be on a high, stoned on 'Hit', useless stupid spray, but still better than any 'Bayer' product. Maybe the German pesticides are weak compared to the Indian ones because the pests in India are a lot more immune and I'm not talking about my neighbor's kids. Running low on battery, I couldn't even call in the National Guard to get rid of these pests. Fortunately, each of us had separate rooms. I must have passed out on what vaguely resembled a bed, the kind of beds one gets to see in Indian porn flicks. This must be a movie studio then, for it was smelling awful and they haven't yet invented words to describe the stench. Maybe the folks from Lobster's or Webster's or whatever dictionary, should spend a night here and they would invent new words. This was 'schmeeze', and this meant 'Brrrrr.....'. Anything goes in India, especially electricity, which went off about two am, never to come back till we were around. Goose was particularly fascinated with the pack of howling wolves that we could hear that night. He was desperate to click them and I saw the gleam in his eyes. It was tough to convince him and make him understand that they were rabid stray dogs and we needed to get away.

There was a place of worship for many new Gods here. All by the road-side. Despite being born, bred and battered in this country, I still couldn't figure out all the deities. Every temple was a monument of belief and that probably one cannot find anywhere. Even Gods would need to keep a Who's-who list if they ever visited this place.

It takes a lot of imagination to come to a place like this. First, one has to imagine a reason for coming here. Second, one needs to conjure up a reason to stay here. Third, one has to imagine that this is not a bomb-shelled place or a concentration camp.

Another lousy part (there were no good memories of this place) was an ugly, very noisy, black and white movie being projected on a tied-up bed sheet to make do as a screen till the wee hours of morning. The sudden spurt in the noise level indicated the falling of the screen thrice during the screening.

It was a true test of one's patience, with a nondescript police station nearby where laws would have trouble existing. Town planning, like any other place in India, would probably have been done with a ruler, a compass, a sharpener, three pieces of string measuring a foot each as the roads are very narrow and of course, not to exaggerate, Fevicol, to hold the gravel together and call them roads. It was horribly warm; I guess that's why they don't bother to build any bridges or flyovers around the place. This place was the unchartered graveyard for good cars. All good vehicles must be coming here to die.

Morning happened and we saw buffaloes and people. It looked like a museum of ugly shops with tin-tops. At least we think they were 'people' because buffaloes don't have two legs nor do they wear clothes or spectacles. Actually, they looked like spectacles as the term sounds like tentacles of some evil thing in ancient Greece. Maybe, a similar creature in ancient Greece would be called 'Spectacles'. We chose to avoid eating anything that was prepared in the kitchens here as we want to live to a ripe old age and this was not the age to die. At least, this was not the place to die. Derek bought a loaf of bread and chose to eat the wrapping paper and threw out the bread. Last night's experience hadn't been good for us when the spicy food had made us levitate a few feet above the toilet seats in the dirty toilets. Anything not bottled or canned or sealed is stale, unhygienic or downright poisonous. So we decided to skip breakfast. It is best to stop where the flies do; so many flies can't go wrong.

I was buckling up in the driver seat when I saw Derek hopping around with the jerry can stuck between his knees and trying to imitate a motorcycle rider. Goose was making a racket while trying to sound like a motorcycle. Suicide seemed like an attractive option. Having these two around me made me look intelligent at this point. And there was a flunkey, trying to get on top of Motormouth to clean the roof. He looked like a Russian acrobat on Roman rings. No amount of yelling would make him get off till he was done with Motormouth. He boasted that he could fix any vehicle in 'My-ugly-soiled-paper-plate'. It was a good thing, for every car would break down over here. We took extra care of Motormouth before leaving and levitated her by a couple of inches after an air fill. I guess, she was swelling with pride.

I wanted to go, get to a real hotel and have a bath. Every other place on the planet had something attractive to offer – be it a Lochness Monster, a Yeti or alien landings. This place has mosquitoes and cockroaches. I guess a child born here would learn to crawl not by instinct, but by watching cockroaches. I wanted to keep moving, move around like a schizophrenic mountain goat (which is a very confused animal, by the way, but more on that later), hoping that I would be able to run away from myself as I was stinking. All of us were. Deo-sprays and pesticides don't quite add up to selling expensive stuff in fancy bottles. Finally, a light-bulb appeared over Derek's head and we saw a glimpse of brightness come across his face. This was a rare moment, rarer than the appearance of Halley's Comet on earth. He said, "We need to get out of this place and get to Kanyakumari, where we should get Motormouth serviced." Brilliant. And this was as brilliant as he could get. The only reason why I didn't kill him then was that it's considered illegal in India.

After a non-stop drive to Kanyakumari (I suspect we flew over the bumps as we decided not to use brakes at all), we finally found a place that looked inhabited by human beings on terra firma. And we decided to feast. Gluttony was the philosophy applied and we must have ordered half of the items on the menu card. Except for the minced meat, which looked more like a goat having been made to go through a painful execution and then having been stuffed into a grinder before being spat upon by all the hotel staff and served on a platter in the name of 'Chef's special', everything was just great.

We had reached early in the morning, taken up a neat place overlooking the sea. The only problem was that our view was obstructed by two very big statues. This is the biggest problem with a beautiful view. After a little while of looking, you need your BlackBerry or your laptop or your iPhone or just about anything to do, apart from just staring into empty space.

Anyways, we decided to stay indoors and spend the day, eating and drinking first, then drinking and eating, followed by yet another round of eating and drinking. And then we passed out. The hogs were appeased. We had been to Kanyakumari and it was now time to head back to Bangalore next morning. And we were very happy to get back.

The currency system in India is quite funny. A US dollar is somewhere around forty-five rupees, a Euro is close to sixty rupees, the British Pound close to a hundred rupees and a rupee is worth nothing at all. Probably better than the Japanese Yen, and I thank my stars not having to live in Japan as everything costs thousands or millions of Yen. Tough for a guy who has trouble counting beyond five.

HOPping to Conclusions

▸ *Never harass a waitress at a coffee shop. She will spit in your coffee and you won't know*

▸ *Four cups of double-shot espresso helps man defrag his brains*

▸ *If you don't take a pit-stop while doing long distances, high chances all of you will float out of the car (A game commonly known as 'Bursting-the-bladder')*

▸ *Opportunity knocks on the door once, stupid temptation bangs on the door every night*

▸ *Never name your kid 'Titty George', it becomes a big joke with morons*

▸ *One man called 'Varghese' should be called 'Vergoose'*

▸ *Munch noodles for dinner; don't have them renamed as needles*

▸ *Peacock feathers only look good on peacocks*

▸ *Credit cards don't taste good. They don't get rid of hunger*

▸ *A 'Plan' is not a four-letter word*

7 Useless Planning

When we made paper boats and set them to sail,
A time when we never had to work and life was a fairy
tale,
Playing in the sun, a dip in the pool;
When counting stars in the night sky was just way too
cool
A time when comic book heroes came out at night,
I could hear the silent screams
When the world of Tintin, Asterix, Calvin and others
shaped our dreams
Nostalgia and Imagination makes you say 'Cheese'
Drive on, that's the philosophy behind 'Horn OK Please'...

The Incredible Hulk is the perfect moron

Five am – I woke up with a start. If I do not rush to the gym, my trainer is going to whoop my ass. I cannot stand his man-tits; I don't want to grow into a new species. I suspected he was a fairy, but this is not a fairy-tale. Give me a break, you moron, for I am a writer, not a jock and you want me to evolve into a different species? Well, the writer was running late, and if the writer didn't make it to the gym on time, he would have become a late author and this book would have been a posthumous publication.

Since we had to clock an average of six hundred kilometers a day with Motormouth, I had to build my stamina. And he was hell bent on turning me into the Incredible Hulk, running bare-backed across the street and getting me locked up in an asylum once the man-in-the-white-coat had come and got me. I call him 'Pinky'. Pinky, my fitness trainer, for I was sure that every night he would be sleeping in his favorite pink thongs with small bunnies and strawberries on them. Whatever, I was improving, for now I could not easily bang on my laptop and it would start sputtering unintelligible alphabets not yet invented. Hell, I must be getting stronger. Protein shake down, I felt like Asterix and ready to thump my trainer up his hooter or cut out his frontal lobe with a nice karate chop. I was preparing myself for our next road-trip, which was to be the full-Monty show of India where we would start from the southern tip Kanyakumari, and drive up to the Northern tip of the country and do at least fifteen thousand kilometers in forty days. We had already messed up the dry-run, and I had to now prepare myself to face a very cute mountain sickness. They called it AMS. It must be similar to PMS. I was worried that Pinky would turn me into something that looked like that dude from 'Avatar'.

It was the same every day, stretch like Jane Fonda on the perverted bars, run like Forrest Gump on the treadmill with the other folks around you smelling like mountain-goats as though we were living in an era where deo-spray had not yet been invented. The smelly old goats would then herd toward the weights and make painful faces and equally painful sounds as though they were being sodomized. Hell, if it is so painful to lift that thing in the first place, why lift it at all? Absconding was not an option, for Pinky would call me up early in the morning (I call it late-night, but this book is not about semantics so we shall let it pass) and threaten me with dire consequences if I didn't make it to the gym on time. The threat included an additional fifty pushups and crunches while Pinky leered at me in sheer sadistic delight. I must have messed up in the initial days for I was slowly developing a washboard back and walking like the Hunchback of Notre Dame. Wasn't the washboard supposed to be in the front? This is what happens when they play pansy music at the gym. I remember as a teenager, when we used to be warned of a gymnasium called the 'Gaylord' in the neighborhood. The jocks would teeter out of the place after doing God-knows-what inside and walk around like they just had their armpits and crotch shaved, after having been dipped in starch for a good one hour.

We like happy. Not gay. With all due respect to the gay community of the world, folks like me preferred our lives straight and simple. I did tell Pinky about wanting to lose weight on my fingers as I was making way too many typographical errors while writing this book. I had seen a frown cross over that dull face before I was ignored. The sauna was no easy thing either, but it taught me empathy. Now I know what a potato feels like in a microwave oven, or how a shirt would feel inside a washing machine. Our towering sauna-man, he had a 'Duh!!" look on his face. One could easily conclude that the appendix and the brain were the two vestigial organs in him. Not everything in life is meant to have a function, and for my sauna-man, the brain was one such organ. It was wasted in him. Why on earth would he turn up the temperature and make us steam and sweat and bake us like fresh tomatoes? We all learn; I learnt too, as you may have noticed, dear reader, for I turned intelligent enough to write this book.

There was this woman who used to look like a 'Helga', who used to come to the gym everyday with her dog. I call her 'Helga', because, that's the name that crosses my mind when I think of an obnoxious and obese middle-aged woman. Every day, she would come in a sweat-shirt with black and white stripes that looked like skid-marks on a road kill. I think she used to consider herself good looking, well, at least somebody did. The more I looked at Helga, the more I liked her dog. Helga also had a golden tooth, and her smile looked like one of those psychological tests which shrinks use to map your brain with. She was a regular for three months and she used to work out every day. At the end of the three months, she looked the same. Probably, the workout prevented her from bloating up, making her look like the Zeppelin. There was absolutely no change in that form of hers even after three full months.

Then there was this middle-aged man whom I called 'Dick'. A formless being, his sole purpose in life was to come in and ogle at all the pretty women at peak-time. He could give Motormouth a run for her money as all he used to do was to chat up all the women in the gym. They say that middle-age arrives when your middle starts giving away your age and he had arrived. For some strange reason, he used to work out in what one can call a 'monkey-cap'. It was like a condom pulled right over his head and he was a dick of the highest order. You know those typical ones with the garrulous laughter and a fake lecherous smile who laugh at all the wrong parts of a joke? That kind. Maybe he comes in just to see if all the machines are being worked optimally. Again, zero change in shape or form.

Then there was 'The Thing'. All bulged up, so stiff that he could have given a telephone pole real stiff competition. Sixty percent of his time was spent on looking at himself in the mirror and striking strange poses, twenty percent was spent grunting with weights, eighteen percent was spent walking around showing off his muscles and the balance two percent was spent finding his way back to where he started off from. I always wonder if he used to eat rocks for food, as they also seemed to have found their way into his head. His face was like a thoroughly beaten up jerry can, and we could have used those arms as a jack for replacing a flat-tire. If we chopped off his legs, they could have been used as beams to hold up two municipality buildings in the neighborhood, built by cheap contractors, to prevent the roof from caving in. And so he was 'The Thing'.

Somewhere deep down, I get the feeling that Pinky got it all wrong. Maybe the fool thought that I was Forrest Gump and was planning to do a marathon run from Kanyakumari to Leh and back? Not drive. That shall forever remain a mystery to me till I kick the bucket and go to hell and roast him alive over a slow fire for all the nasty things he did to me on this earth.

The diet regimen was no better. Oats were in. I was having so much of oats that I had no choice but to stand and sleep at nights like a horse. Oats do that to you; that's why horses sleep while standing. The nuts and crackers made me think like a bird. The meals had to be high-fiber and if I couldn't get a high-fiber meal, I was expected to chew bed-covers and linen. Cigarettes and Bacardi were a strict no-no and I was living life at a discount. They say that living in Bombay or

Mumbai (or whatever the name is today if they didn't change it last night) is equivalent to smoking a pack of cigarettes a day. So we had moved to Bangalore so I could smoke a pack of cigarettes a day and still live the same life-span of a dumb mammal.

I was surrounded by equally insane people, if not more. Under-height people (euphemism for 'Overweight') who would mount the FX machines and whine; over-height people (euphemism for 'skinny') who looked like tape worms or pencils, which would mount the FX machines and whine too. We were perfect, the perfect morons, and prided ourselves on our perfect bodies that looked like chilled cans of Red Bull. We were fat-free and cool. Or at least, we had grand delusions about ourselves, and we didn't need to subject ourselves to the torture at the gymnasium day in and day out and having to pay for it.

A couple of months down, I must have been in shape for the trip for I was relieved of all the excess weight on me like my wallet, the fun and my dignity.

HOPping to Conclusions

▶ *The easiest way to get push-ups right is to imagine that you are doing strange things to a cow with four legs*

▶ *The best way to avoid lifting weights is to grunt very loud, putting pigs and your gym-trainer to shame. You will be let off easier and quicker*

▶ *Abdomen crunches are easier to do when your trainer towers above and sneers. The momentum is built by anger and one tends to do more crunches*

▶ *Getting on a bicycle that doesn't move despite pedaling like crazy is dumb and stupid*

▶ *Take it seriously when you hear a 'crunch' sound; chances are it might have come from you*

▶ *While doing dumbbells, oscillate like a pendulum, at least you can call it the fun part*

▶ *Machines that make you look like the Terminator are super cool*

▶ *Never wear tight clothing to a gym even if you are straight*

▶ *Jocks do not have a sense of humor; they are worse than the security personnel at airports*

▶ *10. Tamper with your trainer's watch when he/she is not looking*

The Loan shark swallows me

Planning for a road-trip isn't cheap; cheap is what I am. Here I was, in a seedy studio on a Sunday afternoon, wasting my time getting my picture taken to be stuck on a loan form so I could buy a new SUV. When I should have been in a swanky resort somewhere in Goa, posing for the cover of 'Time' magazine and signing autographs for fans, I was duly filling out a loan form as the photographer was cutting out those edges from his cheap Polaroid camera for me. Passport size photographs, all twelve copies of them, where I looked like a ruffian from a Rogue's Gallery from Mandrake's Xanadu or the local police station. The trick about getting a loan, I soon learnt, was to pretend that you didn't need the money. While President Obama was preaching change, I had loads of it in my pocket. And that's all I had with me anyway.

The loan-shark. I call him 'Nemo', since I was applying for a loan to buy what would soon become the ride called

'Motormouth' for the road-trip and she was expensive. We had to buy a pile of stuff that cost a pile and all I had was loose change. We were frantically approaching the sponsors to trick them into funding our good times. Fortunately, we managed to sucker a couple of them. We had anyways decided to splurge our measly savings from our pathetic existence in the corporate wasteland and so wanted to do our own thing that could help foster the growth of the right-side of the tiny brains that we possessed. The underlying fear factor was different. Derek and Goose were worried that if they did not explore their creative sides, the right side of the human brain, they would turn into cone-heads and walk with a not-so-sexy tilt. As if they had anything to worry about, they weren't humans. They were Neanderthals. We all were, and we were desperate to evolve.

Having faced a round of rejections from various banks as they doubted my ability to pay and rightly so, I had managed to drag this particular bank employee down to my level of stupidity and beat him with experience in rejections, bank loans etc, and used my charms to wheedle out a loan. Of course, they charged me an arm and a leg for what would barely cover the cost of a spare tire, but beggars cannot be choosers. And I was no Rockefeller. They made me sign in over two hundred places, and I took it in my stride as a practice session for all the times I would get to sign on T-shirts, bras, jeans and shoulder-blades of all those star-struck crazy fans they show on TV. Not that I watched TV after I had to sell it off to pay my credit card bills, but I hope you got the point. And, dear reader, if you have borrowed this book from a friend and are reading this then may the curse of the locusts get you now. After all, a loan with a high rate of interest is like a sexual escapade with a sticky end. Pun intended, as that was exactly so in my case.

Getting the sponsors and explaining the concept of this book was a tough nut to crack as the nuts were tough enough to see through my plans of writing a book that had nothing to say, no cause and completely devoid of any intelligence. Still, we managed to pull a couple of sponsorships through as we managed to convince them that sheer natural stupidity was far more progressive than artificial intelligence. Or maybe, they decided to sponsor the camping equipment out of sheer pity after watching three grown-up fools grovel at their feet, causing public embarrassment to them. The begging bowl trick always works. We see our politicians make a living out of it every day. So here was the deal – Derek, Goose and Chief were supposed to drive down in Motormouth and do a full-Monty of India, stop at various cities, meet the fans of an energy drink company, dole out freebies and T-shirts, party hard and reach Leh. A couple of morons from a circus were to join us at Leh, where they were supposed to smile and pose with smiling kids and talk about education, as if we were educated ourselves. Derek went into a state of panic and we had a tough time trying to calm him down as acting educated and intelligent to us was like asking Osama Bin Laden to sing the Star – Spangled Banner post 9/11 or asking Indians to give up watching cricket. Watching Derek cry was like watching any Enrique Iglesias music video, he cries in each one of them, that's pathetic. Not our Derek, Derek panics only when the word 'think' is used. We had no choice but to sedate him with alcohol and calm his nerves with morphine. The only consolation was the committed free Red Bull supply during the entire trip.

If Life were a marathon run for most, it was an obstacle race for us and we seemed to be tumbling at each hurdle. Now that we had the loan, the SUV and a little money to buy some camping gear, we decided to go for the bare essentials only. After a few hours of intense discussions, broken beer mugs and a couple of cracked skulls, we arrived at the following list of essentials for the trip:

HOPping to Conclusions

▶ *Tents: For us to cover ourselves with while sleeping in the car*
▶ *Cooler: To keep the beer chilled*
▶ *Car Accessories: Back massagers and butt-warmers*
▶ *Cooler: To keep water bottles chilled*
▶ *GPS: To look cool and fancy road-hog types*
▶ *Cooler: To keep the maps and books inside*
▶ *Credit Cards: As we don't have much money*
▶ *Cooler: To keep wet tissues cold*
▶ *Tiffin-box: To keep sandwiches inside*
▶ *Cooler: To keep empty tiffin-boxes in one place*

Maps were made in heaven, for Indian roads are hell

We agreed on naming the trip aptly as the 'Getting Leh'd' trip, for lack of a better name and to let Derek do the planning and come out with the route-map while Goose and I sat and twiddled our thumbs, waiting in anticipation for four hours. Derek surprised us by planning out the route, things to do and chalked out the minutest details with his deep knowledge of India. We knew we were in safe hands now. Here we were, three drivers, who couldn't count beyond five, who had somehow scraped through puberty, poverty, high-school, college and some odd jobs in nutcase nerdy firms, made money through the stock market and worked hard in putting together our life's savings. And Derek had now made it all so worthwhile with his meticulous planning that we were now ready to risk it all and throw it all away for the man who can think so deep. The man could think. Period.

He had worked out the full-Monty of India plans, worked out the route, the distances to be covered, things to do and all those little things that one tends to lose a girlfriend for. The morons that we were, not knowing how to count beyond 5, this is what the plan looked like for us now:

Day	Destination	Halt/ Day	Distance (ft)	Purpose of life
1	Kanyakumari	1	No clue	Get drunk, look at water and rocks from a plush hotel room
2	Bangalore	1	1700	Get Media attention, look cool, get free chicks, get Leh'd
3	Dharwad	1	432	No clue
4	Pune	1	407	Visit Tipu Sultan's Palace
5	Mumbai	2	153	Take a shower, Change the tires. Read in reverse order
1	Ahmadabad	1	562	Shave, Meet the fans, Get drunk, Get Leh'd
2	Udaipur	1	254	Go to Taj Mahal and take pictures.
3	Jaipur	1	395	Try to meet the Prime Minister of , at least drive by his house
4	New Delhi	1	260	Withdraw money from ATM, give away Tshirts, cure virginity

Day	Destination	Halt/ Day	Distance (ft)	Purpose of life
5	Chandigarh	1	248	Get Media attention, Look cool, Get free chicks, Get Leh'd
1	Manali	2	286	Shave, Take a shower, Change clothes
2	Rohtang	2	53	Clean the car, Buy potato chips
3	Keylong	1	42	Meet Nitwit – our local guide, look for beer
4	Baralacha La	0	73	Take pictures, talk to animals, trees and rocks
5	Sarchu	0	36	Meet the Yeti
1	Pang	1	79	Take out garden shears, get a haircut
2	Upshi	2	125	Give Motormouth a bath
3	Leh	1	55	Take a shower, Meet the Chief Nerd, Do good for Orphans
4	Pangong Tso	1	160	Meet Dalai Lama
5	Tso Moriri	1	No clue	Buy Chinese shoes
1	Leh	1	No clue	Get Leh' d
2	Khardung La	1	39	Drive and Pass through
3	Leh	0	39	Look for a McDonalds
4	Khalsi	1	100	Drink with the Indian Army
5	Batalik	1	50	Meet the locals
1	Kargil	1	60	Collect shrapnel
2	Panikhar	0	67	Drive, Camp, Fish, Cook, Drink, Barf, sleep
3	Rangdum	0	65	Drive, Camp, Fish, Cook, Drink, Barf, sleep
4	Sani	0	No clue	Drive, Camp, Fish, Cook, Drink, Barf, sleep
5	Zangla	0	No clue	Drive, Camp, Fish, Cook, Drink, Barf, sleep

Day	Destination	Halt/ Day	Distance (ft)	Purpose of life
1	Kargil	0	No clue	Drive, Camp, Fish, Cook, Drink, Barf, sleep
2	Drass	0	61	Drive, Camp, Fish, Cook, Drink, Barf, sleep
3	Srinagar	0	140	Drive, Camp, Fish, Cook, Drink, Barf, sleep
4	Udhampur	1	226	Drive, Camp, Fish, Cook, Drink, Barf, sleep
5	Jammu	1	67	Drive, Camp, Fish, Cook, Drink, Barf, sleep
1	Pathankot	1	107	Go to the beach
2	Jalandhar	1	112	Go snorkeling
3	Ludhiana	1	59	Give Motormouth a checkup
4	Ambala	1	124	Buy wet-tissues and band-aid
5	New Delhi	1	211	Go to Spa for a Thai massage
1	Agra	1	201	Go to ATM, withdraw money, change under were
2	Ajmer	1	361	Replenish coolers
3	Jaise Imer	1	469	Take pictures of the Vivekananda Rock
4	Gandhinagar	1	55	Meet the Gandhis
5	Mumbai	1	571	Go to India Gate
1	Goa	1	579	Party hard, Get Leh'd
2	Bangalore	0	556	Party hard, Get Leh'd, Take a shower
		40	10129	

HOPping to Conclusions

▶ *Keep your car clean, avoid barfing inside*
▶ *Wet tissues & deo-sprays are very useful if you don't believe in showers*

▸ *Always keep money with you, it is very useful while spending*

▸ *Never chew your credit cards, for swiping becomes a problem later*

▸ *The best cure for a hangover is to stay drunk*

▸ *Actual roads are much bigger than what they draw on maps*

▸ *If you get lost, make more mistakes, till you get back on the highway*

▸ *Man is a social animal, drive for a month, you can drop the word 'social'*

▸ *When asked for a tip, always give advice*

▸ *Plan all the way to the end, throw it all away and let life take over*

8 The Fine Art of Wasting Time

I belong to urban India; I've never milked a cow,
I like fun times with my friends, do some crazy things
and how;
I live in the city and I also get bitten by cupid
Our talks range from Intelligent to downright stupid
We are nice people, like a little bit of fun,
We like to live life, give me my share of rain and the sun
Everyday living can make you say 'Cheese'
Drive on, for that's the philosophy behind 'Horn OK Please'...

An ordinary day: 5 p.m. (Bitten by the writer's bug)

With my Bluetooth device, I look like a Cyborg. I am turning into a robot with my new Sony Walkman. I look like one of those characters from a cheap, horrible, horror B-grade Bollywood flick. The only thing that was left was a placard around my neck stating that I was someone suffering from an acute case of intelligence deficiency, with an arrow pointing toward my head. Instead of being sent across to my literary agents, I ran the risk of being hauled up by men in white coats and thrown into the nearest mental institution. I guess that's what happens to a person bitten by a writer's bug, and I had been bitten in the wrong place by this twisted and perverted bug. I was walking around like a zombie, a man who had shoved his head into the bass drum of Lars Ulrich from Metallica during a show-off session. But there it was, the dratted bug had bitten me in a place that has a direct correlation to the medulla oblongata. I had that bug impact my life – all the signals were messed up. From motor skills to erection, all my signals from the brain were garbled. My brain had died in my body, I was a zombie and I was a drooling idiot crossing the street about to become road kill, had I not been rescued in time by an old lady, who pulled me over from that place on the road where funnily-tanned donkeys cross Indian roads.

Ok, so it's not one of those grab-a-coffee-and-sober-up kind of a situations I was in. Hell, I was off alcohol and nicotine, preparing for the road-trip and was wondering what the hell I was living for. I felt like one of those boys from a clean-cut boy-band, like a piece of cottage-cheese gone mad. The old lady who rescued me looked like a cross between Lady Gaga and a banged-up old car. My veins were overflowing with Red Bull, I must have been high on caffeine, for I looked like Jim Carrey from 'The Mask' who needed a sexy nurse to bring me back to life in her own sweet, special way. But since this is not that kind of a book, we shall let that pass. As I get yelled at by the old woman, I think her voice is about to make my brain explode and come out through my ears. She wants me to think? Thinking is what I'd done all my life and I had concluded that it was an act equivalent to putting your fingers in through your nostrils and trying to scratch the back of your head. And she wanted me to do that? The wicked old witch. Typical of my country where we have people all over the place. I had a few hovering around me, similar to a voodoo dance somewhere in Africa, with the unwanted well-wishers trying to wean out the evil spirits.

Hey! Don't touch that totem pole of mine, else I'll tell your wicker-man. Isn't this supposed to be urban India where at least some semblance of civilization is supposed to exist? And you want me to drink that muddy liquid called water? No thanks! Unfortunately, that was forced down my throat as someone held on to me. I was supposed to feel better after that. Maybe I was now. I guess I was zonked and feeling weird then, while I just felt weird after that dose, thank you very much. Empathize with me now? Then, voila! There came a vegetable puff. Like eating a swarm of roasted bees wrapped in sandpaper. No, there was gratitude in me, just that I had left it at home along with my brain.

The traffic cop came by to check on what was causing the commotion. All I could see were his shiny pearly whites and a phosphorescent jacket and white gloves crossing the street, a trick I had learnt since childhood since the traffic anyways doesn't respect pedestrians and the streets were poorly lit all over India. At least I had managed to dislodge the master from his pedestal and His Highness was leering at me in sheer sadistic delight while there was gay abandon on the road as cars were screeching off, breaking signals. I had managed to cause confusion yet again, something very easy to do in India. I could sense that the traffic cop had sold his spinal cord pre-mortem to his profession as I could read 'money' written all over his face. And I was wearing nice clothes and had a wallet, which is a crime in a third world country, I suppose. My heart goes out to the pretty old lady whose language was much more colorful than any rainbow I'd ever seen; the cop beat a hasty retreat. Leaning on a truck parked wrongly by the roadside, my eyes slowly started focusing on the beautiful girl crossing the street. I could see what I read on the back on the truck, printed on that white skirt, 'Horn OK Please'. It was a sign, yet again. The philosophy behind this phrase was light-years ahead in a country where the trucks were from the Flintstones era. While growing up, I swear I had seen some dinosaurs pee on such trucks parked in our backyard.

In India, everyone needs to know what the matter is. Ten people mean a hundred ways. And all people mean well. It's a different matter altogether that every Indian is a lawyer, doctor or an engineer and of late, every Indian wants to be an author. I mean look at me, with a few dozed geeky and wretched blogs on some nerdy topic, here I was delusional and day-dreaming of selling a few million copies of my first book. Well, you bought it, didn't you? So I guess you need to come along with me for an MRI scan and enjoy those techno-beats inside that rotating coffin. As my hands were itching and I felt like Edward Scissorhands, I needed to write. Better yet, I needed to type as I belong to the new stylus generation. I had to get to my laptop and vomit out all the gibberish that was emanating from the fountainhead of trash aka my brain. I was turning into a cyborg, I was sure now. My old laptop whined and groaned as I let my typographical errors fly at the speed of light.

Well, if you cannot beat 'em, boot 'em, and blame the bad handwriting on Bill Gates.

In convulsions and my hands vibrating very fast, I was glad the muddy liquid therapy was over. Hang on, that was just foreplay, the old witch has other tricks up her sleeve as she starts hitting me on my back very violently in the name of therapy. Old grandmother therapy? My gluteus maximus. I would have choked to death on the vegetable puff. The beating was incomprehensible and gave me a headache. So were my desperate pleas to escape from the mad woman. I was seeing streamlined traffic now because of those violent vibrations, I sure was hallucinating. It was the same feeling one gets inside a rickety auto rickshaw on a very bumpy road. The one that makes a lot of noise and runs on kerosene, where the driver sits at an angle that does not correspond with the trajectory of the vehicle? I now had that kind of a headache as well.

OK, what's my name again? Where do I live? Who is your master? As question marks formed around my head, I finally managed to get rid of the crowd that had gathered around to find out everything about me, my forefathers, my first tri-cycle experience right down to the size of my underwear. At times, I get so taken aback by the first-meeting with a stranger and they start referring to the 'never-ask-anyone-unless-you-know-that-person-really-well' manual and start interrogating me. I'm sure, dear reader, you would be no exception. And we are like that only – a very convenient way to hide a very inconvenient habit.

An ordinary day: 6 p.m. (The fine art of wasting time)

Safely back in my car, I look at the window to see a stray mongrel. It reminded me of Goose who had just been dumped. Again. We had had a hearty laugh and had shredded the sordid love-affair to pieces. He had made a mistake. He had fallen in love with this girl whom he had met up on a social networking site and was going around with two men at the same time. That wasn't the mistake. Every night, he would get into these long distance calls from some godforsaken place in Finland where only potatoes grew. That wasn't the mistake. He had dumped a girl who really loved him for what he was worth, which was not much of course, and that was the mistake. The mongrel had exactly 2,453 fleas on its back, which goes on to prove that I was pretty much jobless that evening and I was spending time counting fleas. Marvellous.

I mean Goose and Derek had it all going for them, but somewhere down the line, things had gone really wrong with them and they had made some serious mistakes. Like being born. They had always had the chance to date the hottest chicks in the neighborhood, but they always seemed to be falling in love with the wrong kinds. It was a case of severe avian flu with them. I revved up Motormouth and made my way to our regular coffee bar, where we would drool and ogle for a couple of hours, then ogle and drool for a couple of more hours after that. When we had nothing better to do, we would sit around and explore the subtle nuances of human relationships, grossly put – the fine art of bitching and we had mastered the art of dissecting people pre-mortem.

An ordinary day: 7 p.m. (Of Derek's culinary skills)

Today was one of those days. Derek and Goose graced the fine evening by arriving in an ancient, beaten-down ride that could put an old Bajaj scooter to shame. Goose was wearing dark Rayban shades in a coffee-bar at night. Anything to look cool. They look good when the sun is up; they tend to look less cooler at nights and can make a person look like Stevie Wonder. It was difficult to decide who looked more stupid – Derek and Goose in that thing or the thing with Derek and Goose inside. Probably, it needed some kind of shaman and voodoo magic to start up, which would take place after the slaughter of a few innocent goats and chickens at the altar, after a young virgin had been offered to the dark Gods before the key could even be inserted into the ignition. Of course, I am exaggerating, that thing of a car would have been invented before keys were even imagined. Probably, it started by the rubbing of two sticks and starting a fire to cause internal combustion in the engine and there I go rambling again, making absolutely no sense as promised in the 'Prologue' section of the book. Maybe, my funny bone is acting up, or maybe you are just getting used to my bad jokes. But they are still better than what Derek could ever cook. I mean, the lunatic has to get back to school just to learn how to boil water. He could only cook up trouble for us. And that was his specialty. There was a time when I had no choice but to try out his cooking. I was famished and barely above the Indian poverty line for a week and had been driven to hungrier pastures than Ethiopia, read 'Derek's kitchen'. Filthy, in a word. One look at it and a man could starve for another week. I had done a month and had now lined my stomach with leather, had kept antacids and a fire-extinguisher along with a bottle of water.

The experience was insane. One spoonful of the frothy soup and anyone could figure that he had drained out the water from the washing machine straight into the frying pan in sheer laziness. The salt was ok, but the soap was in excess. It was a soul-cleansing experience and I had decided to go on without nourishment for another week. Sometimes, I still wake up in the middle of the night, shivering and soaked in sweat when I think of the soup. Forget that, Derek couldn't even cook up an alphabet soup. If such food were to be served in prison, India would not be so populous. Better yet, we should send Derek as a cook to all these politicians who take garlands of currency notes from people or those who create statues and busts of themselves when they are alive. Maybe they should shower under a bathtub full of hard coins, which we can spare, dropped from over twenty feet. We would like to see change too, and this is the best way to rid India of greedy politicians.

An ordinary day: 7 p.m. (Goose's sob story)

As we settled down with bucketfuls of steaming cappuccino, Goose ranted out his sob story. He had been ditched, twice over within a span of six months. The guy was funny, he was a joke. He belonged to that car. The old bucket of bolts, only the horn worked well. His first love had left scar marks on his back and that was alright, but his second heartthrob had left scratch marks on his car as well. And that had left him heartbroken. Derek had a cynical frown on his face, the kind of a frown that one gets to see on a traffic cop's face once you are pulled over. Goose's first girlfriend was right now honeymooning in Spain. He was quite upset about the sex and the Spain part of the affair, not her. It was tearing him apart – like having hot iron rods inserted into his skull and being asked to watch Doordarshan. And now I was forced to listen to his story and empathize. Hurray. Ha! Ha! Ha!

A few barrels of Red Bull and truck-loads of coffee down, Goose was done with his story. Finally, we could get back to planning our next move in pimping up Motormouth. What I vaguely remember from that long and torturous conversation is that his girls left him for someone else. That's all. I mean, it was like a crash course in brain surgery, trying to understand what goes on in a woman's mind. If women were from Venus and men are from Mars, I was looking at a guy who seemed to have been lost in transit. If he was caught breaking promises and trying to hide his porn CDs from his girlfriend as though they were Scud missiles and were about to be used to bomb out some country and its innocent civilians, Goose was nothing short of a terrorist. The second one left him as he spent more time driving across the country and she was jealous of his bucket of bolts. And that's why we saw those scratch marks on his car. Goose considered himself to be ahead of his time, though in no way it can be considered useful. I mean, there are many things and many people out there in this world, who serve no purpose. They are just there taking up space. That's why we are such a densely populated nation. We have many such things and many such people and Goose was sounding like one of those inane objects that we despised. We were not dopeys or crack heads or criminals or terrorists or politicians or traffic police, then where was the problem? And Goose was a guy who any girl would take to her parents if she wanted to kill them and take over their inheritance in a jiffy. Add Derek as the best man and she could get her neighbor's inheritance as well. He was not the grim reaper as his girlfriends had made him out to be and neither this car nor his camera was used for any nefarious purposes other than driving and getting laid in the backseat. It was as innocent as that.

Anyways, we decided not to make too much sense out of it and Goose knew he had made Derek and myself lose interest in his story a few hours ago and was probably talking to a stone wall, clawing at it. Reading a user manual for a scientific calculator would have been a much better idea than looking for sympathy with two morons. I suspected his head was about to explode and his brains would come oozing out of his ears if he didn't let out a few obscenities. Talking to us did help as the next thirty minutes must have been a real spiritual experience for Goose while the dull interior of the coffee bar was decorated by some real colorful language as profanity ruled the place.

An ordinary day: 8 p.m. (Ramblings of a mad man)

I was talking to a cat. A real nervous four-legged cat. The pen is mightier than the sword. Let's just use nice words like 'unconventional' and 'alternative' instead of abusive terms like 'trash' and 'useless' for this book. Looking out at the roads, we surveyed the land our forefathers left us. They seem to have left back a lot of garbage and progeny on the streets. They were like those Incas, or those almost-extinct tribes from the darkest corners of India, who preferred to drink goat-blood or sacrifice animals by the Ganges and leave it all dirty. Problem is, they didn't have a calendar like those freaky Mayans which ended in 2012. The HOPfans community got hold of their secret scrolls and you, dear reader, are going to be privy to some real dark secrets by the end of this chapter. Our next topic of conversation was pointless, ludicrous and foolish, just like any other conversation. Hell, if I were to hold my head up at a slant and stare at the camera with my nostrils flaring, would they call that attitude and award me with a multi-million dollar contract or would I be sent across to the local municipality hospital to get my neck-sprain treated? Just look at those pathetic, anorexic females on TV. Those poor little kids would complete my pencil collection. I think this one is called 'Anorexia' and she is being followed by her sister called 'Bulemia'. If she were to cross the streets in India in those tatters, the show would incur the wrath of the stray mongrels on the street, and they would be pelted by stones by those naughty tykes before they were locked up in the local Women's Welfare association or some other crazy association.

Oh, man-in-white-coat, come and get me, take my personality tests, make me lie down on that couch, take away my dignity till I accept I am a liar either ways, take anything, but please take these guys out of the coffee bar right now. We are now faced with this crazed bunch of boys walking in with hair bands and they must be gay or stupid or both. Is it some kind of a male version of burning the bra? What are you going to wear up next, pal? Pink panties and bling and look like Lady Gaga? Derek stares in disbelief at them, fork in hand. I hope he does something real mean with that fork of his to them. Go on, do something, mate, or these semi-eunuchs are going to haunt me as those nightmares that one gets to deal with in India at various traffic junctions. Take away that hair band, take away that head, take away anything, but get them out of here, Derek! Help!!

An ordinary day: 9 p.m. (Helgaism)

Obnoxious people like Helga, who is symbolic of a typcial, over-the-hill megalomaniac in her late 40s represented in human form, wanting to take over the planet, their failed attempts turn them into bags of pure, unadulterated negativity. Having overestimated their potential, 'Helgas' are the unfortunate victims of their own being. Maybe, that's why so many folks suffer from acute mental constipation and an incurable verbal diarrhea complicated by a persecution complex. I once had a fan on my Facebook page who claimed to be the CEO of some web-marketing firm, somewhere in Hyderabad. One gathers that she is just one of those many people from those shady institutes from Hyderabad. These are the people who battle the now-defunct social paradigms. One dinosaur told me that I couldn't write for life. As you can see, dear reader, I cannot write for nuts and she was right. Maybe, these mediocre dim-wits are actually a boon in disguise now for me, as they have effectively used their negativity that provides inspiration to so many of us by teaching us what not to become in life. That's 'Helgaism'.

Such people in positions of power, who were once dreamers, turned delusional somewhere down the line and now have turned into complete megalomaniacs, building statues, parks and wantonly wasting the nation's wealth and trying to turn impressionable minds into inward-looking and insecure people like themselves. I have been asked to make these types a part of my book and talk about them, so I did. If anyone, gender-neutral, were to be looking at this in an unbiased way, anyone whose starting point of a thought process is at the loser end, there would be exactly double the distance to cover and it is medieval. That is not the India I know or see, where we proudly proclaim the adoption of the girl-child, which was to become the theme of the trip, but give us a break – when it comes to grown-ups, all are equal and we all decide the shape of the world that we live in. Like a great artist, who decided that his balls were cuboids and not round. The nation's changed, the goal-post has moved and you are a dinosaur, Helga. Admit it, and you shall live happily or wallow in your bile till you die. Go on, get that 5-minute private sob in the restroom for you are a loser, Helga.

An ordinary day: 10 p.m. (How to laugh at others and have a great time)

More coffee, mate! In walks a guy with a swagger that makes him look like a Dude-high-on-dope. We wonder what she sees in him. We cannot help but overhear the deep philosophical pearls of wisdom our man is going to mouth to impress the pretty one. We hear a deep sigh once she's told him to change his ways. Deafening silence. And then he says, "Learn from others? Why should I? Isn't it like watching porn?"

"Ha!Ha!Ha! Bad line you fool, not only have you hammered the last nail in your coffin, you managed to get your thumb under the hammer as well!" As the jock watched the girl walk out of the place in a huff, I knew I had just witnessed 'Moronism' in action and this book is full of it. And that's exactly what men talk about in pubs and coffee bars in urban India. Some come in with long hair and pretend to look stoned and deep, while being full of shit and shallower than our collective piddle in the corner of the street. Wee, the nation.

We like to bitch and laugh at other people's miseries and we are morons. So that's cool. You should be roasted over a slow-fire or be subject to Chinese tea or Chinese torture (one and the same for us) or sent to the potato-growing and corn-lovin' Mid-West in the USA for three months as punishment. That makes the four of us now – Goose, Derek, Chief (why am I speaking in the third person?) And Motormouth, our ever sweet lovin' Super-SUV, who would love to make skid marks all over you. Help, he's getting away! Don't! We just got started and I think he slyly noticed our presence. Maybe we were not inconspicuous enough, or maybe we were blatantly obnoxious.

Had he not left the place, we probably would have died laughing that night. Fine-wine. Us. We were more like empty cans of cheap Indian beer.

An ordinary day: 11 p.m. (Welcome to the Hobbit's den)

Everyone must have a plan; we grew up learning that kind of gibberish. After our Kanyakumari dry-run, we had realized that we lacked art, and most of the other arts of life. We needed a cunning plan this time. An evil one. A wicked plan that would have a secret manifesto, where we would form a secret society made public on Facebook. And HOPfans was launched on Facebook. It is my plan to take over young and idling minds of India, take them over and turn this nation into a bunch of drooling morons who would be repulsed by the standard thought patterns of a post-colonial hangover, obscuring any signs of creativity and intelligence in the nation. Look at the IT revolution; our so-called Information Technology Czars, who turned the educated masses into a bunch of educated coolies. And the nation worships them while the media calls them entrepreneurs? Spare me the trash, for Derek, Goose and the Chief are made of a different mould. We stood out like three fingers with me standing in the middle (since I am the author), so that would make me the middle finger. So they can suck me, I guess, if they can read between lines. We are nice guys, as smooth as sandpaper and as straight forward as a cock-screw, destined to unplug the septic-tank of constipated thought created by these megalomaniacs who sway the nation today. That's worse than creating a few hundred nuclear missiles and pointing them at our neighbors and making the world live in fear, if not awe.

We made our way to the iPad, as I like calling my place. No, it has nothing to do with any fruit company, but is the Iyengar's home. It's like a Hobbit's den. Once you walk in, consider yourself lucky if you manage to get out, to escape. It means we haven't cooked you and had your brains for dinner,. At least you will thank your stars for living after that, despite the traumatic experience of stepping on DVDs, books and comics and being bitten by strange bugs that may not be found elsewhere on the planet. Images will haunt you forever, and I'll leave you with that thought. Only Goose and Derek were allowed into my den as even the strange and horrible bugs were scared of them. While I filled up those delicate glass thingies with single-malt and played Floyd, there was Derek, looking at Imhotep (Goose's only remaining pet) in a very lusty way with his 'Come hither, O' sweet wench of mine' looks, as he imagined himself to be similar to Conan, the Barbarian. Goose was very busy fiddling with his camera, and after two consecutive break-ups, he could let Imhotep go on and fulfill Derek's fantasy of making him a part of a sausage. Not that we are animal haters or anything like that, but just to keep it on records, we are die-hard carnivores that eat anything that crawls the earth, swims underwater or soars the skies. Living or dead, it doesn't really matter, as long as they are not vegetables. Only music, no talk, just listening to Roger Waters croon. The more we drank, the better he sounded.

An ordinary day: 12 p.m. (Drunken musings)

An hour of demolishing two bottles of Scotch with these two morons increased our loquaciousness and now we were flowing more freely than alcohol. It was a starry night and we could see more stars than ever before, as we were seeing double. I wondered why on earth I wasted the fine liquor on us especially when after a couple of cap-fulls, even cheap arrack would make any place look like Las Vegas to us. The more we drank, the more we could tolerate each other's idiosyncrasies. But Scotch has this particular effect on us. Single-malt, on the rocks and we find soda or plain water too strong for our system. That's why we always dilute it with alcohol. Alcohol has this particular effect on us. Derek would go from ridiculous to sublime after a few drinks; Goose would go from miserable to pathetic and I would go from moron to insane. There was always a particular trajectory we followed on our path to Nirvana and so we never mix drinks. We were in orbit and the company was stellar.

Tanked up, we were like the three blind mice, effectively turbo-charged and overly delusional like Helga. Trouble was, whenever I mouthed any nonsense minus drinks, folks would look up to me as though I had opened up and shared with them the dark secrets of the universe. Drink in hand, even if I didn't take a sip, the same folks would consider me drunk and dismiss my thoughts as nonsense. Another reason, dear reader, for me to write a book, as you cannot figure out right now my levels of sobriety. Anyways, I love life, get my highs smokin' competition at work and I do not need any artificial stimulant to spin me into orbit. With alcohol, however, we have consistently turned louder, picked up fights or passed out on dinner tables. Just that it opens up the floodgates of our inner being, which of course, is best left caged up, gagged and bound. That's human psychology and individual behavior patterns. So, we always pass on the blame to the Scotch. After all, we were too dumb to deal with psychology when our egos were remote controlled not by the medulla, but by that glass thingy full of golden liquid. Or half-empty. Or half-full. See? The mere talk of alcohol intoxicates me and I prefer to stay off it, save it for occasions. We were drinking as if on a mission to console Geese (as I was seeing double now) and we were stupid enough to start talking about our past relationships.

Derek's first girlfriend

That night Derek did open up, and looking back, we wished he hadn't. Raging hormones and loaded up on testosterone mixed with Red Bull, he had done everything at the time of need. His deep-rooted Freudian instincts had told him that if his parents hadn't had sex, high chances that he wouldn't either. He wouldn't have been there and we would all have lived in a much happier world. But the deed was done as the condom manufacturers may has messed up and left a hole here or there, Derek was born to the world. Our dim-witted friend had done whatever had come his way, right from his baby-sister's Barbie dolls to his pillows. Bruised and hurt and I'm not talking about his ego here, he decided that the best way for him to grow up was to fall in love. According to him, falling in love was like suffering from an advanced case of swine-flu and to an attention-seeking, over-confident, dim-witted nitwit like him, as much as he hated it, he did succumb to it once. Unfortunately, it was his school teacher and his love was pure. Purely one-sided. It had not past, no present and absolutely no future. Ha!Ha!Ha! He just had five finger-prints pasted on his left-cheek before being clobbered by a bouquet and a teddy bear one fine day and he still calls that a break up. We wonder why she didn't break his bones instead. Maybe, she did have a soft corner for him and so she let him live while she decided to mess up our grades in school. Thanks to this dim-wit, we got messed up for hanging out with him in school. When there were normal kids trying their best to grow up, Derek had managed to get himself suspended after being caught humping the study tables and benches in the class room. The only consolation was that he was straight. So we were spared. So much for his sob-story. And now his ideal mate was someone who would start and stop with an ignition key only. But I must say that Derek is always fantastic with the fairer sex. Maybe.

HOPping to Conclusions

According to Derek, men like the following things in life:

▸ *Women: Men like women because they are nice people who can think,*

▸ *Cars: Men like cars as they can start and stop with an ignition key.*

▸ *High heels: Men like women in high-heels as the sound defrags the brain of man.*

▸ *Sex: Men like sex with women as there is no thought involved in the act*

▸ *Power: Men like power as it makes them powerful*

▸ *World-domination: Men like to dominate as that act is like sex. Devoid of thought*

▶ *Men like a combination of all the above as Men like to have sex with women who wear high-heels as it gives them a sense of power and world-domination*

For the first time in his entire life, Derek made some sense. Maybe he was a deep thinker after all. Or maybe he was pissed drunk, no deeper than a bed-pan.

Chief's first girlfriend

My first crush was this girl who had a brother with the same name. I was holding on to the losing end of the stick as I ran a very high risk of emanating brotherly love. Sooner or later, it had to happen when you hear the classic dumping line "You-are-a-fantastic-human-being-and-we-should-be-friends-nothing-more". Yeah right, as if that's what I was after and I had finally found the pot of gold at the end of the rainbow. Hurray. Like with any other dumpee, I had frantically tried to correct the situation and accepted to be called by a nickname. I just wanted to be called. Period. Looking back, I realize that the world is all about the dumper-dumpee relationship. Now, I don't know if there is any such word out there in the Lobster's dictionary or not, but hell, how would a lobster know about my feelings anyways? I gather that in any relationship, the person to walk away smiling is the person who is not the dumpee, so that would make it the dumper. Brilliant.

Not that I could avoid falling in love after that. In fact it intensified, with my falling in love with any object of the opposite sex and I just wanted to have a whole lot of sex, which was quite the opposite of love as I had to prove a point to my pathetic self. Now I don't even remember what was the point I was trying to make at that time, which is not very different from now, as I don't have a point to make right now. There I go, rambling again…Derek's not the only one who was pissed drunk. Goose had already passed out and was snoring noisily. Maybe he was dead; maybe we had just bored him to death. We had wasted yet another evening, just when we had met up to plan our road-trip.

HOPping to Conclusions

According to the Chief (meaning self), men like the following things in life:

▶ *Roads: Men like roads as we can drive on them to avoid walking*

▶ *Cars: Men like stick-shift cars, as they are phallic. Since this is Freudian stuff, go ask Freud or his mother*

▶ *Open skies: Men like the open skies as thoughts evaporate into nothingness. Like clouds*

▶ *Rain: Men like rain as it beats getting under a shower or slinking into a tub any day*

▶ *Rock Music: As there is no other form of music; everything else is just noise and cacophony*

▶ *Women: Straight men like women as there is nothing to dislike about them*

▶ *Success: Men like success as women like successful men*

9 Men are from Mars, Women are from Earth

To choose the right partner is everyone's dream,
Boy or girl, man or woman, it ain't so difficult as it may seem;
You might be the ideal lover or World's biggest flirt,
It's not just in the heart, but could be your skirt or your shirt;
It could be the way you come across, it could be the way you talk,
It could be just how you smell, it could be the way you walk;
For you could get just who you want, get all that you desire,
It's all about your passion, let love take you higher;
I've always wondered what girls talk about all the time,
But read on, dear reader, for this is the last rhyme;
Smiles and beauty make you say 'Cheese'
Drive on, for that's when you go 'Horn OK Please'...

The Incredible Hulk is the perfect moron

A big statue of a naked woman and people drive around it, so many sculptures of all the poses and we call it Kamasutra, but when it comes to the real world, we have multiple standards. But when I watch the same on the internet, people call it pornography and despise me. Done with our irregular dose of porn for a year last evening, it never was any fun. Since they didn't have internet then, maybe that's why we have such sculptures. Just keep the kids safe and we are alright with whatever you do. Talk about multiple standards. Now bugger off and try to figure why we are like that only. After all, I am a typical urban Indian male in a pub tonight with Derek and Goose for company. Oh! Misery. But that's alright as misery loves miserable company. Goose and Derek are real punishment alright and being a friend to them was more like being an accomplice, a partner in crime. And you dear reader, as the over-educated, attention-seeking dimwit like me, shall have no choice now but to read on and figure out what goes on in the mind of a moron in a pub. We call it a 'Think Tank' in legal parlance. We try to think after tanking up. In fact, the best thoughts come through when you are doped, drunk, snoozing under a tree or wanking off in a bath tub. History proved it. And if you have half a brain to understand what I just wrote, dear reader, you are now ready to take up a very strategic position of power in a nation that is gearing up to bomb out the neighboring country. Dim-bulb. I wonder how you survived the past few chapters. My condolences to you and your pet cobra, for you must have some stupid pet like that in your house as you are crazy enough to buy this book. However, if this book is borrowed, may the cobra bite you right now.

As a writer, today I am like the Brainiac's distant cousin, five times removed, living on the edge of the planet. The Terminator's autistic cousin brother and Goose and Derek show mercy on me and we go to a pub. And then it was like any other inane evening of inebriation and hopelessly dumb man-to-man talk. The guy talk, as they call it and I've been often asked by my girlfriends what exactly we talk about. Well, we certainly do not talk about global warming and stuff like that, that's best left to that dude from Maharashtra – Al Gore or someone, who talks about the earth overheating like a pressure cooker with a worn-out gasket.

Heading out to the pub for an evening out, we had a herd of goats crossing our path. The problem with these dumb animals is that they panic and they come in hordes. They come at you faster if you honk more. It goes on to say that the acceleration of a goat's reflexes is directly proportional to the frequency of the horn, multiplied by its loudness. 'K' is the constant multiple here as confusion multiplies in equal proportion. They come closer with their tongues hanging out, looking like a pack of Gene Simmonses from the fabled rock band – KISS. Goose was playing his horrible music, as usual. I think he was playing the same song over and over again and all the CDs have the same song. That was Trance or house or crap or something like that. Some guy 'Dustbin Timberlake' or 'Tiestosterone' or some such. All the songs sound the same and I was glad to have reached our destination.

We go through this metal detector to get inside a pub. What next? Are they going to check my pulse and take a urine sample before I can order a drink? Am I supposed to now have sex with the X-Ray machine and the sniffer dog before we are allowed to enter? All in the name of security. Welcome to Bangalore. Inside the pub, there is more noise than music or chatter, they call it house music or some sick stuff like that, which means that even if you are choking and dying, cannot move or speak, you will be dead in no time. No attention at all unless you have rocket flares or a Scud missile on you. Derek walks up to the DJ, slaps him on his skinny butt and asks him to play some classic rock. Derek's a goon and people are scared of him. So are we, glad he is on our side. The place stops sounding like a real big coffee machine gone mad and the sound of Led Zepellin takes over. We are home.

Life is full of coincidences and accidents. One tends to meet all the accidents in a Bangalore pub and call it coincidence. The moment a back is turned, we bitch and stab. Unless we are pretty drunk so we can pretend to be bum chums with the guys and bosom buddies with the girls. There is a subtle difference, you see. After a few rounds of beer, we see friends in each one of them. Many friends turn acquaintances and vice versa. I have no idea how many party invitations. I have accepted in pubs, all of them to take place at the same time on the same day. And we would be sitting here, drinking and engaging in classic man talk. The more I drink, the better the girls in the pub look. There have been occasions when Derek has even kissed the doorknob of the restroom inside.

The pub looked like a Hobbit's den, all short people as the average height in India is not very high. The midgets make it worse. Hang on, no wonder they look short, as most of them are sitting, so my middle finger to the authors of Super Freakonomics. Maybe, you guys are gay, feeling up all small Indian males and HOPping to conclusions. I don't blame them. Writers tend to put in misleading facts to sell their work. I am no exception to the rule. You remain the victim.

Come on, dumb waiter, if we don't get our table in the next ten minutes, you shall have your head kiss the stone wall a number of times, to the guitar riffs, just to make things fun for us morons. I suspect that the waiter is more of a trainee vampire with teeth to prove it. I am sure he will have to re-apply to join the human race, fill out a form in triplicate at the nearest municipality office, force them at gun-point and make them realize that he is human. For humans are crazy people. Done with the monologues, our conversation shifted from the Oh-so-regular-stuff-that-guys-go-through, to overdrive. And this is the classic man-to-man-talk that most of us would indulge in.

Since we are hungry and ravenous, and we have a great sense of humor, we shall also indulge in what those egg-heads behind the counter are so busy mutilating and roasting over the slow fire. Surely, it will be better than what Goose or Derek can cook. Apparently, the dumb-waiter has managed to trick us into ordering what they call 'The Chef's special' along with a pint served by the chinless bartender. Maybe it will be the carcass of some road kill with zebra-stripes boiled in chef's drool and served with bat's blood, garnished with spinach. I hate spinach!! Grilled and diced, cooked without mercy. I mean, my brain was diced and cooked already with the music, and the dumb-waiter showed no mercy as he shoved the dish into my face. Derek munched and grunted like a pig having multiple orgasms. Goose was licking his fingers. I wanted to call an ambulance.

The pub was like a lap-dancing joint anywhere else in the world, replete with cheap beer which tasted like recycled horse piss. The 'Chef's delight' arrives. Hooray. Chewing on the dead thing is like chewing a raincoat. No, it is like chewing a wet blanket and it tastes worse than doggy-poo. I've tasted doggy-poo here before, so I know. The dumb-waiter tells me that it's good for health as it has very high fiber content. Sigh! Another one of those rotten second best things in life which don't come for free. The beer tastes like Manikin's piss. I've tasted that too. All this is now being served by Helga over here, who looks like a cross between Arnold Schwarzenegger and Grace Jones (not there's much of a difference, truly speaking). It tastes awful and rotten. Awfully rotten is more like it. No napkins on the table, best is to put my hands in my pocket, whistle and try to look cool. That's how I've learnt to whistle so well, I guess.

As the beer started flowing, we were joined by Galileo as well. Goose ordered something that looks like the love child of Julius Caesar and Pamela Anderson. Goose has a great sense of humor; I hope it just doesn't show up in the food he just ordered. That reminds me of his culinary skills, last time when I'd had swallowed a bowlful of his home-cooked special butter chicken, I had felt that a gas cylinder had exploded inside my stomach and my brains had burst out of the skull after the eyes had popped out of their sockets. You know that feeling? Well, it is that feeling that I lived through to write this book every time I think of it. People like Goose and Derek should not only be banned from cooking, in fact such people shouldn't even be allowed to boil water. But in places like this pub where this chapter is being written now, it's not the cooking that's painful, but the sheer effort in how they describe the food in a way that you actually end up ordering it? Now, that is ugly.

As the music played, we didn't want to talk about planning for our road-trip right now. We needed some time off from it all and just wanted to have a good time. So the four psychotics, namely – Derek, Galileo, Goose and Chief, started dissecting relationships, classifying types of men and women and this got really interesting. This is the kind of guy-talk any girl would give an arm and a leg and a what-have-you for. No, I am not talking about getting Leh'd right now, dear reader. A few hours down, out came the classifications, like different genres of music. Not that I am a psycho-analyst or well read in such matters, but this is man-talk and works in the world I have been brought up in.

Types of Girls/Women: (For Guys only)

- **Helga:** She is the ultimate bitch, probably has a false tooth, looks gross, drinks wine and has zero sophistication. She will do anything to be the center of attraction, pile-drive her way through and be any man's ultimate nightmare. She will love her own self endlessly, have a multiple-personality disorder and will stop at nothing to see you in pain. She will be particularly harsh on girls half her age. She will put obstacles in your way in every way possible. Stay away from Helga, for she has grand delusions about herself. As for us, we had locked up 'Helga' inside the small GPS, who is a classic example of the perfect bitch who will do anything to get you lost. Avoid at all costs or lock her up in a cellar. She will be your dark cloud behind every silver lining for she cannot bear to see you happy. She belongs to everyone and yet, she can belong to no one in particular. She is the perfect pain in the ass and a royal screw up. If you ever get a chance, kick her butt. Real hard.
- **Sabrina:** She is the good witch. She will always be mean to you, love you like crazy and will never know how to tell

you that she loves you. She likes lemonade, is elegant and a dream come true. She will always piss you off, but with her heart of gold, she will secretly inspire you. She will be there when you need her....to kick your behind and cast the right spells. Strangely enough, she will be gorgeous in every way, mystical and you just need to be there when she needs you, which will be – all the time. Stick around, for she will make your life worth the while. If you find her, grab her and never let her go. She can be everything you want and she will be fun to be with. She'll never leave you and will always be your sunshine girl. Don't try to argue with her, just listen to her. She will have her moments of weakness, and you need to be there and make her smile. She's worth every bit of it. Life will always be a bed of roses for you with her, no matter what, for she will always wish you well. Truly, madly, deeply. And yes, she will be breathtakingly beautiful. After all, she is a living doll. You will fall in love with her each time you meet her. You are a lucky man if you find her.

- **Slob:** She will pretend to be a Tom-boy, but is not one. She will be a loud-mouth, extremely embarrassing, say everything to sound and look cool and 'one of the guys'. She is a sloth. Extremely unclean, she'll wear the same underpants for days on end and her hair will stink. If she does try to look like a girl, she will wear equally loud and garish clothes. Not the type of girl who will stick around for long as deep inside, all she needs is a companion who will let her wake up at noon on a weekend. Her kitchen sink will always be full. Unclean, unhygienic and a must avoid, unless you have some other friends to hang out with her. She is just perfect to help you get inside a discotheque when they won't let in stags. Interesting to talk to, but that's about it. When it comes down to the real thing, you'd be surprised how conservative she can be. Check out her feet, you'll always note that she needs a pedicure. You can also classify her as a 'Non-male'. A good thing about her? She will always have some extra cash for you when you need it. The bad part is that she would like you to spend it on her, or with her. Slobs go away on their own as soon as they find a sucker, you don't need to worry about them.

- **Glue:** One kiss or a night with her and she will be like a leech on you. What you might have found cute and sweet once upon a time, will start bugging you no end. She will eat into your privacy, want to be your shadow, question your every move and over time, she will be the perfect pain-in-the-ass. Once you get married to her and create a diversion for her by having kids, you can be pretty much sure that you'll be on your own. These are the boring types who will create false images of your personality in their heads within hours and shatter them with ease. They will always be insecure and super-glue in human form. In a few months after knowing her, you will try your best to run away from her and it will not be easy. She will be immature, a giggly school-girl for life, will have a tendency to put on weight by over-eating as that's the way she fights depression. You will always have to buy her flowers, remember things about her, do things to please her till you lose your personality and she loses interest in you. It is best to avoid such types unless you are really desperate. You will keep trying your best to fall in love with her; try to convince yourself that she is the one for you all the time. After a while, she will be the most boring person to be with. She's a nice girl, just boring. You will need to decide what to do with her and you will probably die before making that decision.

- **Snob:** She will have zero credentials all her life. She will know everybody who is a 'somebody', but nobody will really know her. She will have loads of cash and all that jazz, and she will be the perfect someone to be seen around with. She is not the person to hang out with, of course, for she will be boring. She will run low in intelligence, emotions, sex drive and that entire aura around her will be fake. She might sound intelligent to you, that is if you are really dumb. These are the types who will pretend to hate Bollywood, but secretly nurture the desire to be a part of it. She will have an accent that will probably be understood only by her lap-dog. She would not have spent more than three months of her life abroad, but she will continue to yap about it as if she was born there. She may have been to different places, but would have probably spent time at a sister's place and seen only the neighborhood. Don't go by her Facebook profile for she will have all sorts of connections and yet, she will be unknown to them. She will have pictures carelessly displayed that would show her hanging out with celebrities. She is a big 'ZERO' in life. A loser to the core who will end up in boring kitty parties or work for some NGO later on in life. Dump her. Yawn!
- **Heat Seeker:** In a nutshell, a two-bit-half-a-penny over-friendly neighborhood flirt. If she is your girlfriend, I want to know you and will probably hang out with you till you leave me alone with her. You probably are popular,

that's why she is on your list. She is probably seeing a few people at the same time, will not be good looking at all. She is your friendly-neighborhood gold-digger. She'll be around till she finds someone more popular or richer than you. You might be the perfect ugly-duckling and yet she will be with you all the while. Her love will always be plural and universal. If you have your buddies very proud of her, you can bet a copy of this book that she is sleeping around with your friends. She will be found in a small town with extra-large dreams to be realized on the fast-track minus the ability to work hard. Also, her only talent will be to hang on to you. She will always wear garish make-up, carry a fake leather purse and her talk will be so boring that you would rather spend time Facebooking and or try every trick in the book to avoid her. She will always be jobless and bitch about everyone else, for everybody's business is her business. She has no personality or a life of her own. Dump her.

- **Goldie:** In a nutshell, she is the most confused person you will ever get to meet. She is gorgeous, cute, fun and everything you wish for in a partner. She will be forever confused. You will spend a lifetime trying to make her realize her potential and be happy but in time you will burn yourself up. She is lazy and she is forever confused. The Goldie Hawn of today, the best way to deal with her is let her figure things out for herself as you are just wasting your words. She has the ability to make you care for her, not necessarily fall in love with her, for you can never fall in love with her. In time, your relationship will be one of pure convenience. There will be days when you will think she has come around but give it another day, she will waste herself yet again. Stick around but let it be at your will and wish. If she wants she will come to you; if she doesn't want it, she won't, no matter how hard you try. If you are in love with her, then heaven help you. She is a very shallow person, only she will refuse to admit it, Over time, she will become boring, repetitive and predictable. She will be good for a few nights and that's all. She may appear mysterious to you, but the fact is – she has no idea why she was born on this earth. These types just get married to rich people, make babies and wither away. And they stay confused.

- **Rag Doll**: She is the frustrated woman, your friend's girlfriend or just about anyone who doesn't get enough.... attention. Worried about her time running out age-wise, she is your rag doll. Most likely, she is saddled with the wrong guy, a loony or a gay boyfriend/husband or reached a point where nothing but sex matters. She will be loaded, will have all the time in the world, will come anywhere with you and you can do what you please with her. If you are seeing someone of this variety, you are probably out of shape, frustrated or both. If you do not know that you are going after a rag doll, you will find out soon enough. She is not after your money, she is longing for companionship. Don't mistake it for love or fall in love. Just go by your convenience, no extra time to be invested here. And yes, she doesn't drink too much. It's a joy ride, enjoy it.

- **Lump**: You can be rest assured that you have no choice but to marry her or stay married to her. If you are going around with her, then you probably have nothing better to do. She is just that extra pound of flesh God put on this planet for losers like you. You might as well talk to a sack of potatoes. With zero drive and low self-esteem, this kind would never go for a workout at the local gym. If you think she is ambitious, then she is probably that lump of flesh that will have a different ambition every day. She will talk dirty, try to sound cool, but when it comes to the real thing, she will back out. Devoid of any purpose, she will stick on to a job and will become a mediocre worker in any organization. She is plain mediocre, that is all. If you are mediocre as well, go for it.

- **Moron**: For there can be only one love and she is the perfect soul mate, you will know her when you meet her. Keep her for happy and cherish her for a lifetime. She is the perfect one for you.

Types of Boys/Men: (For Girls only)

- **Dick:** The loser variety, he will whine like a lost puppy all the time, try to ride the sympathy wave. What he needs is motherly love. He will go on and on about his past break-ups (if anyone ever dared to fall in love with him) or tell you how he got dumped, how his friends and colleagues pick on him. He would join a Facebook page like "I like to walk in the rain coz nobody will see my tears" and shit like that. He will have a perpetually constipated look on his face, and he will go on and on about how many difficulties he has faced in his life. He will send you mushy messages and give you audio tapes of Boyzone, Akon, Backstreet Boys till one fine day you will get so tired of it all and smack him with your handbag. Piece of advice? Get a real sturdy handbag, punch him on his nose and kick him out of your life today. He is a frustrated loser who can never grow up to be a man. Don't expect him to take care of you. You want a doormat? Get it cheap from the local convenience store and save the best days of your life for someone else. Dick!

- **Nitwit:** Devoid of grey matter, the brain is a vestigial organ for the nitwit. He will be the butt of all jokes when you hang out with your friends. He will have trouble making eye contact with people and will be constantly agreeing with whatever others have to say or plan. He has no control over his life and he will make your image in the social circle come down by three notches. You might just be using him for convenience, do not read that for love. He will drive you around, do your chores for you, and will end up getting sloshed in an all-guy party. He is the kind of person others love to borrow money from. He was born to be a social worker and would do anything to look cool. His pretensions will make him look stupid and there will be a lot of pent-up aggression in him. If you want to find out if you are in love with a nitwit, try a date out with someone else and see what happens after that. Dump him now.

- **Dude:** The regular Mr. Popular. There is something about him if he is popular today. The same fire in him will make him a 'somebody' tomorrow, as he will work towards making himself better. These kinds usually turn out to have very successful careers and make excellent partners. Life will be fun with them as he will treat you with respect. His friends will respect you as well. He is also a charmer, an aristocrat and will always like to live life to the fullest. He will always have a happy bunch of people for friends and a few hanger-ons who will be his piss-boys. If you are in love with him, don't let him go. For his is the real deal.

- **Ass:** He is vain, he is a dandy and he is plain stupid. He will lose out in the long run. His personality is defined by the clothes he wears, the cars he drives and everything that has a funny-sounding French name for a brand will be on him. Since he has no personality of his own, he tries to adopt a personality by hiding under a multitude of brands. He is an ass with a fat wallet. Use him and dump for someone else. Such people are OK to hang around for a lifetime as long as you can keep him wrapped around your finger. A very useful animal to have near you always. Keep him and go for someone else at the same time. Make him your brother or something innocuous. Call him anything, just call him. He will be cool with that.

- **Bro:** The big daddy. Usually, a person who is aged. He would have seen the world, have a lot of maturity and can always be counted on. He is the missing link between two generations. He is a lot of fun, will ensure that you have a good time and stay safe as well. His care is genuine, he is someone you can count on to be there when you need help the most. He is sensible and level headed. If you are in love with such a person, do not ever let go. He will never forget to bring you flowers, remember the important dates and will be consistent in his approach to life. Not the frivolous kind, his love runs deep. His sense of humor will amaze you and he will be a good father to your kids. Piece of advice? Just don't call him 'Bro'.

- **Jock:** Ha! Ha! Ha! Kick, him, slap him, spit on his face, take his wallet and use him to take care of you while you are having fun with someone else. Let him have his share of fun, building biceps and walking funny. Enjoy at his expense forever. Hee! Hee! Hee!

- **Shit-brick:** Bet on a safe future here. Let him study or work or whatever he is doing, but keep him always hanging on. He cannot go anywhere else. Just give him a peck on a cheek once a week and you have a lap dog for a lifetime. Not only will he bring in financial security, he will bring in love and values. With a dope like him in your life, you are in safe hands (read boring). If you are the kind of a person who loves to laugh while reading a piece of Java code or about how he managed to create a utility tool to clean up your registry, he is the perfect mate for your fun evening. This breed is usually vegetarian in India, have no physique or a desire to look good or healthy. If you like vegetables, a sedate life, mediocre existence and lead a life that looks like a flow-chart with everything planned and laid out, he is the guy for you. He is awkward, a poor talker, laughs funny and everything uncool. You can pick a geek like him anytime in your life and continue to lead your life for such people usually don't have a love life.....er.....life. Period.

- **Nerd/Geek/Dork/Dweeb:** The awkward momma's boy who can only talk about good grades in school or college and end up in a job three rungs lower than his actual potential. The amount of pornography they watch will shock you out of your senses. These are highly irritable creatures and usually turn out to be psychos or gays. These are the losers in the world who end up with more than fathomable anger and let it all out someday. If you are in love with a nerd, be prepared for the worst as someday, he might just walk into the neighborhood high-school with an Uzi machine gun and spray bullets and kill a few people. Avoid at all costs. These are creeps of the highest order. You will know a nerd with just one touch, woman.

- **Cheapos:** This is the typical type found in India; they usually come from highly conservative families. The scent of a woman is enough to get a rise out of them. They will always stare at your breasts, avoid eye-contact, whistle and make lewd remarks at every passing girl. If you are in love with a cheapo, well, you must be one yourself. The less said the better. You know it anyways.
- **Moron:** There can be only one love and he is the perfect soul mate, you will know him when you meet him. Keep him happy and cherish him for a lifetime. He is the perfect one for you.

How to win a guy in 69 seconds

- *Look your best*
- *Communicate unspoken words through body language*
- *Have the right attitude*
- *Develop a sense of humor*
- *Be yourself*

Having done with the gender-wise classifications, it was time for us to discuss human psychology. Nervousness was a weakness Derek had once upon a time and he overcame that. For when you are nervous, tiny things take on gargantuan proportions. Small errors have gigantic repercussions when you follow the trajectory of your mistake. We all make mistakes, ranging from a small error of judgment to Himalayan blunders. Since we're close to the Himalayas, we were making really big blunders. Bigger ones than Pamela Anderson's assets and increasing our liabilities while diminishing our chances of success. That's when your over-friendly, all-knowing Indian, who is the free combo-meal of advise as an engineer, doctor, lawyer, match-maker, author and what-have-you comes in. And you make well-informed mistakes. It's meant for convenience alright, but not mine. It is for the staff in this pub. When you see someone reading out the instructions manual for a DVD player aloud, you know you need to have a Plan B for the evening.

How to win a girl in 69 seconds

- *Be natural*
- *Be passionate*
- *Be rich and successful on your own merit*
- *Have a sense of humor*
- *Be a free bird*

Marvellous discovery, this education thing and now Derek felt all educated and wanted to try out our discussions on a complete stranger who was sitting at the next table, waiting for someone to arrive. He sat across the table, looked her straight in the eye and maybe he cracked a joke. We couldn't hear. She didn't like the joke. Derek still has the scars to prove it. It has always been tough for Derek to pull out one foot from his mouth, just to put the other one in and it was tiring.

There was a pause. Her expression was er ... expressionless. A Zen-like silence in a girl's reaction can silence the toughest of the loud guns. It is blank and it is deafening. Her eyes blazed like hell. When faced with a horrible situation in life, like getting caught by a traffic cop, hauled up by a teacher, going through a breakup, having to sit through a boring lecture, forget everything you have learnt till then; just turn around and run like the wind. Derek should have remembered that. Her eyes were transfixed on Derek and I swear we could see some sort of death rays coming out of those peepers of hers. In comic books, those deadly rays become a super Marvel character. In reality, they can make your head come out of your hair.

After having been beaten black and blue, we led a completely shattered Derek to his ugly car. Derek pleaded innocence as he explained the matter to us. He had asked the girl if she believed in free sex. Having got an answer in the negative, he had asked her how much she charged for sex. A seemingly disturbed Derek ploughed his car ahead. The ugly car had left a vapor-trail of well, an ugly car behind. The evening was over for us as Galileo, Goose and I couldn't stop smiling for Derek always gave us those precious and cheap little jokes of life that create memories. These memories make life worth living and 'life' isn't a four-letter word. Galileo picked up the tab, for none of us could afford to foot the bill. No mere mortal could withstand the waiter's strange powers to look away and pretend as if it's not happening. Those awful powers of the pub owner always bloated up the tab, for he had the power to ring up everything twice and increase the price beyond inflation's reach.

Our discussions have always bordered between the ridiculous and sublime. Had this been given the garb of a political conference, we would have probably passed a joint resolution. But since we were so tanked on beer, all we could pass a lot of urine. As countless bottles of our famous Indian beer ended in a piddle that felt like a real orgasm, vivid images of Chennai´s wild tsunami came to my mind. The evening at the pub had been intense for we had discussed everything from guitars, Massages (Tarzan in Kerala and Thai), sexy librarian chicks around the world, a robot having an orgasm and filling out a bottle of engine oil, Somalia pirates, fame and riches and careers. The best part was that it was not over yet. We were now on our way to Derek's house where we would carry on with the binge. This was supposed to be one of those last evenings in Bangalore before we hit the road.

"Darn! Where are the keys? No, Goose, not Solomon's keys. Well, similar, as I can never seem to find them. Every time, it is the same old story – I misplace Motormouth's keys and we all hunt around, taking turns to look at the same place. I guess, this is what they call a 'Turnkey project'...." I decided at this very moment that from now on, I would wear a spare set of keys to Motormouth around my neck all the time as we go on our road-trip.

Having reached Derek's house, we saw this extremely pathetic looking girl open the door for us. She looked as sexy as Shahrukh Khan in a bikini, as comfortable as a stock-broker in a stock-market in downward spiral to let us in. Goose told me that she was Derek's sister. She didn't mind that we were smoking in her house. Actually, she couldn't care less if we went up in flames. Surely, his mother must have used a photocopier to produce such rare gems that she called her children. My heart bleeds for the poor woman. How touching!. The earth spun faster in the past few hours and I was feeling dizzy. If His Highness makes us wait for another five minutes, I'll break open his dump yard door, yank the bastard out with evil spells and cure him forever and leave him constipated for life. And you, dear sister, get off that gluteus maximus of yours and make yourself useful by banging on that bathroom door of his, honey! A crazy, dysfunctional family where the mother looks like a cross between a refrigerator and a coffee grinder, no wonder Derek looks so demented. He looks like an escapee from that Super Mario brother's game. Maybe, that was the effect the pub had had on him and he'd left early.

Goose told me that he needed more time, as though he understood Derek or his bio-clock. Huh! Out walks this girl from Derek's room when the whole world thinks that he was taking a dump. Goose was smiling gleefully as he looked at Raggedy Ann sneaking out of the house before Derek's mom could see. She must have forgotten her broomstick at home today and maybe that's why she was in such a hurry. Maybe, she was the devil. She was wearing a white skirt. It must have been Prada....

Goose told me that I was turning deaf listening to all the Goth and Heavy metal stuff. Maybe he was right for he told me that Derek was making more noises in his room than the chick and the creaking bed put together. Maybe, Goose had sharp ears. When one faculty goes down, the other senses pick up, I told him. He was losing his sense of taste.

Once Derek was out, we kicked him into his kitchen to rustle up some grub for us. We had decided not to sleep and Derek had to now feed us and appease the hungry beast within. We were in his room as Goose started playing those pathetic Trance CDs of his once again. As Derek's cooking made my stomach turn, Goose's taste in music made me chew my pen. The pen may be mightier than a sword. But my teeth had just chewed my pen's pretty blue ass straight down to the refill. We could smell the stench of Derek's cooking emanating from the kitchen. Goose wondered if Derek was cooking his mother's apron by mistake. Derek thought it tasted awesome. Anyone who thinks like Derek not only deserves to die of sheer stupidity, but may the pain be multiplied by severe acidity.

Change of plans happened as soon as we saw Derek bring out his masterpiece from the kitchen. We realized that we needed to get some sleep before we hit the road day after tomorrow, straight down to Kolhapur in Maharashtra. Tomorrow was a send-off party planned for us at another pub and we had much to do. We could not afford to take any risks with Derek's cooking. We could not afford to fall sick. It was 24 hours to flag off. In the forthcoming sequel 'Horn OK Please – The Scrotum Scrolls', I will introduce you to my friendly neighborhood Astrologer. His name is Bhatinda Bedpan. He is good with Sun Signs and Love Signs, but he is horrible when it comes to reading road-signs. Before that, dear reader, allow me to provide a list of some good books that will help you become as intelligent as us. Derek has painfully compiled a list of his personal favorites that make him a smash hit with the girls. Read on.

HOPping to Conclusions

▸ *The stupid, old bandicoot who sold his Lexus*
▸ *Seven irritating habits of highly obnoxious people*
▸ *The mouse who ate my cheese*
▸ *Chicken shit for the soul*
▸ *The Sixty Nine laws of Power*
▸ *The 24 laws of Abduction*

▶ *Victoria's Secret*
▶ *Wee, the Nation*
▶ *Men are from Mars, women are from someplace else*
▶ *Linda Armstrong's Road-signs*

10 Flag-Off, We're on a Roll, Baby!

Of open fields and the swinging scene,
Of hand-sanitizers and an open latrine;
About the ways our nights were spent,
Inside Motormouth or inside a tent;
Of cloudburst and pouring rains,
Of mountainous terrains and open drains
From hope to despair, we bump ahead for a dream,
For ruggedness maketh a man, as stupid as it may seem
Smiling in the face of adversity can make you say 'Cheese'
Drive on, for that's when you go 'Horn OK Please'…

Flag-off

We had to leave Bangalore at five am sharp, if we were to beat the morning traffic and get out of the city. The Goose was late. If he doesn't show up in another five minutes, he'll be the late Goose now. Derek was sure that he would not be able to wake up after our last night's binge, so he had slept inside Motormouth. I was sleepy too, I needed coffee but hell, I'm the driver today and I shall drive these clowns crazy. It was a cool morning and the breeze was making me drowsy and I felt the chill. Yawn and the world yawns with you. Sneeze and you sneeze alone. Ah! There was Goose! Wait, why is he walking around with an over-stretched condom over his head? Is it that cold? And is that a T-Shirt? He looks like road-kill, with skid-marks all over. It was humiliating to head out of Bangalore with a drunk in the back-seat and a loony in the front beside me. Thank heavens, it was pitch-dark and I was saved the embarrassment. It's amazing that even after all the humiliation, I still have any shame left in me.

I wanted to avoid the trucker traffic on the highway near Bangalore as most of the truck drivers in India may have road-sense, but they lack civic and common sense. Having done Kanyakumari, now the basic plan was simple. We party hard on the plains and flat lands, we take it slow up in the mountains. Our first halt was to be Kolhapur, at the border of Karnataka and Maharashtra and it was about 600 Kilometers from Bangalore. We would stop at Kolhapur, Pune, Mumbai, Diu, Delhi, Udaipur, Jaipur, then straight to Manali.

Five hours on the road with no piss-stops, we were playing 'Bursting-the-bladder'. If I didn't stop Motormouth, Goose and Derek threatened me with dire consequences. A few more kilometers and we would have all floated out of Motormouth together. Behind the wheel on the first day, I felt like King-Kong on the Empire State Building. Only the pretty chick was missing. That missing King-Kong chick reminds me of one of Goose's girlfriends. We had met her at one of our orgies in another city. She had looked like an overgrown gold-fish in that yellow and orange dress. She had a great figure but she had a pout like a gold-fish. Like someone stuffed her mouth with five lollipops at the same time and kept it like that for a few hours, blow-dried and now the damage is permanent. I don't remember her name, not that I cared two hoots about it then, but she had one of those funny names which usually gets called out when you are at a police station and are waiting for your turn to pay the fine and get out. Such names get called out for petty crimes, trafficking or indecent exposure. No, she was not pretty. Forget beauty, there was nothing even remotely shaggable about her. Over the years, she would become an ever-expanding woman of girth as it was evident that she was putting that mouth of hers to proper use. With free food at least, for the rest, please talk to Goose. She thought that I am awkward, maybe she already knew of my awkward ways, so I decided not to argue. Not that I am advocating violence in anyway, but some people have this remarkable talent of bringing out the beast in you. She was one of those. I remembered her now as I think of such people when I take a piddle.

Goose was checking out the Kanyakumari pictures and was editing them. Kanyakumari had been nice to us. Also known as the Land's End or Cape Comorin, there is a big statue and a rock. We drove from Bangalore covering a distance of almost 700 kms at breakneck speed, loved that. The best part of course, I managed to set a record of sorts of updating my Facebook status at 169 Kmph (Just kidding – In case you are traffic cop!)

Driving through flatlands to reach the peaks and valleys... to get Leh'd?

I'd rather smoke gunpowder and blow my mind, instead of doing dope. Someone go and tell them that some has got nuclear warheads in Iraq and they'll go and drop a pile of uranium up a civilian's ass. If you want to know more about

Kanyakumari, then you might want to pick up a history book or something, dear reader. Please do not expect any useful information in this book. All I can tell you is that at Land's End, there is a lot of water and one can see the sea as far as the eye can see, well, at least that's what I could see. It is a place where we can see the coming together of three seas namely, the Bay of Bengal, the Arabian Sea and the Indian Ocean. One can actually see the three colors of the waters during low tide. It was here when Derek realized that water colors do not always come in boxes. This was our country and our forefathers had painstakingly worked hard to create and preserve our cultural heritage and created these monuments to remind us of who we are. Derek was confused and got offended. He didn't like the idea of me telling him that he had forefathers. He grabbed my collar, glared at me menacingly and said, "My mother is not a whore. I have only one Daddy. Now, take it back." I apologized to him and said, "I'm sorry that your mother is a whore". Derek was appeased and quietly accepted the apology. Goose had to be caught hold of, before he could fall off the edge of the cliff, laughing.

Kolhapur/Pune/Mumbai/Diu/Gandhinagar/Chittorgarh/ Jaipur/ Udaipur/ Delhi/ Chandigarh

Earlier the plan was to reach Pune directly if we could do 169 Kmph on an average, but because of the crappy weather, we decided to halt at Kolhapur. Surprisingly, it turned out that we had some friends who turned up and ordered some Kolhapuri dishes. To put it mildly, the food was damn spicy. Our levitation level at the commode the next morning was to take on a new high. Thank God for high roofs. Once the hotel chaps got to know of our credentials (and I wonder what those are, the big burly guy of a manager walked into our room and opened a bottle of Scotch. He must have been the direct descendent of a Nazi head torturer at Dachau and we were the inmates. God! What a Dick! Too frightened to say no to him, we decided to play along and helped him polish off the bottle. The big man left after yapping away to glory. The rest of him took about five minutes to leave the room, stench and all. None of us had a clue about what he spoke about. Partying and freeloading across Pune and Mumbai, we reached Jaipur. Derek took us to some extremely weird place where there were men in skirts dancing all around to voodoo music. We must now live the eternal shame of being part of a ritual which seemed like advanced devil worship where you are supposed to slaughter a goat at the altar and offer it to the cook. For dinner comprised of two great balls of fire.

Derek is in a state of denial as he refuses to acknowledge that his plans were all wrong. He denies that we are in the wrong State. This is Uttar Pradesh, not Uttaranchal (if that is a state today). Dude, only the first alphabets of these two names are common, nothing else matches.

I get all confused with so many places we visited, anyways, I remember our flunkey in Udaipur called 'Hukum Singh' who looked like a cross between Igor and the Frankenstein monster. Er....he did look like Derek's twin alright and that's fine as that fits my personality very well, thank you very much. Upon checking in, Igor went all out and scrubbed Motormouth and made her look brand new. Barely fifteen minutes after Igor had washed the beast, Goose and I realized that Derek had wandered off as gracelessly as he had walked into the hotel, scooted off with Motormouth out for some serious off-roading and returns with a filthier version of what once looked like Motormouth. Igor was seething in anger and we had to hold him back before he could do serious damage to our deranged friend. Igor was capable of causing serious trouble as the hotel anyways looked like a mental asylum where I for one would not want to recognize myself in here. The lady at the reception was horrified by us as we walked in. Not by our clothes, but by our behavior. Mercifully, (for her) we were to leave Udaipur the next day- if we could stay alive through the night.

Back in the room, as I watched Goose and Derek do the tango, I realized how useful wearing spectacles can be. I could just stare at them and assume certain things about these two embarrassments I was seen hanging out with. You can never see those features sharply. It's much like staying drunk or being doped out. The benefits multiply when I need to meet someone downright ugly, something I need to do many times in my line of work. I take my spectacles off, they always look prettier, and after that, bliss.

Like any other major decision in life, our decisions were made on the spot. It's only those trivial things like choosing a career, getting through college and stuff like that in life that take up all the time. The fort in Chittorgarh and Diu were two such stops where the locals were treated to real loud heavy rock. We were slowly turning into Indian red-necks in a boom car pimping up the stereo while entering silent zones. Hell, it's a free country and we are alright!

Despite having successfully trapped 'Helga' inside the GPS, she continued to bark out directions for us to follow. Some were right, some were downright wrong. It was fun cursing the evil one all the way and she had no choice but to listen to us, for Goose had nailed her to the windshield and she couldn't move. 'Map my India' maps on GPS are brilliant. As we continued to pile-drive across the country, we were living on free food, free accommodation and free orgies thrown by HOPpers (http://facebook.com/hopfans). They were extremely kind to us as they wanted us to save all the money and give it to charity. We spent it on other useful things instead. Basic essentials like Thai massages were the need of the hour. Derek needed more Red Bull than Goose and I put together. If he had it his way, he would take it as a continuously running intravenous fluid via a drip. Goose suggested jumper cables to be used on Derek while he was sleeping. At the rate we were going, they could have generated electricity out of us.

Derek was snoozing in the backseat of Motormouth. As the trip progressed, the backseat had been now turned into a bed for Derek and was being used and abused for all his nefarious activities. The creature was snoring now. More electricity, Goose, for Frankenstein needs it.

Since we reached late and had to leave early, we managed to visit a few places where they have these sculptures and paintings. Some of the sculptures were good and some pieces of art were downright horrible. I mean, did these people ever see a real tiger? I mean, just look at that. Does that look like a tiger or a schizophrenic pussy cat? Or that camel, no wonder the camel looks so sad in Rajasthan. It would put Darwin to shame and prove him wrong, for God's sakes. Even kids in nursery schools do better these days. No wonder these artisans had their hands chopped off or their eyes pierced and left to wander. I suspect that Royalty was not responsible for the state of such artisans. Maybe the tigers saw their own sculptures and paintings and got even with the artisan community.

Jaipur was our next pit stop before we headed towards Delhi and proceeded to Manali. On the way, one gets to see these tiny farms which barely grow enough grain to keep birds alive. No wonder some farmers looks starved, they ought to buy bigger pieces of land. Maybe, they should stop growing vegetables in Farmville on Facebook, and do more stuff in the real world.

Apple trees with scrambled brains lead one to eternal truth

As I sit under an apple tree somewhere on a mountain in Himachal Pradesh, beside a gushing river, once again, I try my best to think. Unfortunately, every time I've tried to think, I get a headache. So I decide to chuck any thoughts that might try their best to enter my pea-sized brain. I realize that the skull is a cage that has been deftly designed by God's messed up engineers manning the design department somewhere out there. After all, which engineer in his/her right mind would design the structure of a human body that has the sewage line passing right below the recreational area? I've been repeatedly told that I don't listen. Well, like hell, my ears hear and I listen. After all, my ears happen to serve a bit more purpose than just hold up my spectacles that cover my eyes like tentacles and that rhymes and so I could have been a poet as well. Don't think, for thinking is prohibited while you read my book, dear reader, and trespassers shall be executed or electrocuted or executed by electrocution. After all, my mom told me to build myself an electrifying personality. Or a magnetic personality. Mercifully, I did neither. Else, I would be stung to death in a working environment, as a human solenoid, with all those staplers and pins and pens being attracted into my eye. Sorry, Mom, but most of the women I have been able to date in my life have either been morons or cretins or downed a few drinks. Mercifully, I got married to the right girl and my life changed for the better. Any change would only have been for the better.

Here's a theory that I wish to share with you, wise one, for this is not something you would ever have been taught. Sample this – Popeye was a sailor, simply because he loved spinach and that's rich in iron. He would have made all the security gates at airports go ding-ding with his sheer presence. And one can now safely conclude, that post 9/11, any mid-eastern looking male, traveling single should never eat a spinach pizza before going through a security check at an airport as your chances for that special treatment will be higher post consumption. But if you are really hungry, and you must have something, eat chalk or lick those freshly distempered walls, for they are rich in calcium and that's good for your bones. Don't lick too much though, for you might get acidity. But, if you do suffer from acidity after eating chalk for lunch, drink soap water. Soap kills acids or some such thing, as I had learnt during my chemistry classes in high school. And Newton was thoroughly jobless, looking at falling apples or he was plain doped out and wanted to sound deep.

Maybe, apple trees have a strange effect on the human mind, as these random blurbs fill my head. I mean, why on earth would you look at falling apples? Shouldn't you be eating them? Aren't they supposed to keep the doctors away.... if aimed right? You see, dear reader, I share these pearls of wisdom with you simply because you decided to buy my book.

What was Archimedes doing inside the tub? Thinking? Was he out of his mind when he decided to jump out of the tub, run around stark naked and shout 'Eureka!'.....'Eureka!' If I tried that today, like run around naked in an apple orchard, screaming 'Horn OK Please!'... 'Horn OK Please!' Will anyone believe that I have been struck by thought? Oh! These apple trees have some strange and magical powers that take over your brain and turn it into jelly. Better yet, it's apple pies, for we love apple pies. So there.

Since I have the nasty habit of going all over while writing, as you might have noticed in the past few chapters, this one too shall be no exception. It happens every time I try to sound deep. I try, and then fall flat on my face and the deepest thought my mind has explored can be perfectly summed up in three alphabets that define eternal truth. It signifies all the knowledge that exists in the whole universe. It's called....*Duh!!*

Getting Leh'd

It was a very interesting learning experience in the past few days for us. While Goose had a tough time getting away from the party mode, Derek and I were going crazy trying to figure out how to get out of Manali. I was feeling like a sausage caught between two loonies, namely, Goose and Derek. To make matters worse, there was a sudden spurt of violence in the Kashmir Valley, and along with that, there had been an unprecedented deluge of floods in Leh. For the uninitiated, who are poor in biology, chemistry, geography and Moral Science, let me share with you some pearls of wisdom that I learnt during this week of preparation. Derek was all stars and had absolutely no clue about what was going on. Not that he did not care, but the peak of his caring ended with his porn collection.

The first thing was to have Motormouth all stocked up with supplies. While Goose and I went about stocking camping gear such as minus fifteen degree sleeping bags, tents, air mattresses, compass, knives and other such items typically used for camping, Derek did his bit by being thoughtful enough to get us all raincoats. Since we were planning to get Leh'd, visit the Nubra valley, he bought three hundred condoms. Derek was convinced that Leh was a place full of cool towns with hot chicks and the valley of flowers meant something entirely different to him. He had reached the peak of his intelligence. We had nothing to say.

The cutest thing about the preparation for climbing to an altitude of over 18,000 feet was some weird thing called mountain sickness. People call it AMS for short, which stands for 'A Cute Mountain Sickness'. We concluded that it must be something like PMS, which I guess, stands for 'Parasitic Male Sickness', something that women suffer from when they do not wish to have sex. Derek thoughtfully bought a bunch of sanitary pads for us all, in case we had runny or bleeding noses. His brilliance shone through it all and we knew we were safe with Derek taking care of the little details.

An exasperated doctor had loaded us up with some pills called Diamox, inhalers called Salmetrol, more tablets called Dexamethazone. After having spent an hour with us, I would say that she needed it much more than we ever did. Since it was not about distances anymore, but more about altitudes, the ugly fat lady inside our GPS system was locked up inside to steadily help us measure our steep climb. GPS, of course, served an entirely different purpose here for us, as we measured our climb. The ugly woman inside the small triangular plastic cage would keep whining about the altitude scaled and so we could use our pulse-oximeter. A pulse-oximeter is a small obscene-looking device which you insert your finger in to measure your heart rate and your oxygen levels. We were told that the oxygen-content in our body to the brain shouldn't dip below 90% and the heart-rate shouldn't cross 100. So, we concluded that if the oxygen levels were to dip in your body, it would be filled with carbon dioxide and we would all become heavier. If fact, Newton was all wrong about his theory of gravitational forces. It is actually the 10% carbon dioxide and other such gases in your body that keep you rooted to the ground in a world filled with oxygen. As carbon dioxide is heavier than air, the more of that you have in your body, higher are the chances of your being rooted to the ground. Had it been the other way round, we would all be floating in mid-air. The height and weight of a person is actually determined by the efficiency of the performance of all the organs put together. People turn obese when they breathe less, people turn thin when they breathe more. And so, as I tried to explain this to the doctor, she left behind teeth marks on my laptop. *Duh!!* As a preventive step towards remaining intact and safe, we agreed to carry Diamox to stay safe and intact from a very frustrated doctor.

I also have a theory about why your feet are on the ground and the head is up. Since oxygen is lighter than carbon dioxide, all the air that one breathes goes straight to the head. The human head, therefore, is shaped like a filled gas balloon. Since the head is always filled with air, it keeps us up there. And the respiratory system is like an internal-combustion engine that acts as the exhaust fan of the human body. The feet, on the other hand, have tiny pores which prevent the body from bloating into extraordinary proportions. Of course, there are other vents in the body which I shall refrain from discussing as it could gross you out. The hands provide the movement which keeps the center of gravity just right, so we all are able to sit and stand straight and erect. They also help in converting all that oxygen in the body into carbon-dioxide and there, dear reader, the human body is very similar to our sexy talking-vehicle called 'Motormouth'. And so, in order to maintain perfect harmony between man and the gentle ecological balance, we decided to pick up a pulse-oximeter. We didn't want to float in mid-air as that would be so uncool.

The mouth is similar to the fuel-tank nozzle, the feet are the tires, the eyes are the windshield, the heart is the steering wheel, the respiratory organs are the cylinders, the stomach is the engine, so on and so forth. In order to keep the perfect eco-balance, both man and machine have to guzzle in fuel or food and spit out dirty air. In order to be able to spit out dirty air efficiently, one needs to have the lungs functioning just right in high altitudes. So one needs a Salmetrol inhaler. Just like maintaining regular air-pressure in all the tires, we needed to take two puffs of the inhaler to maintain the air-pressure in our lungs. This was also to keep shed any excess fluids that may accumulate in the body. The pressure puff would make the lungs expand, which in turn would exert pressure on all the organs between your lungs and kidneys, which in turn would press the kidneys and make you pee. The human body, as they say, is a force multiplier. We were smart people and we were feeling mighty pleased with ourselves since we had it all figured out. Salmetrol puffs were in. The doctor excused herself for a bio-break. Again. Maybe, she was on Salmetrol herself.

The fine art of pathetic planning

Well equipped with medical supplies now, we decided to stock ourselves up with dry fruits, nuts, oats and candy bars. We decided to use a very scientific approach to select the perfect trader from where to pick up the stuff. Like a homing device, Derek managed to pick out the shop which had the prettiest woman of the mountains. We couldn't be more scientific than this. She had almond eyes, clear, and flawless skin. Also, she had a mouth like the nozzle of a vacuum cleaner. With a mouth like that, with those lips of hers, we were sure that she would be able to do far more than just sweet-talk us into buying all the horse-food. She looked like a rubber cow in that raincoat, yet she was pretty. The only thing I didn't think of was committing suicide, which means that I felt miserable and not pathetic. I see them and freeze in horror as she looks at him lovingly....er....make that 'sympathetically'. I wonder what she saw in that face. I see a Yeti in Derek now.

The last thing to be picked up were those cans which we had to snatch away from someone called Jerry, so we could have some extra diesel once we crossed Tandi, which is supposed to have the last fuel-pump before the vast expanse of the lunar landscape of Ladakh. Goose was excited as he was finally getting to see Jerry as he had never met a talking mouse before in real life. Jerry was an old lady who looked like a rat, with whiskers, selling cheap plastic cans of 20 litres each. She must have been 200 years old. Goose was disappointed as Derek was rolling on the floor, laughing. I wished that the earth would just swallow me right then and there.

We called in a mechanic to do a final check of Motormouth to see if all was OK. We knew everything was OK and he knew that too. But he hung around that little bit longer to see if we would cross his palm with silver. High hopes! Even beggars avoid us these days, dude. If he thought that his lucky charm is going to make him hang around any longer with us, he was wrong. We would have changed him anyways and all that lucky-charm-crap would be shining through six-feet under. It was a bit like my first love. Or my first jerk-off. Ecstatic, Oh yes! That's the word. The engine was so complicated, had we left it in Derek's room, he would have burnt it as a witch. Right-thinking Indians have quietly written him off as an embarrassment to our rich history. Like a blemish or a pimple on a pretty girl's cheek.

We were done with our preparation and now all we needed was a driver from Manali, who knew these 'Jack-and-Jill' hills and valleys well enough to navigate and plough through. One of the several problems that we faced during our initial off-roading was our complete ignorance of what these mountain people called 'roads'. We had trouble understanding what would be called a road and which patch would be called the lack of it. The simple rule by which I learnt to identify a road in the mountains is when you have more than two people near an open patch trying to peddle cheap stuff like fake saffron or hot 'chai', it signifies a motorable road where two vehicles coming from opposite directions can somehow cross each other. If one sees a cow crossing a muddy patch, the patch would be good for one single vehicle to pass through. And if one sees only cow dung through a patch, it means that you have to build your own road.

Morons at cross-roads – cloudburst at Leh, curfew in Srinagar

That cannot be a music composition; it is highly decomposed and simply horrible. Trance, they call it. I am in a state of Trance too, right now, as my eyes roll up as if I'm humping an imaginary Angelina Jolie, down in a 'Mosh Pitt'. I quietly threw out one of Goose's CDs. I plan to get rid of his entire collection this way.

Since Leh had now been completely devastated by floods, there was an entire patch of motorable road missing between Pang and Leh. Firstly, we had a huge problem in pronouncing the names of the palaces in and around the area; it was worse trying to remember them. I mean the place 'Leh', it sounds like a baby sneeze, doesn't it? I mean, how wrong is Derek in being completely off when he goes around gleefully shopping for condoms before entering Nubra Valley? Don't be shocked, dear reader, for the names of some places may sound like a sneeze, a yawn or a fart, but these are really pretty places which bring out the beauty of Mother Nature in full splendor. It was because of these minute details, we needed a flunkey or a driver, or a combination of both. We needed someone who could not just pronounce these names, but remember them as well for they are not easy to remember. Still, many names were easier to pronounce than most places in Europe.

The taxi association in Manali called the approach to Leh 'suicidal' and we had to be morons to even attempt the journey and the Indian Army folks in Kashmir valley called us fools. We had a choice here. Either we could be called morons, which we are, or be shot in the butt by homicidal maniacs in the Kashmir valley. We chose the former. All we needed was a local, who was stupid enough to drive with us through the non-existent wastelands of flood-ravaged Leh-Ladakh, dumb enough to swallow our story that Goose is a photographer, the Chief is an Author and Derek was.....er......Derek. Ten drivers were sensible enough not to accompany us and it was the eleventh driver, who agreed to come with us. Probably because he had a very sick mother at home, had many un-married siblings, a jobless father and a few kids here and there. The usual Indian sob-story, you know? And Santosh, a 4-foot runt of a man, a build like an underfed crow, hawk-eyes and a navy blue sweater, which he would wear for the next twenty days when we would be doing all those things which most of the people tell you not to do.

It was the eleventh driver who agreed. It was our eleventh day on the road. And eleven is made of two 'ones'. Add them up and you get a 'two'. And if you thought I had anything to conclude from all this, dear reader, you are sadly mistaken. I typed it just because it sounded cool and every Indian is into numerology or astrology or biology or like me, writing a book that is a 'frivilogy' (five books). Santosh was on; he also looked like one of us. He looked demented. We were cool.

Foreplay

Nature in full splendour. The sky looked like the cleavage of a pretty woman and the sun shone through like a diamond pendant on her chest. The rainbow that seemed to be following us through the bright sunny skies once we crossed Rohtang Pass on to Keylong was like an angel from the sky who wanted to show us the way to eternal happiness and peace. The climb from Manali to Rohtang Pass was utterly treacherous and as we saw a couple of bulldozers clearing off the debris from landslides all over, with practically zero visibility. We had scaled from Manali (which is about 13069 feet above the sea-level) up to Rohtang Pass (which is 6369 feet above sea level). I was slowly getting my arms around measuring distance and altitude in feet and not losing my head. The cute little thing called 'Mountain sickness' eludes us at 14,469 feet altitude as we went through the serpentine patches of treacherous road-line formations, thanks to Diamox. The roads here in the mountains, I soon realized, were no different from the ones in Bangalore. Just that these roads did not have much traffic and the traffic-snarls were lower, so it was much easier to drive here. Derek was ecstatic due to the complete absence of traffic cops on the patches. The slush and practically zero-visibility between Manali and Rohtang Pass had made me realize how a coffee bean feels inside a grinder, and Motormouth had sturdily scaled those yawning pot-holes in between mud-patches that Santosh referred to as 'roads'. We passed a small clump of huts they call a village around these parts, and this village was called 'Kun Loo'. We stopped to pee.

We were stumped by the beauty this place had to offer and it resembles the smiles of a thousand children from the Tibetan SOS Village where we were headed and hoped to reach. We had been called morons and it was the first time in my life, I took it as a compliment. We all did. For exactly five seconds, there was a strange flicker of niceness in Derek's eyes. The kind of fleeting moments or bouts of thought he suffered from, once in a while. It probably happened once in 76 years, like Halley's comet. This was probably the only time we would see it in this lifetime. I was blessed. The floods had devastated the valley, cutting off all communication, including the internet. They had told us back in Manali that when it rains in Manali, it snows in Ladakh. It was a sunny, bright day in Keylong district and we were nearing Koksar, en route to Keylong. We concluded that it would be sweltering hot in Manali now. Maybe we had carried the sunshine with us to Leh and could give it to the children, if the fury of the rains would let us reach Leh. Strangely enough, we knew we would make it to Leh and cover all the erotic and non-touristy places in the Ladakh Valley. Reaching Koksar, we found that they call this a village too. It was full of cracker-box houses that looked like a bunch of well-kept match boxes among yaks and people. Hold on, they aren't any yaks here, just people who look like yaks. And Derek was trying to communicate with them.

Nature and beauty abound

The local cuisine was simple – rice, pulses, salad and pickle. It barely took us ten minutes to demolish all that was out in front of us. Of course, after the meal, we had to wash our hands and feet. On a shoe-string budget, the meal cost us less than a shoe-lace. Living life doesn't cost money, just needs a whole lot of attitude. We were free men in our beautiful, free country. This is the India we know, this is the India we love. I call it India 2.0

Open skies, beautiful mountains, flowing river and countless waterfalls made the evening sunset look grand. The rainbow, she was still following us, she was the spirit of countless women of India, watching over us, loving us. The cool evening breeze blanketed us in warmth that signified an abundance of love and happiness. Of course, the biggest problem with abundance is that of abundance. I overate, as usual. Barely able to walk a few meters, I felt like a little puppy after a heavy meal, tripping from one side to the other. Having crossed a few more villages that dotted the beautiful Himalayan ranges, we reached our camping ground. A seedy village called 'Tandi' with no public toilets. It is also the last refueling station for the next 369 kilometers. Thank you, Jerry, for this isn't a fun ride. So, as defined by nature, heeding Nature's call, armed with a bottle of hand-sanitizer and a tissue roll, I decided to enjoy the evening light by the river in the most bohemian way that I knew. I was full of shit before. Not anymore.

Oh, for some clean sheets and a proper commode

Pitching a tent was an activity that is loved by people the world over. Derek, Goose and I gleefully got the tents, the picnic chairs and tables out. Of course, lighting up a fire was best left to our man-Friday, Santosh. When you have a flunkey to take care of the rotten stuff, life can be bliss. And we are used to leading a charmed life and this is as rough as we can get. Goose was monkeying around with the user manuals and barking out instructions. Dog. Derek and I were pitching the tent, following His Majesty's instructions. Of course, the flame only lasted till our man-Friday was around. Goose tried to light the fire and gave all sort of scientific theories about the flash-point of diesel, while I watched him play Fred Flintstone with the twigs and rocks. He finally gave up, much to our relief and as soon as he plonked himself on the chair, the fire came up on its own. We heard Derek cuss wildly inside the tent. He was trying out the new sleeping bag and he had got a major organ of his caught in the zip. He never ceased to amaze us. As we sat around the campfire, something deep inside of me told me that it's going to be alright, we would reach the school in time, not just to make a monetary donation, but also to help them in every possible way. Whether we liked it or not, we now had a mission.

Waking up by the riverside with the sun shining bright on the snowcapped mountains reminds us of how small we are in the larger scheme of things that Nature has to offer. It was a sight alright with three tiny specs of the universe sitting like peacocks, going through the morning ablutions, with spectacles on. Maybe that's why the term 'specs' was coined. And we specs were all out to spread our tents (read tentacles) all over the country. Our next pit stop would be Keylong on the way to Darcha, before Sarchu – our first entry point into Ladakh from Himachal Pradesh.

Owing to the flash floods and devastation, the Indian Army had shut down any further movement of civilians. With more than 300 tourists and over 30 Army personnel having gone missing, and with over 150 dead, in the flash floods, Leh had witnessed the worst ever situation in years. An arid desert devoid of much rainfall, most of the houses were mud hutments and they had been washed away. The Tibetan SOS Village School, the place we were to go to, was in Lower Ladakh, and had been one of the worst hit in the region. If there was a time when we could be useful for the children, it was now. Devoid of any communications or radio link, we had no choice but to rely on what was being communicated by the truck drivers who were returning from Leh, having transported diesel, medicines and essential supplies to the region. We had no choice but to stay put in Sarchu for another two days before heading out to Pang, which was to be made open to civilian traffic. We were inching closer to Leh, but it would take us some more time.

Crossing over to the state of Ladakh

We received a very warm welcome in Ladakh, right from the check post in Sarchu, where we had to register Motormouth, Derek, Goose and the Chief. Upon being asked the purpose of our visit to Leh and at the risk of being called a moron yet again, I explained to them 'the-purpose-of-our-visit-to-Leh' – Deliver sunshine and smiles. For the first time in my entire life, I realize I was taken very seriously. The Leader of the personnel of the ITBP (Indian Tibetian Border Police) manning the checkpoint took an immediate liking to me and became a friend of ours, and not only directed us to the best camp-site location, but also gave us other options owing to the extreme conditions of the windy region, while promising to come over in the evening and joining us for a drink. The wind-chill and wind-velocity was enough to turn us all into icicles and blow us away to the moon. We considered ourselves to be uber-cool morons, but this wasn't quite what it meant. This was freezing. Having pitched tent and explored out the region, we were breathless. Derek was panting, Goose was wheezing and I was gasping for breath.

Our man-Friday, Santosh, kept himself warm inside Motormouth. Finally, a flash of brilliance struck us and we decided to de-camp and take shelter in one of the make-do arrangements that the locals set up. These are tents with garish interiors, but with beds and warm blankets. There were also tin hutments that cost 100 Indian rupees per night, which is less than the price of a full-square meal way back in Bangalore. We were in for a big surprise. Our friends in Sarchu now comprised of a very young Indian Army personnel from the Border patrol, a goatherd from Himachal Pradesh, two traders from Zanskar Valley in Ladakh, a policeman and three pretty women from the mountains. For two days, we were looked after, taken care of, by folks who could barely understand us. Our discussions ranged from women, guns, more women, stars, Chinese domination, Pakistani infiltration, many more women, religion, adventures.

We were now out to beat the local record of surviving without a bath for seven days. Freezing cold and severe winds, the desert had only magnificent sights to offer. Derek didn't find the current conditions an aberration. For me, getting used to the Indian toilets or the field, clumps of toilet rolls, heated up wet-tissues, large amounts of hand sanitizers, talcum powder, deo-sprays and mouth fresheners was not easy. Being in thermal wear and layers of clothing all the time is no fun either. In fact, if it were not for Motormouth, this book wouldn't have seen the light of day. With my laptop being charged on her running engine, she took more than good care of us – she had also offered us the back seat of the car, which was being used for all kinds of activities while on the road.

Our hutments resembled igloos. They shall be called 'Igs' henceforth, dear reader, for there are no 'loos' attached to them. It was a circular place, large enough to house eleven to twelve people at the same time. The entrance was a small aperture, slightly larger than a window, and there were only beds around the place. It was warm and cozy, manned by three beautiful women and one ugly male, who looked like a big bandicoot. There were mattresses and blankets and pillows all around with two broken tables in the center. There was a counter as soon as we entered, well stocked with woolen socks, noodles, chips, confectionary, biscuits and packets of milk. The place offered hospitality, warmth and a place to get together with people from everywhere, as well as to some life-forms that vaguely resembled people.

Livin' on a prayer

I had never seen the sunrise like this – perched on a rock like a peacock, a roll of toilet paper and hand-sanitizer in each hand, somehow balancing precariously, talking to Goose and Derek, who were watching the sunrise along with me, separated by thorny bushes. It wasn't nice at all; it was shitty – in the true sense of the word. Also, the sunrise is supposed to leave one breathless, but in our case, the severe breathlessness was a result of the least amount of physical exertion, like the morning ablutions, being a part of our two days of the acclimatization process. When they tell you that mountains can leave one breathless, trust me, dear reader, they are not talking about being spellbound by the sheer beauty of it all.

Today, Goose and I would head out to the Army Headquarters and try to see if we can call home and tell them we are alive. Fortunately, the skies had cleared up, but I guess the TV people – that 'Helga' who keeps spreading rumors based on 69th-hand information – have to be countered. These are over-rated and over-excited people, who love to take pictures of a leaky drain, and show it as a busted water-supply line. Tsewang, a native of Leh, gives us the hutment for three weeks, until the roads are open for public. The valley shuts down from September 15th till April of the following year. Tsewang's nephew studies in the Tibetan SOS Village School and we offered to give him a ride. The five of us now would reach Leh with money, food and medical supplies and see what we can do for the children.

Within two days of our stay in Sarchu, we knew practically everybody, sans names, and Motormouth became a beast of delight to many. She loved the adulation, for sure. She had stickers around her that screamed 'Horn OK Please' along with the logo, and she was basking in the glory of the local population and the Army folks, who couldn't get enough of the gizmos that powered her.

It had been over a week since we had called home. With absolutely zero communications or telecom signals around the place, it was probably the first time I realized that all the things that I used to take so much for granted back in Bangalore were the basic necessities of life here. In Sarchu, we went to the Army camp, directed by the Indo-Tibetan Border Police and used their Comsat link to call up home. The telephone operator there looked like a Headmistress with a beard. I've never felt so useless in my life, with all bits of communication down. My HTC android on my left holster, my BlackBerry in my right holster, data-cards and the different cell phones and iPhones amongst us had all gone black. All communication links were down, and this was when we realized that all the Social Media tools that we were using were now so useless. Standing in a queue at the local Army headquarters, like a common man, only to call up home to tell them that we are safe and not extending the call beyond one minute is not something that we spoilt morons were used to. Dinner was simple chicken and rice. A bird in hand makes an ugly mess. Had it been alive now, it would anyways have shat in my hand by now. Which fool said that a bird in hand is better than two in the bush? Does he have any clue as to how many men dream about getting their hands into a bush?

I grew up on the main road....Well, not exactly, but it was the first house by the main road, so that makes it the roadside, I suppose. I've always lived in cities. It was always dark there too. Not an overabundance of dark, but just an absence of light. Whereas, in the rural areas, dark would make the sky look like a leaky blanket, riddled with holes and stars shining through. I mean, what's the point? Might as well have a few streetlamps and avoid getting hit while crossing the roads as cars hurtle through at break-neck speed at night. In the city, however, I had mastered the art of crossing the street, smiling. Brushing my teeth twice a day gave me shiny teeth, which act as reflectors at night. Therefore, brushing your teeth twice a day keeps you alive, I guess. If the car didn't hit you, maybe a thought about this chapter will. Anyways, you are pathetic and are about to go insane by the end

HOPping to Conclusions

▶ *In India, It is impossible to get on Facebook while doing high speed*

▶ *Not all four-letter words are cuss-words. 'Free' is one such*

▶ *Red Bull also doubles up as shampoo*

▶ *Rain is liquid sunshine*

▶ *If you spend too much time with sheep, you start looking like one*

▶ *Spit works well on windshields*

▶ *An underwear on a tripod looks like Darth Vader in drag*

▶ *A bird in hand makes an ugly mess, a hand in the bush is a lot better*

▶ *Not all monuments are pieces of art; some are really dumb*

▶ *Thinking and driving do not gel*

11 Through the Eyes of a Moron

When hope slips away and depression laughs in your face,
About obstacles everywhere, we all have those days;
Ploughing ahead with the heart of a moron,
Praying hard to make a difference, to be reborn;
Of undying faith and wishful thought,
Waiting for a new tomorrow, do away with the rot;
Radical dreams shape a brave new nation,
And 365 Kms away from the nearest fuel station;
Dark Clouds clear and the sun shines through, it makes
me say 'Cheese'
Drive on, for that's when you go 'Horn OK Please'...

Depression 2.0

2500 were feared dead in China, many more in Pakistan
and we were stranded with all kinds of people who had now
become our friends. This evening, we had been invited by the
Border Police for some spicy mutton and we were looking
forward to it. It was our last night in Sarchu and we were to
try out a new route to Leh, which cut across a place called
'Chooha-ground', which means a ground full of bandicoots. It
was an 80 kilometer extra-stretch and Tsewang was to guide
us through this off-roading route. There are no roads over
there, one is supposed to carve one's own. Nothing better.

After all, that's what we had been doing in this trip in every possible way. An arid desert with flat lands and awfully smelly people all around us. A driver who smelt like an abused jerry-can from World II, a hutment owner who smelt like scrambled eggs and the plan was being created along with our goat-herd friend. Our friends from the Army and the ITBP had their own share of whims. And here we were, with all senses intact, except horse and common.

It's the middle of the afternoon now, and we are here in a bar. I have been limping for the past one week like a one-legged Tarzan because of a wound on my foot. As I try to strike a conversation with the waitress, she reminds me of the usual bitch of a secretary of an undead boss. She has an awfully sweet mop of hair, but is a wee bit skinny. Hold on! That is a mop I am talking to for Helga over here comes in with three cold beer mugs and a bottle of 'King-pisser' beer as she calls it. She has fat, with hairy arms and the subtle hint of a beard. The biceps are bigger and stronger than mine or Derek's. Help! For this must be Helga again in a different shape, size and form. Of course, beauty might be skin-deep, but ugly goes straight to the bone. So we aren't your typical chunks of cottage-cheese with the perfect set of those pearly-whites from the neighborhood who can dazzle you with our brilliance or make your mom feel good about you buying this book. Derek is wearing a jacket that looks like a dead animal on his back. Goose wears a condom on his head. Motormouth needs a wash else she will also commit suicide like my previous car for my not having been nice to her. As we re-visit our plans to reach Leh somehow, Derek drools, staring at Helga, our waitress now, and reminds Goose of a dripping tap. The poor, dumb animal is frustrated. God save the yaks.

So we weren't our chirpy selves today as we seemed to be hitting a cul-de-sac everywhere. Hell!! What's the point of getting Leh'd when we cannot be there when they need us? They needed help. We wanted to be there anyhow, even if it meant throwing Derek to the vultures, appease the Gods and get a move on. Helga went back to her cave, I presume, for there were only the sweet ladies of the hutment who were ever-smiling and extra-nice to us. Maybe they were sure that we were no threat to them in our current state of sobriety and zero libido. And we were about to get Leh'd, no matter how. We looked like those typical hungry, jobless, out-of-work aliens from a neighboring state, replete with persecution complex, homicidal tendencies and other such behavioral problems. Maybe that's why they were being extra nice to us.

Goose was constantly being badgered by our new friend from the Indo-Tibetan Border Police, a spirited youth who loved bikes, girls, guns and singing. Everything was alright with us except for the singing part. He had been deputed to guard the border near the Tibetan SOS Village, which separated part of China, and I suspect that it was his singing that made the clouds over valleys burst above Leh, China and Pakistan-occupied Kashmir, all at the same time. Or maybe it was his singing which made the Army send him to the Indo-China border as punishment. The man was unstoppable when it came to singing. With a gun-throat like that, we were hoping to unleash him onto the Chinese, use him as a sonic-weapon, make him croon till they beg, plead, get down on their knees and give Tibet back to the Tibetans.

A handsome young one who taught us the wonders of Sikhism, it was probably the first time we understood the real meaning of religion. It must be good to have a religious bent of mind, I suppose, but his was so bent out of shape that he was probably demented. Demented, but straight for he had a girlfriend. But, never mind. With over ten people now teeming in the hutment, each one with a different dialect, Derek was going crazy and got really worried that he would forget how to speak English and the urban-Hindi that we are all used to. Goose was happy and grinning gleefully as it would have been a dream come true for both of us if Derek just woke up one fine morning and forgot how to talk. If wishes were horses, I would own a Derby team and would be all rich and famous by now.

Again, we were joined by a driver and the goat-herd. Funniest part is, the goat-herd got us some raw, dried and salted goat-meat that tasted like an old shoe dipped in formalin and sun-dried. As if that wasn't enough, he also got us some goat-milk and 'lassi'. It is said that goat-milk is high in protein and is good for patients with asthma or for those climbing high mountains. It must be true. Have you ever come across a goat with bronchitis? The rum was flowing in the funny desert land, the wind-chill in the air, bright sun and one could burn into a crisp in the heat. Here was our friend, tanking up in the midst of it all. Not only was he a goat-herd, he looked like one, smelt like one and spoke like one. It is so easy to get sun-burnt by day and get frost-bitten by night. You take your pick. Derek was depressed as there was no way he could get an erection in the funny mountain climate. Maybe, that's the reason why mountains are thinly populated and there are not many people around. Put a sexy, naked girl in front of our friend, the goat-herd here, he is sure to cut her up into pieces, dip her in formalin and sun-dry her and make that extra buck for those few more bottles of rum. With fantasies like that, it's good that he is a goat-herd.

It got so cold in the evening that when we tried to talk, my words turned into icicles and fell to the ground and broke into pieces. Thinking anyways wasn't an easy task for us, and now the power of speech was being decimated by the Snow-Queen. It was time for alphabet soup now.

People manning the borders have no contact with civilization for months on end. Our friends from the border police told us that months would pass before they returned to some place where they would catch sight of the superior gender and they would start throwing coins into water and go berserk. In simple terms, they would behave like Derek at the sight of a woman every time they returned from the border, one job that doesn't sound very exciting.

We were to attempt the road to Leh the next morning, so we were to feast tonight with the who's who of Sarchu, which wasn't much, as everybody in Sarchu was a nobody. We blended in perfectly. Tomorrow morning, we would leave and attempt to reach as close to Leh as possible. Though we were barely 300 kms away from Leh, in spite of the newly plotted course, every few meters seemed to knock our breath out. The cold was harsh, the wind was fierce, the days were burning hot and the nights were icy cold. It just got worse with every inch closer to our destination. But the spirit of India that we experienced here made our resolve only firmer, for everyone wanted to help and they did.

The local cops from the checkpoint arrived and threatened us in particular not to leave Sarchu as the situation was very bad in Leh. The roads had been washed away, hundreds were dead or gone missing and the body count was rising. Ladakh had never witnessed such rains and people were homeless.

We had tried our level best to reach Leh by road, were stopped everywhere, and since the local cops had stopped us, we went ahead from Sarchu to Pang, tried out the 'Chooha ground', tried alternate routes, but all the bridges were washed away. We had ploughed ahead since the cops had told us not to. From Pang, which was about 80 kms ahead of Sarchu, we went to some place called 'Rectum' or something. The rains, the desert heat, the cold climate and an utter absence of roads had toasted us for a week. Add to it the fact that we were living like animals devoid of any good food or sanitation. Derek concluded that they cannot even boil water. Over time, we got so sick of living like animals. Of course, we are animals, but we were thoroughbred, totally spoilt, party animals. Goose was fast plunging into a major depression, running low on oxygen and worse – Red Bull. All the mountains, after a point in time, get onto you. I mean, how long can you stare at stony mountains and ice-caps? Especially when you run the risk of getting sun burnt by day and frost-bitten by night? The gentle rain which sounds so romantic when one just gets enough to keep things green and at night was now the same force that kept slapping me on my face every time I tried to plough ahead to reach our destination. And poor Derek, not even powdered rhino-horn could get him his mojo back. He was in tears. We were just 80 kms short of getting Leh'd and it was not to happen for another two weeks. And even if it did, the fear of an epidemic breaking out loomed large. It was time to rework the plan.

Planning is a waste of time

The breaking point was when we were in Pang (North of Leh) and while being asked not to go ahead to a place called Upshi near Leh, we were tortured by being made to drink something that I suspect, was goat-pee. Neatly kept in dragon-painted thermos flasks, it was a sight to watch Derek and Goose give up after a few sips. The goat-pee got us pissed off and we decided to do a U-turn. And we did. The wild-mountain goat, Tsewang, had deserted us. The mountain rat.

Since both Plan A and Plan B had failed, we decided to come up with Plan C and Plan D and give up only when we ran out of alphabets. Plan C was to get back to our base camp i.e. Manali, and get back our lost communication link, get in touch with the world first. Then the next thing to be done was to book our airline tickets from Chandigarh and get Leh'd. We were yet to come up with Plan D, but since it always sounds cool to have a backup plan, we just named it 'Plan D'. The treacherous road ahead had become worse along with worsening weather conditions as now the clouds had accumulated over Himachal Pradesh and Ladakh border, right above us. These are two adjoining states and civic authorities have yet to understand what a motorable road really means. This was worse than Bangalore or any other patches of roads we had ever driven on. We halted for the night in a place called 'Darcha', in between Keylong and Sarchu, if one knows the major towns here. Having stayed in yet another dirty, rotten, filthy, stinking hutment overnight, we decided to flee early morning. We did. Unfortunately, the rains lashed our path and somehow we managed to reach the peak segregating the two states- Himachal Pradesh and Ladakh.

An Open note to the Government of India

The first thing the Government of India must do is to ban these Indian lorries. Collect all of them and provide them with a totally indecent burial. These dumb Indian lorries with ugly faces that dot the Indian highways slow down our progress and slow down our nation. Not only are they eye-sores, they are heavy polluting vehicles which can barely carry 9-10 tons of material, on an average, are perpetually overloaded owing to the greed of the traders, carry 1.5 times their prescribed weight, are assembled with primitive parts, built in primitive workshops, by primitive people. Compare them with the trucks used abroad for similar purposes, and you will see that there is no comparison.

The second thing that the Government of India needs to do is to blast the shitty molehill of a mountain and flatten 'Rohtang Pass' to the ground. Despite living through inhuman conditions near Leh, owing to the weather conditions, this Pass is a particularly horrific place and is one more self-imposed and self-created miseries we have in India. In a perpetual state of gross neglect, this mountain is of little use to India. Pundits might tell you that this would be a strategic buffer-zone, but hell, any fool can come up with lame-brain excuses to justify anything that is an undoing. I learnt new cuss-words from our man-Friday, Santosh, and taught him some new ones. The second thing that these fools need to do is quickly execute the plan of drilling a tunnel all the way through Manali straight down to Leh. Yet again, you will hear of all these plans on paper, but with absolutely zero skills to execute them. It is high time we folks in India learnt to outsource work to developed nations and eat our own dog-food that these pathetic IT-Czars have used it to their advantage by selling cheap, educated labor to the rest of the world.

The third thing which I will tell our Government is that having flattened our mountains of no strategic significance (unless our armed forces people consider this as a buffer zone to prevent hostile nations taking over us and marching right in and straight on to Delhi…*Duh!!*) put all these Indian lorries and other pathetic vehicles into one giant mixer, add your gravel, tar and stuff and use them to build new roads. While you are at it, Honourable President, throw in some of these truck drivers, politicians and some jail-birds as well. Not only will we have better roads, better vehicles and a faster, cleaner and a better nation, we will also not have those traffic jams where I've seen centipedes, goats, cows, buffaloes and sheep overtake me on many city roads.

While I continue to whine having been stuck in a traffic jam for over six hours at Rohtang Pass, my pain runs deeper with Goose snoring behind me and Derek playing his porn CDs. The deep ravine, inches away from my door, does seem a very tempting thought right now, albeit a bit suicidal.

You, dear reader, might get all puffed up with pride and glory about our nation when you hear, read or understand (that is if you can do any of the above) the 'Great Indian Jugaad theory', but I personally detest that. I mean, dignity of labor and things like that are all fine, but there are some absolutely pathetic and downright stupid forms of employment that people indulge in today. You can call me iconoclastic or insensitive, that's cool, and anyways I call myself a moron, so there.

What do you feel about a young chap from rural India running around with six cheap bottles of even cheaper smelling oil and pestering you ad nauseum, that he would give you a very healthy massage? That too, a full-body massage with that pink-colored cheap liquid that smells like shit? You can call him what you want, but to me, he is nothing more than a pesky beggar, who hasn't explored better ways of self-employment.

Or consider this – we came across the official road-blockers and road de-blockers on the mountain track, which comprised of four people working on a contract to an agency called GREF, which works the Army Infrastructure when it comes to roads and things like that. My ass. They only work from 10:00 am to 5:00 pm, so say the locals. Now, that's a lie. Do they have any clue how hard they work to carve out a rescue operation such as the one we witnessed? Despite the onslaught of rain, fog and falling rocks (one barely missed Derek), they parked two bulldozers facing each other and carved out another make-shift road with the debris. A classic example of the same 'Great Indian Jugaad theory'. We watched in awe, for hours on end. The road was still blocked by the land-slide, which mercilessly showed no hint of subsiding. I wonder what kind of a cock-and-bull strategy will all those eminent people of India come up with when they talk gibberish on television talk-shows. What stops air rescues of vehicles like the one they did when I saw the movie 'Godzilla'?

If they can ship dinosaurs and large reptiles, why can't we airlift bulldozers and find a permanent solution to such issues? I am not trying to romanticize the Indian Army or GREF or the ITBP or the armed forces here. But I do believe that it is the abundance of poor leaders that we have in our country today who have a full time job of robbing our nation's wealth. They are those slimy, pathetic reptiles who should be flushed down the biggest flush known to mankind – the black hole, which I tell you, dear reader, is actually the big commode of the universe and leads to a very big septic tank called Hell. Heaven, of course, belongs to you – the reader of this book, who actually bought a copy of the same and did not pinch it from someone or borrow it from the local library.

Ranting of a mad man

It has been close to 22 hours since the landslide and all we see is a bulldozer. A rich state that grows only potatoes and peas, can they not afford any chopper teams that could clear the mess? Are there no advanced means to bring a crack team up and clear the landslide that happens day after day in this season which anyways doesn't last for too long? If these places are of such importance, strategically speaking, can they not even put some nets on the rocks that could hold them or at least reduce the chances of recurrence? That's how important Rohtang Pass is. Some jerk in a hurry (like most of us Indians who are in a perpetual state of hurry), parked his van full of peas right beside us and disappeared. We, like normal citizens, had parked Motormouth in a queue, like the others, in a narrow pass so the oncoming traffic in a narrow one-lane stretch would not suffer. Since this idiot carrying bags of peas had parked smack in the middle of the road, blocking relief work, Goose filled up a bottle with his holy water and Derek was liberal while filling up a paper bag with his biologically hazardous waste and emptied both on their cargo of peas. I did my bit to clean his windshield. Well, maybe only some people can understand this language.

I shudder to imagine how smart our engineers and civic bodies are about Khardungla pass, which is the highest motorable stretch, beyond 18,069 feet. We just want to get out of here, having wasted a day in a traffic jam and all we see is one bulldozer which has taken hours to come – somehow. That's the 'Great Indian Jugaad theory' at work for you, by which the driver somehow reached on top with a bulldozer after fifteen hours. Give me a city-jam any day. At least, one sees people who have had a bath, look like human beings and don't smell like wild-goats.

Now, out of the blue, four guys from Bihar appeared in front of us. Two of them blocked our path and asked for money while the other two pretended to carry iron roads from one end of the road to the other end of the road. I call it extortion. Things get worse, when these goon-types saw a foreigner and went about betting/extortion in the most despicable manner known to humanity. Now, these are the kind of people, who extort money from foreigners, who should be castrated and sent home with a boxful of condoms. Surviving a cold climate, making that extra buck by lying to people with a veiled threat – that's the 'Great Indian Jugaad theory' at work for you. Or cutting an empty bottle of Aquafina and using it as a funnel to tank up Motormouth, when our driver could have easily bought a new funnel, that's the applicability. So much for management jargon.

Let's stop gloating over the current state of affairs that we live in, for sometimes, while most of us are not vocal about it, we would like to see a very large percentage of our fellow-Indians vanish, cease to exist or simply drop dead. Just drop the pretensions and explore those dirty little secrets of yours. Derek, Goose and I have many such discussions, and we represent that large chunk of urban India that is constantly rattled by such sights and incidents.

It is wrong to say that India has not progressed. Of course, we have. And since we are right now stuck in the mountains and surrounded by the mountain-types, I measure the progress that they have made over the past two thousand years or so. Earlier, two thousand years ago, they lived in hutments made of cloth, yak-skin and leather and other such stuff. Now they dwell in hutments made of plastic.

Earlier, they would carry earthen pots to go potty, now they carry an empty container of engine oil to wash up after the big job. Or consider the usage of packet noodles to make chowmein, crude leather jackets with the name of a heavy-metal band that is unknown in these parts – now, compared to those crude leather jackets thousands of years ago. Yes, we have progressed, though we are going slightly tangent to our vision. I mark the progress, dear reader, for let's not say that this book didn't teach you anything.

It makes one wonder why all those tourists from all over the world come to suffer such pain and agony in the name of tourism. Maybe, they have a death-wish or like to suffer such pain in the name of a holiday. But, it was truly remarkable to see those fleets of bullet-motorcyclists, campers and bicyclists who were enjoying the devastating scenic beauty of a fabulous state called Ladakh. While Derek couldn't stop laughing and passing inane remarks at many of our fellow Indians huddled in cheap shawls looking like nuns, so totally unaware of the beauty that surrounded thcm. These were our local tourists who were loud, packed like sardines in a tin-can of a Tata Vehicle, taking ridiculous snaps of themselves with those 'I-have-been-there' intentions and leaving the place all littered up after exactly five minutes. I know it was five minutes; as I've told you this before, dear reader, I cannot count beyond five.

Kings of wishful Thinking

Goose wished he were a giant so he could knock those ugly trucks into the ravine and make way for Motormouth to go through peacefully. Derek wished he were a midget so he could sneak into the SUV of the pretty woman behind us. I wished both would disappear and I could be transported back to civilization.

China, for instance, builds fantastic roads. Of course, it's a different matter that they nibble on our lands to do so. Or look at the power of those weapons that they build that we Indians use to kill each other. Goose and Derek had a point to make here, all said and done – the Chinese were progressive. At least they built stuff, and lots of it and sold it to the world cheap. So unlike our other hostile neighbor, who's fighting over Kashmir for apples? So what if they cannot even manufacture a shoe, at least they have created a very safe haven for all those terrorists in the world who use Chinese weapons to kill people all over the world. At least they put their heart and soul into it and are slowly crafting a nation that gets funded for all these activities by the world's greatest democracy. Now, they are indeed morons. Who else on earth has the ability to foster terrorism, create a healthy breeding ground for fundamentalists the world over, mooch off money from a nation to bomb their own asses? That's our neighbour for you. While we Indians like to live in pieces, our neighbors like to see us in pieces. But, Indians? Hell, we rock! When we left for our road-trip to complete the final chapters of my book, there were forty-odd states (I mean odd!), and I am not sure how many states there shall be upon our return. We take our states, break them into pieces and create many more for all those young tykes in school to suffer trying to memorize them all. I mean, if there were no states being created for a reason, we prefer to go on hunger strikes and make it to the national headlines, burn a few people alive, destroy public property and create new forms of employment – like changing those sign-posts. If nothing works, we shall rename our cities. Newer ways of creating employment? That's the 'Great Indian Jugaad theory' for me. *Duh!!*

We had never had such an intense discussion on such matters; we must have been at the nadir of our depression. It showed on everybody's faces. I knew it was coming. As Goose was skimming through his photographs, Derek let out yet another pearl of patriotic wisdom. He said, "We must re-define our nation. We should do it like dogs and mark them with territorial pissings. We should redraw our maps, rename all our states and cities. This way, all those terrorists in the world would be at their wit's end trying to re-do their 'Hate-manuals', change their hate-speeches and all this would leave them utterly confused for the next few years, while we'll gain some time for ourselves without having to worry about wars and shit like that. They wouldn't know what to hit, what to destroy and anyways they are dumb people'. Pause. Applause. He reminded me of a great president who once led a great nation to many wars, once upon a time…*Duh!!*

When asked about the flow of traffic, if and when the pass was cleared, (hopefully within the next 24 hours,) whether they would let the vehicles from the top come down first or let the vehicles below go up first (since we drive on the left-hand side of the road and there is a very deep ravine inches away when one drives, like most of the stretches in Ladakh), pat came the answer, "Since the vehicles coming from the hills carry potatoes and peas, we will have to give them priority. So the vehicles coming from the top will get preference."

I wanted to barf. Goose wanted to pee. Derek spat on his rain-coat when we were not looking. Plan A and Plan B had failed. We fell short by 80 kilometers of road. We were asked by the Indian Army to do a U-Turn and return by the route that we had come. Entry of new vehicles into the flood-affected Leh was hampering their task of re-constructing the washed away bridges. We had to abide by these orders but we were not about to give up yet. We would find other means of getting Leh'd.

One night in Rohtang Pass

Pitch dark. Derek whispered that he saw a Yeti. That too, a female one. He had never slept with a Yeti before. The closest he had got to sleeping with a Yeti was a very hirsute girl from college. The dark figure vaguely reminded him of her. His face was twisted and contorted, not that it wasn't otherwise, but this Yeti-thing he wanted real bad. He had gone on for a week without sex and he was like a rabid dog on the loose now. Again, unless and until you know Derek really well, it's really tough to spot the difference in his behavioral patterns. He was delirious now. Goose said he needed to be culled. Fortunately, there was a big bottle of whisky in the trunk. Whisky does work in the mountains and can put you to sleep – another one of those mountain yarns. Fortunately, there were a couple of pegs in it. I took a good swig of it, emptied the bottle and hit Derek on the head with it. We slept in peace at night. The whisky had worked.

Day 2 in a traffic jam in Rohtang Pass

Sleeping inside Motormouth yet again, amidst falling rocks, rain and icy cold weather, started doing things to our senses. Goose woke up at five am and started pleading with us to make the authorities understand that the peas being transported would get all spoilt if they didn't clear up the mess and let us all go. GREF had stopped working last evening and in the mountains, dawn breaks out soon. The debris-clearing work would not start for another five hours from now, as the royal highnesses of GREF would be sleeping right now, to be woken up by dancing girls later. At least, we were seeing the classic Indian apathy at work, so it would be wrong to say that they were not working.

We had these typical half-brained, moth-eaten monkeys of taxi drivers in a hurry to ahead of the queue. As if others were fools. A 20-feet patch of dirt-track, and these fools would go breaking the serpentine queue of vehicles, trying to go straight up front. Ever notice how we Indians are in such a rush always? Education levels hardly matter. Each time I try to board or disembark from an aircraft, a bus, stand in a queue for movie-tickets or just about anything, we would all be trying to save that extra minute in life as if the whole world is about to end. Maybe, it is some kind of a post-colonial hangover that extended from some kind of a Freudian-like, deep-rooted insecurity that makes us manifest the 'Me!Me!Me!' syndrome, even if it is at the cost of others.

The 'mad rush' syndrome is so evident to us right now as Derek and Goose begin to lose it. This isn't what fun is all about; this is not what we bargained for. We have enough and more mountains in India. We were imagining how easy it would be to have a few B2 Bombers sent in the dead of night and raze the blasted mountains to the ground.

Armed with hand sanitizers and toilet rolls, we battled the rains, going about the morning ablutions. I was worried that would get to become a habit and that once I got back home, I would forget to use the flush. Goose was finding playing with the dynamo of the torch a very exciting activity to indulge in. Derek could not get enough of his smutty magazines, which was his idea of keeping himself warm. We were stuck and badly so. If it wasn't for Motormouth, we would not have survived the night.

As if the slush, the cold and the fog were not enough, we now had mules coming and littering our path and adding to the confusion. They were carrying peas – uphill. I wonder what's wrong with these people? Why couldn't they simply make up their minds and decide where they wanted their peas and potatoes? Up in the mountains or down in the plains? Goose vowed that he wouldn't eat peas for a year. We all joined him in his resolve.

I think it is the immigrant-thing. Any city, any country, any continent, is definitely more progressive when it is teeming with outsiders. If one has locals, too many of them, everything tanks. Immigrants are progressive, hard-working, they follow rules and shit like that. The locals, on the other hand, play with not-what-you-know, but whom-you-know. Can you imagine the US of A looking all green and spruced up without Hispanics? Or driving up education standards without the Jews, Chinese and Indians? Of course, I shall reserve my comments for the United Kingdom, which could have been a bit wiser in terms of letting people in. I long for the day when we shall have an influx of Europeans, Americans and Brits into our country, the way we do today. If every second person in Hyderabad who aspires to live the American dream (of course, one doesn't really call 10-12 people living in an apartment in Fremont living the American dream, but that's a different debate) or every goods carrier from Punjab full of illegal immigrants aspiring to go to Canada or United Kingdom, can be stopped or nipped in the bud, we would probably give a bit more respect to our motherland.

Maybe, they should stop the very concept of immigration. You were born here or there, stay here or there. Come, visit us and we visit you. Do not try to confuse cultures, making a mess of both. Keep the immigrant population flowing. Maybe a year or two here and there, but that's it. I hate to meet ugly, unhygienic kids visiting us from abroad and speaking with a silly accent that doesn't go with their personality at all. In Rome, do as the Romans do. Don't try to give your stupidities any fancy names like 'melting-pot' or sticking to your so-called cultural roots. Sometimes, I do believe that Indians are the biggest racists. Calling it 'Casteism' doesn't change a thing. And we are the ones who whine about racism or outsourcing or things like that when it doesn't work in our favour. We have so much to learn from our Western counterparts and progressive nations of the worlds. Of course, there are some despicable nations which teach us what not to do, but they are best ignored. I told you I was delirious and a moron and I just proved it and I cannot stop rambling and I have stopped making sense even to Derek? Hell!! Get us out of here!! Get us out of this landslide in Rotten Pass or whatever is the name of this place. I need to have a bath and need to see some washed faces. And stuff those peas of yours!!

GREF worked hard in making sure we were out of GRIEF soon. The classic 'Great Indian Jugaad theory' had been put to work. Another temporary road was built that would last for a few more hours before the next landslide. They hadn't locked their bulldozers at night, for no one would have stolen their bulldozers at night. It is true; the mountains are very safe when it comes to such things. Goose and Derek watched in disbelief – not at the way GREF was working the mountains, but at the way the jerks were trying to cut through the queue and about to create another traffic jam.

We would be out of this shit-hole in a few hours. And we needed to pamper ourselves after a week of torture. Clean sheets, good room, internet connectivity, hot water and edible food it would be. The mountains sucked. That was that. We would now start work on Plan C and Plan D to reach the school to help the little tykes in Leh.

Clueless but with absolutely no intention of giving up, one of the HOPpers helped us get flight tickets to Leh. That was Plan C. Plan D was to meet the Honorable Dalai Lama, seek his blessings and see if we could hand over the check to him for the kids at the Tibetan SOS Village School. Having failed twice in a row, we decided to do both. Our next move would be to get out of this God-forsaken place called Manali, and in the three days before we could get to board the flight from Delhi, go on a chase of his Holiness, the Honorable Dalai Lama. Starting off from Jispa in Himachal Pradesh, we started tracing his holy steps straight down to his holy residence in holy Dharamsala.

The drive from Manali to Pathankot is probably one of the best drives that a road-hog can ever experience. I'm not sure if the jokers from the Guinness book of records have been here and measured the hair-pin bends, but it can sure put any hirsute man's crotch to shame. This probably has more curls than known to most of the folks who come to our country. Dharamsala, the city where his Holiness, Dalai Lama stays, falls in this route. One gets to see a bunch of these morons from all over the world come to India and get on their bicycles or motorbikes and attempt to cross over the stupid Rohtang Pass over to Ladakh, and ignore this route. They should try this route instead, where one doesn't really run the risk of being run over by a bus, caught in an open drain or getting stuck in a traffic jam full of jerks who do not understand the very concept of 'the right of way'. Whereas this stretch can give anyone multiple orgasms. The roads are long and winding, the scenery is perfect, safety is at its best and there are no traffic jams. This was probably one of the best routes that I have ever driven Motormouth on, with the three of us fighting to get behind the wheel.

The glory of a beautiful sunset appeared in full splendor as I took to the wheel. Sun-kissed and loaded on Red Bull, driving through the terrain with the wind caressing me, Motormouth was being loved by the roads. The subtle hint of a peeking sun from behind the clouds that kept shying away from us time to time, the straightness of the pine trees in the region, unlike the barren landscape of Ladakh or the unruly look of the palm trees in the south. It was so much better than those dense forests that dot most of the North Indian terrain with clumps of trees that just don't know how to grow. Add cobwebs to them, they look worse than Jimmy

Hendrix's hair on fire. But this was mind blowing. Simply awesome.

Now, here we were, sitting on a holy stone-thingie right outside his holy gates. It was the 15th of August and it was a Sunday. A double whammy! A Sunday combining with Independence Day in India is the pits when it comes to reaching out to any Government official. Not that it is easy otherwise, but still, here we were in a complete *Duh!!* moment of our lives. Derek was silent for a change, which was good, else we would have been bludgeoned to death by the holy guards of His Holiness. Goose was glued to his iPhone, chatting away with his girlfriends. I was writing this chapter down. Armed with a laptop, a camera, two cell phones, a dossier that contained our credentials, we managed to talk to his Holy Security guards, a holy tree, a Holy gate, three Holy mosquitoes near his Holy Residence and not to mention, his holy gate. We had 24 hours to kill on that Holy stone-thingie. It reminded me of my first love.

When I was in school, I had fallen for this chick, who was smart enough not to continue the so-called, long-distance affair with me for eight long years. I was so absolutely smitten by her that I think I was beyond repair. We used to live in this two-storey house in a small town, and I would diligently park myself on the parapet of our terrace, day after day, rain or shine, just to watch her ride her lousy moped by my house so I could get a glimpse of her. We were not meeting then, she was not talking to me, and there was no way I could reach her. I had no clue why I used to do that every morning, walk many miles every day, traversing the trajectory of that blasted two-wheeler, simply with an undying hope that someday, everything would be alright. We had had a break-up as she couldn't take my bohemian ways and our relationship was pretty much intense. She did come back, on her own, one fine day when she called up my college and reached out to me and it was the time when Eric Clapton's knock-out single 'Laila', was released. Those days, we didn't have cell phones or Facebook. She left me as she broke up with me the second time, on a railway platform, exactly where it had all started, just that the city was different. This time, she took the wind out of me, left me cold and knocked out for a week and I spent three days being totally numb. As the train chugged out of the station, I did cry a bit, dunked a soda and went back to my room and listened to an album called "The Sound of White Noise" for three days in a row. Very little sleep, a few bananas, some water and loads of nicotine. The fourth day, I had bounced back to life, but I can never forget her. May the force be with her, wherever she is. All I need to know, still, is the reason why she left me. That is all. Maybe, someday I will. Or maybe I won't. But the point I am trying to make over here, dear reader, is this – sometimes a wait or an act is not without a reason. I am sure she would have had one, for she must be a successful doctor somewhere out there, today. I've never tried reaching her since that day. And that happened over a decade ago. Waiting for the Honorable Dalai Lama fills me with the same feeling right now. Empty, hollow, depressing, fruitless and not knowing what to do or how to reach the Honorable one. Just that this time, I have the maturity to handle the wait. And this wait is selfless…it must be worth it, I suppose.

I guess, some of us are born stupid. I was stupid enough to write this book and you were stupid enough to buy it. So, that makes two of us. Imagine a network of all of us and I am sure, there would be something good about it all. Security guard after security guard comes and questions us, they understand our purpose. Our sole purpose of getting to the Tibetan SOS Village School, which is under the aegis of the Holiness of the Honorable Dalai Lama, all we want to do is to meet him, seek his blessings, hand him a cheque that comprises all the savings we have right now between the three of us – Derek, Goose and the Chief. A measly amount of one lakh rupees. We want to hand it over to him, go to Leh, provide whatever is physically and morally possible to help the children of the school. Getting Leh'd now has a completely different meaning for all of us. For the first time, it was not about sex or fun for us anymore. This was serious shit. Derek took off his glasses, Goose stopped playing with his hair and I left my android phone aside. This is what we do when we try to get serious in life. This was as sincere an attempt as it can get. Somehow, all those comic book heroes whom we had grown up reading and idolizing, came to life. Derek said he felt like Conan, the Barbarian, who was out to battle evil sorcerers and their mad magic in Leh. Goose felt like Asterix, out to battle a pathetic Roman army, loaded on Druid Getafix's magic potion and I felt like Calvin, out to rescue my Hobbes and his brothers who studied in the school.

Funny, how the comic book heroes of yesterday, whom we grew up reading, so form the personality of the modern Indian Youth. Urban India thrives on Tintin comics, where Captain Haddock, Professor Calculus, Bianca Castafiore, Snowy, Rastapopulous and their cronies like Allen or Pablo explore the world, save people and do a lot of do-gooding while having fun at the same time. Or that tiny little village, which the Romans were never able to conquer, thanks to

Asterix, Obelix, Dogmatix, Druid Getafix and the rest of the loveable village folk who got together to fiercely defend themselves from the megalomaniac Julius Caesar (And I remember the great Roman Emperor every time I have my salad). Or Calvin and his inseparable imaginary tiger friend – Hobbes, a friendship that defines the subtle balance between being an adult, yet not losing the child within. I mean, a person ceases to be a sensitive soul the day the child within dies. And we morons never let go of that child within us today, it was because we were still devouring comic books, while the whole adult-world was devouring those smutty, trashy novels. I like it this way and it's alright when someone calls us morons.

The urban India scene is full of those educated, middle-class types who have grown up like any other kid anywhere else in the world. Underlined by fantasy, magical beings, fun-worlds, imaginary worlds and all of us want to be super-people in one way or the other. The only difference between the world of super heroes and reality is, in India, we do not wear our innerwear on top of our outerwear for fear of being arrested. Nor would I ever dream of roaming around M.G. Road in Bangalore wearing a cape for fear of someone blowing his nose into it, or wiping his pollution-impacted face. But we are super-people, nonetheless. We like our beers, we like girls, we like fast cars, love flirting, so on and so forth. The very stubbornness that we were demonstrating right now, with this head-strong attitude, right in front of the Honorable Dalai Lama's residence when we didn't care if they put us behind bars, beat us to pulp or make us drink that horrible salted-tea like we were made to do in Pang, Ladakh, it didn't matter. We wanted to meet His Holiness and that was that.

After all, we are morons and incident is a testimonial to the fact. No appointment, no protocol, no sense. Armed with just Raybans, attitude and a cheque book, the Men in Black wanted to meet the spiritual leader of many.

You must have experienced it sometime in your life. As far as I was concerned, my entire life had been without a reason. It was like a very long *Duh!!* moment till the time this book happened. But is there a regret? No. But sometimes, we all must do something that might kill you today, but would breathe life into you tomorrow. Like my subsequent relationship, this one worked out very well. In between the two, life was one big party. Not that it is not now. The party just got better. Derek was humping a tree that stands right in front of security guards. He had to kill time and this was his idea of fun. We had to get him Leh'd. Sheesh! That day we were unable to meet The Dalai Lama but were promised an appointment after returning from our visit to Leh.

HOPping to Conclusions

▸ *Every second male living in the mountains spits with full vigor, every sixty ninth second. Maybe, it's a man thing out there*

▸ *Every fifth person in the mountains either grows peas or potatoes or both*

▸ *Every fourth person in the mountains owns a 'Dhaba', (Local cheap hutment of an eatery) but they cannot even boil water properly*

▸ *Every third person in the mountains eats chowmein, moo-moo, yim-yam, zing-zing, bam-bam and tick-tock. I have no clue what these\mean but we've eaten most of their stuff*

▶ *When you climb the mountains, all you need is a flashlight, reams of toilet roll, hand-sanitizers and Red Bull.*

▶ *People in the mountains have to use water, as the hot and spicy food they consume would burn toilet-paper*

▶ *If someone near you smells like a goat, he must be from the mountains*

▶ *Anything that is unrecognizable, hard or smells awful would be considered to be a delicacy in cold climates anywhere in the world*

▶ *Indians are poor road-builders, we draw them very well on paper*

▶ *Never eat or drink anything that doesn't taste the way you think it should taste like*

▶ *There is nothing romantic about the mountains in the cold. They only look good in pictures, on you tube or post-cards*

▶ *If you play video games, you can be an awesome driver on Indian roads*

▶ *They should not felicitate some of our Helga- leaders with garlands, instead, they should fill a bathtubs full of coins, hoist them to 5*5 feet and shower them with those coins. Rinse\the coins to reuse and spread the cheer*

▶ *If you are one of those starry-eyed types, all smitten by mountains and shit like that, get to your local shrink – pronto!! You need a check-up from the neck-up*

▶ *Any place that grows potatoes and peas alone as major crops, should be best avoided for a vacation*

▶ *Never ask a local taxi driver for good places to visit. 95% of those places will be religious places, 3% will be a crowded valley for a sunset, 2% will be dirty, rotten, filthy, stinking places of zero significance, teeming with equally dirty, rotten, filthy, stinking tourists from nearby places who will be loud, will litter, take pictures of their own and go away after 5 minutes of boorish behavior to seas, forests and anything of yore. I can write sonnets for you to make you happy about them, but that's that*

▸ *You've seen one mountain, you've seen them all. Same applies*

▸ *Hand sanitizers and toilet rolls are more useful than a flashlight or camping gear*

▸ *Mountain people also wear socks, condoms, hand-kerchiefs, bandanas, plastic sheets and towels for head-gear. Many tourists from nearby places also wear funkier stuff*

▸ *Never trust any peddler in the mountains who tells you that their stuff is one of the following:*

  a. *A-One*
  b. *Top-Class*
  c. *Imported*
  d. *A-Class*
  e. *Export material*

12 Others Before Self...Got Leh'd

Children without a nation, they teach us how to smile,
Putting others before self, they learn to walk that extra
mile;
Walking on a tomb after the dance of death and mayhem,
Can we lend a helping hand, can we feel for them?
A slow revolution, a silent storm and they stand tall
Education can be a powerful force, and that can change it
all;
A faith, a dream suppresses a silent scream,
But to live with pride, the Tibetans shape a dream;
The strength of character shapes a human being, it makes
me say 'Cheese'
Drive on, for that's when you go 'Horn OK Please'...

Day one in Leh

It was one wild night in New Delhi, at the karaoke bar when we decided to party a bit. We were on our way to Leh and this was an awesome pit-stop. I had lost my voice screaming to sing along to one of my favorite songs from a band called 'Hoobastank', a song called 'The Reason'. Goose had just come back from a date and was getting drunk, and Derek was with two bubbly girls who were smitten by him. They made the perfect threesome. I was sounding like a frog with a bad throat. As I croaked out for the bill, Goose had to be stopped and told the party was over and we were the only ones in the house now. Derek made me gargle with some crazy stuff that tasted like toilet water (yes, I have had a soda called Dr. Salt or something like that in the Mid-west). Goose was gleeful as I couldn't speak. Derek told me that I should paint my face and try walking around like a mime-artist. The night went on till two am and we had to leave for the airport at three am. The wound on my leg was hurting and as Goose changed the bandage, I was howling in pain. Having Goose play a male nurse is worse than getting your chest waxed. Of course, I mean that if you are a male.

Goose had caught a bad cold. What's a good cold anyways? We know for he is the only person known to all humanity who can sneeze with the same intensity for five minutes in a row, that's how I learnt to count beyond five. That's the only thing good about his cold. Goose -The Trance lover. The only people I know who like Trance turned gay or turned dope-heads or both. I mean if you want to get that high, go blow your brains out by chewing dynamite sticks. Or eat green chilies in New Delhi, the kind of stuff we had been served as part of the salad at dinner tonight. It was all salads and stuff. Food for lambs along with lamb for food, that's alright as Delhi is awesome, foodies. The waiter, our man 'Cadbury', with a condom-like cap stitched to his head, was constantly at our table hovering around us like those military drones they send out for recce before a bombing spree, waiting for a tip. I'd rather tip those roadside food-joint guys, not these well-fed and over-paid Cadbury-like butlers in these hotels. Would you tip a lawyer or a doctor ever? The bill was a bomb. Cadbury had carpet-bombed my wallet.

Goose kept the background score up with his sneeze. It came like a punctuation mark after every sentence that Derek spoke. And Derek's sentences were very short like, "Grunt! Can I touch?" or "Duh! Can I have some wa?" Goose's cold was getting worse and we all needed to get a bit of sleep.

It was a dark, rainy night. Sweet drops of liquid sunshine fall on my head; Goose and I love getting wet in the rain. And the gentle sound of thunder now....Wait! That was thunder? It was Derek after the crappy food. Man down! May Day! May Day! One moron with a Godawful cold, another with a throat gone wild, and now the third one with a tossed-out stomach, we need to get rested before we got arrested for walking around tipsy in underwear. We decided that the best way to avoid a hangover was to stay drunk and not waste any time sleeping. We had become smarter during the trip. By the time we reached the airport, we were so pissed with each other, as that one hour between leaving the pub and leaving for the airport had been a torture. A feeble attempt of a nap and here we were, rushing to the airport. The flight to Leh was in one hour. Still drunk, we somehow tottered through security, boarded somehow and passed out in the plane. We were open-minded people and the cops seem to mistake open-mindedness for a hole in the head. Else, why would we have our home parties getting busted at three am by greedy cops banging on the door? We needed to play it a bit safer and saner, so Goose suggested we don some clothes and pretend to act like humanoids and do our research about the history of Tibet and China by listening to some smart person. Listening to smart people is so much easier and better than reading, so we heard our friend out with whom we were staying. She is a smart one. At least she was smart before she edited this book and got all jumbled up. Smita is the one who edited my manuscript first. So read on….

The Tibetan Settlement in Ladakh in the 70's was the most remote and least developed of all the Tibetan communities in exile. After China ate up Tibet, nomadic refugee camps were scattered all along this Indo-Tibet border region where communication and physical contact were almost entirely cut off from the rest of the Tibetans in India. Today, for example, in Leh, there are 12 Tibetan refugee camps. There are nine more such camps in the no-man's land between India and Tibet, which is about 280 Kms from Leh. This is the place Derek really wanted to visit. For him, he had visions of a 'No-man's' land to be like a ladies toilet. A place where no man had gone before – Star Trek. Sheesh!

There are about 16,500 kids that the Tibetan Children's Village (TCV) provides education to 16,500 tiny little morons under the CBSE (Central Board of Secondary Education) or (Central Bureau of Selective Entropy), whichever way you want to interpret it. I choose the latter. These tiny tykes include orphans, senior orphans and the destitute. The idea of TCV is to provide them with education (God knows why!!) till they turn self-sufficient. You can find more information about TCV at http://www.tcv.org.in/ They also have a branch near Bangalore. But since every other place is far from my Bangalore, they come here. Back home in my country called Bangalore….er….Derek's messing up my geography. Back in my city Bangalore, we can hear crows at 1:00 am, owls hooting their lungs out at 2:00 am, blasted chimes going ding-ding all around at 3:00 am before some blasted cuckoo making a racket at 4:00 am and no, dear reader, I am not an insomniac.

With initial seed money of Rs.10,000 from His Holiness, The Dalai Lama and land donated by the local Indian government, TCV set out to build a children's village near Leh, Ladakh in 1975. Today TCV Ladakh is a thriving SOS Children's Village with its own school and other facilities. The school includes classes from pre-school through grade ten, after which students can join other TCV branches for further education. Out of 24 children's homes or Khimtsangs, seven are allotted to destitute Ladakhi children.

Besides the main Tibetan SOS Children's Village at Choglamsar, there are now seven schools, three in Jangthang and one handicraft-cum-vocational training centre, one agro-nomadic farm and one old people's home. Nicknamed "oasis in the desert," TCV Ladakh has become the pride of the region, serving both the Tibetan and Ladakhi communities in the best tradition of universal responsibility and care. Beyond just the Tibetan children, the TCV, under the guidance of His Holiness, The Dalai Lama, had extended the cover of education to Ladakhi and other children of the backward areas of Ladakh. Living as refugees, with no motherland to call their own, here they are, dreaming of a free Tibet as they live on the lands of the World's Greatest Democracy that has embraced them, my Motherland. India.

Forget the political leanings of any country of organization, dear reader, for we are humans first, rodents later. With education as the prime drive, these folks seem to be doing a pretty good job of it. Since they are hell-bent on destroying innocent minds with education, maybe, that's the only weapon they have today in order to dream of a free Motherland. And it costs pittance in India to get oneself educated. There are 28 family homes all around as I walk around, with each family home culturally bifurcated into groups of 25 children per home. 25 loud children can drive anyone crazy. Another interesting part of my day-walk was around the six hostels, where girls and boys are separated once they reach their teens. Teenagers, the world over, are a different species. And then you have similar groups of morons, like you, dear reader, who bought this book. With a well-rounded multi-lingual education that teaches these tykes English, Hindi and Tibetan, the alumni list of the same now goes beyond 70,000; such bright young people infused into the world. A great and a wonderful network effect that reminds one of the movie 'Avatar'; this is very similar.

Tenzin Rabatan, our friend, who works at the TCV, explained to us the philosophy and the concept of the place. I think I would have registered round 20% of what he said as he is an intelligent man. After all, he is an alumni from TCV, Ladakh. He works in the school primarily because it gives him job satisfaction. He is married and has two kids and both of them are studying in TCV. I realized then the vicious trap that I am caught in. Here was a person, who has absolutely no need for money, makes do with what he has and all he lives for is a greater cause. He is not alone. Like him, there are hundreds of others living their lives selflessly, propagating the tenets of Buddhism, and all they aspire for is to churn out good human beings. We now proceeded to visit the most impacted flood-hit areas.

The floods had completely devastated Leh. At least 103 people were killed and another 370 injured when flash floods triggered by torrential rains struck this Himalayan town in Ladakh region, northeast of Jammu and Kashmir, leaving a trail of death and destruction. Massive rescue operations were underway involving the state police, paramilitary forces and the army in Leh town. Security personnel were also rushed from Kargil to assist the civil administration in rescue and relief operations. Nobody really had the body count of those missing. They would never ever be found. It hadn't rained like this in Leh, or so they claimed, for the past 50 years. The stupid cloudburst had exploded over Leh like a septic tank gone wild and had led to this deluge with absolutely no mercy. Derek and self had updated our status messages on Facebook asking God to stop the rains, after all, that was all we could do on the fateful night of August 6th, 2010. It had worked, even though God was not there on our friends list.

While many villages like Sabu, Phyang, Nimoo and Choglamsar were affected, the city bore the maximum brunt of the calamity. The communication equipment of BSNL was also washed away in the flash floods and rains that hit the town and adjoining villages in middle of night at around 2 AM. Various buildings and mud-houses in old Leh town were wiped out in the incessant rains. The cloudbursts left a trail of death and destruction. The district hospital was flooded, bus stands flattened and vehicles were seen floating in the town. Leh is located at a height of 11,500 feet above sea level, 424 kilometres from Srinagar.

Jammu and Kashmir Police had set up two camps and were providing food and shelter to nearly 2,000 people and the camps would remain operational till alternate arrangements were being made. Not being allowed into Leh by road was one thing; there was no way to get into Leh, as the so-called roads and bridges had been washed away. 50 CRPF jawans were rescued from the flooded areas, Khoda said, adding the JKAP building was also washed away in the rains.

The dead included three Army Supplies Corps jawans and three Jammu and Kashmir Armed Police (JKAP) constables. Home Minister P Chidambaram had said that over 6,000 security personnel had been deployed in Leh to carry out the rescue operations to see what and who could be saved after the dance of death that destroyed Leh in less than an hour. The district hospital and two buildings housing offices of the Union Home Ministry were also affected. All commercial flights from Delhi to Leh were cancelled and somehow, thanks to friends, we managed to get into one of the first empty flights to Leh. A defence spokesman said many civilians, including foreign tourists, were stranded at various places and efforts were on to rescue them. The affected areas stretched from Pang Village on Rohtang-Leh Highway up to Nimmu on Leh-Srinagar Highway, a distance stretching nearly 169 kms.

Now there was no internet connectivity, no TV, no newspapers and absolutely no semblance of happiness in the place. As we visited the Sonamlin Tibetan Settlement at Leh, my mind was racing with thoughts. They were swirling. In fact, any thought has a lot of place to do any kind of acrobatics in my head, there's lots of space for thoughts in there. There were makeshift camps around the place. Smiling faces greeted us in spite of such adverse conditions. And that sight was enough to make one think. Derek reeled, I was nauseous and Goose was all teary for we had not seen so many happy, smiling faces since the karaoke night in New Delhi. We continued to walk and move towards the piles of upturned vehicles, dried up canals – which would be the burial grounds for all those who were killed in their sleep after the vulgar dance of death a few nights ago. As I walked, I saw people around me with masks, trying to salvage what they could. One problem with Leh is that even during normal conditions, it looks like a place devastated by floods. Similar to many towns in India that look all bombed-out after a war. But this was real and we knew it. I was walking on what was once a canal; no one knew how many bodies had been buried underneath. Everywhere we went, there were reminders of life. An open book on integral calculus, a pink bag with Cinderella on it, a notepad with nursery rhymes, comic books, toys and dolls amidst upturned cars and trucks, muddy waters and dry patches. As I stood on a mound, I wondered how many children had been buried alive that night. Right in the patch that I was standing on. They were still pulling out bodies, parts of them. The place was filthy and stank of death. The fear of epidemic was large. I think I saw Derek cry as Tenzing

Rabten explained to us how the water from the mountains had come surging down and devastated places in and around Leh and Choglamsar. There was a huge shortage of drinking water and medical supplies all around.

Of course, Death knows no nationalities, religion and things like that. With over 400 dead in Pakistan, over 3000 dead in China....the hearts of people from around the world bled for all. And the stupid politicians across countries were acting like jerks when it came to relief funds. Thank God for United Nations. I hope someday all the important cities of all countries become Union Territories like Chandigarh. I'm told that a Union Territory comes directly under United Nations and is not impacted by the territorial pissings of world leaders and greedy nations. As we continue to walk on mangled tin shutters from shops and broken doors, which now form part of the road, one cannot help but look around a wider patch of devastation where I see Nancy Drew novels, dictionaries, study books, utensils, piggy banks and sleeping bags – all semi-buried in mud with the nearby canal loudly gushing out muddy water.

Having seen the devastation caused by the floods and all the good work the TCV staff was doing, under the guidance of the Director of TCV, Ladakh, Mr. Tsering Palden, we decided to go ahead and sponsor a few girl children over there. We were travelling over dusty traces of former roads in Leh now, while listening to some painful Tibetan song by an NRTI (Non-Resident Tibetan in India), our guide Dorje, all of 32 years and a person we shall always remember for taking us to the worst hit areas of Leh. Having experienced the network effect of humanity, born of good, happiness and love, we ended up sponsoring three children between the three of us. As we stayed on in the school premises, overnight, our caretaker from Tibet – Njima, told us horror stories about what happens to Tibetans in Tibet and how they get tortured when they try to cross over the mountains and escape Chinese rule. Politics is not my forte, not shall it ever be. At night, we lit up three candles, stared at them and experienced the change that was slowly taking place in each one of us. Of course, any change that we went through would only be for the better. Day One had taught us much, after all, I am an educated illiterate of India like many of us. I dozed off as the candles lit up our room and we didn't have anything to talk about today.

Day two in Leh

It is so cold that I don't feel cool anymore; in fact, my words are turning into icicles and dropping to the floor. We are going to find Jack Frost and we are going to bury him alive in the snow. Morning happened, as I scratched my....head and crawled out of bed. Goose was trying to call his girlfriend and by mistake he dialed his Dad's cell phone number. Derek timed out....what was Goose's father doing with his girlfriend so early in the morning? Derek was the reason I became hooked to cold icicle baths every morning. Anyone who used to take a shower, we would know as one could hear the teeth chattering all over the house. After all, we were going to meet the three children we had sponsored and were eager to meet them. I had picked up a Barbie story book, some fairy tale books, a pencil box and some scrap stuff and had taken care to have everything wrapped in pink. Women and girls the world over like pink for some strange, funny reason. You want them happy? Wear pink. As confusion reigned supreme with these clowns around me, I was finally rescued by the Mr. Tsering Palden and his Man-Friday, Rabatan, who had come over to help us plan the day that included spending time at the school, the facilities, other areas and devastated structures in Leh, and a visit to the Thikse Gompa, followed by a formal dinner.

Watching the kids gather at the basketball court praying for courage, strength and fortitude, Derek concluded that fortitude is equal to two twentitudes. There were about 400 children and 17 teachers in the morning assembly and a very sick feeling engulfed me as my blood froze in horror. The fear that I used to experience many years ago came back to me as I realized that I stood right in front of the scariest place on earth – the 'Staff Room'. A place that breeds teachers, principals and lecturers, a place worse than mosquito breeding grounds. Derek decided to pay homage to all teachers that night by bringing out a bottle of Scotch with that name, the same night. He was always respectful, that boy, Derek. I passed two signs brightly pasted on the walls. The first one read "Others before Self" and the other one "The greatest mistake a man can do is to be afraid of making one". Derek concluded by combining the two mistakes and for a strange reason, it made sense. It read "The greatest mistake a man can do is to be afraid of putting others before self". Those rare mistakes in life that turn out alright? Well, this was one.

And then I saw Tenzing Choekyi and Dawa Lhamo, both of them wearing blue trousers, striped blue shirts, green pullovers with yellow borders. Choekyi wants to become a Doctor and Lhamo wants to become a teacher. They will. Both are like angels fallen from the sky. Short cropped hair, a hint of a smile as they know Derek and I are watching them. Goose is going crazy with his glass eye. The innocence in a child's eyes, he concludes, cannot be captured by any camera. As I sit on the aisle by the playground, memories of my happy childhood engulf my puny mind. Sitting by the side of the School Gompa (Temple), I see boys and girls in their uniforms loitering all around the place, cramming up before the exams at the last minute. A visit to the Computer lab reveals 40 computers with state of art configuration. The assembly of each machine, coincidentally, costs INR 18,000/- apiece, same as sponsoring a child's education at the TCV for a year. Derek, Goose and self have blown up multiples of these amounts in one single night.

Next we proceed to the assembly of the secondary section and watch Goose's child, Tenzin Londen as Derek and I ogle at those pretty, pretty higher secondary teachers. I remember one of my mathematics teachers from school, whom I squarely blame for my inability to learn to count beyond five, ogling and learning don't go together. As we watch the assembly of the higher secondary children at the school, I see that nothing has changed in the past few years. There are always those four categories of children in any school world over – Nerds, Geeks, Dorks and Jocks. The jocks will always be found at the back of the classroom, the nerds in the front, the geeks on the side and the dorks....er....um...a bit out of place.

The last leg of the facility visit is the library where there are over a thousand books on Philosophy, Psychology, Religion, Social Sciences, Applied Sciences, Mathematics and Technology. I see Ayn Rand's epic 'Fountainhead' under the technology section. It is true, the librarian is a moron and I do agree with him in terms of the placement of this book. Kunchok Tsomo now walks me over to the most important section of any library – the comic books section. Tintin, Asterix, Marvel and Jataka tales. I know the kids will learn much more here than in any stupid class room. TCV can lead the children down the right path. Their selection in comic books is just right.

As we cross over to visit a dormitory that houses little teenage girls, we watch two girls playing with four pebbles and a ball. We join in and have a gal (or gala? 'Gal' is apt too) time. Before leaving, I try to count the number of toothbrushes near the sink. I'm told there are 25 of them and a matron. Maybe, the matron doesn't brush her teeth. As we pass by the kindergarten section, we spend some time inside the classroom taking pictures. I learn the terrific levels of patience demonstrated by the teachers. A successful visit to the school after all, I now know where the money goes and how it is spent. It is enough for me to walk away from the school with a commitment I make for myself. For the Women and Children of India. This was too much to handle. In fact, way too much to handle for all of us. I needed some spiritual healing. Like right now.

Thoughts from Thiksey Gompa

Thiksey Gompa is one of the most beautiful monasteries and is approximately 18 km from the town of Leh. I am given to understand that it belongs to the Gelukpa Order of Buddhism, and was built on a hilltop near the Indus River, by Sherab Zangpo in the 14th Century. The original monastery was built at Stakmo. There are temples, numerous artifacts, ancient paintings on the walls and other things that spell 'Peace'. The monastery also plays host to the Gustor ritual, organized from the 17th to 19th day of the ninth month on the Tibetan calendar. Sacred dances also form a part of this ritual, which takes place on an annual basis. As I drive up the road to the hilltop, a spectacular sight unfolds. Climbing up into the monastery and just sitting there, gives one immense peace. As I sit in front of a few idols, a surreal ray of light fills the room. We are there. Inside the sanctum sanatorium where the idols are so serene and calming, something we really needed after what we had seen in the past few days.

Notes from inside a Gompa

Needless to say, the aura I feel in here is beyond description, beyond ordinary words. The sound of silence, the voices in my head – not the nasty ones, but those calming ones as if a bunch of angels are singing in unison, the happiness in my soul I feel now as I write from barely three feet away from the idols, I am blessed. I must keep my pen down now and take in the silence for a while. The smiling picture of His Holiness, the Dalai Lama, is here as well. And it is the first time in my life I note that no matter where I go in Ladakh, wherever this is some good work happening, or there is happiness, there is a picture of His Holiness. I want to meet him all the more. The sentiment is echoed by Derek and Goose as well. A living God if you will, he intrigues me and the desire to seek his blessings overwhelms us. The dim light inside the sanctum sanatorium comes alive. Like a ray of sunshine, it falls on the peaceful idols in front of me. A sense of calm and serenity fills me so completely now. There is this small window to my left that lets the sunshine in and illuminates the idols. It inspires me. Peace fills the room. I notice that this is a small room, paved with flagstones, as I walk across to see the splendid landscape dotted with rugged mountains and open fields. The monastery has been untouched by the floods. It stirs the soul. It makes me smile. While Goose tries out all kinds of stunts to capture the beauty of the place, Derek is all confused yet pleasantly surprised. Derek had walked into a monastery for the first time in his life and was expecting a lot of 'Monasters' in here, just like those in the Hobbit movies. Instead, he sees monks in pink robes and now he is desperate to get one of those cool pink robes. Goose gives up as his dumb glass eye fails to capture the beauty of the place and hates it when the shutter makes such an out-of-place sound inside the monastery. The eyes of the idols fill my heart with warmth not known to me before. This must be heaven and I must be on Cloud # 69....

Notes from…er…outside a Gompa

A visit to the Druk Prema or the Druk White Lotus School after the Thikse Gompa stirred the heart yet again. The devastation here was complete. Driving from the monastery down to this school of day-scholars, the devastation was total. The infrastructure is wiped off. Classrooms filled with mud and slush scream a silent scream of agony as the place is devoid of any children or their laughter now. As I stumble from one classroom to another classroom, the images of what it used to be once flashes before my eyes. Out of breath, as I park myself in what was once a classroom upstairs, I hear the sobbing of an overgrown gorilla of a Frenchman, sitting inside a classroom, holding his head between his hands and taking in the reality of this washed-out place of learning for children in place of what it once used to be. After this visit to the 'Druk Lotus' School, all we wanted to be was to get 'Drunk, which was more a lot-like-us'.

Everywhere I go, the devastation is so visible. As the relief work continues, the 6000+ relief personnel from the ITBP (Indo-Tibetan Border Police) toil to bring back the town of Leh back to what it once was. Locals say that the town has been set back by 20 years. Derek cannot comprehend that as we have seen towns in worse condition during this trip, and they have not been hit by floods. For us, the loss of lives is more important than those run-down, beaten hutments and mud-houses. For one can sure about the fact that the run-down, beaten hutments and mud-houses will spring back once again, all over Leh within days. People like us tend to mistake regular houses made of mud to be devastated, flood-hit places and choose the wrong charities to send money across to. Same applies to so many of these so-called, useless NGOs and Social Service organizations, who tend to pick up really sorry-ass people from equally sorry-ass dwellings from the region, make brochures and websites and market them all over the globe. I mean, these sorry-ass faces tend to do a thing or two to melt your heart and one ends up sending money to the wrong organizations, with no serious intent behind them.

I once remember looking at a brochure of an NGO near Bangalore which had pictures of young and old people., That's when a thought, which probably reflects more sensitivity to the real cause and motives rather than some of these organizations, occurred to me – have you ever noticed how they deliberately pick out those real sorry-assess, who would look sad and pathetic no matter how happy and young they might really be? I mean, there are some people in this world and specifically in our rural areas who just look sad. Period. They could have had the best crop this year, they might have found buried treasure while ploughing their fields, they might have had five of their huge loans from the government waived-off after threatening to go on a hunger strike and would be considering to marry two thirteen-year-olds in the absence of one twenty-six year-old in the village, yet when they face a camera, they suddenly tend to shrivel and look all sorry-assed the moment they smell a fat wallet behind a camera or inside a passing tourist vehicle. The point I am trying to make here, dear reader, is that you need to pick out the right social cause. And that's exactly what we did. With the Tibetan School Village in Leh and Mahesh Memorial Foundation in Chennai. No fancy stuff here, just real people trying to do some good work in the real world. As we walk around the Leh market now, which wasn't impacted by the cloud-burst at all owing to its geo-political position (God knows why I typed that, but it sure sounds cool!), a medley of thoughts plague us all. Sometimes, it is good to have a lot of free space in your head, just like an empty hard-disk. So, if your computer is fast or slow, you know what I mean. As we covered the Shanti Stupa and sat in a local place of worship over there, a sense of calm took over my soul. Goose was quiet and so was Derek. This was probably the first time I had seen them numb without alcohol. The "Jewel in the Crown of India", as Leh is popularly known as, now resembled Jimi Hendrix in full bloom. As we continued to drive across a land full of dust, slush, upturned vehicles and people wearing masks, there were some people with small black thingies, barely the size of a human male-nut. To be used like smelling salts, they keep sniffing that and staying alive.

As we reached our humble abode at the Tibetan School Village in Choglamsar again, we were greeted by Mr. Tsering Paldin (Director), Mr. Chogyal Tashi (Principal) and our Man-Friday and the coordinator of TCV, Leh – Tenzing Rabten. Listening to them speak that night was like tanking up on Bacardi and Redbull. The humility and selflessness in them was like having a few Jägerbombs, minus the ill effects. Instead, it must have been like drinking some kind of holy water, for as we left in the morning to catch a flight out of Leh, we were not morons anymore. We had become morons with a noble cause, devoid of political or religious leanings. We just wanted to do something good for the women and children across the world. We had learnt much about history. But since I have been historically messed up, a history lesson about Huns, Manchurains, Mangolians, Turishtan and Tibet sounded no different than cuisine we should be trying out or had been missing for a long time.

Well, this is as good as it gets then, for we decided to take a little break and get deeper into....having some serious fun on the roads.

HOPping to Conclusions

▶ *Raincoats do not always work; sometimes, you have no choice left but to die*

▶ *Walking on graves is no fun, in fact, walking is no fun when you re dead*

▶ *Education doesn't save lives, but can give you a better life*

▶ *When you run the risk of being tortured in any country, just run like the wind*

▶ *There is more to life than getting Leh'd without a reason*

▶ *Too much water is never good for mankind*

▶ *The Human Network is far more useful than a dumb cell phone Network*

▶ *Politics is not good for health*

▶ *Someday, soon, HOP Nation, along with Credit card companies will break down physical and geographical boundaries, so get yourself a credit card today and keep your ratings clean*

▶ *Tour guides in Leh play horrible songs*

13 On the Road: No Sugar, No Milk...Back After Getting Leh'd

When nothing works your way, it is best to drive like hell,
For once the head clears up, it all ends well;
A little slice of life and a fun ride through the hills,
Of crazy antics, some loony driving and cheap thrills;
Livin' the way we were born, all truth and no lies,
You die as a human, the day the Calvin in you dies;
Foolish behavior and weirdo acts, it makes me say 'Cheese'
Drive on, for that's when you go 'Horn OK Please'...

The Fountain Head of Trash indulges in masturbation after getting Leh'd

I am sitting in an aisle seat as I scratch my...head. When I rub my chin, people think I'm deep, but when I rub my crotch, people think I'm a pervert. As I sit in the aircraft on our way back from Leh to New Delhi, some really deep and *Duh!!* moments take over my mind. The inside of the aircraft is so bright red and so are the air-hostesses, I'm glad the flight will land in a few more minutes. I skim through my notes and I rub my chin so, dear reader, you now know what it means. Ladakh had reminded me of New York minus buildings. There was not a tree in sight for miles and I saw people of many nationalities loitering about. The 'Jewel in the Crown' of India had seemed more like cheap imitation jewelry from one of our neighboring countries, peddling cheap stuff from sweat shops.

As I watch an air-hostess pushing the trolley, I wonder why some passengers cannot behave themselves and instead end up harassing these hard-working young girls doing their best to provide you with good service. I mean, many middle-aged men are lecherous bastards who fail to understand the difference between 'harass' and 'her – ass'. Sigh! I guess, middle age is when your middle starts giving your age away and that's when they suck in the air, show sallow cheeks and fake a flat tummy when all they have to boast of is no chest, but man-tits, a double chin, an ugly paunch and zero likeability. Fitness in Indian males in this age bracket continues to be a myth. Talking about myths makes me think about nothing to seem intelligent, deep and cool, the way we do it in Bangalore pubs. After hours of thought about nothing, the conclusion would be that thinking is of no use, no sir, none at all. In fact, thinking is bad for health. If you are thinking while driving, then it gets you closer to the nether world as anyways, dear reader, no one is going to give you a free pass to heaven now that you've bought this book.

A deluge of stupidities came to my mind as we were getting ready to land at the New Delhi Airport. I was going to be getting back on the road again and I was happy.

Random musings from Cloud # 69

In fact, thinking about nothing is what I attempted once upon a time when I was sitting in front of a waterfall in Himachal

Pradesh en route to Manali. We had tried thinking while looking at the same object and I reached different conclusions. Sitting in front of a waterfall, beer in hand, it made me want to pee in exactly thirty minutes. After sixty minutes, staring at the same waterfall and post two sandwiches, it had made me want to take a dump soon as I touched the hand-sanitizer and a napkin. Staring at the waterfall and listening to Goose and Derek talk their hearts out made me want to puke in just five minutes. So we decided to leave the place and head out towards Manali. As we ploughed Motormouth through a place called Raison towards Manali, a pretty commercial hill station that is the gateway to Ladakh or J&K by road, I couldn't help but admire the pine trees that dotted the hills around us. You see, pine trees are how trees should be. They know how to grow, they are straight, well groomed, green and make the country side look pretty. Compare the same to what one gets to see in say, Madhya Pradesh or Bihar, there are these wretched trees with cobwebs and you'd feel like razing them to the ground with a B2 Stealth Bomber in one go. We should all plant trees, pine trees. Pine also rhymes with wine, so it sounds cool. Unruly Banyan trees are worse, they look so shaggy and have roots all over. In India, they are supposed to be the abode of demons and ghosts as well. Isn't that cool? I can visualize it in tomorrow's headline news and all over my RSS feeds, "Funky old witch named Helga falls off her banyan tree and kills hundreds of goblins with her horrible looks". Banyan trees should be banished and all their seeds or saplings and what have you should be sent to Africa. At least Tarzan can go all 'Kreegah' and 'Bundolo' and be the real swinger that he is over there. Same applies to some dumb, funny looking, stray animals found all across India. If PETA loves them so much, they should take them home with them or dump them in no-man's land where there are no people anyways. Let them live, let us live; for such animals are very unclean people. Here I go rambling again…..

Most of the times while on the road, it would be me with my notes when I was not driving, Goose fiddling with his camera when he was not driving, Derek thrashing some cat in the backseat when he was not driving. Usually, Motormouth would be a mobile concert house. Like any other road-trip by road-hogs the world over, we were no exception. Having thrown out the entire collection of crappy Trance and house music that Goose used to listen to at the beginning of the trip, the music for us was always Hoobastank, Metallica, Collective Soul, Kid Rock, Blink 182 and other such decent bands. Derek maintained that Trance and other crappy offshoots of House music were very similar to the kind of stuff that was invented by the Germans during World War II. An experiment gone wrong when Hitler's army was trying to create the sound bomb. Or maybe, they did succeed. Driving through those long winding roads, listening to Michael Buble's 'Sway' was an exception as that can probably be the best song for the curvy roads between Manali and Dharamsala, both in Uttarakhand or Uttaranchal or Uttar Kingdom or some state like that. Pardon my ignorance about the latest statistics as I write this chapter after 50 days of being disconnected from the Indian political news. The number of states might have gone up, some names of cities may have changed, some new states may have been created, but what the heck – everything else stays the same.

The long winding roads, off-roading and camping had left us with nicks and bruises here and there. While I was walking like Long John Silver, Goose was walking like the Hunchback of Notre Dame and Derek was walking as if he had grown thorns in his crotch. Out in the wilderness, where technology and gizmos can go for a toss with absolutely zero network connectivity, I was walking around like that fascinating cowboy of yesteryear called 'Lucky Luke', just that my six-shooters were all smoked out and all our gadgets were down. The holster on my left hip had an Android phone and the other hip sported a blackberry. Goose was an iPhone addict and Derek was a sex-addict. He was right now desperate enough to hump a Yak as well. He just wanted to get out of Himachal, Ladakh and all such places where he had got massively disappointed as getting Leh'd was not exactly what he had in mind. He very clearly wanted to go to Rajasthan next to see 'Camel Toes' and watch the camel's hump when he was done. Now that tickled our man very much. The pretty women of the mountains were the only respite for us for days as we got sick and tired of looking at trees, waterfalls, breath-taking views, and the like. We needed to get back on good roads to get our lives back. People in the mountains walk a lot, therefore hilly regions in India have no proper roads as they have been worn out by pedestrians, cyclists, hikers, cyclists and other such despicable beings on earth.

Slowly, with the humming sound of the plane playing on my mind, I drifted into a dream. Having been through the flat lands at varying speeds between 120 Kmph and 160 Kmph, the hilly region was forcing us to crawl. I swear I once saw a centipede overtake Motormouth and we were so devastated. And Motormouth has not come in contact with water since our trip through Rajasthan cutting through Jaipur, Udaipur and some other dirty villages that need no mention in this book. Pick up a map and check out the route if you are so curious. Coming back to the point, we had this real goon of a flunkey in Udaipur, who just couldn't bear the sight of dirty ol' Motormouth. Having driven all the way from Gujarat and off-roaded in Rajasthan, she was dirty and we had run out of spit. In Goa, when we had visited the Daman Fort, it made absolutely no sense to Derek. We had a tough time convincing him that this was built by the Portuguese in India and it was not because they had run out of space in Portugal. The boy had a point you see, it's like going to New Jersey and watching all those people from Hyderabad over there. Similarly, we saw only Indians here in a Portuguese fort in Gujarat. But the best fort I would recommend to any Tom, Dick or Harry would be the Chittorgarh Fort in Rajasthan. Nothing can beat that experience and locals, like any other locals in any locality, claim that it is the largest fort in the whole world.

Hukum Singh, our flunkey in Udaipur, spent hours cleaning and washing Motormouth. We were pissed drunk and had passed out in the afternoon. We woke up and decided to go to this commercial palace on top of a hill and explore the surrounding areas. By the time we go back at night, Motormouth was once again covered in layers of dust. I swear we heard Hukum Singh howling in pain that night and in the morning we saw scratch marks on the door. No, wait, they weren't scratch marks, they were his teeth marks as he had tried to bite through our door. We had quietly slipped away in the morning before the goon could wake up. I guess, we just got lucky. There is a superstition that I had heard when I was a kid and it was about bird shit being lucky. If this is true, well, we had so many birds splattering on our windscreen, we must be really lucky then. That's probably how we managed to escape the curse of Hukum Singh, who looked like a cross between Frankenstein and Mayawati.

Back on the road, Derek complained of some un-mechanical sounds that were coming from Motormouth. It took us a while to figure out that we were hungry. Derek needed iron as he believed that is what is needed to have a magnetic personality. I was worried that he would start chewing on Motormouth. At night, I decided to chew on my bedcovers so I could make up for the low-fiber diet on the road as I hadn't had a well-balanced diet in weeks. Goose' stomach has a life of its own and would growl and demand crap at its own whim. The Oh-so-painfully-slow trucks and toll gates take their toll alright, maybe, that's why they are called 'Toll gates'.

Somewhere, in the midst of nowhere, we saw this horrible looking shack in the middle of nowhere, where all the lowest levels of living beings must come to feed. Since we were anyways the remnants of an after-scrape barrel exercise, it suited us just fine. Just that, the food was a wee-bit too spicy. A very big 'WEE-BIT' at that. So we whined and dined and griped and sulked. Of course, nobody cared. I could now understand why we Indians use water instead of toilet paper; the shit would burn toilet paper any day and take us to newer heights of levitation the subsequent morning. It becomes worse when you get drunk and pass out in the night. Then you have this booting-up syndrome in the morning and a severe case of acidity, so you must have a fresh glass of soap water to neutralize the aftermath.

There was this small hair-cutting saloon beside the shack where we decided to go for a haircut and a massage with horrible smelling oils. We now knew what it takes to smell like shit. In order to beat the odor, I had to keep on moving, lest the stench get into my nose and choke me to death, before discovering a nearby stream. We must have bathed for about a half-hour to get the stench off. Now we smelled of fish. So much for a bath. We now decided not to have a bath at all for the next one week. We'd rather spray ourselves with all kinds of deodorants and walk around and pretend to be human beings. Derek caught the fancy of a mountain girl over there who was womanning the place. He is a doer, that nut. He got lucky and he decided to do her in the backseat of Motormouth. Yet another reason, Derek explained, why SUVs make so much more sense than dinky cars. He had yet again defeated a young cat in the backseat. The old cow who was getting us 'chai'...while Derek went about doing the deed, Goose took some real cool pictures of her udder-side as part of Derek's collectibles. All we wanted now was a night in a decent hotel with clean sheets and a microwave oven. Clean beds to sleep in and the microwave to dry our clothes after washing. Of course, a microwave oven works best on the classic 5-pocket blue jeans. We had become smarter and were learning to overcome the fury of the elements, as you would have noted by now, dear reader.

Back in the saddle again, onward Himachal Pradesh, UK, UP and what-have-you

The aircraft landed and I am wide awake and happy to get out of the red flight. It was more like getting from Leh to New Delhi inside a flying tomato owned by some rich and fat dipsomaniac. If they call this 'Incredible India', I endorse it. I call it 'Incredibly Funny India'. Have you met some of our leaders? Which fool said we lack a sense of humor? Try eating what I ate somewhere in the armpits of Bihar and you'd call it 'Inedible India'. So when you don't like the food or wish to complain, stuff yourself with bananas till you go 'Cheep-cheep'.

We leave the airport and head towards Motormouth and pay the parking attendant, whose constipated face looks like she's just been made to drink some really bitter medicine. Part of her face is covered by her hair, maybe she thinks it makes her look kind of cute. Yeah, I guess, she does. Maybe, if I were really nice to her, she would let me chop off some of that hair that falls on her face and we could use it to clean Motormouth's windshield that always seems to have splattered bug-shit-marks, blood stains of confused or drunken birds flying too low, or some stray mutt with a death-wishor a dumb pussy living out its ninth life. The hair would be super-cool, lady. Can I take you out on a date, cover your face with a paper bag and poke you…in the eye for a clump of 'Helga-hair' in return, please?

Derek and Goose walk like Siamese twins in front of me. I realize that we are all wearing the same cargos, same smelly socks, same hiking boots, the "Chief", "Goose" and "Derek" T-Shirts, contacts, Raybans and attitude since the beginning of the trip. And we walk with a swagger, trying to look cool and I guess we're alright and life is cool. Derek tries to clean the windshield before he slips behind the wheel and pumps up the stereo with 'Blink 182', a cool song called 'What's my age again' and we zip through New Delhi to reach the highway. We gloat over the woes of some poor fool who has been pulled over by a traffic cop. Pulled over for driving at 80 Kmph in the city? That too in a dinky car that looks like half-a-car or a half-butt Helga? For driving an ugly car? He is talking to them right now. My heart bleeds for him. Again, he was pulled over for driving such an ugly car.....or was that a spray-painted wheelbarrow? Anyways, really happy to see these high-octane alpha-males with a sprout of a beard get into trouble. With lard bulging and oozing out from all over, they have some hopeless misconceptions about mixing 'Desi ghee' in their fuel and running their pathetic beasts. Anyways, half of Delhi's population lives for others, the other half is from outside. On the good side, there is no better place for a foodie than up North of India. People here love food, live for food and just simply love to feed people. The concept of a hungry, third world poor country is not what Delhi and the surrounding states is known for. I have always left Delhi with a heavy stomach and a light heart and this must be 'Paradise City' as sung by 'Guns n Roses'. Axl Rose must have had New Delhi in mind and knowing what a prized jack-ass he is, I am sure he would have love the concept of a 'Langar', just like Lemmy from Motorhead.

Passing through Punjab, the Langar concept hit us straight in the face with over 150 makeshift establishments stopping us at every place, filling Motormouth with fruits, lassi, dessert and an invite to come and join the party. The term Langar, from the Sikh religion, stands for free (yes, free!) vegetarian food served in a Gurdwara. They care a hang about your dietary restrictions, your calorie count or your weight watching exercise as they feed you and plead with you to eat with so much love that you don't really mind watching your weight grow. Everybody is an equal here and one has to experience the hospitality of the Sikhs and Non-Sikhs to believe it. All that food left Derek sick. One tends to wonder why the fools from around the world who come to India looking for poverty and illiteracy do not report of this concept. These idiots would prefer to paint a gory and a starving picture of India, else all their money spent on video tapes and movie tickets on Indiana Jones and monkey brains would go waste and their myths would be so shattered. So they report hunger and poverty only.

Since we had all the time in the world to kill, and as we had no plans, and there wasn't even a semblance of a route map to be followed now, we figured we had about a week to cover this part of Himachal Pradesh and Uttarakhand. Goose wanted to check out Dehradun and Mussoorie, so Dehradun and Mussoorie it was. Derek wanted to see Kasauli and Haridwar for some strange reason, so Kasauli and Haridwar it was. We had crossed New Delhi thrice and it was kind of getting on our nerves, crossing the same rivers and densely populated areas. Somewhere down the line it became clear that if we had to spend another night in the same city, we would sulk or get mad at each other or both. So, cutting across some places of no relevance in Uttar Pradesh and Haryana, we cut across to Himachal Pradesh and UK, as we like to call it. Half of UP seemed to be on the road, by the side of it or squatting like mile-stones in their white-kurtas and black moustaches. The roads also included some politicians, red lights, eight vehicles in front, eight vehicles in the back and all the police force and security personnel with booby toys et al, and all we wanted was out of such places.

I must say that though we hated that obnoxious woman whom we had managed to trap inside the black rectangular box called the GPS, the 'Map my India' maps were the only way we could reach wherever we wanted to. We drove like crazy, we drove like mad. City to city we went, we had our

HOPper friends, thanks to the fan following around this book. They helped us, sheltered us, partied with us and somewhere down the line, each one of them shall have a very special place in my deep, black heart always. As we went zipping through some towns of UP, where hygiene had not been invented, I also noted that there are some villages in India, who have managed to cunningly trick Darwin. Evolution has not touched these villages and people had managed to trick civilization. Maybe once upon a time, when the waves of evolution were travelling across the earth, these tiny villages cunningly avoided getting on the radar of the evolution people. They still belong to the Fred Flintstone era, pick their mates by hitting young girls with their clubs and fight over castes, religions and sub-castes or what-have-you. We must have passed many of those villages which would either be hit floods or droughts throughout the year, after all, politics is a very dirty game.

Since we were, maybe, heading toward Mussoori, we did some heavy amount of off-roading, just to confuse the bitch called 'Helga'. After all, Helga is a depiction of that evil woman who is full of shit and negative things like that. She hates us. She hates anyone who is happy. And now, we were confused and at the mercy of Helga. I thought we were in UK, we were in Uttarakhand. Derek thought we were on our way to China. Goose thought we were on our way to Manila. And Helga was all set to push us off a cliff. It rained and poured during the day, it poured and rained at nights and so we were happy to have that as a pleasant change. The confusion arose when we were to go to Mussoori…need I tell you more?

Up from Dehradun, which is a town of dinky cars, tricycles, truckloads of kids, burgers dipped in oil as though they have a contract with an Arabian Sheikh and are out to finish all the oil reserves in hurry, and the prettiest places and the nicest people as well. There is something warm about the place where I forgot my license in a hotel of which I have no recollection of the name. A sneeze away from Dehradun, up there is Mussoori. If you peed in Mussoori, it would rain in Dehradun.

Somewhere in Mussoori, we went and checked out some place called the 'Sisters Bazaar', since Derek wanted to watch some pretty girls lick ice cream. We saw some bizarre sisters devouring pizzas instead. The serene places of interest for me were of course the places where I could get my cup of tea and Maggi noodles. With peas. Hills are all about peas and potatoes, if you remember this lesson from a previous chapter. Farmers on top of the hill grow peas and potatoes, bring them to the plains and sell them at a premium. Farmers who live on the plains also grow peas and potatoes and cart them all the way up to the mountains and sell them at a premium. That's what farmers around these parts do. It's all about growing peas and potatoes, selling them where they can be sold at a premium, for whatever reason. So now you know, dear reader, why inflation in India is fast moving towards a double-digit. It's all because of a few people who control the growth of peas and potatoes up in the mountains. If inflation needs to be checked, stop eating peas and potatoes from now on and life will be alright for all of us. Goose wanted to tell the time as we were all lost when it came to time, day, date and so we checked out the Clock Tower, which was a big clock and an equally big disappointment. Thanks to a friend, we could go to a place called Robber's Cave in Dehradun, which was very similar to the Jesse James Hideout near Saint Louis, Missouri, USA. And the similarity between the two nations just increased. A place of gushing water, surrounded by rocks and cliffs on both sides, you could wade through a stretch of 1.5 Kms.

After that, a drive to a peak called the 'Lal Tibba' or something, where we did the typical touristy thing of staring at clumps of trees on top of hills, going Oooh-Aah about it and a couple of keepsake snaps. We were done with it in five minutes and were hungry enough to eat an apple attached to a pig. Somewhere down the line, Goose and Derek had taught me how to pretend to enjoy all these nauseating touristy spots in all these hill-stations just to look a part of the crowd. Anyways, our attire, loud music and an equally loud vehicle with loud people in it always tends to raise eyebrows. The least we can do to appease them is to pretend to enjoy these filthy, unhygienic places which are daily peed-upon by these truck-loads of regular tourists, and make them feel as if they have come to the perfect place on earth.

Haaalp!! Get me outta here, Goose, quick!! For heaven's sake!! I cannot take this touristy shit anymore!!!! Derek, stop leching and get us outta here now!!

Of course, the best place we visited was a food shack called the 'Lovely Omelet Center'. There is something special about this place and the two brothers who run it. The Lovely Omelet Center is a small shop that sells Omellettes…*Duh!!* and is world famous, if for nothing else but the attitude of the owners who walk that extra mile for children on weekends. Nice, hygienic and very simple, we ate like there was no tomorrow, just like any other time, of course.

Derek's curiosity fetish took us to a place that's full of tourists, Godmen and well….Gods. We cut across to a place near Haridwar where Derek stopped by a hardware store to buy some nails and a wooden board. He had heard that many Godmen here sit on a bed of nails, sleep on them, passed a few fakirs doing some crazy rope tricks while avoiding those elephants and flying carpets. He had been told by some dumb, broke tourist from some cheap-shit nation in the Western world, the name of the place I just cannot remember or pronounce. Instead the town was so spiritual that we saw so many people in their innerwear bathing in the Ganges. Devoid of any religious leanings, we took in the true spirit of India. And we were all blessed out and all set to pass out before heading out to someplace else now.

We had taken this cheap-shit hotel in Mussoori where all we could do was to watch the rains from the balcony, which looked like a pile of leaky diapers in the sky, and kill moths in the room with no electricity. Of course, one tends to feel very powerful after killing a few moths. We were THE 'Pathetic Losers' today with nothing better to do in a hotel, where one has to park his car on the terrace. While Goose and I twiddled thumbs in the room, Derek was lucky enough to set himself up with a blind date. Now let's not be too rude, well....um... she wasn't exactly what one would call blind, but she could barely see a few inches away and had the figure of a very large eucalyptus tree. She smelt like one too. Goose concluded that she must be good for a cold. And Derek really didn't mind doing a sackful of potatoes in the past either, so she was cool. But when he started taking off her clothes, his blood froze when he saw that she had 'Golden Tent House' written on her shirt as a label...and he went downhill that moment. There were now three of us musketeers killing mosquitoes with sheer passion that night.

We next decided to appease Derek, who didn't know how and why we needed to go to this town called Cuss-Ollie and why everyone in this town wants to cuss Ollie. Worst of all, he didn't even know who Ollie was. The journey to the place was simply brilliant. I am not sure about the route we took anyways, as Helga barked the orders (the bitch). A few twists and turns for a few hours visiting Solan and Kasuali, listening to Michael Buble's 'Sway'.

Life with toilet rolls and hand sanitizers

Goose had meticulously planned the route, plotted the distances and we had worked it all out, down to the minutest detail like what to eat for breakfast at that location. Derek had taken some real neat print-outs and copies of the same before throwing it all away and letting life take over. Now all we had was attitude – the right one. That had helped us secure an appointment with his Holiness, The Dalai Lama, and we were very excited. We had time to kill till then. With three more days in hand, we started to move toward McLeodgunj, which is where The Dalai Lama stays. Helga wanted to go over a very big garbage dump on a hill called 'Shimla'. A highly overrated place, we couldn't figure out the hype around it. We thought we would halt for lunch as Derek was hungry as usual, Goose was thirsty again and I was exasperated, as always. But when we stopped at this local shack barely on the outskirts of Shimla, out pops a truck driver in his underwear proudly displaying his ringworms as Goose places the order and starts having a bath barely a few feet away. Goose goes first, Derek follows, and then I barfed. That was Shimla for us. We decided to skip it and move on as the experience was way too much for us to handle.

Driving towards Kasauli, a very pretty place not far from Shimla, it's where Derek wanted to take us. We wanted to give Goose a good two days to perch the tripod, make him feel like a real photographer first and then watch a dream unfold. Also, we needed a 'cleanliness-and-hygiene' break big-time. While the images of the Leh children at night were haunting me till now at night, it was Goose or Derek who haunted me all day. And now add to that our friends with ring worms. Goose wisely pointed out that some famous movie called '1969 – A Love Story', a Bollywood hit, was filmed here. As we ploughed our way mercilessly through the traffic of the crowded city of Shimla, we realized that Motormouth needed some loving after the off-roading bit we had done near Mussoori. A wheel cap was off, some nuts were loose, and there were quite a few splatter marks of dead birds and road kill of cats and monkeys. We rattled our way through the beautiful town of Kasauli, which looks like any other proper hill station – replete with an old church, a graveyard, a mall road and shit like that. I couldn't help but wonder why every hill station in India has the same pathetic mould of mall roads, scandal points, suicide points, sunrise and sunset points, cheap-shit chocolates and ghost tales as well. A night at the graveyard in Kasauli and after peeing near a giant tree there, we wanted to see a ghost and hump the living daylights out of her. And so the night began. A very cold and a moonless night, here we were, three morons of the highest order, walking shirtless at two am, searching for a sexy vampire or a ghost or any woman in white, lantern in hand. Sitting on a grave didn't help either. We returned to the resort early morning, disillusioned and shattered. No ghosts, witches or sexy vampires here as well. We need to do something more drastic.

We had checked into a nice resort, into a room with a microwave oven to dry our washed clothes. Since Indian microwaves are very poor in toasting wet underwear, Derek pro-actively set up Goose's tripod and we hung our underwear to dry on them. That sure did the trick. Having achieved this feat, it was really nice to see Goose snoozing, so oblivious to the goings-on. Derek dragged Goose out of the bed as we headed for breakfast; it was getting late and we are never late for anything that is free. Goose and Derek picked out the most expensive items from the menu as I was instructed to learn from the camels, from the way they can go on without water for days. We were to attempt eating a free breakfast, and making it last at least through till dinner. So again, we ate as if there was no tomorrow. Like those dratted puppies who eat too much, we were done with the grubbing and crawled back to the room somehow. Having dozed off the food, the next item on Goose's agenda was to 'borrow' all the complimentary stuff that was kept in the room, the bathroom and all over the place. Derek liked the towels and bath scrubs.

Noooooooooo!!! Goose!! Not the TV, dammit!! Get off the carpet, Derek!! No!! We do NOT need a new carpet!! Haaalp!!

The concept of a 'Goodie-bag' was born in Kasauli for us. We now had a new piece of luggage, that we called the 'Insanity bag'. This housed all the free shoe-polish, shampoo, moisturizers, foot-scrubs, barf-bags, conditioners, soap-bars, wax-apples, soap-stands and just about anything that was free and could be 'borrowed' by us. Who knows – maybe all the shampoo collected now and during the rest of the trip would keep my grand-children free of dandruff; Goose's posterity would save a pile of cash on bath-soap, while Derek's girls would never have to invest in barf-bags ever again. We are smart people now, worldly-wise.

We now had to proceed to McLeodgunj and so we were back in the saddle again. Passing the same funnily named towns again that don't seem funny at all if you happen to be associated with it. Sample a town called 'Sissu' or 'Mandi' and you happen to be born there. It would go like this, "Dear all, meet my friend, Goose, from 'Sissu' and Derek from 'Mandi'. *Barf!!* Thank God, I was not born nor do I live in a town like that. Would you buy a book called 'Horn OK Please' written by some random moron from 'Bhonsari'? As we drove through a random village full of males in Haryana, Derek got a bit upset when he saw many sign-posts on shops that loudly proclaimed "STD". Goose ignored us when I slapped Derek. Passing through Haryana villages was a breeze, a rhyme. With a cuss word here and a cuss word there, here a dick, there a prick, everywhere a hick-hick, it was that regular Scottish farm that now sells burgers and other junk food.

Stopping by for a quick bite, we tried this road-side stall for an early dinner. The cook quivers as if nearing orgasm as he tosses the stir-fried vegetables in the pan with one hand and sprinkles spices with the other. With a frame like a pencil, he shakes rhythmically to the beat of the strenuous act. His mouth open and his face covered in sweat, it is an ugly sight that kills and buries our appetite. We decide to have papayas for dinner instead.

Once again, we did the zig-zag snake thingie at high-speed and spent the night in a town called 'Joginder Nagar' (Imagine a place called like 'Bush Town') in the same cheap-shit motel with our man Friday known as " Monty Python" whom we had convinced to join the Pakistani army last time itself. The guy was a loser. He looked like one. We made him run around to our whims and fancies till the three of us were comfortably numb, got drunk and passed out and waited for the morning again before heading out to Dharamsala and McLeodgunj to meet the Big Daddy.

HOPping to Conclusions

▶ *Always carry a goody bag when you check into a good hotel*
▶ *Never play with a hair dryer pretending to be a rock star in a wet bathroom*
▶ *Remembering names of towns is one thing, pronouncing them right is another*
▶ *Clothes dry well inside a microwave oven. Best for 5-pocket jeans*
▶ *When you don't understand a conversation, it probably makes sense*
▶ *Choose a birthplace that would go with your name before being born*
▶ *Ghosts exist only in movies and books. Some living beings are uglier by far*
▶ *Eat lots of peas and potatoes if you want mountain people to prosper*
▶ *The earth is spinning at an angle because it is tilted by over population*
▶ *To get things done your way, one needs to be born, for which one needs parents*

14 Pride, Not Arrogance

It is not about religion, it is about knowing how to live,
It is not about politics, it is all about being positive;
I didn't change, my thought process did, and it feels
sublime,
For we are the morons, and you gave us so much time;
A life changed, a purpose formed in my head,
Thank you for all those kind words you have said;
You just made us the happiest people on earth,
I'd so like to give it all, for there is no dearth;
A sense of purpose in life, it makes me say 'Cheese'
Drive on, for that's when you go 'Horn OK Please'…

The Morons are back

Mother Nature seems to have been partial to this part of the country. Or maybe, God's just been kind to this part of the planet for it houses His Holiness, The Dalai Lama. As I savor the sweet sights of waterfalls, lush greenery, winding roads and the break of dawn, looking at those pretty angels peeping through the cracks in the sky, Derek and Goose shuffle the music and pump up the volume with Metallica's anthem "Master of the Puppets". Ah! What a perfect morning as we break the silence of these sleepy villages to cross over to McLeodganj to meet His Holiness. Goose has so much fun in watching the other birds get scared and cheep away as Derek downs his gargles with Red Bull. I wonder, am I really blessed? The book-box inside Motormouth breaks the monotony of those irritatingly repetitive and predictable natural sounds of chirping birds, whistling woods, bustling natural springs and the same old crappy shit that one gets to hear in these parts day in and day out. Wow! It must be so painful to turn all silent and serene. Here I am, a blessed soul in the company a dodo bird and a Unicorn with a horn in the wrong place. And I wonder, how folks like us have survived the world till date and continue to drift like flotsam through the journey of life. Without a meaning or a purpose, we just seem to have grown up. The world sure looks at adults differently. Anyways, what the heck! The morons are back with a bang and maybe, just maybe, this meeting might just change a few things inside of us. Any change can only be for the better, I realize when I see Goose chewing on his leather belt for the taste or having to watch the hand of Derek going up and down at six am in the backseat, in the name of morning ablutions. Yeah, I guess, the morons are back when I realize that I feel a bit odd, driving down Motormouth in T-Shirt and underwear. Maybe, that's why Hobbes is still alive in us, as we grew up into bigger Calvins. The goodness in us remains since childhood and it is now time to take it to the next level....whatever that means, but it sure sounds deep. So there.

The Head Quarters of the Tibetan Children's Village School is in Dharamsala, slightly before McLeodganj, where His Holiness, The Dalai Lama resides. We decided to spend a day over here first, check out the facilities, infrastructure and spend some time meeting all those who live so selflessly, trying to create a better world for our children. An absolutely chaotic place, Dharamsala, full of traffic jams and human butter on the road. We cut through the city somehow, on two wheels, with Motormouth tilted on one side and if you believe this, dear reader, you will believe anything.

Before starting our day at the TCV here, all we wanted to see was one place of interest, so we could do some fishing in the evening, as

Derek was super excited to do the same. We reached the Dall Lake, for it is supposed to be a very nice fishing spot on top of the hills, away from the city. We did and I think we parked on the bed of that dumb lake or the *Duh!!*-l lake, for there was not a drop of water in there. Goose concluded that maybe someone shipped out the water as people here might have needed more land to expand the city as it is so congested. We decided to go in search of the lake. Driving up the hills, negotiating treacherous paths where most vehicles would have been stripped off their chassis, Motormouth must have created a few roads that day. But still no lake. Derek concluded that the maybe the sign-post was taken off from Srinagar and some weirdo might have come and plonked it on an empty ground here to trick naïve tourists like us. He had a point. And carrying a sign-post anyways is a lot easier than using a bucket to empty out a lake. We dropped the idea, couldn't find the lake and went straight to the TCV, where we met up with our pretty hostess, Kinchuk Tsomo and Lobosang who walked us through the campus, explaining everything that was explained to us in Ladakh.

As we alighted from Motormouth, we were surrounded by these lovely, giggly schoolgirls who mistook us for celebrities, wanted our wrist bands, badges, posed with us, scribbled on Motormouth's layers of dust that adorned her. They made our day as we connected up on Facebook later, on the HOPfans page and bullied us into giving away more goodies. That was the fun part. After all, teenagers, the world over, they are the same and fun. Some of the kids get all educated and smart and get into good B-Schools. No, Derek!! One doesn't 'Pass-out' of school; that only happens after too much alcohol. One graduates from high school and makes it into college. You then make your own life the way you choose to. No amount of preparation can help if one has the wrong attitude in life. For life is like a one long urine test, no amount of preparation can help and education is like learning how to beat all the wrong things from showing up in the report card when God takes you to task once you're all dead and gone. Derek insisted that his life is a stool test, as he tapped on the nearest bench to sit on. Well, we are talking about normal people here, so Derek may not really be the right sample. And our talks got more stupid after this. It was always like this. Our discussions started off from ridiculous and moved to sublime.

Once again, it all went over my head as I continued to nod my head, trying to look intelligent, while Goose pretended to be an ace photographer adjusting and changing lenses and filters. Derek had no pretensions while ogling at the teachers. Having met the staff and heard them out, I am not sure what really happened as I couldn't help but jump into the basketball court and try out my hand beating those mean little kids hollow. The mean little brats beat me hollow as I panted and wheezed and I realized how smart and well-trained they are. The TCV folks do put their heart and souls into making a better world for the children and they sure have succeeded.

The kind hosts that the Tibetans are, we were ushered into a 'modest' hostel on campus. We pretended that we were so used to luxury that we indeed found the quarters to be very modest. Derek, Goose and I were jumping for joy as soon as they left us alone and when we were sure that nobody would see us. Having lived in tents for the past few days, having shared the bed with truckers, goatherds, piss-doped foreigners and smelly people who hadn't had a bath for months because of the cold climate, this place was far beyond our expectations. A proper bathroom, with two taps that we could share, and a dump yard with loo-rolls, and a mirror as well. That evening, as I went through my notes and we prepared ourselves for the meeting with His Holiness, reading bits and pieces of history and making those small notes to ask questions to the Dalai Lama, we realized that we may have not known much about history, but the three of us shared a very deep-rooted sense of doing something right for the children at TCV. So 25% of whatever moolah I make out of this book goes to the TCV. Another 25% of the proceeds goes to the Mahesh Memorial Foundation that takes care of cancer patients from backward classes. Primarily women and children.

Before hitting the sack, we pondered on how the TCV staff works so hard to create a better world while all these people in the Corporate Sector were busy trying to trick tax authorities by feigning false trusts and foundations trying to evade taxes. Here they were, the Tibetans, working selflessly without a land to call their own, shaping the world into a better place. All under the teachings of His Holiness, The Dalai Lama. Surfing the net, checking out Wikipedia, here I was struggling with a slow internet connection. Derek suggested that next time, I get myself a thicker internet cord so that more signals would flow in with ease, like a fat pipe. I plan to heed his advise and probably take up a house closer

to my internet Service provider's servers and office as Goose suggested. I knew I had very smart people with me, with brains practically coming out of their nostrils and ears. I now knew I was in safe hands and we were all set to meet The Dalai Lama, ask the right questions and sound intelligent......
Wait. Maybe, on second thoughts, I need to take out that thread and needle from Motormouth's Medical kit and sew a few lips if we were to avoid getting thrown out.

That was it. And so we all fell silent as we watched this dumb, stupid lizard on the wall trying to commit hara-kiri. We watched as the stupid one repeatedly climbed on the wall and came falling down into the dustbin. The pathetic fool of a reptile didn't even know how to die. We left it as we continued to read up about His Holiness, about TCV and about Tibet, like school kids cramming up for the exams. I had this nagging headache which refused to leave me since morning. Derek suggested that I hit myself on the foot with a hammer to divert my attention. Goose wanted me to try his newly discovered 'Flash Therapy' with his Nikon D5000 on me. I was made to keep my eyes open while Goose used the flash on me. Now I know what Jim Carrey from the Mask looks like. Or why Susan Sarandon looks like Susan Sarandon. With nothing registered after our cramming sessions, an intensified headache and a persistent lizard in the room apart from these two morons in the room for company, I passed out and dreamt of 'Tintin in Tibet' that night.

My dreams are in multi-color, Dolby-stereo, with rewind, pause and forward options, 4-D effects like at the Universal Studios, and I am an active participant in shaping the dream. I was with Tintin and Captain Haddock, along with Snowy, Goose and Derek, looking out not for Chang, but for

Panchen Lama. We didn't find him though. If life was a box of chocolates as told by Forrest Gump, the human mind is where these dreamy chocolates are made. If you dream good, you get the most expensive ones, if you don't dream, you get only the wrappers. Or, er…lemon enough to make your own lemonade and struggle all your life.

A shriek in the bathroom a few hours later indicated that it was morning again. As we saw Goose dart across the room, ashen and pale-faced, he barely made any sense. Not that he did anyways, but this one also brought out that constipated look on his face. That meant that he was scared. He had gone to take a core dump a few minutes ago, and had levitated a few feet up from the commode on seeing a gigantic spider with hairy legs that had got him all screwed up. Brave Goose. A big, fat bird who couldn't stand his morning worm. Not that Derek or I are any braver, so there was chaos in the dormitory. Like the three Ghostbusters, here we were, equipped with deo-sprays and lighters to create those massive-blow torches, sprain sprays, bottles of water as the battle with the hairy beast began. It was a tough one, the beast was a sprightly one. The battle-cries wouldn't scare it one little bit. Nor would the scalding hot water from the geyser deter it. The blow-torch only blackened the mirror and the commode seat. As the screams got louder and as Derek surged ahead as the lone ranger to annihilate the beast and as we looked away from the gory scene, the sound of a dull thud and a tight slap resonated in the room. There was the matron in the apron who had thrown a slipper and crushed the beast, eradicating the hairy-one off the face of the earth. That was the thud. Maybe, the sight of Derek covering his cheek with one hand, blow-torch in other, explained the slap. Helga quietly walked away and we resumed breathing. Anyways, we won. Helga had used her rubber slipper, shame on you, Cinderella! This 'Helga' looked like a cross between a frog and Attila the Hun reigns. Victory was ours!! So was the shame.

We quietly filed up and got ready, checked out of the dorm and now we had to go to McLeodgunj to be blessed. It was the greatest moment of my life. Also, for Derek and Goose. Though we didn't know why we were so eager and excited to meet The Dalai Lama, maybe it was a total lack of purpose in the lives that we led all along. This isn't a spiritual journey, hell, it is just one hell of a party to celebrate life and our country, and then why were we so keen? Maybe, we just wanted to get an answer to a question that didn't exist in our minds today. I was taking notes in my little black book with my pencil as Goose drove. I asked Derek for a rubber and the 'matron-slap' was forwarded to me as he corrected me, saying that I needed an eraser. Not a rubber. Rubber was in short supply and Derek had stocked it only for the chicks in the back seat of Motormouth. It was amusing to see flashes of brilliance in that boy. Goose was gleefully smiling adding that I needed to do something about my verbal skills, since he didn't know or care about my oral skills. The funniest part is, these are those moments that make you go *Duh!!* and add the fun part to life. It's like the music that forms such an important part of our lives and how this concept has so effectively made it to the Bollywood movies. We had learnt so much about world history from our discussions with all those people we met at the TCV, at the Mahesh Memorial Foundation in Chennai and some of the intelligent people we met on the way. "No, Derek, 'Arsenal' is not a gay word. It is used by straight people like you and I. It has nothing to do with sex. And 'Infantry' has nothing to do with a hole in the rubber *Duh!!*. Anger management in full force, I try my best to make Derek understand as Goose chuckles as he plays with his dumb glass-eye.

Arriving at McLeodgunj, straight into the parking lot, we fussed over our hair, our clothes, our stubbles and our attire. While Goose and I were in our uniforms of black cargos and black t-shirts with 'Chief' and 'Goose' written on it, with the HOP-Symbol of 'I love you' imprinted on our backs, Derek was the sharp dressed man. He had neatly tied his long hair into a pony-tail as he wanted to look cool. Cool? He was right now freezing in his brand new shirt and well-polished shoes. I gather that was pinched from someone called 'Tommy' as that cunning fellow had stitched his name on his collar. Dumb Derek had no clue. He was fussing over his shoe-laces now, neatly done straight to the aglet. Sometimes, one wonders, were the people who made the English language, really jobless? I mean, a word like 'Aglet', which means the plastic or metal bit at the end of a shoelace, did it really need an identity? A name? I'm sure the consultants would have charged them a bomb and there must have been someone like McKinsey defining corporate strategies for an organization like say, Golguppa Industries, or something like that. Goose and I were cool. A dirty t-shirt that hadn't made contact with water since it was manufactured, we believed in spraying loads of deodorant on it and giving it a loud, dust-off shake. The louder you shake it, the louder and cooler it sounds. One can make music with this kind of stuff, mix it with the sound of blaring horns, granite-cutting sounds, yelling sounds and cut a CD out of it and call it 'The Typical Sound of a Developing Country' and market India in a big way. And that would be a million dollars as my consulting fee.

The crows in McLeodgunj are certainly bigger and scarier than Goose here. Noisier too.

The excitement in us was showing as Goose was going crazy. Derek was running behind him, trying to stomp on his feet. Don't ask me why, but I guess this is what one would call a 'wild Goose chase'. As we went through the security check, we exchanged smiles and pleasantries with the security personnel whom we had seen and met before during our last trip. We knew that they were instrumental in getting us an audience with His Holiness. We crossed the familiar monks clapping their hands in a group in a way that would encourage a debate. My heart was pounding like a hammer; Goose was fluttering like a bird and Derek was subdued. As we entered The Dalai Lama's residence, we were escorted to the queue. I don't think people have ever been this kind or nice to us ever, at any point. The warmth, the respect and the sheer calmness of the office staff and security personnel must be a result of being around a great soul and a God of a man.

A huge campus, not even a small part is visible as it is all covered by trees, the buildings were a true reflection of the spirit of pride and humility. As we waited in the queue patiently, there was no holding back our excitement. It showed. It was tough to control Goose and I was delirious myself. To say we were lucky is to undermine the presence. A personality that people around the world worship had been gracious enough to grant us audience, thanks to those around him. People were kissing the soil he walks on, praying in all humility with folded hands in front of the gates as we saw a group of monks who had crossed the mountains from China on foot to seek his blessings. People from all over the world come to seek blessings of His Holiness, not for any religious purposes, but for a more spiritual purpose. One can feel the calmness in the air, addled morons like us could feel it in the air. A sense of serenity, calm, and tranquility filled me as I waited in the queue, behind Goose. We were politely told that we are the first ones on the list to meet His Holiness, but are being pushed to the last so that we get maximum air-time with His Holiness. On hindsight, I suspect that this was done by the staff to avoid embarrassment to themselves by letting the premises get empty of visitors before letting the morons in.

We are sitting in the same place as we were sitting last time except there was a huge sense of happiness this time. We had learnt much in the past few days. Having heard so many Tibetans talk about their cause and history, we had moved from the *Duh!!* zone to a *Double Duh!!* zone. The children at the TCV had given me a very strong purpose in life. Devoid of any political learning, my mind has singularly focused on a group of people without a nation. It reminded me of the movie, The Terminal, as the guard waved out to us. We were now to enter the passage to the chamber where His Holiness was meeting the chosen visitors. Devoid of thought, Goose was humming the famous Pink Floyd song 'Comfortably Numb'. Not that we had to come down all the way from Bangalore to McLeodgunj to be devoid of thought, but this was different. So was Derek. He was devoid of thought and different at the same time. He was busy working on his shoes, polishing it with his spit. He was looking mighty stupid with a hair band. A real pansy. I wonder why people do this to themselves. What next, Derek, a skirt? You think you look cool? You look like a she-monkey with gelled hair. We waited for them all in the serene atmosphere. However, I could never figure out why people talk in hushed tones and whispers when they are in a silent environment. I mean, it is silent because you are not talking, isn't it? This is not a library, damn it!! We don't see any sexy librarian chick around the place. Goose was unstoppable, all chirpy, and was a major embarrassment. Maybe, I should have spat on his sugar-coated cream buns or puked in his coffee.

We were moved along the passage to the chamber, where there were a few monks who aided in easing out the meetings, made those dozen people in front of us comfortable. I wonder, who was making them comfortable when it came to Goose and I? Derek was not to be seen, we gathered he was somewhere, groping, trying to spot a mirror to groom himself before we presented him to His Holiness. And then it happened, then the moment came. Our time had come. For we had now been led inside the chamber along with his trusted aides. My heart was pounding like a hammer as I entered the chamber along with Goose. I realized we had folded our hands in awe and reverence, and it was not something I was used to doing. And in the presence of our Guruji, our inspiration, here we were, two morons in front of what I know as God. As we walked in and as we were introduced, he already seemed to know us as we touched his feet and sought his blessings. But what was to follow was something that would spin my life totally out of control till the day I die.

The Dalai Lama patted me on my chest and said, "I see a lot of passion here. Keep the fires burning". He took Goose's right hand and my left hand and held it to his chest. He would continue to do the same for the next 15-20 minutes that we were to be in the Holy presence of a person that the world worships. All my words, our preparation, our questions, our pretensions went out the window as tears welled up in Goose's and my eyes as all we could do was go *Duh!!* and stare at the Dalai Lama with a stupid smile on our faces. From quantum physics to Geo-political equations, from religion to mathematics, he spoke. I remember vaguely mumbling what came to me at that time which now haunts me every day. That was a promise we made to him – to do something good for the Women and Children of India and Tibet. That was a promise made, a promise I aim to keep. His aura humbled us. He said to us, "Be Proud, not arrogant". The sound of his voice still echoes in my ears as his comforting presence and his warmth was similar to an elderly person in the family showing the way to his children. The way to salvation. He was smiling and as he spoke, the world moved in slow motion. What may have been 15-20 minutes as known to the world today in this warp was probably a few years in time when it happened. For the words he spoke, the love that was given, the warmth that I felt touched every nerve, every cell of my mind, heart and soul. Maybe this is as spiritual as one can ever get. Mind you, I do not say religious or political, but at a level far greater than that as though he was the embodiment of all the positive energy in the whole universe and we were being blessed by the Holy one, who was worshiped by millions across the world. I briefly glanced at Goose, I could see he was welling up and for a moment, I saw a fleeting glance of the person he was going to become someday and make a difference. Derek was invisible or was not around. This meeting was enough to give meaning to my existence till date and my life ahead. I was humbled and I would guess Goose felt the same.

As our meeting with His Holiness got over and we were leaving the chamber, I looked back. Here was God as I know him or her, waving out to us and wishing us a safe trip back to Bangalore. As we went out through the hallway, out through the security gate, I think we were walking on air. Once out of the gate and having said our goodbyes to the security guards, Goose and I hugged each other and started jumping for joy. This was the highlight of our trip, the defining moment of our very existence and we had found a reason to live. The Reason.

There was no other reason for us to hang around in McLeodgunj. The only problem was we couldn't spot Derek, for he had missed out on this meeting. We were a bit worried till we found Derek in front of Motormouth, staring at his reflection on the tinted windows, combing his hair, getting all ready for the big meeting. Goose delivered a tight slap to Derek as I whooped his arse. With no words spoken, we ruffled his hair, pushed him into the backseat of Motormouth as I revved up the engine and Goose played with the iPod and pumped up the volume. Happy and proud, we now headed to Rajasthan via Haryana. Derek would take a few hours to understand.

We had been blessed. We now had a reason to celebrate our lust for life.

15 Of Camel Toes, Getting Humped and Desserts

The morons are on a roll again and we kick some butt,
Anything to get out of the regular corporate rut;
Of misadventures and learning galore,
Give me my adventure, else life can be such a big bore;
I want to drive like the wind, I want to feel wind in my hair,
I want my loud heavy rock, of life, I want my share
High speed and going crazy, it makes me say 'Cheese'
Drive on, for that's when you go 'Horn OK Please'...

Hurry, Ana, Hurry

Blessed and blissed out, while driving down from McLeodgunj, having met the Dalai Lama, Derek was in the pits for having missed the meeting he had been planning throughout the trip. Not meeting His Holiness was not something that was making him happy. Goose and I were feeling bad for him and so we decided to make him happy. Derek told us that we would be now cutting across Haryana and driving down straight to the deserts of Rajasthan where he could feast his eyes on some camel-toes. He could hump all that he could as there would be belly dancers and night safaris for some serious off-roading. Those dim-lights that formed Derek's peepers lit up and we had once again successfully managed to trick this dim-wit into submission and Goose and I tried our level best to suppress our laughter. We did it, for exactly 69 seconds. HA!HA!HA!

This part of the country is simply awesome, very pretty. The beauty of Mother Nature seems to have been partial to this part of the country too. As we continued with our descent onto the plains, it had just stopped raining and there was this beautiful rainbow that cut through the sky and divided the world into two parts – the cool side and the not so cool side. We were on the cool side and the rainbow kept us on the cool side. Goose let put a loud cry as I pulled over and Derek was making some wild animated gestures to get those words out of his mouth that seemed to have got stuck in his gullet. He had eaten humble-pie having missed the meeting. Maybe, those crumbs had him all choked up with emotions. What we saw was this beautiful waterfall cutting through the rocks which looked like the intestines of a man dead for over a month and left on the operation table, all cut up and with maggots coming out of every pore.. Umm….bad analogy, I guess. Gross! Let me try again, so here goes.

What we saw was a piece of art, hand-crafted and delivered to us by Mother Nature. In full splendor, she wanted us to take in the lovely weather, the beauty of the mountains, the kiss of a rainbow and the gentle caress of the wind before we took in the sheer imperfection of what formed a waterfall, cutting through the rocks and shrubs. The sound of the gushing water that fell on the rocks barely ten feet above us was Nature's way of telling us to have a bath before we hit civilization (or the lack of it) before we headed out to the plains. Funny, how refreshing the experience can be under a waterfall. We dumped our clothes inside Motormouth and frolicked under the waterfall for an hour. Refreshing – Goose was like Priety Zinta from the 'Lyril soap-bar' ad that made her famous. Since we now had to hang our swimming trunks out to dry and continue on our journey and to reach Haryana before sun down, I reeled under the sheer impact of being struck by a thought which was not really a great idea. As Goose made a clothes line in front of the bonnet of Motormouth, Derek hung our swimming trunks. In case I haven't mentioned this before, dear reader, we had learnt a lot during this journey and we had become very smart people. Just that we had overlooked one teeny-tiny aspect, which was soon to hit us smack in the face by evening. Smart-ass Derek had hung the swimming trunks a bit too low and the license plate was not visible anymore. Motormouth was now a cop magnet and we didn't know it.

Helga barked out the orders and I obeyed her. GPS with 'Map my India' works. The only trouble is when you are following Helga, trapped inside the GPS and with the ever-changing names of cities and States in the country, you are totally confused between Uttaranchal, Uttarakhand, Himachal and every place and we cursed ourselves for our ignorance and ineptitude. I was not even sure how many States we would be returning home to after fifty days. All I wanted was to be respectful to the locals by at least being politically correct while asking for directions, while beating the hell out of Helga inside the GPS and telling her she was always wrong and we didn't like her one little bit.

We reached Haryana and darkness had started to settle in. I've heard that pockets of Haryana are very dark and casteism runs deep. People are hell bent on marrying off their kin within the same community and trespassers are executed. So much so that if they had it their way with God, they would have turned hermaphrodites and married themselves. But that is a very false image that is portrayed to the world at large, I mean, which part of the world is devoid of jerks? One cannot generalize, for the majority of Haryana is full of nice people and I'm not trying to be politically correct over here. And so, as luck would have it, here we were, crossing through a seedy town, deep in the crotch of Haryana, and we had these cops on bikes chasing us. With goon-like thugs escorting them, speeding through was not an option. We were surrounded by 7-8 cops who looked ready to bite. That was an exaggeration; for they only looked ready to chop our heads off before beating us black and blue, so we were cool.

Flexing some political muscles in India can do wonders. Thanks to a letter that I had received from the office of our Honorable Home Minister, P.Chidambaram, flashing it in front of the cops made everything change. Once the honchos saw the seal of the Government of India and the signatures, they did an absolute volte-face and what was to follow was beyond our imagination. A flock of cops who had never seen a GPS, had the instrument explained to them by Goose, replete with her horrible voice. The tracking systems within Motormouth and how we were using Social Media to have our back-office track and trace our exact position via satellite was explained and they posed for pictures with us as one of the junior officers was running around getting us fresh juices and water. It was enough to trigger off the ambition in me to become the President of India. Oh! For that Neolite, a free

PhD degree and a title to make a difference for free, what more could I wish for?

We had the flunkey-boy escort us to the seediest hotel in the neighborhood. We were also told that it is the best cheap motel to stay. Goose was suddenly looking all constipated as the angry mutt at the door started barking loud. The flunkey was dressed in weird striped underwear and was holding a very handsome dog by the leash. Derek was accosted by a completely inebriated man claiming to be the editor of a local newspaper who wanted to interview us. I declined politely as he threatened the hotel staff. Derek was pissed. He went to the editor's car and emptied himself through an open window. I mean, how can you give an interview to a strange-looking stranger who finishes up all the liquor up by himself and refuses to show you an identity card? Before leaving the premises, he got all abusive and threatened the hotel staff, the manager, the waiter and the flower pot – as he was piss-drunk. Bad vibes kept us awake all night after we saw a very expensive car parked in the backyard of that hotel, where the last guest had checked in exactly eight days ago.....and had never checked out.

Hey Goose! Is that your new hairdo or are you shitting bricks?

Fright is a contagious thing. The scared Goose started telling us horror stories from all the horror flicks he had watched, actually they were more horrible than horror stories, where guests check into random motels and are accosted by loony psychopaths and other horrible stuff like that. Well, this was it then. We were in this seedy motel in a seedy town where everyone looked like a member of Derek's family. Brrrrr! A loony psychopath is an understatement. Goose was scared and wanted to fly away. He got us scared right now with his stories, Derek and I were scared that he would tell us more of those horrible stories and he is a pathetic story teller. So we were scared, thanks to the Goose. Maybe, this is what they call 'Bird Flu'. The big bird had pooped more than enough for one night and so we decided not to sleep. Wee 'o' clock in the dead of night or early morning happened, we scooted from hick-town, ran into cul-de-sacs and got back on the road. The scariest part of this was that we had no choice but to listen to Helga inside the GPS to get back on the highway. For once, we were thankful to this evil witch called 'Helga' inside the GPS. Suddenly, at the break of dawn, we heard the broken-hearted wail of Derek from the backseat. It was Derek in tears, bawling away. Derek had just spotted a camel and seen its toes. He knew he had been had. We all laughed our way into Rajasthan.

The nightmare was over. Or so we thought. But Rajasthan would be another basket of surprises for us. We had a long drive ahead of us that day, for Jaisalmer was our destination and that was land's end for India bordering Pakistan. As I pulled out a packet of roasted nuts for a snack to chew on, Derek was shell shocked. He couldn't believe how many make-cooks must have been killed to fill a small poly-bag of tasty nuts. Goose was driving like crazy, maybe, this was his idea of fasting. I wanted him to slow down as I was finding it difficult to juggle between answering Derek's pathetic queries and writing down my travel notes. Dear reader, appreciate the fact that this Chapter was written at the speed of 169 Kmph inside Motormouth.

Looking for a Desert Rose

Having worked the cheap-shit accommodation for more than a month on the road, we decided to pamper ourselves big time. This meant going way beyond clean sheets and beds. We wanted more stuff for our goodie-bag, which now occupied a lot of space inside Motormouth. Goose was getting greedier by the day. As we checked into one of those extra-classy joints and took the most expensive suite in a once-upon-a-time-palace. Potty-mouth Derek was still inside Motormouth, thinking that he was staring at the sunrise and going 'Ooh-Aah' as he stared at the light-bulb through his Raybans. He had just woken up at the end of the day – another reason why Goose and I needed to take a very big suite with many rooms. Maybe in another hotel away from Derek. Maybe in another city altogether. Better, as we needed to crash for the night. Unfortunately, Derek got into a talkative mode and we had it. All I remember vaguely as I was too tired to protest as he started ranting about what he would do with all his money when he became all rich and famous and telling Goose of his ambition of buying up a sperm-bank and selling his progeny online. Having driven down all the way through the desert belt, close to the India border in Rajasthan, we all wanted to get to no-man's land. Derek was excited with the prospect of finding loads of women over there. The desert belt had been devoid of any female species and was like a chastity belt across the state. The only place we had taken a pit stop while driving down from Haryana was a town owned by one of the co-founders of Microsoft Corporation. The town was called 'Balmer'. Goose was hopping mad at India Incorporated that night, for we had outsourced an entire town to an International product company that has made life miserable for millions of geeks across the world. The software that Microsoft sells puts Indian roads to shame; they are full of holes and horrible bugs and things that tend to crash. Still, Gates is alright for pobody's nerfect and we were duckin' frunk now...Good night.

Sunrise in the desert is grand, but the sounds of the pigeons in our balcony was horrible. Sunset is worse. Having escaped from the crows of Uttaranchal, I was now subject to the torture of these horrendous pigeons who sounded like Helga having multiple orgasms. Pigeons are among the most horrible creatures known to mankind. Just like crows, God made them with that little bit of extra meat, after making skinny people. Compared to crows and pigeons, camels are a lot better. The deserts of Jaisalmer are infested with these four-legged slow-coaches that can eat, shit, fart and walk at the same time. Tourists from all around the world come to take camel rides in India. We wanted to know why and so we decided to hire a flunkey in the name of a tour-guide who would take us to the dunes and make us experience the rich cultural heritage India has to offer in this part of the country. Yeah, right.

From getting Leh'd to getting humped

So the day was all laid out by this dim-wit of a tour guide, whom we promptly christened 'Nitwit' as his name sounded something like that. I don't remember his name, not that it would have made any difference to my life. Nitwit was to take us around city palaces and attractions, get us humped around on camels across the 'Sam dunes' (pronounced

'Some' dunes and rightly so), then get us to a resort in the middle of nowhere so we could be subjected to the torture of shrieking folk singers with absolutely no melody in their songs, wrapping the night with female dancers who would dance with colored pots on their heads and we were supposed to enjoy it all. Or at least pretend to look blissed out. Come on, we were road-hogs, we wanted the dunes, nice 4-wheel night safaris, belly dancers and hookahs while they roasted skunks and squirrels on a spit and waited for Imhotep. Nitwit maintained that not only would he have us get on the night safari in a desert called the 'Khuri' desert, he would also make sure that he would show us a ghost town, since we don't have pyramids in India.

They sell chilled beer on the deserts of Rajasthan. Nitwit, our man Friday in Rajasthan, in his funny accent, urged us to have a bottle of chilled 'King-pisser' before we got humped around the dunes on these ridiculously *Duh!!* looking camels. The nightmare of a ride began as Goose made grunting sounds and Derek made some equally ridiculous pained faces. It was sheer pornography in motion as the camels walked, farted, ran, ate, squatted and humped us all around. Definitely, these were not joy-rides and we paid heavily to get sodomized. As the nightmare in the desert got over, the tourists around us must have seen three bow-legged morons walking into the sunset. I suspect, I saw some Japanese tourists click pictures of us as well, since tourists from Japan take pictures of anything and everything when they come to India.

Nitwit now wanted us to enjoy a night in the desert and had arranged for a cultural feast replete with dancers, singers, countless frogs and snakes. Hooray! Just get me out of here. Nitwit was quite a character, though I am not sure if he had any. He seemed to enjoy the evening much more than all of us put together. He put on quite a spectacular show for us by dancing the rain dance like an Apache around the campfire, dirty dancing with folk-dancers, and feeling himself obscenely with his tongue hanging out like a lusty camel when the star dancer came with a backless blouse. Derek had competition that night. Goose was pissed as he could not take many pictures as the dancers were moving around way too much. I was pissed with the sheer cacophony that the lead singer of the Dune-band created in the name of folk-songs. I love folk songs, we all do. They are the best touristy things to see, take pictures of, as long as they can wind up within fifteen minutes without getting too carried away. Our man over here was right there screaming his head off as though someone from the eight-piece orchestra with some primitive instrument from the Flintstones era had pinched his butt real hard. It was worse than being subject to the torture of Luciano Pavarotti in full form. I so wanted to pull down his skirt and give him a real tight slap to make him shut up.

People in some parts of Rajasthan wear skirts just like they do in Scotland, where they call them 'Kilts'. This bard in the desert would have been 'kilt' too if he hadn't stopped singing. Since that was not an option, we decided to tip all of them heavily and bribe them to shut up. Nitwit got an earful that night. We punished him by making him sit beside Goose in the front seat as Goose drove like a maniac and without a seatbelt on. Nitwit was visibly scared as he counted the road-kill by the time we reached our hotel in the dead of night for God alone knows what all Motormouth had crushed as we counted the sound of 'Crunch!!' thrice, "Snap!!" twice and 'Splat!!' a few times.

Wow. Some desert dudes sure can sweat inside an air-conditioned vehicle at 18 degree Celsius. We must have run over a few snakes, crushed a few rodents and squished countless zoo-zoos that night. Good job, Goose. It was wicked fun to watch Nitwit crawl out of Motormouth. Goose was gleeful. I was ecstatic. Derek was in a different plane, for he wanted to sleep with a sexy ghost tonight and he was adamant.

The haunted village of Kuldhara

To appease Derek's mojo and cravings, we had no choice but to visit a ghost town. Rajasthan is full of folk-lore, rich in horror stories and mystery. For those seeking mystery, this is the perfect place. Nitwit was at his wit's end when we decided to drag him to a place where he had never gone before. Being born, bred and battered in Jaisalmer, he has been wisely brought up not to stir up the evil spirits. The only spirits he had been exposed to had been of the drinking variety. That helps when one is confronted by the wicked spirits of the Chief, Goose, Derek and Motormouth. He had no choice but to succumb to our demands of being taken to the ghost town and spending the night there after being soaked in whiskey for two hours before lunch time.

Derek had done his research on the village and this is what he had to say: "The story about Kuldhara is that it was once a very prosperous town populated by the Paliwal Brahmins of Rajasthan, who were a very prosperous community then. They had garages, big houses, duplex penthouses, pretty women, loads of money and that made it all very lucrative just like it would make any village lucrative today. Greed is as old as man's desire to get behind the wheel of a fast car......maybe, much older than that. The daughter of the head honcho of the village was a cute, hot chick and some royal chappie from Jaisalmer's royal brigade got all horny over her. Now, this horny guy was notorious, like any other horny guy from anywhere. Some regular nut ratted on his royal horniness. The villagers sought a fortnight for their decision on getting this chick married to this royal pain-in-the-ass. The entire village scooted from the village one dark, moonless night and left it completely empty. Not just that, they put a curse upon the village. The curse now applies to anyone who comes to the village. Archeologists found some skeletons in the cupboards of some of the villagers who left their belongings behind. And now the ghosts of horny, naked women dance around in the village at night."

Knowing Derek, we knew he would exaggerate and play on our baser instincts, I mean, who in their right mind would not like to see a ghost? Of course, Derek wanted to get a good 'look and feel' of a feminine ghost. The closest he had gotten to a ghost was his first girlfriend, who looked and behaved like a witch. She owned a vacuum cleaner, of course, not a broom. I've always wondered if I would ever get to see witches flying about on vacuum cleaners in the dead of night in this modern day and age. Surely, progress impacts everyone and witches are no exception. I know a few witches myself and we now call them 'Helga'.

What followed was straight out of a horror flick, replete with a deserted old town, 200 broken houses, empty wells and canals, empty temples and old men telling tales. The old men who man such places are far scarier than the ghosts themselves. Maybe, that's why ghosts do not come out. I mean, tourists like you and I would get all scared and go all shitless looking at these people and when the ghost finally comes out to do its thing, it wouldn't be half as scary compared to what these watchmen look like. So we tanked up, took some snaps and inspired by horror flicks, I left the video camera on. Absolutely nothing. Derek was randy as hell. Somehow we managed to yank him away from a stray mongrel in the dead of night. Not a peep, not a whisper. Came morning and we got back into Motormouth and back to the hotel. Maybe, the ghosts had been warned of our visit and had heard horror stories about Derek. Disappointed, Derek had no choice but to befriend some vague tourist from some obscure country in Europe. She was scary and horrible enough to appease Derek's fantasy of doing a witch. She was a 'Helga' for sure.

Territorial pissings and the border

The next morning dawned with the dratted pigeons and it was a day of getting the permissions in place to visit the border that separates India and Pakistan. A point called 'Pillar 609', now manned by our brave peace keeping security forces from BSF of the 15th Battalion. This is the same point where insurgents from Pakistan had tried to make their way into India, and the Indian Army had then mercilessly thrashed their butts and driven them all the way back to Lahore before we decided to give them a big piece of their country back to them, way back in the year 1965. They still haven't learned their lessons from their past and continue to irritate us around Kashmir now. This is my Indian side of the story. The same paragraph could have been written in a completely different tone, dear reader, had I been a Pakistani national. We are birds of a feather being played by China and it would be so awesome if India, Pakistan, Bangladesh and other tiny nations around us aligned with us and saw through the smoke and Chinese mirrors. After all, nobody wins a war and as a great man in the history of mankind had recently said, "War is a very dangerous place....*Duh!!*".

We headed to Longewalla, Tanot and the border today. For those who don't know, the border is a place where politicians from two countries indulge in territorial demarcation and marking out their area for copulation. Having clearly trapped the population of a country within a somewhat circular cage surrounded by barbed wires and electric fences, they then start humping the citizens of the country and bleed them to death. We wanted to take Motormouth to where Indian roads ended.

So armed with our legal documents and loads of attitude, Derek and Goose went to the BSF Headquarters in the region and got us some special permissions to visit the farthest point of the country. About 200 Kilometers of vast desert separates Jaisalmer from the border. Dotted by bunkers and secret helipads all around, driving through the desert reminded me of 'Area 51' and the Mojave Desert, so this place shall henceforth be referred to as 'Area 69'. Motormouth stuck to the roads as there was sand all around. This is the biggest problem we have with deserts in India, there is way too much sand. You run the risk of getting stuck in the sand if you get off the road, if not, there are high chances of pieces of your ass and shrapnel flying through the desert skies if you happen to drive over a land mine. Therefore, it is advisable to stay alive if you want to avoid getting killed.

We had left for the border in the wee hours of the morning and were now on the way to see a relief truck and a lot of mangled iron in the name of a dead Patton tank, having paid our tribute to war heroes. Since morning, we had been inside bunkers, seen unexploded shells that look like chopped pieces of alien-green sausage from Pakistan, heard the soldiers speak and explain to us the various nuances of the fencing around the border. That's not just a piece of barbed-wire running all the way down from one part of the country to another, but a depressing piece of mesh invested in by our country to prevent infiltration. One can safely conclude from this that it is to prevent the Pakistanis from crossing over into India as this is an investment made by India. I suppose that the Pakistanis would build roads into India if they had to invest around the border. We had climbed up check-posts, understood the concept of rigging or how they study sand around the border, seen the 'Pillar 609' (69 is my lucky number), learnt about army gear and a lot of other things and had driven Motormouth to the very end of Indian roads in this part of the country.

Stranded in the desert

After doing the border thing, we now proceeded from Tanot, which is the point closest to the border onto Longewalla. Some Bollywood blockbuster was shot there a few years ago. There had been a sandstorm the other day and so the roads were half-covered with sand. Close to the border, it is said that temperatures soar up to 69 degree Celsius, just like at the Siachen glacier; they say that hell freezes over at -69 degree Celsius. Himachal Pradesh, Uttaranchal and some other state are in between the Himalayas and Rajasthan and so we concluded that these places are so cool to stay in. Give or take

5 degree Celsius for exaggeration purposes, still, it makes the place very hot. (In statistics and Science, they term 'Bullshit' as 'Degrees of freedom' to make it sound academic and esoteric). Such soaring temperatures can make you behave abnormally. Therefore, we decided not to let Derek drive as it would then become way too risky. Since today was my 'driving-day', it was my turn to drive people crazy. And I did.

Even vultures do not dare to soar in the sky here for fear of getting their feathered butts roasted in the desert heat. It is said that if you threw some peanuts on the sand here, you can so easily fry them in minutes. I said it because all folklore starts with the phrase: "....It is said". Sounds cool, doesn't it? Having come from places where they have landslides, we were now driving through a place where there are 'sand slides'. I suppose that's what one calls all that sand that is on the road. However, unlike ice, sand doesn't melt. It's people who melt in the desert heat, and that is why you don't see many people living in the desert. The heat also takes the mojo away and so the desert continues to remain devoid of people. Since there are no people, there is very little shit and since there is no shit, there is no fertilization of the ground. Therefore, you don't find mud in the desert, only sand. I guess one can safely conclude that wherever one finds people, there is shit and that leads to more people being born.

Exactly half-way between the border town of Tanot and Longewalla, our destination, is a patch of desert near a place called 'Sadewala' where people go crazy. I just made this one up because this is where I went berserk and got us all into trouble. Nine am now and the dratted desert sun was high in the sky. Driving at 169 Kmph, listening to Sting, I don't know what bit me for I suddenly found this dune to my left so irresistible that I just had to try to get off the road and try to scale it a bit, then get back on the road to continue our journey. It was a very stupid thing to do. Goose and Derek had absolutely no time to react. The road caved in as the sand from underneath the tar road gave way like a big, broken, hour glass.

Within the next few minutes, Motormouth got firmly stuck in the loose sand and came to a grinding halt. Nothing I did to make her move would help. The smell of burning rubber, diesel and then dead silence brought out the beast in Derek who punched me real hard on my chin. We had no drinking water in the car as we were not very smart, running on spare fuel from jerrycans, bought off the cheap tin-shops in Tanot for there are no fuel pumps for miles around. And now this. We were terribly stuck in the worst part of the desert between the border and the closest town of Longewalla and the sun was beginning to climb. Strangely, I didn't feel like Clint Eastwood right now, rather I felt like a clit who never knew what morning wood was, if I was not out of place. Goose couldn't stop laughing at my stupidity. The next one hour was spent shoveling out the sand from under Motormouth and filling up with broken road-pieces. Nothing worked. We were stuck and in deep desert shit. There was nothing we could do but wait to be rescued.

What followed for the next eight hours is not something that we would forget in a hurry in this lifetime. Pulling out our umbrellas, we spotted the rubble of four mud huts, which now seemed like a bustling economy to me, had it been populated. All our efforts to pull Motormouth out of the dune were in vain and she had just gone down deeper into the sand. We were thirsty, tired, irritable and in our bathroom slippers. Far away, we spotted a man and a half for as they neared, we could see that one was a shriveled old man who would drop dead any moment, maybe he was a few hundred years old, and the other person was lame and demented. That was our only support system right now, which carried a plastic bottle of sweet water. They gave us information which wasn't nice. We had to get into the shade so we had no choice but to leave Motormouth behind and go to the other side of the dune where there was a deserted village. Of course, there was a well but that was near Longewalla. And the Pakistani Army had poisoned the water in the well before retreating and many people had died after drinking the water. Gory tales told, the information we got from them was not very encouraging. It seems like there are exactly three vehicles that pass through this place every day and we were in the middle of nowhere yet again and were twenty-five kilometers from 'Yes-where'. This had happened to us before near Kanyakumari, only this time, survival was a lot tougher. If we were to stay alive, we had to get to the shade, wet our towels with sweet water so we could squeeze it and keep our mouths wet and wait for evening to happen. Not that there was any rollicking party scheduled in the evening, but the possibility of a BSF (Border Security Force) relief truck passing through, if we were lucky. internet or cell phone signals are not known around the place. The sand was boiling hot and Goose was boiling. Derek was chewing on a wet towel. I felt horrid for I had got us into the mess. The old man and the lamed duck disappeared into the rubble and we waited for a sane human being to arrive who could help us with a few drops of water.

The desert can do strange things to people. And worse things to strange people. After a few hours of laughing our heads off to Derek's jokes, we knew that that was the best thing we could do to survive. I mean, here we are, three spoilt city-hicks who couldn't survive a few hours without air-conditioners, bottled water and luxury and this trip had made us realize how spoilt we had been. All we had now was a bottle of water between the three of us, very little fuel, no food and not much sense. If we were to die today, the world would be ….well…..lesser by three people tomorrow. If the bottle of water between us got over, we would probably kill each other and drink blood to survive. The day was getting hotter and it was like breathing in fire, spitting out sand, waking on lava and this could lead to madness.

We were done rummaging through the ruins of the deserted structure; at least we had some shade. Even to walk ten steps was an effort. Strangely, there was goat shit all around the place which meant that this was obviously a pit-stop for all goats. In walked a 'goatly' figure of a goatherd with another bottle of water and we drank some before exchanging any pleasantries. At this moment, if someone had told us that the water was poisoned and we shouldn't be drinking it, we really wouldn't have cared. The temperature was soaring high today, close to 60 degree Celsius and ours was the only vehicle which had come through since morning. And since we had left the Border area, no one would come looking for us. We had no choice but to wait for evening to happen, when there could be a water tank going by and that could take one of us to Longewalla and we could contact the BSF for relief. By now, we were cool in this heat to take in anything, as we were now prepared to spend the night here. He also pointed out an underground water tank that is filled once a month to prevent people from ending up dead here. About a kilometer away, we trudged and took in all the water using a bucket to pull it out, removing the bugs, cow-dung and beetles from it. This was the kind of stuff diarrhea is made of and we would be lucky to get diarrhea later, at least we would be alive to end up in a hospital for such small stuff.

This person, heaven-sent, was a goatherd and it was evident that he was in love with his goats. For he used those round black balls goats pass out in the name of crap to make a point. In fact, he even used three of those round balls and gave them our names and explained to us where we were and what we could do to stay alive. We felt like shit and this goat-who-walks had just called us that. Around five pm, when we were all drained out and dunked in the well, inside the water tank full of crap and dung-beetles, Derek went berserk and starting yelling like Tarzan. Goose wondered if he was having those things called 'hallucinations and garages' or something like that, for we could see a convoy of vehicles and an Army truck nearing us, a few kilometers away. Since we were about a kilometer away from the road and Motormouth, we had to run. We just got out of the water tank, ran like the wind, God knows where the energy came from, in underwear and screaming out for help. The rescue team was here. Within the next thirty minutes, we would be given water to drink, Motormouth would be towed out of the dune and we would be back on the road to Longewalla. These are our heroes and this chapter is dedicated to those good Samaritans from the BSF and ordinary citizens who love to drive – our heroes who rescued us. India 2.0 citizens.

Back on the highway, Goose and Derek insisted that I get behind the wheel and drive us to our planned destination of Longewalla before we headed back to the desert. I knew these were my real friends, for in spite of me getting them into trouble that day, they wanted me to retain my confidence behind the wheel as we drove back via the martyr town of Longewalla, back to Jaisalmer. Derek stared at the battle tank for a long time and was sobbing. The tank reminded him of his first girlfriend.

As we crossed those insignificant villages, the same villages we wouldn't even have glanced at in the morning, they now seemed like big cities with smiling faces despite the tough conditions these people live in. However, I can never fathom why people live in places which are not at all for habitation – up in the mountains, in the desert or in New York.

Hit the road, Jack? Duh, hit the sack!

Back in the hotel, we had a new bard and a dance troupe arranged for us by Nitwit to make up for the other day's fiasco. I tipped the singer in the man-skirt real big for not singing and graciously taking a flying saucer to the moon with a one-way ticket, on a spinning donut. I was beside a very big and pooped out bird called Goose and a demented road-hog called Derek and all we wanted today was dancers, a puppet show, lots of water and some beer. Next morning we decided to leave the miserable desert. Derek bought a very ugly five foot Rajasthani for his nefarious activities.

I was pooped out and needed an over-doze and was checking on our finances, all our money had vaporized, the desert sun burnt a hole in our piggy-bank. Derek had gone back to that ugly tourist and had been caught by her husband. We could hear Derek screaming for innocence in the hotel lobby, "Isn't that my room? I thought it was a garage! Was that your wife? Is this a bed? Holy Carp!" We let that pass.

The pigeons came, out went an empty bottle of beer from Derek's room. The sound woke me up. Good morning. Checking out of the hotel, we decided to see some Royal umbrellas in Jaisalmer. They looked like a Royal clump of mushrooms and are a sight recommended to every tourist who comes to this part of the world. We decided to drive via Pokhran. Pokhran is a place in Rajasthan with a big crater. Our military had carried out some nuclear explosions here and the hole in the ground had gotten so big that they, the locals, had no choice but to fill it up with onions. It had led to an inflation then. It had poured the night before and we were so happy that Motormouth would get a free wash. But as luck would have it, the dim-wit called Nitwit had safely parked her in the garage of the hotel and all the layers of mud and sand on her were intact. Dick! Not only that, but Nitwit had lost the keys to Motormouth and hence had tied her to a tree. That moron was so used to dealing with camels only. Goose was at the door yelling at Nitwit, "OK, Dimwit, had it been a camel, where would you have inserted the key to wake him up"?

It was our last night in Rajasthan and so we decided to have some real expensive booze that night. And since it was pouring cats and dogs in the land of camels, we decided to drink in the rain to make the drink last longer. A dead bull, a tired bird and a demented person soon passed-out as we had a long distance to cover again the next day.

As Motormouth roared out from Rajasthan toward the party scene in Mumbai and Goa, we realized we had not changed, learnt nothing. We were on our way to Goa and our friends had planned for a party in a place called 'The Blue Toad' or something like that. We were born to party and live the life we had chosen to. Or, maybe, the one we were destined to. From animals, we had grown up to become party animals, and that was all the growing up we could do. Also, we now had an ugly puppet doll in the back-seat for a change, which was good, for unlike Derek's other girlfriends, this one wasn't so ugly and she wouldn't talk endlessly or foolishly. But we had learnt the art of giving and that was nice. The smiles on those children's faces would remain etched in our hearts forever.

My rucksack was a mixed bag of emotions and I was carrying it like a monkey on my back. Motormouth told me to put it into the trunk and forget all about it and drive. Life is cool, we're alright. And Goa was our next destination.

HOPping to Conclusions

▶ *Bathing under a waterfall can make you famous, look at Priety Zinta*

▶ *Camels are dumb animals. People who sit on them are dumber animals*

▶ *If you decide to visit a ghost town, make sure people don't know about your plans, especially dead people*

▶ *If there are many people in a town, there is bound to be loads of shit*

▶ *Filling a crater up with onions leads to double-digit inflation*

▶ *Never tie your car to a tree, it doesn't really help*

▶ *Folk-songs are good, but the singer needs to stop after awhile*

▶ *It is easier to deflate the tires and fill sand underneath and avoid getting stuck in the desert*

▸ *When in the desert, always carry water with you or at least hang out with people who do*

▸ *If you must get lost, get lost at a place where there is snow. Snow can be melted into water and you don't die of thirst. Sa d doesn't melt to form water.*

16 The Big 'O' at Goa-Aaah!

Give me the sun and give me the sea,
Let me watch the sunrise, let me be free;
For the spirit of a road-hog can never be tamed,
I lust for life and I am not ashamed;
My beautiful country and my chilled-out friends, it makes
me say 'Cheese'
Drive on, for that's when you go 'Horn OK Please'...

Here comes the fake photographer and
crappy roadie – Goose

A whole day spent in navigating amidst pot holes as we drove towards Goa. The ugly woman 'Helga' inside the GPS doesn't know shit about these things. Heading towards South Goa from North Goa, we crossed a place called 'Mudgaon' or something similar, where we stopped for a snack. Given the name, Derek had imagined it to be place full of huts made of mud. He was mistaken. It was a beautiful town with beautiful people. The calmness and serenity of the place made the people progressive and they had somehow managed to keep the population under control. Derek had those typical images of unhygienic villages, full of ugly chicks. He had concluded that that's why the population in such villages is very low. Another myth busted.

South Goa. Lazy place, beach shack and no dumb hawkers. Goose and I tanking up on beer. We have asked for a barrel of beer with three pipes that we can guzzle straight from the barrel without having to move a muscle. We are hoping they oblige. They don't. We just named our flunkey 'Dick'. This is South Goa. People here do not move. There are some equally pathetic ones around us. As Bob Marley songs play in the background, I see this trashy tourist from somewhere who just passed out. She looks like 'Helga'. I guess she is dead and since she looks so stiff, Goose concludes that she must be a Brit. Or wait, maybe, this is what they call 'rigor-mortis'. Derek has finally found two extremely sexy Brazilians and plans to stay back in Palolim. We're cool as long as he takes 'Raggedy-Ann', that five foot doll from Rajasthan, out of Motormouth. He has dropped the idea of buying up a sperm bank and instead wants to open up a resort in South Goa and call it 'Pubes'. Since there is another place around town called 'Curly's', Derek wants to take over their clientele. The evil one is finally happy. And we are happy for him.

Goose and I plan to turn entrepreneurs as well once we publish our respective books. I have already become rich and famous thanks to morons like you who continue to lap up all that I write. Galileo is planning to join us in our venture and so will Craig. We all plan to do our bit for the women and children of India and Tibet before I become the next President of India. Our journey continues as our fan base continues to multiply. More suckers, more customers, more Indians 2.0 who live for a greater cause.

The next three days are spent in absolute bliss, not a shred of activity and just living the good life. There are inane conversations and moronic talks. And the stupidity never ends with Derek finally giving up trying to learn to play the piano. He doesn't need to play his flute anymore, not after getting those two absolutely stunning Brazilian chicks. Finally. Goose needs to shed all that puppy fat or lard and must dump the policy of 'Weight and watch' for he has been watching his weight grow. As the thought weighs on his mind, he watches the pretty one take to the water in a teeny-tiny string bikini.

We have learnt much during the trip and today is Teacher's Day. Sho we dechide to order shome fine Scotsch wishkey. (Hic!!) I idle around the place looking at a man lost in the menu card. I can understand his pain, for this is what happens to me every time I visit Europe. Come to my country, dear International readers, for I shall get even with you for making me starve every time I visit your country. Goose, Derek and I now have a deeper bonding. Our friendship has reached a new high. We can even understand what each of us speaks. Our words have became shorter as we can understand each other really well. Derek and I know Goose is hungry when he says 'Grunt'. He needs to be fed then. Goose and Derek know I'm thirsty when I say 'Wa'. And Goose and I know Derek is horny and thirsty when he says 'Cock'. He needs a woman and a Coke then.

There were some unwritten rules like these that had now become a daily part of our lives for the past 69 days we had been either driving or partying. Like every time we would be at a railway crossing, we would all go silent, count the number of bogeys and make a wish. To me, that still remains a struggle as I cannot count beyond five. So every time the fifth bogey would pass, I would start counting from one and make that many wishes. Like you, dear reader, I was born greedy, with a lust for life.

On the road, Goose learnt the fine art of photography, not just driving like hell. Every time we would see a shoulder on the road, he would get out to pee. His best pictures have come out this way, so if you decide to buy his picture book 'Goose's World', you know the secret now. We made a pretty decent bunch of drivers on the road. Goose cannot read, Derek cannot write and I cannot think. We're alright. Not really all that shitty like that goatherd in Rajasthan had made us believe. Sure, we are dung-bits, but we don't really eat that for food like him. Just like the best pictures are taken during piss-stops, the best YouTube videos are made while taking a dump. If you don't believe me, dear reader, watch the Discovery channel or the Animal Planet. If someone has to make movies of, say, two flamingos mating or record a pregnant seal deliver a baby, you really don't expect the photographer to ask the horny flamingoes and the mother seal to wait, go to a proper toilet, take a dump and get back, do you?

That reminds me of a big problem we have in India. In every state, they eat the same food every day. Like the boiled rice cakes down South, cook's balls in hot garlic sauce near the China border, Great Balls of fire in Rajasthan, deep-fried ball sandwiches in Maharashtra, momos in the East. When I become the President of India, I'm going to make all these cooks travel. In Goa, right now, our lunch was stir-fry noodles. A misnomer. With so many of these noodles which like ugly earthworms on my plate, they should call them 'Stir-fry Needles'. Again, part of my manifesto to change our Nation's way of thinking.

We've been around and seen a bit of our country in the past few days. We have tasted some tasty dishes and some downright horrible food. Maybe, some are acquired tastes, like those ridiculous and horrible smelling cheese they eat elsewhere on the planet. Like snails and eels. I've had stuff for which I may never be able to acquire a taste – in India and abroad. Sample the mutton delicacy in Kolhapur which tastes like lava salad. Too spicy. Or momos in Ladakh that taste like they've yet to be cooked. Or idlis in South that need no teeth. And parathas up North that are loaded in bad cholesterol. Or some Delhi cuisine which is food for alpha males. Being on the road with my middle finger well exercised, my stomach also was now well-lined with leather. And these bleary eyes that can irrigate a vast desert wasteland. So just give me plain food with little spice and healthy vegetables.

Now, I'm done with dead animals, mutilated fish and gutted entrails of birds loaded with spice, dipped in unhealthy oils and served on my plate in the name of food. Many times on the road, I've thrown out the shitty food and eaten the plate and spoon instead. This trip sure turned die-hard carnivores like us into vegetarians and that doesn't seem like a bad choice at all. Of course, to each his or her own, anyways. That's the reason why this book which you are reading, dear reader, is the world's first low-calorie book and I have been talking about it on Facebook like that. "No sugar, no milk, Horn Ok Please". If you are hungry now and don't want to eat any further, just use some tomato ketchup or any bread-spread and start chewing this book. It's multi-purpose. Go on, try it. It will make you turn vegetarian. *Burp!*

They were shutting down the bar and we had no choice but to get back to our rooms. Having successfully crawled back into the hotel room, Goose switched on the TV and they were showing something very ghastly and horrible. It was all about cooking some dish called 'Haleem'. Gak! How can you eat something that is called 'Haleem'? It sounds gross and misplaced like 'A fish called Wanda' or Derek's first girlfriend called 'Pretty'. But now we know everything about it and we have learnt to respect it. Anything you don't like or understand, I guess it is best to 'respect' it and avoid any conflict.

Since Derek had gone off with the Brazilian chicks, Goose took out Derek's iPod to the TV as we wanted to watch some porn and Derek's iPod was full of it. We tried out Indian porn. What we saw was worse than watching two stray dogs making out on the National highway. We tried this horrible desi-lesbian show, which has some cheap-shit whores with lactating tits and beer bellies trying to make out like two dung beetles in the Jaisalmer desert. Ten minutes through the show, we watched with glee as Goose flushed down Derek's iPod in the toilet while I recorded that for posterity and to host on YouTube. Nothing better than the real thing, dear reader, and best to keep it straight and natural the way it is meant to be.

I switched on the radio and the RJ played some real crappy music. I should have brought my radio from San Diego instead of giving it way. My favorite Rock Channel over there used to play some really awesome rock on my radio through the night. Had I had that radio now with me, she would be playing the songs which I like to listen to. Goose was growing up, for he had been weaned away from crappy Trance music by some guy called 'Testosterone' or something like that to the pleasures of real classic rock and Alternative. I had succeeded in that one. It was like weaning a baby away from the bottle of milk, making him grow over eighteen real fast and getting him hooked straight down to rum.

In Goa, tourists can afford to be lazy or drunk or both. You can have a morning coffee or morning rum or a morning coffee with rum and not feel tipsy. We woke up in the morning after getting completely sloshed the night before. We got up in the morning, went straight to the shack, gargled with beer, prawns and fish and drank all day before a dip in the sea. Goose advised me to go easy on water as South Goa is not a place where people like us come to drink water. He always made sense, the fat bird. So we got back to the shack and continued the binge and as Goose and I stared at the sea silently, tanking up yet again, a deluge of memories came to my head and we started rambling again, it happens to anyone who spends too much time staring at the sea. For the sea is like an ocean. You see water all across the sea. You see, I make less and less sense with every passing page. Well, we aren't morons for nothing.

One cannot but help but notice those skinny lifeguards on the beaches here. It really doesn't matter if they can swim to the rescue or not, but they would surely float like matchsticks and reach the victims. Rescue is an entirely different matter. I mean, having grown up watching 'Baywatch' and Pamela Anderson, who wants to be rescued anyways? And I'm quite certain she doesn't know how to swim but I've read somewhere that silicon bubbles float on water. As we majestically survey the beach early morning, I see a woman sweeping a beach. Awesome. I can bet my life on it that such a sight can never be seen anywhere else in the world. I've heard of beach combing for God's sakes, but sweeping it clean? What next, are we going to see vacuum cleaners on these beaches?

Sun and sand – a slice of my life

Palolim Beach is a very pretty sight in the morning. You can see the sea all around, watch the sunrise, look at the local fishermen who could be far more productive in their fishing techniques or watching a dog pull a girl on a leash. This beach is as pretty as any other beach in India. As long as there are fewer people, the place is always pretty. Unlike North Goa which is full of hawkers and two-legged pests, South Goa is paradise. People who tend to watch the sea for prolonged periods tend to become lethargic and run the risk of getting their senses dulled by thought. The same applies to people who watch mountains, lakes and anything overly serene. But the road, it keeps you on your toes, keeps you sharp and alert. I wished I could drive Motormouth on the beach instead of bumming around near a boat now. As we waited for Derek, we stood near a boat, as I wondered who belonged to this boat. The term "stink" was definitely coined here.

Derek joined us as we watched the fishermen pull out the fish from the sea. The boy had to be taught that fishes come from the sea, not supermarkets. Derek continued to ponder as to why these fishermen don't go to the super-market to buy fish as they're a lot cleaner over there. Goose delivered the much-needed slap on Derek's face as he explained to him that milk still came from many cows, one cannot go and milk a milk-van. The *Duh!* expression lingered on Derek's face and we decided to change the topic to something he would understand easily. Like girls.

So Derek started talking about his first girlfriend and how they had broken up in the morning. He had met this girl at a party we had all been to. Goose and I had wondered what he could have seen in this girl who looked like a battle-tank in her green dress. He had fallen in deep lust with her and spent the night with her. The same chick looked so horrible to him in the morning that he decided to run away from her. But just to sound deep and cool, he maintained that she was a woman of substance, as if that mattered to him. She was a woman of substance, he had said, and the world had abused her. Maybe, this is what they call substance abuse and in the morning, she wore a purple shirt. She had looked like a brinjal which had sprouted arms and legs. Goose and I were very happy for Derek that morning. OK, so Derek could have been a little more sophisticated in breaking up with her. No breakup is a piece of cake and for our friend who had been run over by a battle-tank the previous night, that really wasn't a piece of cake. It was more like a bar of soap gone wild in his mouth. But that is the problem with truth. It tastes worse than soap and it is very bitter. Surely our friend could have used some saccharine to make it seem nice and normal.

We hadn't had a bath for days now. We had learnt a thing or two from the nomads near Leh. Goose had taught me how to avoid going in for a full bath and instead indulge in a 'near-shower' experience. You just put your arms and legs, one at a time under the shower, make groaning noises, rub yourself vigorously with a towel and spray yourself with deodorant. Also known as a 'Crow-bath' in urban India, it's alright to live with this experience, if you happen to be straight. That was the reason, as Goose wisely justified his action of bloating up our Goodie-bag which was getting fuller and fuller with pinched stuff from various hotels across India. Not as mementoes, we were told that we never 'stole' stuff. We just 'borrowed' them. Of course, it did reduce the guilt.

Cock tales and more

The cocktails kept on coming, Goose educated us well on them. For Goa was his playground. Derek was quietly playing with the umbrella on his cocktails, wondering if that depicted the size of the people who lived in the basement of our resort, locked up. They must have all taken a slow boat from China as everything here is 'Made in China', served by a 'Maid' from China today. Goose quipped wisely, "40% of world climate comes from Tibet, 60% of Chinese population drinks water from there, therefore they waste 100% of their energy gobbling up nations." The boy was deep. Deeper than that crater we had seen in Pokhran. Only difference was the filling. The crater in Pokhran was stuffed with onions, while Goose is full of shit.

Goa was a refreshing change from all that we had seen across India so far. Anywhere we would go, they'd point us to religious places. I mean, do we guys look like the 'religious types' to them? From any angle? We were self-proclaimed morons. We had conferred the title of 'Dr. Chief' (which sounds silly) and Dr. Goose (which sounds like a cool DJ) and Dr. Derek (which sounds like a porn star) as we now believed that we have an advanced degree in humanitarian arts, very far removed from civil society. When Goose graduated, he was titled 'Certified Pervert', when I graduated, I was titled as a 'Sex Worker' and when Derek graduated.....wait a minute....he hasn't graduated yet. But still, we are spiritual people, not religious. We respect everything we do not have a comprehension of without being judgmental.

And here we were, amidst a vast stretch of a clean beach, surrounded by green hills. This is a clear blue sky as a gentle breeze brushes against my face. I am inside this simple shack as I feel a surge of happiness inside me. We are now having lemon tea with some 'bed-pan fried potatoes' and Goose is happy for this is the good life for us. We wish peace and happiness for all humanity. Could this be 'Nirvana'? Derek has his shrimp, that's his choice. Who cares after they are dead and over-cooked? Where does religion fit into our scheme of things? It doesn't. I am not speaking for all Indians over here, but this is the life I love, we love. Maybe, this is how many folks like me think across India 2.0. We like doing good to others and we have been doing it all our lives. It is far better than the world of superstitions which we saw across the country. Some crazy chap seems to have made a horse of cloth and tried to fly away. He came back to find himself on every wall in a city. Blind faith or a ridiculous belief? A superstition of getting rich by watching snakes copulate. Voyeuristic? It seems like if you put your handkerchief on them, you would become very rich. Isn't that worse than watching animal porn and dreaming of getting rich by doing so? Another superstition that was told to us was that saving a cat's placenta after the deed would make one rich. Does it mean that pussy juice can make people rich? A cat crossing the road is bad luck. Since when is a pussy crossing the road, bad luck?

As our conversation got more inane, the sea got more violent and noisier. If only we could do something about the volume. These seas should come with volume control buttons. If not that, at least, God, you should have made a "Power Off" button for all lazy people who sit around and watch the sea like us. At least we could have blanked out dumb sights like the one where we saw dumb, stupid tourists from the world over come to India and take pictures of poverty and animals on the beach. They are worse than cows and dogs on the beach. These rejects from their countries come to India on a shoestring budget and take pictures of beggars, garbage and stray animals. Just a shade better than pedophiles and junkies, I can never understand why they wish to paint an ugly picture of India. Goose was busy taking pictures of a dumb tourist who was taking pictures of a cow on the beach. Derek was rude enough to take pictures of his girlfriend in a string bikini while the dork was busily clicking a cow. Give me this two-legged cow any day. Of course, the cow is dumb to be sitting on a South Goa beach waiting for grass to grow in the sand. Well, don't blame the cow, but blame the tourists. These dumb animals, I'm talking about cows here, must have been told by some stupid cow that one does find grass on the beaches of Goa. This is why one finds a cow on the beach. If there were no trashy tourists, the beaches would not be teeming with junkies selling grass and dope. Cows are dumb enough not to understand this, but are tourists smart enough not to get in the way of local authorities and let them do their job of educating the cows? That's why you find cows on Goa beaches. They come for grass. The tourists just don't understand. Sloshed, we went back to bed.

It's a beautiful day

Woke up in the morning, I took a cold shower, and since we were running low on toothpaste, I forgo brushing my teeth and instead used a mouthwash called "Latrine" or something. Goose hadn't woken up yet. Derek crawled out of one side of the bed only to get back in from the other side. Lazy bums! They're turning into regular lazy Goan tourists. I decided to go to the beach and watch the sunrise. As I watched the sunrise sitting on a boat, I scribbled these notes. Dear reader, before you conclude I am weird, please understand that I have written this book sitting in a boat, inside a palace, inside an SUV, in a pub, in my tent, on the beach, in the forest, on top of a mountain, by the lake and inside a toilet. So, no wonder the book is weird. And since you bought this book, so are you.

I see about fifty-odd people on the beach who look like fishermen. They do look odd. They must be fishermen as the place is now stinking of fish. I knew it was the right time to look stoic, put on my strong and silent face, keep my mouth shut and watch them pull the net out of the sea again. Let people wonder if I am a fool rather than to open it and remove doubts. And thank God, Derek's not around right now, else he'd get quite worried watching the fishermen pull out so many fish from the sea every day. At this rate, there will be no more fish left in the sea soon enough.

It was time for breakfast and our boys were famished and on time for the sea-show yet again as we ordered a round of beer and muffins to start the day. It is a vicious cycle for us in Goa. The circle of life spins around a bottle of beer. That's why the earth is round as well and this is how Galileo or Kepler or some scientist of yore had it all figured out. If you sit on a beach with a pint and look at the horizon, you will see that the earth is round. Since everything would have fallen off from the edge of the earth, they invented gravity. Gravity is that apple thing that Newton kept blabbering about. In fact, gravity was invented to keep things on our earth as they belong to us. Gravity also pulls the sky closer to the earth. And since gravity was also invented by a woman, it continues to keep the earth round with no sharp edges.

Derek was famished and ordered lobster for breakfast. Yes, he was weird. Lobster, muffins and beer for breakfast is certainly not had by most people the world over. If you go by common sense, you'd note that 100 shrimps = 75 prawns = 1 lobster put in a gigantic cockroach shell. But what's really weird is an Indian having an English breakfast at an Italian joint in India. Now that's a weird global world and we love it. The moment these territorial boundaries are broken, it would be the end of xenophoia and we can drive across the globe. Imagine a world of International highways, we help a five-minute silence around the thought and got back to cuss words. Fuck!

Now that's a term I have been desperately trying to avoid using in this book. Not for any moralistic reasons, but the word has now become so generic that it is the perfect expression used to denote anger, excitement, agony, pain and ecstasy. "Well, fuck off mate!", "I so fucking love you!", "I cannot fucking drive any faster!", "The roads are so fucking good!", "You are so fucking brilliant!", "You are so fucking full of shit!", "That was fucking good, lady!". "The brake!! Use the fucking brake!", "Are you fucking deaf?", "Ahh!! The fucking sea again. See?" Of course, the sheer excitement and passion is highlighted with the use of an exclamation mark while ending a fucking sentence! We had a fucking good time discussing!

Our intelligent conversation was rudely interrupted by the sudden howling of stray mongrels on the beach. It was one of those dratted tourists trying to feel up a dog and the mate seems to have disapproved that. Good for 'Ed', for we call such tourists 'Ed', which is an abbreviation for 'Erectile Difficulty'. Well, Ed, If you like stray dogs and stray animals so much, please take them home to your country with you, where you have them for breakfast anyways. Stop cootchie-cooing them here and trying to act like a good Samaritan, we have enough mouths to feed anyways. Also, we don't like these mongrels mauling children. If it weren't for these PETA folks, we wouldn't be so kind to them. Of course, we all love animals, as long as they don't hurt people. Do you know that there are more vegetarians in India than the entire population of your country, Ed? Take some pictures and eat them for breakfast if you wish.

A newlywed Indian couple passed by, rattled by this noise, the husband clutched the wife's hand tighter. As if someone was going to snatch her away from him. We wondered how she could lift her arms with so many bangles. No wonder, she had big biceps. We promptly christened her 'Mrs. Armstrong'. Ho! Ho! Ho! As the music played, the dumb-waiter got us a lobster. Lobsters look like gigantic cockroaches. Ours looked like an open dictionary. That's how the 'Lobster's dictionary' was born. The look on Derek's face indicated that he had those question marks around his head as Goose explained to him, "Right Derek, Just like when the world came to know that Wren & Martin were gay. Gay like those two guys who wrote 'Freakonomics' . Happy people, Happy and Gay (sounds like a gay couple from Punjab or Canada). These two few minute foreign noodles wrote trash about Indian males. Not two, but few-minute noodles with dicks the size of a pea-pod found in Himachal Pradesh. Studies indicate that they are gay, done by an Indian handwriting 'analyst'. No, Derek! 'Arsenal' is not a bad word, it has nothing to do with 'Arse' or 'Anal'. And 'Infantry' as nothing to do with defective condoms! *Duh!*" Trying to suppress my laughter, I gaze at a schizophrenic crow that's trying to hop. Sheryl Crow plays in the background as

I realize that there's something very lazy and magical about Goa. I mean, you could sleep with any woman of your choice in Goa. Any woman. You both will sleep off.

Three days in Goa, getting drunk the whole day, listening to Coldplay, Bob Marley and Sheryl Crow, loads of food being washed down with loads of beer. This is nirvana. No wonder I feel enlightened. It was time for us to head back home. After all, home is the place where all homies belong.

The men in black with cool shades were on the move again. Goose was now a man. Having gone through two break-ups, a string of nonsensical one-night stands, he was all set to straddle the corporate ladder of success with a quest for knowledge. He would find a girl, settle down, make babies and get back on the road with us. Trance was out, Alternative rock was in.

Derek was finally appeased. The less we talk about him, the better, else I'd have to rename the book as 'Porn OK Please'. I was inspired. The canopies and lemonade coupled with Michael Buble now left me even more confused than before. In the company of Goose and Derek, my IQ had taken a severe beating and I have decided to go back to Kindergarten.

Motormouth looks like a gigantic dustbin on the move, with two trashy people inside, who now vaguely look like human beings after 69 days on the road. Not fit for civil society – Tom Hanks from Castaway. We were breakaways. Derek has no intention of leaving Goa as he waves out to us, Brazilian chicks in arms, the man had finally got it all figured out. Au Revior, Goa, for we shall be back soon enough.

HOPping to Conclusions

▸ *A 'muffin' sounds like 'chewin' or 'nibblin' and has a lousy feel to it. So it must be unhealthy*

▸ *Potatoes and baked beans in beer taste like shit dipped in hot garlic sauce*

▸ *A Canopy of trees on the road means a place where you should not stop by to pee. I've tasted. I've been to China.*

▸ *The difference between 'Class' and 'Crass' is more than just a typographical error*

▸ *One can never get ducking frunk in Goa*

▸ *Peeing is like reverse osmosis. On a full bladder, the feeling is next to orgasm*

▸ *If you want to punish somebody, gift him/her a CD of Indian porn movies*

▸ *8.   iPods make a racket when being flushed down a toilet*

▸ *'Goa' & 'Leh' are unfinished words and remain so*

▸ *Cows in Goa are very confused people*

Epilogue – Born OK Please

It was 5:00 am. I had never seen such a constipated tube of stubborn toothpaste. Which idiot made the hole so small for the toothpaste to come out? And they should have called it 'teethpaste', by the way, as I use the same paste for all my teeth. Same goes for my toothbrush. Who in his right mind would ever use one toothbrush per tooth? No one is that foolish, dear reader, sorry, not even you can be that stupid.

As my darling wife, Rose, tries to pack our rucksack, she curses and mutters under her breath. The camping gear is broken, we've run out of supplies and she needs a check-up from the neck-up for having married me. Worse, this 50-day road-trip seems to be getting on her nerves as we are now hopelessly lost in Zanskar Valley. We had spent time with the children of the Tibetan Village School last week and had decided to explore the interiors of Ladakh. Khardung La Pass had been awesome and we had a few nicks and bruises having done some serious off-roading on the bumpy terrains of Hundar.

We can hear the voices getting louder as Goose seems to be getting cooked by Jane. Jane doesn't like the loud, pulsating Rock music that Goose plays all the time. She argues why Goose cannot be normal like the other guys and listen to Trance instead. Ouch! I think I cut myself now as I shave and am about to bleed to death. Goose and Jane make a nice couple and Jane can be a great navigator. Helga, our GPS, has been safely bitch-strapped and tucked away. Not a peep out of her anymore.

The four of us have been on the road for the past forty days and the stress shows on us. We were stressed out, not because of driving, but because of Derek's new found passion for the guitar. He is not bad, my friend Derek. He is downright pathetic. I wonder how this pretty woman can stand him. We don't know her name, but he calls her 'Angel'.

Driving at 130 Kmph, Motormouth purrs her way back to a patch of rubble which the locals term as a 'main road'. As she eats up the distance, I take a deep swig of lemonade. I want to get back to Himachal as we all would like to see some greenery around us. I want to drive through a canopy of trees on the road. Goose cranks up the stereo and a book comes hurtling at him from the rear seat. Derek whizzes past us in his new beast he calls 'Thor'. Thor and Motormouth create symphony on the road. Thor seems to love Motormouth.

We are heading back to Leh right now as the sun rises through the mountains and the sunshine comes in straight into my heart. It's a beautiful county we live in, a beautiful life. As I am almost done with my next book titled 'Horn OK Please – The Scrotum Scrolls' now, I am reminded of the words spoken to us last year by His Holiness: "Pride, not arrogance". Yes, I feel proud of my country and the world that we live in. I call it India 2.0.

A lust for a beautiful journey called life. For it is my way and the highway…

Community Speak: The Fishing Pond

Compiled by Craig Cmehil and Yadavendra Yadav

> *I want the world at my feet;*
> *I want sunshine upon me now;*
> *I want the moon to lead me on,*
> *I want the wind to feel me now,*
> *Give me my 4-WD, for my beast will set me 'free,*
> *Drive with me now, I'll show what I see;*
> *If smiles and imagination makes you say 'Cheese'*
> *Drive on, for that when you go 'Horn OK Please'…*

About the 'Horn OK Please' Community on Face book

http://facebook.com/hopfans
HOPfans is a Global Ecosystem, a network of individuals from around the world who share a passion for life, driving and a walk on the wild side. While the book is the first as part of a trilogy, 'Horn OK Please' is aimed at changing the world and creating the New World order with Social Media. Also known as 'HOPpers', this community cuts across geographical boundaries and obliterates the shackles imposed by race, nationality, religion, gender, social standing and every archaic

term that segregates human beings spread across an ever-shrinking world. Welcome to a brave new world of Social Media. Here, at Planet HOP, like-minded, educated and progressive people connect in a heart-beat, disconnect in a sneeze. As one of the world's first reality shows on Facebook, thousands of HOPpers live their life with us vicariously as I try to spread sunshine and smiles on this planet, with this book being practically lived through and written by fans from around the world who were connected with me day and night. I just happen to be the lucky person with a pen doing a two-month road-trip across India, a journey lived by thousands of fans around the world.

As the World watched, Craig Cmehil (Social Media Expert) from Germany, Yadavendra Yadav (SAP CRM Expert) aka 'Hound' from United Kingdom, Kunal Kant (SAP GRC Expert) aka 'Galileo' from France and Venkat (SAP geek) aka 'Geek', from India along with a virtual back-office that cut through the United States, APAC, Middle East and Europe connected with us via Social Media and every gizmo and Social Media network via satellite from around the world. Our positions were tracked and recorded by Craig Cmehil and Galileo as my colleagues from Capgemini, the world's best workplace, blogged about it and tracked us throughout the journey when we were driving across the country. This section is a tribute to all the stars of Planet HOP. Many of the HOPpers from Planet HOP left their foot-prints about a journey called 'HOP' and this book. Craig Cmehil and Yadavendra Yadav put this all together for us. And here's what they have to say:

Goose: 'You won't get any fish here, Chief. The currents are very strong.'
Chief: 'Hmmm...lemme go and create my own pond, then.'
Goose: 'Err…….and the fish?'
Chief: 'They will come flying one day, Goose. You just wait and see….'
Derek: Yeah….*Duh!!*
Motormouth roared.

And yes, they came flying… as compliments, as good wishes, as their own experiences. They came, they wrote and they HOPped on. Each one is as precious as the other. Whether it was a few lines or a few paragraphs, the underlying sentiments were the same. A latent strength for some, an inspiration for quite a few, a sunshine smile for many….Horn OK Please has touched the life of its fans in many ways. It has made a difference in their lives and will continue to do so, and why not? It is after all, about making a difference and HOP the world one day!

We went fishing into the 'Fishing Pond' to *get* good catch but got drowned hook, line and sinker and hit the bottom very hard. Gasping for breath, we did manage to surface alive and when we dug deep into our pockets….we found a few pearls. Here they are:

Craig Cmehil (Germany): *"When Kartik first told me about his ideas for writing a book and doing it all almost entirely within Social Media channels on the web I thought he was nuts; I mean writing a book is not an easy task to begin with and now he wanted to put the extra pressure and stress himself by being so open and public about the whole process and bringing a ton of strangers into it. However, I've known Kartik for years now and I knew* *that if anyone could accomplish this crazy feat, it would be him! So here I sat in Germany, so far, far away and watched the story unfold and frankly I was amazed as the dedication, inspiration and sheer fun of the process began to infect one person after the other. I created some videos and posted about it as well but there were folks within India who literally were living the experience with him!*

What really blew my mind about the whole process was despite the fun and crazy side, Kartik never seemed to falter in his determined course to help others. HOP, for me, is about changing the world! They began to do this as they travelled through India and beyond. Visiting the Tibetan Children's Home, helping to start scholarship funds for them, stopping to meet and speak to the Dalai Lama and stopping along the way to meet and speak to fellow HOPpers all over. HOP is about changing the world and HOP is all of us."

Yadavendra Yadav (United Kingdom): *"Horn OK Please … A phrase I grew-up on. It was on the back of almost every commercial vehicle on Indian roads. A phrase that to me meant 'please honk if you wish to overtake'. The honk was almost like a leap of faith those years whilst making an attempt to overtake the dilapidating, gas-guzzling monsters on six wheels. I am glad that what I understood was what it meant and I never needed an ambulance. Then a few months back, a good 'ol friend of mine came honking by and... he said he was writing a book. He also said that he will write it on a road trip. [Good luck!!... *<mumbling>* Crazy! Fingers crossed at the back] He then went on to say that it will be a book written by its reader's! [WTF!! ... *<mumbling again>* This guy must be outta his mind] It has been many months since then. The phrase 'Horn OK Please' took on a new meaning, I started laughing and* *smiling again a thousand times a day. The wit, the humor, the attitude and the social cause...everything connected. And, more so, in this journey I found a new me that I never knew ever existed. HOP is an attitude. HOP is the will to make a difference. HOP is a social cause. HOP is you and me. HOP is all of us together. And finally, thank you Chief, Goose and each and every fan of HOP. I wish you well. And the show must go on for as long as it can ... so sez the Hound on the Merry-Go-Hound."*

Kendra Robichaud (United States): *"It's not very often that you find a treasure... But every once in a while, in the most unlikely of places, not at the bottom of the ocean, but at the bottom of a pond that's full of HOPpers (and I don't mean frogs even tho there are a few!), you find the ultimate gem, of all things, a book – Horn Ok Please ... That is so much more than just a book.... A true inspiration ... Thank you for taking me on your far away journey and inspiring this frog to become a true HOPper! :)"*

Melani Strachan (South Africa): *"Kartik Iyengar, the HOP page you created has not only connected me (form miles across the 7 seas) to India, but also to HOPpers, people who love life and love laughing, morons I have come to love. The humor and wit that you shared everyday on this journey became a platform for all of us HOpers to interact, dream, care and most of all LAUGH. You gave us a stage to perform on and it brought out the best in us. So thank you, Kartik HOPper. HORN OK PLEASE! *Smack* Your sugar plum always."*

Anusha Wickramasinghe (Sri Lanka): *"Love your absolutely SUPER sense of humor... haven't heard anything like it in years!!! So looking forward to reading your book, so hope it will be available in Sri Lanka. And if it is, can we get a signed copy?*

I've never seen the signature of a 'nobody'. Humour makes us forget the tough, rough and difficult times we face, even if it is just for a moment.... So 'Thank You' for a never-ending humourous experience at Horn OK Please ..."

Chitra Mahesh (India): *"In life's unfunny junctures, I have laughed and laughed. Spirits have soared for the sheer pleasure of living and laughing for the moment. I HOPPED on. And, I'm still alive to tell the tale!"*

Deepthi Narayan (Australia): *"I am absolutely amazed and gob smacked by the infinite abundance of energy and enthusiasm that you have in you for HOP and an even greater zest for generating the same excitement amongst your thousands of fans within SUCH A SHORT SPAN OF TIME! Your wall posts and comments are humorous, naughty, chirpy, witty, inspiring, completely WHACKY and HIGHLY addictive amongst all your followers. U have succeeded in creating this exclusive HOPper community and your all- India road trip was a very entertaining daily news feed =) And above all I am VERY proud of my big bro for your massive achievement and I look forward 2 seeing u grow rich and famous and do lots and lots of good things towards India 2.0. India is in your hands, dude! Keep HOPpin'!"*

Rupa Gandhi (India): *"You dreamt, chased and succeeded. Having shown the way to 12000+ morons and still counting, your journey across the country has revealed your golden heart to those who read between those whacky, frivolous, smartass one-liners. *Inkheart* wishes for more of your ilk and we see India 2.0 already shining!*Smack!!*"*

Acknowledgements

Roses are red, violets are blue,
All poems rhyme, but this one don't

- To all you HOPpers on Facebook, thank you for being a part of the journey.
- To my parents, dear Mom and Dad, for without your love and my love for your money, I wouldn't have become the world's greatest nobody.
- To my wife, for you inspired and helped me find a reason with my book, you make me complete.
- To my colleagues at work, you should do what you want, not just what you must do.
- To each one of you from my professional world who supported me in this endeavour.
- To our Honorable Home Minister, P. Chidambaram, Mr. M.A Siddiqui, Rahul Gandhi and my country's leadership.
- To everyone at Wikipedia, *The Hindu, The Indian Express* Group, *The Times of India* group, *PTI* News Agency, Facebook and all Social Media vehicles who have helped me every step of the way.
- Tibetan Children's Village: To all folks at the Tibetan SOS Village.

- To Mr. Tenzin N. Taklha and everyone at Dharamsala who were really nice to us.
- Mahesh Memorial Foundation: To Chitra Mahesh, for igniting a spark of humanitarianism in me.
- To all my childhood friends. God only knows why I need to thank you.
- To my publisher, editor, cover designer, book designer, printer and all those who believe in me, a sincere note of gratitude from the bottom of my deep black heart.
- Without the support of Kausalya Saptharishi, you wouldn't have this book in your hands. Thank you, angel.
- To each one of you who wishes to make the world a better place for our children
- To Rohit Tiwari, aka Goose, thank you, bro. Let's roll again soon.
- To a silent HOPper, who works from behind the shadows to make the book *happen*.